HAUNTING
BOMBAY

HAUNTING
BOMBAY

Shilpa Agarwal

SOHO

To Mom, Dad, and James
for your enduring faith in me

❊   ❊   ❊

Copyright © 2005, 2009 by Shilpa Agarwal

Published by
Soho Press, Inc.
853 Broadway
New York, NY 10003

Library of Congress Cataloging-in-Publication Data

Agarwal, Shilpa, 1971–
Haunting Bombay / Shilpa Agarwal.
p. cm.
ISBN 978-1-56947-558-4 (hardcover)
1. Young women—India—Bombay—Fiction. 2. Family life—India—Bombay—Fiction.
3. Family secrets—Fiction. 4. Bombay (India)—Fiction. 5. Domestic fiction. gsafd I. Title.
PS3601.G37H38 2009
813'.6—dc22
2008040703

10 9 8 7 6 5 4 3 2 1

CONTENTS

THE BRINK: 1947

The Sea Inside 3

BEGINNINGS: THIRTEEN YEARS LATER

The Bungalow 11

A Bolted Door 21

Watery Presence 26

Cascading Foliage 36

A Witch 48

The Drowning 54

Sinking Sunbirds 61

Devilry 69

Drinking Moonbeams 80

Famine Amidst Suds 89

Husband, Husband-Eater 96

The Brass Bucket 105

Elements of Death 111

The Ghost 117

A Blinding Vision 125

BORDERS: 1960

An Inauspicious Sign 133

Monsoons & Miracles 140

Rain-Swept Tamarind Tree 149

Lightning at the Green Gates 166

Puddle of Pink Gum Boots 179

Captive on A Rainy Night 184

The Caliginous Ocean 196

Chalice of Desire 205

Slums & Sewers 218

The Tantrik 225

Death & Disinheritance 231

Fishing Village 243

Water-Elimination Plan 249

Crystal Vials of Attar 263

Scriptures & Sex. 275

Phantasmal Fog 285

The Haunted Coastline 294

A Trawler & Truth 306

Silver *Puja* Vessel 315

Stormy Retribution 327

Return of the Ayah. 336

The Vampire Curse 344

A Scalding Sacrifice 351

EPILOGUE • 353

THE BRINK:

1947

Can the subaltern speak?
—GAYATRI CHAKRAVORTY SPIVAK

Might they not be the cracks and chinks through which another voice, other voices, speak in our lives? By what right do we close our ears to them?
—J. M. COETZEE, *FOE*

THE SEA INSIDE

The girl moved like water itself, unthinkingly toward the darkening horizon. She was only sixteen, or maybe seventeen. A brilliant red sari clung to her body. Tangled hair lashed at her face.

Now, as the thickening dusk closed in upon her, the girl stood on the outskirts of the village, little more than a cluster of thatched huts huddled at the water's edge. A solitary coconut tree rose to the sky, straining against the heavy winds. Somewhere a dog barked incessantly. She took a step back, waiting for the moon to slip behind scattered clouds. The mirrorwork on her sari cast pale, misshapen circles of light upon the ground. She tried to touch them with her left foot, the dancing lights illuminating her toes, the middle one adorned with a silver ring, the stub of a sixth gracelessly curled under. She pressed onward, fighting a feeling that she was being repelled by some invisible energy, a collective fear.

Her destination was not the village itself but a solitary hut on its outskirts. Unlike the others, this one was badly weathered, its coconut-frond roof rotted, its interior pitch black. The wind stung, as if in warning, pulling her back, back. She did not stop until she reached the decayed bamboo mat tied to the doorway, dimly remembering weaving it as a young child. Here it was, proof that she had once inhabited this place at the world's rim, before she had begun to bleed, before the women had gathered, their salty voices crooning the ancient tale of the menstruating girl who caused the waves to turn blood-red and sea snakes to infest the waters. She should not be here. She knew this. Yet she pulled the mat away and stepped in.

The first thing she saw was the glint of the moonlight on bangles. A figure squatted in the corner of the hut, rocking back and forth on her haunches.

"You've come back," a voice said.

The girl nodded, wanting nothing more than to weep. But this was not a time to be weak. She wanted something from this woman, this blind midwife who had powers, unspoken powers. "Help me."

The tinkling bangles fell silent.

"You must," the girl pleaded, eyes shining with loss, "you were the one who cursed me!"

The midwife cackled.

The girl dropped her face, remembering the taunts, the bits and pieces she gleaned from the other children when they dared speak about her ill-fated birth.

It had been Nariyal Poornima, the day that the fishermen returned to sea after the long rainy months during which no fishing was done. Monsoon season was the breeding time for the fish, and the men had stayed away while the ocean's bounty was reproducing under the turbulent waters. Women, too, emerged that early morning, walking in the opposite direction, toward the shrine, to offer prayers to Ekuira, deity of the seas, patron of the Koli fisherpeople.

"Your Ma walked slowly," the midwife offered in a glutinous voice, "her belly pushing out so far that we thought there were two inside. She went to pray."

The girl knew of the small *shamiana* that rose from the treacherous rocks, its thick cloth canopy decorated in colorful patchwork. She was never allowed to go near but once visited it in secret, a single velvety marigold clutched in her small fingers to offer at the small stone shrine devoted to Ekuira, the orange-faced goddess with eight-arms, born from the body of Lord Brahma, Creator of the Universe. *O most compassionate Goddess,* she had recited a prayer of fisherwomen for their husbands, *your oceans are so vast, and his boat so insignificant.*

"Afterwards, your Ma cracked a coconut at the goddess's feet."

The girl braced herself, knowing what came next, that her mother's birth-water had broken open, defiling the shrine. The other fisherwomen had dragged her away, spitting accusations. When her father's boat failed to return that evening, no one had been surprised.

The midwife cackled once more, then as if suddenly tired of the old story, she pulled out a small, rusted lantern and lit it. Her face—dried and weathered as salted shrimp—cast eerie silhouettes upon the wall. "You've been banished again," she stated.

Had I been there *just this morning?* the girl wondered, remembering the warmth of the body next to her, the scarlet-tinged light filtering through the colored glasswork of the wall. "I must go back," she whispered, unable to keep the desperation from her voice.

"Once you've been banished, you can never go back, not in life, not in death," the old woman muttered. Her unseeing eyes bored into the girl's face. "They will have done a purification ceremony, just as we did the day you left, to block your spirit from entering. That's why you can't go beyond my hut into our fishing village. That's why you can never return there."

"There must be some way," the girl implored, her eyes wild. It had been home, that bungalow. She was only a servant there, true, but for a little while, she had been much more. She pulled out the merciful stash of money that Maji, the bungalow's matriarch, had given her and placed it in the midwife's gnarled hands.

The old woman seized the cash and bit into the wad with broken, blackened teeth. A line of saliva dripped down her chin. "There is one way," she said slowly, her tobacco-stained mouth curling into a smile, "but it involves an exceptional sacrifice. You must be strong, unwavering."

"I will!" The girl gritted her teeth as if to underscore her determination. She was nothing, nothing if she could not be there.

"I was right to banish you. Someone else has died."

"An accident, a baby—"

"I thought you had learned the ways of birthing," the old woman sneered, "always lurking nearby so others couldn't see you."

"I delivered the baby safely, there wasn't time for the lady to go to the nursing home. It came too fast. Maji ordered the boiling water and sheets. I told her that I knew the way so she let me deliver it while the others waited outside. I did it exactly as I had seen . . . and then—" Her voice broke.

"You were away when the baby drowned."

The girl nodded.

"Just like with your father. An accident perhaps. Perhaps not. There will be other deaths, other fatal accidents."

"Other?"

The midwife hooted once more, her tongue lolling to one side. "You defiled the Goddess, your birth-water and blood raining down upon her altar. You were exiled when you began to bleed. You are dangerous—unknowingly, unconsciously—during your six days of bleeding. You draw dark powers from impure blood, blood of any kind from that region—birth blood, menstrual blood, virgin blood."

The girl felt the stickiness between her legs, she had begun her cycle that very morning, an alarmingly heavy one.

The old woman began to mutter, "Exiled at thirteen, thirteen-year exile." She lifted a mat on the earthen floor and stuck her arm down into a hole. One by one, she pulled out tiny packets wrapped in old newspaper and lay them in front of her. From somewhere inside her ragged sari, she pulled out a small coconut: raw, smooth, green.

"Why go back?" she asked. "What do you desire there?"

The girl looked away, remembering the feeling of tresses entangled in the thick of the night, skin so fragrant she had only to be in the same room to be intoxicated by it. A forbidden touch in a scarlet-tinged room.

The midwife crowed horrifically as if she had read her mind, and then, regaining her composure, opened the newspaper packets. In each lay a powder, some velvety yellow, others a gritty brown, blue, black. She began mixing them together, all the while chanting in low tones. The dog's barking drew closer and with it came the snapping of footfalls upon dried palm fronds. The girl glanced over her shoulder, regretting that she had not pulled the mat back over the doorway. Moving quickly now, the old woman cracked the coconut open with a sickle-shaped *koyta* and poured in the powder mixture, stirring it into the coconut milk. The concoction smoked, filling the air with a foul, polluted smell.

The girl drew back, horrified.

"Exiled at thirteen, thirteen-year exile," the midwife muttered again. And then her blind gaze fell upon the girl. "For thirteen years you cannot go back."

"No!"

"The fulfillment of your desires carries a price, an unfathomable price."

"I've lost too much already," the girl whispered as the smoke coiled around her. "I won't lose this."

"Think of that then," the midwife commanded, holding the reddish, snaking liquid to the girl's lips. "You must think of that as you drink. What you desire will become your truth."

The girl hesitated, touching the mole upon her cheek for luck.

"Fast now, fast, someone is near!"

And the girl once again remembered the feel of warm skin, the sweet breath of laughter. And the loss was so deep, so intense that she felt a deep hatred boil up inside her chest for those who had cast her out that morning, severing her from the only place she regarded as home.

As the first drops of the elixir touched her tongue, her desire was not love.

But revenge.

BEGINNINGS:

Thirteen Years Later

We have to build the noble mansion of free India where all her children may dwell.
—Jawaharlal Nehru
Speech On the Granting of Indian Independence
August 14, 1947

⁂

Hich: A person who is nowhere, a thing which has no place, no identity or personality of its own, from 'hichgah'—nowhere.
—From the Old Pahlavi Persian
Zia Jaffrey, *The Invisibles*

THE BUNGALOW

Pinky Mittal's earliest memory was of glistening water. It splashed and crashed along with the sounds of wheels straining to push forward, the crack of a switch upon a bullock's bleeding back, shouts of men, whimperings of hungry children. There was a buzzing, a screeching, like the sound of a kettle of vultures, their formation like blackened bubbles rising from the river.

In this memory, so primal that it came to her only as a dream, Pinky stared at a woman in a sari, golden yellow like the *champa* flower. The woman looked to the barren sky as if beseeching the gods, and then—slowly, very slowly—began to fall into the current. She was carried swiftly downward, the sari *palloo* trailing behind her like the fluttering of a dying bird. Pinky cried out, the sound coming out as a baby's inconsolable wail, but the golden woman sank without a sound.

And then came comprehension.

It was her mother.

Pinky woke with a start in the strangely stifling room. Sweat poured from her skin and pooled in every crevice of her body, between her fingers, behind her knees, into her eyes. She opened them, feeling the sting of salt, the blurriness of tears, and instinctively reached up, grasping for something solid in her dream-induced haze, and knocked over a covered steel cup by her bed. It clattered to its side, spilling water across the polished wood floor.

She lifted herself up on to her elbows, taking a moment for the recurring nightmare to fade away, and the familiarity of the room to offer comfort. From her vantage point, upon a mattress positioned at the side of her grandmother's bed, Pinky could make out the hulking outline of the cabinets lining one wall, each painted with fanciful, ocher-colored chinoiserie murals. As a child, she had spent hours tracing the long, tapering branches which occasionally meandered from one panel to the next. She had woven endless, circular stories about the exotic birds who inhabited the trees: the cruel, sharp-beaked crimson one with the white-tipped feathers, the quiet russet one who pecked amongst the thatches of long grass, the little baby one who chirped longingly from her tiny nest. On one rectangular panel, the painted branches ended in a cluster of vermilion-colored berries that Pinky had long ago ordained with magical powers.

She drew out each story, peppering it with obstacles and twists, as if to delay the final moment, to savor the thrill when the sole, gossamer-winged butterfly on the panel swooped down and saved the berries from the cruel bird. And then, spanning the breadth of the six murals, she distributed the berries in a queenly way. And by magic, the one-legged bird grew another leg and the blue bird with faded feathers received shiny new ones. Pinky always saved the final berry for the sad, little baby bird who had lost its family. *Eat it*, she whispered to the baby bird, *it will bring them back.*

Rubbing her eyes, she stretched as if to push the last sticky dream remnants away and then opened a small teak chest inlaid with intricate enamel work on the floor next to her. It contained her most precious possessions: fresh pencils that had arrived by ship, a box of sticky oil pastels, a tin of enameled jacks sent as a gift from a relative in Haridwar, a swatch of emerald silk, and a faded magazine photo. In lieu of actual photos of her dead mother, of which none remained, Pinky had torn out a picture of the actress Madhubala from an old copy of *Filmindia*. In it, Madhubala is looking out into the distance as if lost in thought, her face and hair framed by an ethereal glow. She is stunning, her lips parted slightly, a pearl choker at her neck. Over time, Pinky had forgotten that the photo was not really her mother. She knew very little about her, except for a few stories about her childhood and the fact that she drowned while crossing a river.

Pinky carefully returned the photo to the chest, pushing it against the wall next to a heavy dresser with a small brass mirror overturned on top. Just above her on the imposing Edwardian-style bed, her grandmother's enormous belly rose from a faded sheet like a snowcapped peak, her snores already at deafening levels. A mosquito coil burned in one corner, releasing a bittersweet smell, where a temperamental air-conditioning unit jutted out from the wall. Pinky clicked the knob and the machine sputtered to high, offering a blast of cooling air. It was early June, the hottest, most unbearable, most humid stretch of the year, and sleep without the AC was nearly impossible.

She sat on the bed, pulling her grandmother's warm hands, knotted and thick with bluish veins, into her own. They were life-giving hands, ones that had held her, clothed her, and fed her ever since she had been a motherless infant thirteen years ago. When Pinky was younger and still sleeping in the huge Edwardian bed, she used to hold on to one of Maji's hands through the night and perform a little ritual whenever she was afraid or sick. Turning it face up, Pinky ran her finger along the lines in the palm, starting with the thickest one that curved around the thumb. She meticulously touched a line for each of her years, as if to somehow map herself into the infinite universe within Maji's hand. She incanted a small prayer: *I am in you.* Even at thirteen, Pinky still continued with this small assertion of belonging.

After she had finished, she wiped up the spilled water and retrieved the steel cup. Peering down the dark east hallway that ran from a locked teak door on the front verandah and across the entire length of the bungalow, she could barely make out a dim glow from a large window overlooking the back garden. A parallel hallway ran down the other, west side of the bungalow, dividing it into roughly three sections with bedrooms, bathrooms, and the kitchen in either wing, and the front parlor, the dining hall, and living room in the center. The one-story bungalow had been built over a hundred years earlier by a high-ranking East India Company officer as an architectural symbol of the British Raj. His wife, longing for the tidy coolness of

Home, however, had irritably christened the bungalow The Jungle. Pinky loved its elegant symmetry and grand teak doors, its Moghul-inspired archways, and the lush, tropical garden in back with its grove of mango trees.

During the season, the trees dripped with the fleshy, golden fruit and Maji gave away all they did not need, sending baskets to friends and relatives throughout Bombay. Mango-picking day was a festive day in the bungalow, a holiday unto themselves. The gardener arrived at the crack of dawn with extra workers and they collected huge basketfuls of the fruit, while Pinky and her cousins sat under the trees, biting into the sweet flavor, their faces smeared bright orange. *They are Lord Ganesh's favorite, too,* Maji always told them as she clipped a handful of auspicious mango leaves to hang on the front verandah. Later in the day, she supervised the distribution of the mangos in the ornate dining hall while her daughter-in-law, Savita, sauntered around the long, polished dining table, squeezing and prodding the fruit to ensure that the best ones were earmarked for her relations.

Pinky stepped into the stifling hall, deprived of the artificially cooled air that the bedrooms and the front parlor typically enjoyed. The wooden floorboards, which normally creaked and sighed with the slightest pressure, absorbed the lightness of her feet. Pinky knew these floors, knew where they gave way and where they were supported. She walked across them with unthinking familiarity.

She crept past her uncle and aunt's room, stopping to peer through the crack at their door where their low voices diffused into the hall along with the soft whirring of their modern air conditioner. Wedging her body against the crack, she indulged in the rush of chilly air that dried the sweat along one leg, arm, and cheek.

"As if it isn't enough that we've taken in Pinky," Savita sniffed, her delicate features tightening with anger. The upper ribbons on her imported silk nightgown lay untied, revealing the tiny glitter of a diamond dangling between her breasts. "I can't believe you just sent ten thousand rupees to her father."

"At Maji's request," Jaginder said as if to assure her that he would not have been so generous on his own. The years had added a slouch to his once proud shoulders, a shadow of stubble fell across his handsome face. "A loan only."

"Loan?" Savita's voice grew shrill. She pointed a slender, manicured fingertip at him in accusation. "We have nothing to do with them anymore. Why should we give them money?"

"He's Pinky's father after all."

"What father," Savita snorted. "He's remarried, he has other children now, he hasn't even bothered to visit since Maji took her in!"

Outside in the hallway, Pinky felt a hot sting of tears in her eyes. Savita never let an opportunity pass to make her feel unwelcome in the bungalow, like a beggar. *She's not your sister,* she would admonish her sons whenever Maji was out of earshot, *she's your destitute cousin. Remember that.*

Pinky retreated into the comfort of darkness, making a quick left under a scalloped archway, breathing in the bungalow's aroma of sandalwood, peppers, and fried cumin. It was so dim, that for a moment, she thought there might be a power outage. Then her eyes fixed on ruby stains of color flickering upon the walls emitted by series of stained-glass and brass *handis.* She pressed her hand to the wall of the corridor, watching as the color settled upon her skin like a kiss.

At the west hallway, she turned right, into the kitchen where a tall, decorated earthen urn of boiled water stood on a marble countertop. Pinky glugged down the tepid water with relief and refilled her cup. A wave of sleepiness washed over her.

Turning down the corridor to return to her room, she unexpectedly heard the scrape of a door and backtracked, first peeking around the corner, then tiptoeing to her cousins' bedroom. The three boys were the only inhabitants of this side of the bungalow. Pale moonlight filtered in through the window, revealing the sleeping bodies of the fourteen-year-old twins. Dheer's pudgy body was thrown carelessly across the mattress, his mouth gaping open, while Tufan's lean one was curled tightly into a ball as if he were still a baby. The third bed, that belonging to seventeen-year-old Nimish, however, was empty.

Thinking she had a few minutes before his return, Pinky crept to his bedside and placed her cup of water on his night table next to a cluttering stack of books, bookmarks sticking out midway from each one. She leaned in and inhaled his salty, sensuous scent and then, blushing, glanced at the slumbering twins to ensure they had not awakened and seen her. Dheer let out a reassuring, rumbling snore.

Pinky touched her hand to Nimish's warm pillow and inhaled again. A book peeked out from underneath it and she reached for it, fingering its odd title, *The Fakeer of Jungheera*. It felt old and dusty and she knew immediately that it belonged to the musty library at the end of the hallway. It fell open to a page where a miniature chart titled "An Ideal Boy" was carefully taped inside the book, covering an entire page. The chart detailed the twelve most essential behaviors, including "Salutes Parents" and "Brushes Up The Teeth," each one accompanied by a gaudy illustration. Pinky could not help but smile. Nimish had received this chart in primary school. He had showed it to her and the twins when he returned from class that day, the four of them rolling with laughter and taking turns pretending to be the upright little boy in the pictures with his clean, white shirt and knickers, dutifully "Taking The Lost Children To The Police Post." And yet, even though they had mocked it, Nimish had kept the chart all these years, taped inside this random book. Perhaps Dheer or Tufan needed daily behavioral cues but Nimish already, effortlessly, embodied the dutiful son.

Curious now at Nimish's lengthy absence, Pinky replaced the book and decided to look for him in the library. She hesitated as she passed the children's bathroom, which consisted of two separate doors, one leading to a tiled bathing area and the other to a toilet and sink. The door to the bathing area was like all the others in the interior of the bungalow, made of shiny wood inset with three panels. A delicately carved chakra occupied the center of each panel. What made it different, however, was the vertical bolt at the very top of the doorframe, out of reach.

For as long as she could remember, this door was unexplainably bolted at night, the thick metal rod sliding into place with an echoing crash. The children were forbidden to touch it after sunset. In place of a rational explanation for this nightly ritual, the children came up with their own wild theories. The twins were sure that the bathroom was transformed nightly into the headquarters for their father's superhero activities or perhaps into a hideout used by the infamous criminal Red Tooth. They, of course, dared each other to get out of bed to touch the door or wiggle the handle, which they did before racing back and throwing themselves under the covers. Once they even rigged a pair of chairs so they could reach the bolt. But as Tufan touched it, he tumbled over. The weight of the seats left ugly bruises and cuts. At the sound of the crash, Savita had come running at them hysterically. *What do you think you're doing?* she had yelled, slapping them each several times across the face. *Do you want to die? Do you?*

After that, none of them dared to try again despite their claims of bravery and the shrugging off of Savita's ominous warning. Yet they could not account for the sound the water pipes made at night, the odd rattlings, the strange whooshing that did not settle until just before dawn.

Pinky pressed herself against the wall to be as far away as possible. She did not want to look but of their own will, her eyes fell upon the bolt. A chill shot to her fingertips. She raced to the library.

"Nimish?"

The library must have been grand in its day, with its elaborately carved bookshelves, dark paneled walls, heavily upholstered couches, and glass chandelier, but by the time the bungalow passed into Maji's hands several years before Independence, it had already suffered from neglect. The once-plush carpet was bare in ever-growing patches, the chandelier housed an intrepid family of spiders, and even though they were thoroughly cleaned once a year, the thick, gloomy curtains stank of stale cigar smoke.

Its faded, forgotten glory soothed Pinky. When the rest of the bungalow had been updated, this sole room remained as it was, lost in the past. Nimish spent hours in here with the books, breathing in the residue of another era. His plan was to read every single book that the library contained, from the hard burgundy or green leather covers richly engraved in gold to the small ones dressed in cloth dust jackets, all the while imagining what it was like to have been a *pukka* English sahib. So far he had read every single autobiography of the English Indian Civil Service officers—the elite competition-*wallahs* who governed India and then vainly penned their memoirs upon retirement—the works of Kipling, and the entire, paperback series of *Wheeler's Indian Railway Library.*

A faint sliver of moonlight filtered between a crack in the heavy drapery and fell in a jagged line upon the threadbare carpet, across a rectangular table adorned with a large, multiple-piped hookah, and onto several books with intense blue bindings. Pinky felt her way to the window and looked to the sky. The moon slipped into a dark haze. The clouds had started gathering that afternoon, little billows of smoke in the bright, sunlit sky that foretold the monsoon's impending arrival. Oh, how they had obsessed about nothing else all that scorching day but the joy of those first drops of eagerly awaited rain from the heavens.

The moon brightened and Pinky's heart stopped as she caught sight of Nimish. There he was, on the driveway, his tall, slender frame, finely chiseled face, and copper brown skin glowing. He was pacing back and forth, his fists clenched as if in determination, eyebrows knitted above thin, wire spectacles. Pinky wiped the sweat trickling from her hands onto her pajamas and rapped on the window. But Nimish had already turned away, heading toward the back garden.

Pinky raced down the hallway, out the side door, and past the garage which Gulu, the driver, shared with the black Mercedes. A frisson hummed in her chest as the humid air drenched her thin pajamas. Above her, a gust of wind rustled a broken kite impaled upon a tree branch. And just past the bungalow, a grand white-marble lotus fountain stood in the grassy center of the garden surrounded by a pond, a stone pathway, and a ring of rosebushes. Beyond that lay the thickness of the trees.

Pinky stood breathless, pressing her back against the stone wall that separated their bungalow from their neighbors', the Lawates, on the other side. She called to Nimish in sharp whispers. A love song from the hit film *Dil Deke Dekho,* took root in her head as she cut into the expansive garden, which was exquisitely groomed by the gardener who arrived every day with nothing more than a rusted sickle for landscaping and a fresh coconut for quenching his thirst.

She had always loved Nimish, even as a little girl, drawn to him as if he were the father she never had. When she was younger, he had hovered over her, shielding her from unkind remarks and accidental harm. In the last years, however, as her body began to change, Pinky wanted more from him than simply this . . . this paternal affection. She had begun to notice, with a flush, the soft tones of his laughter, the gloss of his hair.

He was so carefree with his younger brothers, teasing them, guiding them, and occasionally throwing a sympathetic arm around them after they were punished. But with Pinky, he had become more distant, his communication limited to passages read out loud from his countless books or professorial monologues if she asked for help with her schoolwork.

"Nimish?" she whispered again. *Could he be right there, behind that tree, waiting for me?* She reached out, imagining the feel of his strong hand in hers, on her.

She could almost picture a flash of silk behind a tree, betraying the presence of a troupe of dancers that was waiting for the lovers to meet before breaking into flirtatious song and dance. Nimish had led her out here, she was sure of it, to confess his love. This was her Bollywood moment.

Somewhere in the distance a door closed.

Pinky snapped out of her reverie.

Had Nimish gone back? Had she somehow failed in her scripted role? She raced back through the foliage, carelessly treading upon lovingly tended flowers until she reached the edge of the bungalow. And then she dashed across the moonlit driveway.

The bungalow's darkness embraced her.

Back in the air-conditioned coolness of the boys' room, Dheer snored in loud, choppy breaths and Tufan lay in a sweaty, satiated slumber, his hand tucked into his pajama bottoms. But Nimish's bed was still empty. Pinky hid herself behind it, slowing her pounding heart and fighting off the cold, clammy feel of sweat beginning to dry.

"Where are you?" Pinky whispered into his pillow.

She could not imagine what he could be doing in the dark garden alone, behind the immense stone wall that surrounded the bungalow on three sides, the fourth protected by an equally imposing gate complete with welded-iron arrowhead caps. But then, as she mentally walked the yard, she remembered that the wall was not impassable after all. There was a way to get through, to get out. *Could it be?*

She once again picked up *The Fakeer of Jungheera* and glanced at the poem opposite the gaudy "Ideal Boy" chart. *My native home, my native home, Hath in its groves the turtledove, And from her nest she will not roam—For it is warmed with faith and love. But there is love, and there is faith, Which round a bleeding heart entwine, To thee devoted even to death—And oh! That love and faith are mine!*

Slowly, meticulously, as the urgent words sunk in, she untaped the chart from the opposite page. There, hidden behind the "Ideal Boy" was his not-so-ideal truth, his turtle dove in a tamarind tree. Yes, the stone wall had a small opening that led to one and only one place, the Lawates' next door. And Nimish's little bird was none other than seventeen-year-old Lovely Lawate, beaming exquisitely in black and white.

A BOLTED DOOR

A stinging pain took root in the center of Pinky's chest, its poison-ous tendrils radiating outward, tightening, tightening around her heart.

She panted in small, wet breaths: *Lovely. Lovely. Lovely.*

She should have known. Pinky still wore her hair in two oiled braids. How could she compare to a blooming beauty like Lovely with her thick mane of hair delicately adorned with flowers? Neighbors always commented on her enviably fair skin and the delicate shape of her eyes to which Lovely's mother, Vimla, applied a broad, black smear of *kajal* every morning to ward off the evil eye.

Lovely had been Pinky's playmate for years, especially when they were younger. They had hidden away in a shaded part of the garden, constructing makeshift *puja* altars with branches and decorating them with flowers and sacred *tulsi* leaves, and placing a miniature sandal-wood idol of Lakshmi, Goddess of Prosperity, within the soft interior. Lovely was always the priest and Pinky the supplicant who kneeled as Lovely sprinkled water upon her bowed head and marked it with vermillion.

As Lovely entered her teenage years, however, she had lost interest in this childhood game, and the four years that separated the girls felt like a lifetime. Still, Lovely occasionally invited Pinky for a picnic in the park and, away from watchful eyes, they could speak as friends, sisters even. It was at these moments that Pinky glimpsed what the others never saw—a transient shadow upon Lovely's beautiful face, a hidden recklessness.

The air conditioner started up with a noisy clanking and Pinky crouched by Nimish's bed fighting a surge of jealousy. She felt small, insignificant. Wiping away tears, she tried resticking the "Ideal Boy" chart back onto the page of the book, her fingers fumbling with the yellowed tape.

She was so immersed in this task and deafened by the AC's toiling engine that she did not hear Nimish's returning footsteps. And then, before she knew it, he was whispering her name. She closed the book with a snap.

"What are you doing here?" He sat down on his bed and leaned toward her. "Are you okay?"

She nodded, her head still bowed.

He put his hand lightly on her shoulder. That weight, that warmth, should have comforted her but it did not. Is this all she would ever get from him? A concerned question, a consoling hand? She pushed his arm away.

Nimish sat back, surprised, and adjusted his spectacles. It was then he saw his book in her hands. He stiffened and reached out to take it from Pinky but she held tight. Inside lay the photo that Nimish treasured.

"Where were you?" she whispered boldly.

Nimish disregarded her disrespectful tone but did not respond. Once again, with gentleness, he asked, "Are you okay?"

Tears began to fall from Pinky's eyes. She was not immune to him, to his soft voice, his tender manner.

"Please tell me," Pinky asked, testing to see if he would lie to her, he who never lied.

He shrugged. "Out on the driveway, in the garden."

"I came outside, I looked for you."

Nimish raised an eyebrow. "You shouldn't be outside at night. If Maji found out—"

"And what about you?" Pinky shot back, wiping away tears. "What if they found out what *you* were doing?"

"Just give me the book," Nimish said, his voice stern now. He reached out and grasped it but Pinky held on tight.

Their eyes met, his so soft. Pinky felt her grip slacken.

"Why her?" she whispered, just as the air-conditioning unit cut sharply to silence. "Why not me?" Pinky's hand flew to her mouth in disbelief that she had said those words at the very moment he could hear them. She saw him recoil.

"What do you mean? Oh, Pinky. . . ."

He shook his head.

Pinky could not breathe, the stinging in her chest pulsed. She could not see. She did not want to live. *How had this happened?*

Fragments from the ancient epics flashed in her head, shards from the *Puranas* and the *Mahabharata* that Maji was always recounting to her. The fearless Princess Draupadi married five men, all brothers. And the beautiful Princess Sanjana and her shadow Chhaya shared the same husband, the Sun God Surya. If their legendary loves were possible, surely what Pinky desired of Nimish was not so horrible.

And yet it was.

"You should go," he was saying, his voice sounding faraway.

Pinky stood. There was a humming noise inside her, as if the stinging in her chest had traveled up, up past her throat and into her ears.

"My book. . . ."

She looked down, allowing the book to fall open to the "Ideal Boy" chart that was haphazardly stuck to the page. It jeered at her now, the photos of the knickered, little boy with fair skin and impossibly rosy cheeks.

Nimish took it from her.

Pinky continued to stare at her upturned palms, now empty of their treasure, his treasure.

"Go now," he said, the kindness gone, replaced by subdued anger.

She could not leave his room like this, with the bite of his fury, with him thinking that she had purposely violated his privacy, with their relationship changed forever.

Yet, taking her steel cup of water from the table, she put one foot in front of the other and walked out.

The door shut behind her.

Pinky slid to the ground, sweat dripping into her eyes, tears falling out of them. The wall warmed with her heat, offering silent, stoic assurance. In front of her stood the shiny bathroom door. Once again, her eyes traveled up to the bolt.

Tufan once let slip that the door was first bolted at night the same year Pinky came to live in the bungalow—thirteen years ago, the year he and Dheer had turned one—but that was all he knew. The children, of course, had questioned the adults about it but stern faces and an occasional slap kept them from probing too deeply. Nimish was the only one who never seemed intrigued by the bolt, accepting it easily as he did most of his parents' governance. He, in fact, was the one who scanned the papers for the time of sunset each day, taking care to slide the bolt into place a full half hour beforehand.

The bathroom was unlocked at sunrise by the housemaids, Parvati and Kuntal, who savagely beat the laundry upon the tile floor. Afterwards, the children, one by one, were allowed to take their baths, squatting upon a low, wooden stool with a bucketful of water and *lota*. The room was small, windowless, and flat except for a rectangular cement ridge that had been built around the faucet to keep the water from spreading out of the bathing area. It was so ordinary in the daytime. And yet . . .

New tears sprouted in Pinky eyes at her foolishness that night, at the unnecessary ruination. What else had he been keeping from her? What was behind this door? She was certain he knew. She approached the door, placing the steel cup upon the floor. She pressed her palm to the wood. The door appeared to sink into its frame as if protecting an internal wound.

She stretched her arm up, up to reach for the bolt but it was too high.

The confining space in the hallway seemed to pull her back, to hold on to her, but Pinky broke free and raced to find the old rickety kitchen stool. The floorboards squeaked in warning but she did not care if Nimish heard. She *wanted* him to come out of his room and see her. She wanted him to stop her. She thought of the ancient tale *Ratnavali*, of how the king had saved the princess as she strung a noose around her neck, he at last confessing, *I can't live without you.*

If there's anything truly dangerous, she thought, *he'll come out.*

She climbed upon the stool and reached up; her fingertips touched the bolt. The metal felt cold, unnaturally cold. The bungalow shuddered in a sudden gust of wind.

The forbidden door.

Tears fell freely now. She glanced at Nimish's bedroom door, but it remained firmly shut. Her heart filled with the poison of rejection, screaming out for a sign, any sign of his love.

She lifted herself up upon her toes, reaching toward the bolt. The door seemed to lean back, the bolt moving further from her. But she held onto it, held it for dear life, as if it were the only thing that could return him to her.

Nimish!

The floorboards lurched and the stool toppled over, but in that split second before she fell, she slid open the bolt.

The water pipes whispered all around her—all of them suddenly rushing, rushing towards the bathroom.

Pinky landed hard, knocking over the steel cup of water.

And then the bungalow's shadows pushed her out of the hall, out, out, out as fast as her legs could run.

WATERY PRESENCE

M aji woke and turned her eyes to the window, noting the exact hue of the sky. Yes, it was dawn, not a moment before nor after. She felt pleased, the day had begun auspiciously. She noticed that Pinky lay sleeping in the bed and not upon her mattress as usual, and gently touched the smooth skin of her cheek.

Maji slid her legs off the bed and into a pair of worn *chappals* that were conveniently lined up on the wooden floor and then grasped for her cane. She stood up with great difficulty, arthritic knee joints crackling and popping at the sudden weight thrust upon them, and adjusted the widow-white sari she always wore. Then, shuffling around, she stole another glimpse of Pinky, huddled under a thin, cotton sheet. Despite the pain surging through her obese body, she smiled.

The sleeping child was the light of her life.

Yamuna, Pinky's mother, had died as a refugee, crossing from Lahore into India during Partition. The military had disposed of her corpse, saying only that she drowned. The pain was breathtaking, like a vengeful blow from the heavens. There was nothing left of her possessions, her dowry, her brief life—except for Pinky. She was the tiny bit of Yamuna that was still alive on this earth. Maji remembered the day she had laid claim to her, the sun already fiercely scorching, crackling, in that desolate place, a full overnight train journey from Bombay. The *tonga* cart stopped just in front of an ugly dark olive building next to a factory where a huge pile of metal scraps had been dumped. Workers sifted through the metal, carrying it away piece by piece in baskets atop their heads. Nearby, a phalanx of black-limbed, pot-bellied children sluggishly stuck their scrawny arms into the dirt and trilled for their mothers. One walked towards her with hand out-stretched, his body naked from the waist down, a talisman tied with a black thread just over his little penis.

Maji remembered hearing the clicking behind her and then the gait of the *tonga* cart retreating upon the makeshift road, the horse evacuating noisily as it was whipped to a trot. A *falsay* vendor passed by on his rickety bike, calling out in an empty, echoing voice. A silk-cotton semul tree drooped in front of the stairwell leading up to the second floor of the flat.

The door was already propped open for circulation when she reached the landing. As exhausted as she was, Maji was resolute, her eyes revealing nothing as they fell upon Pinky's other grandmother whose thinning grey hair billowed behind her like a spider's web.

Maji uttered a little prayer of gratitude for this child, marveling—still—that she was hers. She glanced through the windows, noting the hazy clouds outside that ineffectively hindered the sun. The monsoons would be here any day now to bring relief to this parched city. She tapped at the AC with her cane, turning it off, then shuffled slowly to the bathroom where she leaned over the shining Parryware basin. She concentrated on opening nasal and throat passages that had been in-filtrated with phlegm in the night. Loud hawking and blowing noises like the trumpeting of an elephant ensued, and then Maji stepped back into the hallway visibly refreshed.

She started down the long hallway as she did every day at dawn, making her usual rounds within the lavish, one-story bungalow. Maji had started this routine when they first bought the bungalow from a portly, cigar-chewing Englishman who fled India, leaving his belongings and unscrupulous business dealings behind. She had spent the quiet mornings then discovering her new home, its cracks and crevices, the antique furniture, all of which now belonged to her. When the fascination had faded into a comfortable acceptance, Maji realized that she had actually come to enjoy this routine, this matriarchal stroll through the bungalow while her family slept. It was also her belief that a hundred rounds each morning allowed her to indulge in the cook's homemade ice cream that evening, a hundred and fifty if he was serving the dessert in a sea of rose-flavored sauce with pink *falooda* noodles on top.

The first doors she came to were on her left, grand paneled ones that led to the dining hall. She opened them, taking in the long teak dining table occupying the center of the dark, polished room. She began to think about the day's menu, settling upon a combination of cooling foods such as yogurt with cucumber, cauliflower cooked with coriander, saffron rice, and green lentils. She walked past Savita and Jaginder's room, her face sagging into a slight frown as she pondered her daughter-in-law. From the day she entered their household as a bride, Savita had proven herself difficult, lacking in what Maji considered the fundamentals: selflessness, respect, restraint. Just yesterday, in fact, Savita had flung a *thali* of uncooked rice into the ceiling fan after shouting at the servants. The basmati grains had rained down upon all those in the vicinity, including the unsuspecting priest who mistakenly attributed the shower to a divine blessing.

Maji sighed, passing the *puja* sanctuary on her right and, to her left, the etched glass doors of the ornate living room, throwing them open to allow the morning air to circulate. Then she cut under the corridor archway, inspecting as she went to check for signs of neglect. The floors shone, the walls were clean and bright, the brass *handis* were free of dust. Maji felt reassured.

She strode down the west hallway unhurriedly, her heavy step and swish of white cotton sari in tune with the rhythmic thumping of clothes being washed by the housemaids. And then, coming full circle to the front of the bungalow, she opened another set of glass doors and stepped into the parlor. Her gaze immediately went to the unsmiling photo of her late husband that hung near the entrance, garlanded with a sandalwood rosary. Although so many years had past, fifteen almost, she still felt a pang of loss in her heart. A film song floated into her head, the one her husband had murmured into her ear as he lay dying: *Sleep, princess, sleep. Sleep and sweet dreams will come. In the dreams, see your beloved.* He did keep this final promise, appearing in her dreams and sweeping her into the timeless past when her life did not carry the burden of so many losses.

The parlor was carpeted by two enormous, wine red Persian rugs. The far wall leading to the dining hall consisted of a series of carved wooden screens inset with sandblasted glass panels. The room was elegantly furnished with an array of fine, plush covered furniture and global curios. One table displayed a blue and white Cantonese Export porcelain candy dish, another a set of eighteenth century European ceramic bowls. A cabinet contained a shelf of silver inkwells and chalices, each brightly polished and set upon a lace doily. A Victrola Talking Machine stood in one corner, imported all the way from exotic-sounding Camden, New Jersey. It had a multiband radio, a turntable, and high-gloss cabinets for storing records. One of the housemaids had thoughtfully adorned it with a vase of fresh yellow roses.

Maji began her next round, moving at the same pace, looking for-ward to her dearest friend Vimla Lawate's visit from next door so they could sit sipping chai and dipping salty *muttees* into mango pickle. Their daily chats were a respite from the hectic demands of running the bungalow. Maji made a mental note to ask the cook to replenish their stock of Gold Spot and pick up a box of fried *jalebi* dipped in syrup and immodestly dressed in edible silver.

Her thoughts went on like this, round after round, sometimes mak-ing lists, sometimes more meditatively reflecting upon the lessons on morality from the great epics, the *Mahabharata* and the *Ramayana*, sometimes snagging on a memory of her late husband or daughter. Maji always ended her rounds in the parlor, hoisting herself upon a cushioned, antique dais that may have at one point belonged to the raja of a small fiefdom before it was done away with by the British. The dais was heavily ornamented, its brass base overlaid by a dense mattress, a silken saffron cloth, and finely embroidered bolsters. Lean-ing against their solid girth, Maji offered a dignified, even regal pres-ence while presiding over the sitting area where no business, domestic or otherwise, could take place unheard or unseen.

"Kuntal," Maji called out to the housemaid, her legs painfully tucked lotus-style in front of her, "bring my morning tonic."

Kuntal appeared with a small silver tray in hand on top of which was a tall glass tumbler of boiling-hot water mixed with fresh lime juice and honey. Though she was in her midthirties, she still carried herself like a shy, plump girl. Maji reached out and gingerly grasped the rim with her thumb and middle finger, the other fingers splayed out to protect them from the rising steam. She took a sip and sighed, her stern mouth sinking in a sea of flesh. It was then she noticed that Kuntal lingered.

"Is something wrong?"

Kuntal bit her lip, she did not like to be dishonest with Maji whom she deeply respected, revered even. "No, nothing Maji. I just didn't sleep well last night."

This was not entirely a lie. What she did not say was that she had discovered the bathroom door had been unbolted this morning, that there had been an overturned steel cup alongside the kitchen stool, that she had hastily summoned her elder sister Parvati, and that Parvati had said, *No, don't tell Maji, not just yet.* They had beaten the laundry in the bathroom without incident and pinned it up in the back garden. The clothes now hung, crucified, to lines of jute, bleeding their dampness into the air.

The Mittal family's laundry used to be sent out to the *dhobiwallah* to be cleaned. But as Maji grew more and more obese, she became concerned with the indignity of a strange washerman rubbing soap into the crotch of her gigantic undergarment. So when Parvati and Kuntal were hired in 1943, the expectation was that, in addition to the full array of housework, the household's laundry would be done at home by them too.

Relieved to find work, they had taken on this task without complaint. Over time, though, as they became an indispensable part of the household, the sound of Parvati's wooden paddle hitting the clothes echoed through the bungalow each morning, infiltrating its inhabitants' dreams with loud smack-smacks of resentment.

Maji inspected Kuntal's face more closely. *No, something was definitely wrong.* She decided to let it be for the moment because the rest of her family was at last waking up. The bungalow stirred to life,

filling with the sound of running water, the clanking of Cook Kanj
in the kitchen, the gradual crescendo of voices. She rocked back and
forth until she could dislodge her legs, then laboriously stood and
hobbled to the front gate where Cook Kanj met her with a with a
thali of rice and curried vegetables in her hand. Though she rarely
left home because of the crippling arthritis in her knees, Maji never
missed a day of giving alms to the famous hopping *sadhu* who came
by the bungalow every morning.

The *sadhu* traveled on one foot, the other bent like a triangle at the
knee, completely naked but for a small loin cloth that immodestly
flapped upwards with every hop. He had traversed the same route
for twenty years, becoming an object of veneration for the pious,
local debate for the men, and endless fascination for the neighborhood children. He possessed nothing more than three white stripes
of ash painted across his forehead and a small group of devotees who
followed him around, one of whom scurried ahead to sweep dung
and debris out of his path. The *sadhu's* hopping leg was muscular and
distended with blood while the other one had simply withered away
from neglect and had to be tied via prop system to his shoulder. He
received the alms from Maji, gave his blessings, and ceremoniously
hopped away. Maji felt at peace.

By the time Pinky emerged from the bedroom, the first shift of breakfast was already laid out on the table. Patties of *aloo tikkis* were piled
upon a plate with spicy mint and sweet-sour *imli* chutneys, and a
bottle of ketchup. There were thin slices of toast smeared with softened butter, chunks of fresh fruit, and chai. Jaginder was popping
the *aloo tikkis* into his mouth at an alarming rate while scanning the
Hindi-language *NavBharat Times*. Savita sat next to him, simultaneously heaping more food upon his plate and taking delicate bites of
guava sprinkled with rock salt. Nimish, who was the only one of the
boys allowed to read at breakfast, ate while using his elbow to prop
open a book, *Hindoo Holiday.*

Nimish often expounded on complex topics at the dining table,
which earned him irritated looks from his father, proud smiles from
his mother, and sharp elbows from his younger brothers. After Nimish

reached adolescence, Savita had declared him off-limits for general slap-ping and other disciplinary actions such as ear-pulling and nose-pinch-ing that involved his face. *You mustn't jiggle his brain cells out of place.*

What rot, Jaginder had replied, *judging by the nonsense that comes out of his mouth, he could use a bloody shake.*

Nevertheless, he obeyed the injunction against slapping his eldest and instead, much to Dheer and Tufan's dismay, augmented his disci-plinary efforts toward the twins.

Dheer was chatting away now, expounding on the composition of various street snacks. "*Bhelpuri* should be served in a malu-leaf cone with a squeeze of lime and enough *imli* chutney on top to make it sweet," he said, his voice strained with longing for the sour tamarind paste amply mixed with sweet dates, sugar, and wrinkled *bedagi* chilies.

No one appeared to be listening.

Tufan ate sullenly next to unopened stacks of comics, including *Palladin, Annie Oakley, Roy Rogers,* and *The Lone Ranger.*

"Oh, *wah,* look who's decided to get up finally," Savita remarked, spotting her niece in her pajamas.

Pinky's face fell. After unbolting the door the previous night, she had thrown herself into bed with Maji, holding onto her hand and imagin-ing the worst. Exhaustion and tears finally overwhelmed her and she fell fast asleep. Now in the morning, she felt a little better. The family was sitting as always, eating their breakfast. She stole a glance at Nimish.

"Good morning," he offered quietly before returning to his book.

Pinky could not bring herself to answer, to pretend nothing had happened to keep up appearances. Had he erased everything that transpired between them last night? She felt strangely relieved, and perhaps a little foolish too. She slid into a chair and began sipping from a cup of tea.

"Nimi, darling," Savita said sweetly, popping a fresh, spongy almond into her son's mouth to nourish his brain. "Read something from your book so I won't have to listen to that slurping."

Nimish chewed quickly and swallowed.

"It's written by an Englishman named Ackerley who recorded his stay with an Indian maharaja," Nimish said with a blush having just completed a passage that morning in which Ackerley noted that, for Indians, a kiss on the mouth was considered a complete sexual act.

"Read something from it," Savita encouraged while Tufan held his ears and Dheer sucked on a mango pit.

Nimish obediently opened the book. "The other guests left this morning, and just before starting Mrs. Montgomery gave me final advice. 'You'll never understand the dark and tortuous minds of the natives,' she said, 'and if you do I shan't like you—you won't be healthy.'"

Savita glared disapprovingly and popped another almond into Nimish's mouth for good measure.

☆ ☆ ☆

"Come now Pinky-*di*, Maji's already done with her bath," Kuntal said, meeting her in the hallway with a bundle of the previous day's wash to take next door where the unruffable ironing-*wallah* set up his stand in the shade, servicing the entire street.

He started at dawn, lighting a fire to heat the coals before transferring them, red-hot, into the iron itself. Then spreading the material onto a covered table, he flicked water at it and began ironing with fast methodical movements, all the while placating Mrs. Garg from down the lane who blamed his errant ironing for the mysterious lipstick-colored spots on her husband's shirt collars.

Kuntal steered Pinky to the children's bathroom. For a moment, Pinky hesitated, remembering her terror from the night before, but now everything felt so normal, dull even, that she almost laughed. All these years, they had been bolting that door. Nothing terrible had happened last night after she had opened it. Nothing.

She sat on a low wooden stool, reflecting upon Nimish, her long hair heaped on top of her head in a froth of bubbles, eyes shut. The ache in her chest grew stronger. She thought about the way he told her to go, his voice empty of affection, cold even. Slowly, she became aware of feeling chilled and reached for the *lota* to rinse off the shampoo. Down, down, her hand continued into the depths of the brass bucket. But instead of feeling water, she touched dry bottom. Although the low wooden stool she was crouching on had already begun to swell with the day's heat, she shivered as she reached for the faucet. Blindly, she pushed the bucket underneath, hearing the whoosh of the water as it surged through the pipe, the hollowness of the bucket's changing tones as it filled.

The bathroom was a source of constant irritation due to its faulty piping and strange metallic odor. That, along with the pile of fermenting clothes in the corner, lent the space a certain unsavory quality which the four children had to endure each morning, Pinky most of all since she was the last to use it.

The chill grew sharper.

Pinky wondered if she had simply forgotten to latch the door and Kuntal had sneaked in to grab her unwashed clothes, letting in a draft of air.

Cautiously, she reached into the bucket again but, though she distinctly heard the faucet spewing, there was not a drop of liquid at the bottom.

She knocked the bucket over with her foot and opened her eyes, frantically trying to wipe the shampoo from her face. Her eyes burned, her vision blurred.

As far as she could tell, the door was securely latched. The walls held not a single window. Then she looked over to the overturned bucket, drawing back in shock as she saw water gushing out of it, overflowing, flooding.

Hurling herself at the door, she yanked her top down over her head and began to pull at the handle.

It would not open.

She felt something damp rise up behind her.

"Kuntal!" Pinky yelled, fists banging on the door. "Kuntal! Kuntal!"

Her voice reverberated against the walls as if she were sealed in an underwater tomb.

"Parvati!" she cried out to the sharp-eared servant who was always waiting to catch the children in some indiscretion so she could complain to Maji and gain importance in her eyes.

Pinky banged on the door with all her might but still no one came.

"Maji!" she screamed. "Anyone, help!"

Suddenly, and with an unearthly wheeze, the door swung open.

"Why all this shouting? I'm not deaf."

It was Parvati. She was followed by Dheer, cheeks bulging with Cadbury Gems, and Tufan with his jute-rope gun.

"Why didn't you come?" Pinky cried, heart pounding in chest.

"Oh pho!" Parvati shouted, stepping into the bathroom. "Why have you left the faucet on? The whole room is flooded!"

"I . . . I . . . I . . ." Pinky wept.

"Pinky's crying!" Tufan gleefully announced to the household. *Bang, bang.*

"And why's there still shampoo in your hair?"

"Oi," Maji's voice boomed from the parlor as she struggled to propel herself from her seat. "*Kya ho gaya?* Is Pinky okay?" Ignoring the surge of pain through her arthritic joints, she reached for her cane and made her way as hastily as she could to her granddaughter's side.

"The heat makes the door stick, *nah?*" Parvati said, sighing audibly. "Silly girl."

"But . . . but . . . the bucket," Pinky sobbed in between hiccups, angry at herself for being overcome with emotion. *Emotion* had always been a bad word in the Mittal bungalow, spoken of in the same disapproving whispers reserved for the mentally ill. Too much of it led to a host of other afflictions such as insolence, disobedience, and the need for privacy, all which proved ruinous to girls and their future marriage prospects.

"What's going on *now?*" Savita asked out of the side of her mouth. The other side was full of bobby pins which she jammed, one by one, into the mammoth bun on the back of her head.

"She got stuck," Tufn answered.

"*Hai-hai,*" Savita sighed, eyeing Pinky's distress.

"You must be coming down with a fever," Maji declared, deciding that was the only plausible explanation. She pressed a palm to Pinky's forehead.

Dheer lumbered away. Tufan galloped after him as if he were a fleeing buffalo, pretending to fell him with two clean shots from his jute gun. Savita strolled off in the opposite direction, still loudly tsking. Maji and Pinky slowly shuffled towards the parlor. Parvati swung the bathroom door closed.

It could have been the hinges, the warped swell of door against frame, but Pinky thought she heard a soft moan as the door pulled shut.

CASCADING FOLIAGE

S quinting against the bright sunlight, Pinky and Maji strolled across the back garden to pick flowers for the *puja*. Maji inhaled deeply as she walked past the shameless, carmine-colored hibiscus and coy, pink frangipani and stopped under a line of jute, the fresh smell of the hanging laundry an alluring promise to cleanse her body of any stray pollutants she might have missed during her morning bath. It was hot already, the sun's unforgiving rays beat down with an intensity that burned.

"I feel tired," Pinky said, her voice still shaken.

"The rains are in the air," Maji said. "It makes everything feel lethargic. The lightning and thunder will start tonight, then the monsoons will come." She stopped and eyed her granddaughter with concern. "That's it, right? Nothing more?"

Pinky shook her head.

The mundane activities—the quick sweeps of Kuntal's short-handled broom upon the back verandah, the gentle flapping of the wash on the jute line, the buzzing of the bees in the flowers—made her feel a little silly about her fright. She must have misplaced the bucket, putting it just to the side of the faucet instead of directly underneath. The tap had still been on, after all, when Parvati had come to the door and Pinky had not been able to see very well with the shampoo stinging her eyes. It was possible that she had misjudged things.

And it was equally possible that Tufan had bolted the door from the outside. He had done that before, taking advantage of the outside lock, making her beg to be let out. He reminded her of the guavas sold on the roadside at Chowpatty Beach: sharply sliced with an overabundance of chili powder that made even the most ironclad stomachs churn. He had been named after the tsunami that hit Bombay in 1945, at the exact moment of his birth, sweeping away fishing boats and flooding the coastal communities. True to his name, Tufan left a path of destruction in his wake.

✳ ✳ ✳

In the *puja* sanctuary Maji painfully lowered herself onto a seat near the ground in front of the black marble altar adorned with brass and silver figurines of the gods. A huge carved stone *lingam* stood under a framed painting of Saraswati, Goddess of Knowledge, seated upon a white lotus, a brilliant peacock at her feet. Pinky placed the flowers next to a small silver bowl of sweetened *halwa*, and another one containing fresh apples, bananas, and a coconut. They lit the *diyas* and, with folded hands, chanted the Gayatri Mantra. *Om bhoor bhuva suvah.* O Creator of the Universe, the Giver of Life and Happiness. . . .

Pinky sprinkled satiny orange petals before Lord Krishna and his divine consort, Radha. She loved this time inside the *puja* sanctuary with her grandmother. It was as if they were sealed away from the worries of the rest of the world. After they finished the prayers and tasted a little of the *halwa*, thick and buttery with almonds, Maji always recited a story from the great epics. She sat back, her eyes misting over.

"Once there was a great king who yearned for a child. He prayed for many years and one day a daughter was born to him. She grew into a beautiful, intelligent woman but no man dared to ask for her hand so her father sent her on a journey, telling her to find a husband worthy of her brilliance."

Pinky knew the story of Savitri from the *Mahabharata*. In it, the princess meets a noble prince who is fated to die in one year. She nonetheless falls in love and marries him. On his last day on earth, they go to the forest where Yama, the God of Death, takes his soul from his body. Not ready to let him go, the princess follows Yama through the thickening bramble and desolate terrain, her determination never wavering. Finally, on the outskirts of his kingdom, Yama grants her any boon except for her husband's life back. *Please then grant me many children*, she asks, *and let their father be my husband.*

"Lord Yama smiled, knowing he had been outwitted," Maji concluded. "*Go*, he told her, *you have won back his life.* She ran back to the forest and found her husband, waking up as if from a long rest. They returned to his kingdom and lived as king and queen for the rest of their days."

Pinky smiled distractedly.

"So you see," Maji added, her lessons these days always focusing on the topic of marriage, "a wife must always be courageous, especially when it comes to her husband's well-being."

Pinky remembered her confession to Nimish, and how she had not considered his happiness that night, but her own. It had been her broken heart that compelled her to unbolt the door. "The bolt," she blurted out. "Why, Maji, why's that door bolted at night?"

There was a flash of pain in Maji's eyes. "There are some things best left alone."

Pinky hung her head. She could not bear to see her grandmother's sorrow. It prevented her from pressing her further. It was the reason she rarely asked about her mother even though there was a lifetime of things she still wished to know.

Maji touched Pinky's cheek. "Now go, the *darjee* will be here in a little while with your new outfits. Take my keys and get money from the cabinet."

※ ※ ※

The heavy key holder, made of ornamented silver and tightly packed with two dozen keys, usually stuck out from Maji's fleshy waist like an instrument of torture. As a safeguard in case they were ever robbed and to thwart temptation of the servants, anything of value in the bungalow was stashed behind locked doors, including clothing and aging, duty-free items from abroad. Every room had at least one row of cabinets, each with its own lock, and Maji rarely let her keys out of her sight except as needed by Pinky for errands. Maji even slept with her set tucked securely under her pillow at night.

The chinoiserie cabinets creaked in protest before yielding to reveal their contents: old pants from the Raymond's Shop, a box of clay *diyas* smelling slightly of mustard oil, yellowing aerograms bundled together with string, aftershave, a Japanese transistor radio still enclosed in its leather case, a row of bright Terylene shirts, and an assortment of silver figurines of Lord Ganesh encased in clear plastic to keep them from tarnishing.

An elegant, richly cream-colored woolen coat too warm for Bombay's tropical climate hung in one corner, loosely wrapped in a gauzy cloth and faintly smelling of Yardley's talcum powder. It had silver buttons down the front and on the cuffs, each etched with a crest of two imperial-looking lions. It seemed so empty hanging alone there, devoid of a body to fill it. Pinky imagined that her mother might have worn it, picturing Yamuna sliding her slender arms into the sleeves, laughing at the unfamiliar wintry bite of her new home in Lahore, and thinking she had all the time in the world to get used to it.

Pinky stroked the coat, touching the buttons that her mother might have once touched.

"Come *beti*," Maji said, entering the room with a tray of mixed nuts balanced against her hip, "come eat breakfast."

She caught sight of the coat and an old, persistent ache rose up inside her. It had been a gift from her daughter soon after her marriage. *Come visit in the winter time,* Yamuna had written in a letter which Jaginder had to read out loud since Maji had never been schooled long enough to read or write. But Maji had not visited, not wanting to be a guest of Yamuna's mother-in-law, who had postnuptially, proven herself to be a petty and cruel woman. *Come here instead,* Maji had asked her son to write back, *for the holidays.* Before they could solidify plans, however, there were outbreaks of Hindu–Muslim violence. *Get out now, while you have the chance,* Maji had urgently warned, *relocate somewhere safer, to a Hindu-majority area.*

But this is our home, Yamuna's husband had insisted.

And then the unthinkable came to pass: the partitioning of India into three separate geographic areas, the forcible separation of Hindus and Muslims. Suddenly, Yamuna found herself a refugee. She was one of the many, the too many, who never made it across the border.

· · ·

In the parlour Lata Mangeshkar's melodic voice emanated unreliably from the brand new Victrola.

"Oi," Maji said with a dignified burp to the *darjee* as he arrived, "while you're here, measure me for a new blouse and petticoat. My best white blouse was ruined with those chutney-leaking samosas at the Mahajan's wedding."

The tailor circled around her, attempting to take her measurements. He was a lanky little man with thick black nose hair, whose thin arms and fraying tape measure combined were not quite long enough to encircle Maji's massive hips.

Jaginder lumbered into the room, kurta pajamas tied loosely around his substantial paunch. He preferred not to reach his office until well after breakfast, and spent the morning situated at a small corner table in the parlor simultaneously talking into three phones at once. He managed this feat while delicately drinking a cup of piping hot chai, his arms, mouth, and chin working in fluid motion like a modern avatar of Lord Shiva. "So what if the lorry toppled over," he said into the first phone. "The payment is due today." And to the second, "Do I bloody pay you to lose money for me?" And then to Laloo, the ratlike manager at the shipbreaking yard, "Idiot! *Dimaag kharab ho gaya hai, kya?* Has the heat affected your brain?"

On the occasions Jaginder later required something at his office in Darukhana along the city's eastern docks—legal documents, a forgotten briefcase, or a box of sweets from Ghasitaram's shop—the driver was dispatched immediately. If Pinky and the twins were done with their schoolwork, they sometimes joined Gulu on his trip. From the backseat, they listened to him weave intricate tales that bore marked similarity to the latest Hindi films, except they starred Gulu himself as the drama's handsome hero. Just last week it had been him as Rajendra "Jubilee" Kumar in *Kanoon*, forced to investigate his own father-in-law for murder.

Savita fluttered in, holding yards of pomegranate-colored Kanjeevaram silk in her hands. "I changed my mind, I need *this one* done in two days," she said to the tailor.

He hobbled over and fingered the costly material with gasps of pleasure. "Measurements," he squeaked, artfully lowering his eyes from Savita's voluptuous body.

"Oh pho," Savita complained, setting down the sari, "you just took them last time."

Slowly, lingeringly, he pressed his tape measure against her slender waist, delicate neck, bare shoulders. And then, satisfied, he pulled the pencil stub from his mouth and scratched some incoherent numbers upon a scrap of paper.

* * *

That afternoon, seventeen-year-old Lovely Lawate arrived from the bungalow next door in a sapphire-colored *salvar kameez* with the golden *dupatta* that she wore with almost every outfit, draping it across her chest and shoulders where it fluttered like the wings of an *apsara*, a celestial goddess.

Savita had initially teased her about it, *Oi, Lovely darling, what is this same-same* dupatta *all the time?* But Lovely had only smiled and pulled the scarf tighter. She had spotted it when she had gone shopping with her mother along Colaba Causeway, the intricate hand-sewn pattern of cascading foliage glittering in the boutique's window. One superb miniature bird, an image of the fire-breasted *phoolchuki*, no bigger in real life than a thumb, was embroidered in dark gold with a red breast. The restless flowerpecker, India's smallest bird, was caught in a thick cluster of emerald petals as if lost, trapped, crying out—*chick-chick-chick*—for its crimson-hearted mate.

Lovely had begged her mother for the *dupatta*. *I'll buy it for your dowry,* Vimla had promised. *Such an extravagant thing is only meant for a new bride.* But Lovely had insisted, and softhearted Vimla relented. Since then, Lovely was rarely seen without it.

"*Namaste* Maji, Auntieji." Lovely smiled demurely as she entered, proffering a box of *mithai*. "Mummy went to Ghasitaram's shop this morning."

"He makes the best *pakwaans*!" Dheer splurted out, recalling the crispy fried shell topped with steaming *channa* lentils that he bought whenever they visited his father's friend on Narayan Dhuru Street, just two blocks from the shop. And where, just a lane away on Kalbadevi Road, workers pounded small ingots of silver into the impossibly thin sheets of foil used to decorate sweets.

"I've only brought *laddoos* today," Lovely said, opening the flap.

Dheer immediately circled around her like a moth, curling his pudgy fingers around a sticky, yellow ball of sweetened chickpea flour.

"I have this for you, too," Lovely said, handing him a Cadbury chocolate.

"Thanks *didi!*" Dheer said, respectfully referring to her as elder sister before pocketing the chocolate and vanishing into his room.

"For me, for me?" Tufan greedily inquired.

"Nothing today," Lovely patted him on the head. "But when the next *Popeye* comes out, I'll bring it for you."

Tufan grabbed a *laddoo* and trudged away.

"Don't have bad thoughts about anyone while you're eating," Savita called after him, "or you'll get a tummy ache."

Nimish remained on the outskirts of the room, a stack of books in hand.

"What are you reading today?" Lovely asked, turning to him.

Nimish looked down at the books, trying to make sense of the titles as his heart raced. He had loved Lovely from the time she wore knee-length frocks. Loved her so much that he sneaked to the opening in the wall that separated their yards and gazed every night at the tamarind tree that grew in their backyard. The tree had been planted at the turn of the century when the Lawate's bungalow on Malabar Hill had belonged to a Sir Ryfus Peyton. According to local lore, Sir Ryfus had gone on business to the Portuguese colonial port of Goa, on the coast just south of Bombay, when an impudent local boy spat out an insult before darting away.

Tamarind-head, Sir, the guide had told him, shaking his mosquito-bitten fist in the air. *The bloody coolie just called you a tamarind-head.*

Ryfus quickly learned that his fellow colonials placed tamarind pods in one ear when having to cross into the native quarter. *The bloody natives actually believe that the pods are inhabited by evil demons,* the guide further explained with a guffaw. *Sticking them in our ears is a great trick to keep them from harassing us.*

When Ryfus returned to Malabar Hill, he immediately had a tamarind tree planted, hoping that the tree's special powers would work in Bombay as well. They did work, too well perhaps, driving Ryfus back to England long before the rest of his countrymen followed.

The little tamarind tree continued to grow undisturbed, pushing out green feathery foliage adorned with clusters of small yellow-and-red-striped flowers, and bearing sour fruit every winter that was plucked and used for the treatment of ulcers, constipation, and fevers, as well as a souring agent in cooking. Lovely had always had a fondness for the tamarind's long pods with their brown, edible pulp that was both sweet and sour.

Stay away from the tree, her mother Vimla had warned her since she was a girl. *It's unwholesome. Evil-evil spirits live in it at night; see, even the tree's own leaves curl up in fright.*

But Lovely had not kept away. The tree had become her solace, the only place of escape in her overly protected life. At night, while her family slept, Lovely often climbed from her window to rest against the tamarind's cool, gray bark.

And Nimish watched her every night, creeping to a small opening in the remote end of the dividing wall and peering through it. He urged himself to approach her but, paralyzed by uncertainty, always returned to his bed desolate, with a tortured mind.

Nimish, of course, told no one of his feelings or of his nocturnal escapades. Romantic love was *filmi*, not daring to appear in a proper Hindu household like theirs. He knew that his marriage, like those of generations before his, would be arranged to a woman whose astrological chart matched his. His family was Punjabi, originally from the northwestern region of India, while Lovely's was Maharastrian, from Bombay itself. Their families, however close, would never consider a marriage outside of their regional communities. Yet, where Lovely was concerned, Nimish's usual rationality fell away.

Nimi, your future wife's already written in the stars, his mother had always told him.

But from the time he could remember, Nimish had decided that he would break with ancient tradition and, come what may, marry Lovely. He struggled to contain his emotions now, and fumbling with the stack of books, wiped his spectacles with the edge of his shirt.

"Tell her, *nah*, Nimi," Savita jumped in, pointing to a book with the title *Scinde; or, the Unhappy Valley* by the famed explorer Sir Richard Burton. "This one looks interesting."

"'How lovely are these oriental nights,'" he obediently read from a marked page. "'How especially lovely, contrasted with the most unlovely oriental day.'"

How very Lovely, Pinky thought, her chest tightening.

Savita snorted. "And what's so lovely-flovely about English sky the color of rotting rice and cold so severe that it sucks the heat from their big-nosed faces?"

Lovely hid a smile behind her hand, demurely casting her eyes away from Nimish.

And then adjusting the string of aphrodisiacal mogra flowers tucked into her glossy hair, she turned to Pinky. "Come, *hawa-khaneka hai?* Maji thought it would be good for you to have some fresh air. Let's go to the park."

Pinky nodded, noticing Nimish's flushed cheeks with a stab of jealousy.

❀ ❀ ❀

After they left, Maji turned her attention to Lovely's mother, Vimla, who had just arrived to discuss the latest marriage proposals brought over by eagle-nosed Mrs. Garg from down the lane, a meddlesome woman who considered herself the neighborhood matchmaker despite a remarkable record of lack of success. The first offer had come when Lovely was merely fourteen, but now that she was of proper marriageable age, the trickle had become a veritable flood.

Mothers across their Maharastrian community wanted seventeen-year old Lovely for their sons, not only for her stunning looks but also, more practically, for her family's wealth and their reputation for absolute strictness with their daughter. Modern girls, Maji and Vimla often lamented, had lost all sense of dignity, wearing makeup and prancing about town after college classes as if they were shameless film stars. *These* padi-likhi *girls think they are royalty simply because they can read and write* was Maji's stark assessment.

"My Lovely will be compliant," Vimla declared.

"Yes-yes, she's a good girl."

"And her dowry's almost ready now. My jeweler brought the final sets just yesterday. All the pillow cases have been embroidered and even the refrigerator's ordered."

"And that Singer-*finger* machine?"

"That too, though I've left out the sewing scissors."

"Yes-yes, nothing sharp to brandish at her new husband!"

The two women chuckled and then, intently sipping their chai, proceeded with the business of finding a suitable groom.

"She's so stubborn sometimes," Vimla Auntie bemoaned, opening her cherry-colored cloth satchel of proposals which she kept tied with a bit of gold thread procured from the temple. "Finding fault wth every single boy."

"In our day, girls had no choice," Maji said, studying a black-and-white photo of a young man with a heavily oiled mustache.

"Whattodo? Children don't follow the old ways anymore," Vimla chirped helplessly as she remembered her late husband's frequent beatings, his merciless fists at her stomach, her face, her spine.

"Lovely will do as you ask," Maji said, patting Vimla's knee.

"I have this uneasy feeling," Vimla suddenly confessed, tears welling up in her large eyes. "As if something terrible will happen before I get her married."

"You're just feeling sad that you will have to let her go soon. It's only natural. Daughters don't belong to us."

Vimla nodded, wiping her face with an embroidered handkerchief. Still, that feeling persisted, like an encroaching shadow. She busied her hands leafing through the pile until she found the most recent one: a young doctor with wheatish complexion whose hobbies included collecting American cars and lepidoptery. "How about this one?"

"No," Maji said with a click of her tongue, "*Dekko, nah?* See his eyes. They are hard-hard like stone. He will not treat your Lovely well."

Vimla glanced at the young man's handsome face, the curve of his nose, the trim moustache, before studying his eyes. Yes, they were hard eyes, she noted with surprise. And they bore an uncanny resemblance to her own dead husband's.

Gathering storm clouds widened their hazy sway, but the sun still beat down with feverish intensity. Pinky and Lovely found a shady spot and spread out a sheet. They sat silently for a while, their thoughts falling into separate realms with the effortlessness of windswept leaves. A wig-shaped cloud of flies collected over the penguin-shaped trash receptacle. Nearby, children screamed in delight as they played in the giant Old Woman's Shoe. Young men stared openly at Lovely, trying to catch her eye as they swaggered by while old men stole longing glances only to be thrashed by their wives' purses and led away by their leathery ears.

Lovely was immune to the attention, as if unaware of her own beauty. Pinky meanwhile tried to contain her envy and suspicions about Nimish. *Does she love him, too?* Lovely had shared many things with Pinky over the years, advising her on her pending menstrual cycles and suggesting a diet of sky fruit and ashoka bark to stimulate her growing breasts. But despite their intimacy, their implicit trust in each other, there was a line beyond which Lovely fell into a brooding silence, her face dark and unreadable. And so, knowing that she could not ask about what transpired in the garden at night, Pinky decided to broach another topic, one that had pressed against her thoughts with equal urgency that day.

"Do you know, *didi*," she began, "that one of our bathroom doors is bolted at night?"

There was a look of confusion on Lovely's face, then a sudden realization. She brought a delicate hand to her lips. "Oh?" she said.

"You know, don't you?"

Lovely shook her head.

"You know!" Pinky shouted, grabbing Lovely's arm. "Please tell me!"

Lovely sighed, remembering the day it had happened. She was only four then but had climbed into the tamarind tree that morning while her parents slept. She had spied her older brother, then still a boy, cut across the yard and into the passageway to the next-door bungalow. He entered from the side door, which was unlocked at sunrise to allow the servants to come and go. Time passed and then he returned with packets of biscuits stolen from Maji's pantry, already stuffing the contents into his mouth. She had not told her parents, especially not later, after what happened that day. All these years, it pained her to have kept quiet and now there was no point in telling.

She sighed again. "It was Savita Auntie who made that rule about bolting the door. You know how she can sometimes be, believing in all those old-fashioned superstitions."

It was true, Savita was always battling shadowy beings and malevolent neighbors, both of which she believed caused all sorts of trouble with the good fortune she had worked all her life to secure. She brandished her *kajal* eyeliner pencil like a sword to protect her sons from any ill will that might be circulating about, drawing black dots behind their ears to ward off the Evil Eye.

"But *her* bathroom door is unlocked at night," Pinky said.

"I don't know anymore than that," Lovely said, turning away from Pinky. Her golden *dupatta* slipped from her shoulders causing sharp intakes of breath from passing men. And her sloping hips flared the ridge of her *kameez* just so.

A WITCH

The AC whirred; thunder rumbled across the night sky. Even as the dense air lay upon her like a stack of bricks, Pinky had the sensation of a thick drapery falling away, of something lurking just beyond.

She stood and paced the room, waiting for Maji to fall into her usual deep sleep pattern which included talking, whispering, and sometimes even praying, her fingers moving in sync as if handling a rosary. Pinky's insides itched; her thoughts raced, each one of them leading back to the bolted door. She had asked Dheer about it yesterday and had even tried to bribe Tufan, but neither twin had any answers. She had no choice but to go directly to her aunt.

Savita was the only daughter of an influential family from Breach Candy, the old and exclusive British enclave. She had learned her lessons well: how to choose the right set of coruscating jewelry, how to butter up her husband's business partners, and how to drape her fulgent body in exorbitantly priced chiffons. But most successfully, she had learned how best to make her friends jealous: with words spoken over a cup of piping hot chai. *Nimish is such a good boy. Will no doubt take over his father's shipbreaking business one day. One spoon of sugar or two? And Dheer, he has such a good memory, I tell you. Remembers each and every item he ate for dinner the week before! And little Tufan, so clever. Scored first in his maths class! Biscuit? No, no you must try one, they're imported.*

Competing with her friends for who had the Most-Number-One-First-Class-Life had become a veritable athletic event, with a new tally calculated each week in the minds of the contestants. One week, Zarine placed first when her cousin-sister announced her engagement into an influential automobile family. The next, Anjali, because she registered for a painting class despite her in-laws' objections. Mumta sneaked into the lead when she hired a second driver with an uncanny resemblance to film star Dev Anand. And Zarine's perpetually youthful face kept her in the running long after she eloped with a skinny foreigner who had come to Bombay on a Fulbright.

If Savita had one goal in life, it was to win. Just last month, in fact, she had battled to deny a neighbor membership into her exclusive luncheon group. After a few discreet phone calls to a flock of gossip-prone ladies, concocting a story about how this neighbor rubbed rose-infused curds into her breasts in broad daylight, Savita succeeded in not only barring her from the group but blacklisting her in the entire seaside half of the city. As if to further cement the woman's humiliation, for months afterwards a rabble of well-bred boys converged at the neighbor's front gate sporting indecent bulges and binoculars.

Yes, Savita was a formidable opponent and Pinky, more than anyone, had been on the receiving end of her wrath.

The AC unit sputtered loudly then died out. Pinky walked over to it and clicked the knob but no sound came out, not even a wheeze. She sighed. It had broken again.

Maji began muttering, growing restless upon the bed.

Pinky quickly pushed open the two windows that overlooked the driveway and was immediately enveloped by the oppressive night air. Everything outside felt still. Not even the crickets sang. Sweat soaked her nightdress. Thirst gripped the back of her throat. She turned on the ancient ceiling fan which struggled to life, then merely stirred the soupy air rather than bringing relief.

Maji suddenly moaned, gnashing her teeth together. And then her eyes flew open and she shot up to a sitting position, a feat she had long ago ceased being able to do while awake.

Pinky gasped.

"I know, Savita. I know everything," Maji said, her voice flat, her eyes staring unblinkingly at the opposite wall, saliva dripping from her mouth.

And then with a snort, she fell back in bed and reentered her dream that had been interrupted just as the hunky Prime Minister Nehru leaned in to nibble her ear, cooing *Oh my darling, darling Mother India.*

Pinky stood there, her heart pounding in her chest. On the bed, Maji continued with her sleep-talking, now whispering something incoherent.

A flash of lightning lit the sky.

"They said she's a witch," Maji was whispering urgently, her breathing harsh, fast, almost panicked. *"She's a witch! A witch! A witch!"*

Pinky ran out the door before even the thunder had a chance to boom.

❊ ❊ ❊

The heat in the corridor enclosed Pinky like a hug as she waited in the shadows, her breathing slowing. A few minutes later, Jaginder swung open his bedroom door and slipped into the hallway, his white kurta pajamas flashing in a shaft of moonlight. Soon enough came the muffled sound of an ignition and then the hum of a car, the creak of the front gate. He left the bungalow almost every night. Pinky had no idea where he went, but she knew that his nightly escapades caused Maji considerable distress.

Pinky crept to his doorway and peeked in.

A dim light cast a faint glow across the room, which was decorated in stylish white upholstered furniture covered in hand-beaten metallic sheeting. The furniture had been brought as part of Savita's dowry, delivered just before the wedding.

Take it back, Maji had said, inspecting the silvery-sheened chairs in horror, recoiling at the thought of bringing white, the color of mourning, into her house at this auspicious time. She did not add that this stark modern set clashed with the majestic hues of the bunga-low, *her* bungalow. Jaginder had remained mute on the topic, secretly intrigued by his future wife's underhanded power play—she had been to their bungalow after their engagement, after all; she had known its colors, its style.

It was Yamuna, Maji's daughter, then still unmarried, who had intervened.

No Mummy, she had said, *it's not white. It's bluish white like that Seijakuji pottery bowl we have from Japan. Almost a milky white.*

White is white, Maji had muttered, finally giving in because the dreadful set would be confined to Jaginder and Savita's bedroom.

Savita sat now in front of her elegant dressing table and lit a candle which glittered off the silver sheeting like a thousand fireflies. A mirror hung on the wall, veiled under a tissue-thin cloth. Mirrors were a rarity in the Mittal household, mainly because Savita felt that malevolent spirits lurked in them, waiting to cast their evil eyes at her boys as spirits often did to those they considered young and beautiful. She kept a thin cotton sheet across her mirror when it was not in use and the only other one, a small oval looking glass on a shiny brass pedestal, was tucked away on Maji's bureau.

Savita reached past crystal vials of attars, touching each one as if a ritual. She rearranged a collection of colored glass jars from Uttar Pradesh, the candlelight reflecting off them with a glow. She unclicked her silver-plated compact and held the powder puff to her nose.

For the briefest of moments, Pinky missed her mother.

Savita lifted a small, polished silver box that contained her forehead *bindis* and set it down in front of her. She caressed the box, one hand upon the lid as if to keep herself from unhinging it. Lingeringly, she opened it and rummaged through its contents. She pulled out a small square-shaped paper, staring at it for a long time without moving. Touching it gently, she began to weep.

A shaming heat crept into Pinky's face and she backed out of the room, accidentally knocking into a string of tiny silver-belled birds that hung in the doorway.

Savita looked up, her gaze eerily distorted by the shrouded mirror.

Blindly, Pinky raced out of the hall and down the corridor. The kitchen absorbed her into its shadows where she flattened herself onto the ground.

Moments later, she saw the drape of a robe dragging across the floor, strangely illuminated. Delicate feet adorned with diamond toe rings slowly walked down the west hallway, past the boys' bedroom, and then stopped.

Pinky lifted her face.

It was Savita.

She carried a candle in one hand, held aloft, and was gazing intently at the bolt on the bathroom door.

There was no time to think. Pinky ran down the corridor to Savita's bedroom and threw open the silver box of *bindis* on the vanity. Dheer, she knew, had once sorted through it, rapturously organizing the forehead adornments by color, shape, and occasion. *To wear to temple*, he had narrated, *To wear to lunch, To wear to shopping, To wear when angry at Papa.* Savita had unexpectedly returned early from a luncheon and gave him a slap that nearly sent him flying across the room. *Don't ever touch that again,* she had hissed before storming away. Dheer had curled up like a slug on the floor and laid in a puddle of slimy snot and tears for the better part of the afternoon, unresponsive even to Pinky's offering of Perk wafers.

Just inside the *bindi* box lay the square-shaped paper that had caused Savita to weep. It was a black-and-white photograph. An out-of-focus arm hung across the top, thin bangles huddled together at the wrist. A rattle lay nearby. And just below, wrapped tightly in a cloth that rested in sharp juxtaposition against a mirrored Jaipuri blanket—*a baby.* On the back was scribbled one word, *Chakori*, along with a date, 1947.

A baby.

Pinky felt a stinging in her chest, a humming in her ears.

She dropped the photo and turned to go.

There, standing in the doorway, was Savita, her face white with rage.

She quietly closed her door then strode up to Pinky and slapped her.

Pinky reeled backwards.

"How dare you," Savita hissed. "How dare you come into my room like a thief!"

Pinky stammered, holding her cheek. The humming in her head steadily grew into a cacophony of voices. She stuck her fingers into her ears but the urgent, overlapping voices did not go away.

Savita wrenched Pinky's hands from her ears. "You want to know why I hate you so," she said, grabbing the photo from the table and pushing it into Pinky's face. "You're here because she's dead!"

Pinky saw the baby's swelling cheeks and shiny hair that carried the slickness of one just born. She saw its eyes, closed to the world, its thick eyelashes dewy with moisture. Those chaotic, ethereal voices filled her ears with lamentations.

"You should have been the one to die, you were so sickly when Maji brought you, so malnourished, your skin oozing pus." Savita's mouth curled with disgust. "Yet, you lived and *my* child died." She began to weep, tears slid down her cheeks, down her neck, and pooled into the crevice between her breasts.

"I'm sorry," Pinky managed to say, the voices crashing upon each other, deafening.

Savita flicked back her hair. "This will never be your home," she said. "I will send you away. I swear to you, I will."

THE DROWNING

Pinky stood absolutely still inside the bathroom the next morning, her back against the door. The floor was wet from the boys' baths and the bucket half-filled with water. *A baby girl died,* Pinky reflected miserably, *and I'm her replacement.* Yet, it had not worked out exactly like that. Savita had not wanted her, and neither had Jaginder. All this had been kept from her even though goings-on behind closed doors were strictly forbidden in the Mittal household.

Indeed, a closed door in the daytime, however temporary, invited reprimands and a thorough questioning of activities, motives, and general morality. The only legitimate excuse for locking doors involved one of the three tiers of daily purification: discharging internal toxins, cleansing external toxins, and purifying invisible toxins. Thus, anything personal in nature had to be done in the toilet, bathing area, or puja room. Or, at night.

Pinky apprehensively remembered her terror from the day before. Her three cousins had all already taken their baths without incident, however, appearing fresh-faced with towels wrapped around their waists. Sustained by this fact, she quickly clipped her braids to the top of her head.

Right away she noticed that the square of hard brown soap which usually rested on the stool was missing. Resisting the urge to panic, she sighed loudly as if to appear irritated, reasoning that Tufan had forgotten to replace the soap after he had finished. Nonetheless, she grew anxious as she made her way down the hall to the kitchen pantry. *What if he hadn't forgotten?*

The pantry was perpetually dark, having not been deemed worthy of a light when the bungalow was outfitted for electrical lines. The daylight filtering in through the small passageway leading to the kitchen was just enough for Pinky to make out the sacks of basmati rice quietly aging on one side and canisters of snacks—turmeric-stained puffed rice and salty *chevda*—temptingly lined up on a shelf. There was a small second fridge in here, a castaway from one of the ships in Jaginder's shipbreaking yard. It rattled sporadically as if suffering from a bout of the flu. The room smelled old, like paper and dust and dry biscuits. It was usually a comforting smell, but today it made Pinky feel on edge. Almost frantically, she felt around the corner of the top shelf, where she knew that the soap was stacked, and pulled away a dented bar of Lux—*the film stars' choice*—which only Savita used. After more fumbling, Pinky located a brown bar and ran to the bathroom, the stillness chasing her all the way there.

"Still haven't taken your bath yet, Pinky-*di?*" Kuntal asked as she swept the hallway.

"No soap!"

"Oh? I just fetched a new one yesterday," Kuntal ducked her head into the bathroom. "Why, there it is, right on the stool!"

Pinky halted in a moment of terror but remembered Tufan's laughter from the day before. "I didn't see it."

"Brown soap on brown stool, sometimes even I have trouble locating it," Kuntal said kindly.

Pinky relinquished the new bar and stepped inside the bathroom.

She opened and closed the door three times, ensuring that it did not stick to the frame, and then latched it. Undressing, she sat upon the wooden stool and poured a *lota* of water over her shoulder. She splashed her face, washed with soap, and splashed again.

The room grew chilled.

She did not have to open her eyes to see the sudden light.

An immaculate luminosity emanated from the brass bucket.

It was so blinding, so intense, that Pinky covered her eyes with her hands.

Hand over mouth as if to stifle a scream, she stumbled to the door, pushing herself against it.

"Help!" she yelled, eyes shut against the brilliance. They began to water, stinging from the brightness. Pinky groped for the door handle, her fingers trembling. Unexpectedly, she recalled something Maji told her in the *puja* room yesterday: *Beti, Lord Vishnu never sleeps so he can always look out for you.* And then she had popped a handful of golden raisins into Pinky's mouth. It was still inside her, the *prasad* of raisins and almonds blessed by the gods. She felt strength returning to her. Lord Vishnu, embodiment of mercy and goodness, was with her and, due to this morning's rare bout with constipation, still half-digested within her intestines.

"I'm not your substitute!" Pinky yelled into the light as her fingers found the handle and unlatched it. "Maji loves me!"

All at once, there was blackness.

Pinky opened her eyes, taking a moment for them to adjust.

The room looked the same, ordinary, dull, empty.

She grabbed her towel and dashed out of the room.

She was safe once more.

In the quiet protection of the *puja* sanctuary, Pinky tearfully confessed to Maji.

"There's something in the bathroom!"

"What is it, *beti?*"

"There was a light, a bright light. My eyes were closed but I saw it."

"You must be coming down with a fever," Maji said, feeling Pinky's forehead. "Sometimes this terrible heat gets stuck in your head and makes you see white spots."

Pinky shook her head. All her life she had heard stories about lurking ghosts and evil spirits casting spells upon their unsuspecting victims. Even her favorite teacher at the Catholic convent school, Sister Pramila, who kept a small figurine of baby Lord Krishna in the pocket of her habit, once told them about a classmate who suffered from terrible stomach cramps after picking flowers from the fragrant field behind the school. *Naughty girl that she was,* hahn, Sister Pramila spoke with a tight gloom-and-doom voice, *the bad-bad spirits went right into her belly and now her poor parents have to take her to Mehndipur all the way in Rajasthan to have her cured. May Christ have mercy on her!*

"But it was not heat," Pinky insisted, "I felt cold and it was terrifying like a . . . a . . . a ghost—"

"Sit," Maji cut her off with a wave of her hand and a puckered brow. She paused, searching for an appropriate story and then pulled her granddaughter toward her. "Do you know the story of the Rani of Jhansi?"

Pinky hung her head.

"She was a queen who fought the British during India's first battle for independence. When her province came under attack," Maji continued, "she cast away her veil and became their leader. She had no fear."

Pinky lifted her eyes.

"She went dressed like a soldier, but like a true queen never forgot to wear her gold anklets into battle."

"What happened to her?"

"She was mortally wounded. Her compatriots took her to die under a mango tree."

"She died?"

"She died but her name is revered all over India." Maji began to recite a line from a song sung by village women: *Her name is so sacred we sing it only in the early hours of dawn.*

There was a long silence.

"When people are frightened, they turn to dark, unnatural things. If there's something that frightens you, you must instead confront it." Maji said. "Remember the Rani. You have that very strength inside you."

"But—"

"You're no longer a child," Maji concluded. "It's time you came out of your dreamworld. I don't want to hear you talk about ghosts. You are not one of those uneducateds living in the streets."

"But Savita Auntie believes in them."

Maji frowned. "She told me that you went into her room last night. Why?"

"I saw her crying. She was holding a photo . . . . I wanted to see it. It was a baby. A baby girl!"

Maji's face went blank as if unaware that such a photo existed. She held her forehead in her hands and pressed her eyes. "*Kyu? Kyu?* Why bring all this back?"

"I just want to know what happened," Pinky said softly.

Maji leaned her upper body heavily against the wall. Memories came rushing at her.

"Go!" she suddenly shouted, waving Pinky away with her hand. "Just go!"

Pinky startled. "Maji?"

But Maji did not hear her. She was already drowning in a merciless darkness.

★ ♡ ☆

She was sinking, sinking back to that long ago morning when she had been taking her early morning rounds around the bungalow. *As the sun, who is the eye of the world, cannot be tainted by the defects in our eyes,* Maji had been reciting to herself from the four-thousand-year-old *Upanishads, so the one Self, dwelling in all, cannot be tainted by the evils of the world.*

She had just passed the library when she heard Jaginder call out for the milk-production cereal, a steaming sweet concoction that promised to swell Savita's barren breasts. The young ayah, the end of her flaming red sari tied around her waist to keep from getting wet, rushed out of the children's bathroom and toward the kitchen. Almost immediately, she reappeared with a lacquered tray and entered the corridor, going toward Savita's room.

Maji had come full circle and was traveling down that hallway once more when she heard a gasping. There was a trail of damp footprints leading away from bathroom. Stepping across the threshold, she watched as the ayah shook the baby as if to force life back into her tiny lungs. Her eyes on the child, she had only one thought.

The bluish hue that clung to her at birth has not yet left her at death.

When it was clear that nothing more could be done, when Maji herself held the lifeless body weighing less than a half-dozen *hapus* mangos, she ushered the ayah to the front verandah in silence.

"Oi, Gulu," she called for the family driver in her low, gravelly voice.

He appeared within seconds, though he had been in his personal quarters in the back garage combing his hair. One section had been carefully oiled back into a careful wave, but the other half still stood up on end, as if it had already heard the shocking news of the ayah's dismissal. Whispering a command into his ear, Maji took a fold of damp rupees from within her blouse, where the uppermost flesh of her breast strained against fabric, and handed it to him. Gulu wavered, reluctant to execute her orders, but the ayah wordlessly slipped into the backseat of the black Ambassador, her red sari damp from the baby's bath, eyes hooded.

Maji did not wait for him to pull away, to refasten the rusted green gates verdurous with jasmine creepers, to enclose her in a fortress of grief. Hastily returning to the bathroom, she cradled the beloved child one last time, naked but for a gold-and-black-beaded amulet upon her neck, and rinsed her of any impurities she might have gathered during her brief stay on earth. Tearing the end of the cotton *khadi* sari she wore upon her body, she wrapped the baby in the colorless hue of mourning and nestled her to her bosom.

Somehow she found the strength to knock upon her son's door. Inside, Savita lay, eyes closed, reclining against the thick embroidered pillows, her dark hair cascading over her shoulders like lush vines of bougainvillea. Jaginder sat on the bed next to her, tenderly spooning cereal into her mouth.

Maji stood in the doorway and watched this display of affection. Fleetingly, she thought about her own daughter Yamuna on the other side of the country somewhere, then still alive, a refugee.

"Ma?" Jaginder said resting the spoon in the cereal bowl with a clack. "Is something wrong?"

The air grew sharp, bright, flecked with a thousand colors as if Jaginder and Savita already sensed the gravity of that moment, that ephemeral second when their lives hung in precarious balance.

Maji squeezed the stiffening baby, her head shaking, just once, just a few centimeters.

And that was enough.

Savita screamed.

Maji met her son's wide-open eyes. In that split second, she understood that the baby's death was a gathering juggernaut. The worst devastation was yet to come.

Jaginder tried to stand, then faltered. He clenched his jaw and stood up. "The ayah," he said. It was not a question, not a question at all, but a knowing.

"An accident," Maji whispered.

Jaginder was already racing out of the room, his feet pounding the floor, head thrust forward, fists tightened in attack.

Somewhere in the far end of the bungalow, the twin boys started wailing.

"Give her to me!" Savita shrieked, grabbing the baby to her bosom, her cries filling the room.

Maji stood nearby, fighting the infinite blackness inside her.

She was the head of the household.

She would not cry.

She would not allow herself to be lost.

SINKING SUNBIRDS

Pinky locked herself in the toilet, stunned by Maji's harsh tones. *Go! Just go!* Maji had never before pushed her away. *If Maji stops loving me,* she thought, *I'll have no one.* Whatever lurked in the bathroom—and Pinky was certain it was *something*—was already pulling her away from her grandmother. She wanted nothing more than to close that gap, to crawl back to Maji's side, to make everything between them the same as before. Yet Maji made it clear that Pinky was never to bring up such matters again.

"Oi, Pinky?" a voice said through the door.

Pinky held her breath. Of course, not only were closed doors regulated in the bungalow but timings too: twenty minutes for morning bowel activity, twelve for bath, ten for other toiletry needs. A grand total of forty-two minutes per day of privacy. And Pinky's had just expired.

"What are you doing in there for so long?" Maji called out. Her voice was gentle now. Tired.

"Just an upset stomach," Pinky said, already feeling better now that her grandmother had come for her.

"I knew you weren't well," Maji called out loudly, mentally adding an additional thirty minutes to Pinky's allotted behind-closed-door time. Forty-five if her diarrhea was especially virulent. "You must stay away from *puris*. And no fried food today. *Achha?*"

"No chili, onions, garlic or *garam masala* either," Savita chimed in from the dining hall, ticking off her list of food items that enticed malevolent spirits. As it was, she made Cook Kanj prepare food in two different batches, one for herself and her sons, and the other, spicy version, for the rest of the family. After marriage, she had tried to curb Jaginder's eating habits as well but, though taken by his new bride, he had flatly refused.

Eating garlic causes bad-bad thoughts in your mind, she had insisted.

It's not the garlic, he had responded with a wink.

So Savita inflicted her dietary zeal upon her children instead, except during social engagements when she was too busy to keep such a close eye on them. Nimish was too engrossed in his books to care about such things. Tufan simply bribed Cook Kanj to give him onions on the sly, threatening to tell Maji of his wife's lapses in housework otherwise. He ate these onions raw, mouth burning, tears pouring down his face, whenever Savita was napping. Poor Dheer suffered the most from the restricted menu though no amount of whining lightened his mother's injunction. Impatient with the desperate look in his eyes, however, she had imported chocolates delivered to the house each week.

Whenever possible, Pinky slipped Dheer a part of her flavorful meals under the table. But now that her stomach ailment had been broadcast throughout the bungalow, vegetables, mangoes, chutneys, and pickles were all eliminated from her plate to be replaced by bland rice-and-lentil *khichidis* and watered-down yogurt *lassis*. Worst still, Dr. M. M. Iyer, their family physician, was called in and prescribed a regimen of pink fizzy tablets, salted lime water, and asafetida-laced lentils.

Afterwards, Pinky was duly sent off to bed. She lay on her mattress restlessly. There was still so much she did not know. Who was this baby, this infant girl, whose untimely death led to Pinky's salvation?

⚜ ⚜ ⚜

Later that morning, Lovely's mother, Vimla, came over for lunch, using the narrow passageway carved into the far end of the connecting wall during a brief time when the adjoining bungalows had belonged to the same owner. For at least half a century thereafter, the opening had been sealed by overgrown shoeflower shrubs, thickets of pale purple phlox, and tender blue vinca blooms. But after both Vimla and Maji had become widows, their days freed from attending to husbands, the foliage was cut back to allow visiting without the hassle of having to unlock and lock their bungalows' front gates. Maji was too large to squeeze through the passageway. So by unspoken agreement, Vimla always did the visiting.

Vimla was a fragile-looking woman with slender arms and large, doelike eyes. She always wore white saris as custom dictated, though allowed herself small indulgences of color such as a magenta hibiscus bloom tucked neatly into her glossy black hair. Before her husband died, Vimla had taken much joy in her kaleidoscopic collection of saris, which included brilliant purple Bengali Balucharis, square-patterned Gujarati Gharcholas, Moghul-influenced Benaras Brocades, and gold-bordered Nayayanpets from Kerela. In fact, in the privacy of her bedroom, she often fantasized about managing Sweetie Fashions or one of the other exquisite sari shops along Colaba Causeway.

Bring out the Mysore crepes, she imagined herself commanding one of her workers who would scuttle across the brightly lit show room, opening the tissue-like saris with a snap of his hand while the heavily ornamented ladies oohed and aahed, cash-filled purses tucked under their armpits, fizzy Coca-Colas in hand.

When her husband had died in his early forties of a heart attack, Vimla had mourned not for him but for the loss of her sparkling saris. Confined as she was to achromatic clothing, she coped by refusing to part with her collection, tenderly tucking the most expensive ones into a locked *almarie* in her bedroom. Only when her children were out of the bungalow and the servants safely napping did she dare to open the cabinet and spread the rainbow of cloth before her, pressing her face into the silky fabrics, draping the golden *rangs* against her bosom, and losing herself to the days when she, too, was gazed upon with breathlessness.

Vimla's husband had been a wealthy industrialist, friendly with the British, and feared by Indians. He was a brutal man, caring nothing for the lives he ruined on his way to prosperity, nor for the happiness of his own family whom he sought to trample into submission. Once, when they had been at a dinner party overlooking Bombay Harbor at the Taj Hotel, the conversation amongst the Maharastrian crowd steered toward their decades-long battle with their Gujarati neighbors to annex Bombay city as the influential capital of their own state.

"We control Bombay's municipal council," Vimla's husband stated heatedly, "so it's only a matter of time before the city will belong to us as well."

The group of men cheerfully clinked their iced glasses of Royal Salut.

"Best is to buy a gun from one of those Parsi Bandookwallahs," concluded one man.

As if on cue, a small explosion sounded in the distance. Even though gunfire was typically unheard of within the city limits, the shot was far enough away that it almost did not register above the blaring *filmi* music or their drunken conversation. From their vantage point in the majestic Taj Hotel, they were safely shielded from the street violence below, from the Samyukta Maharashtra Samiti foot soldiers living in the city's slums who provided the muscle behind their demands.

But Vimla, too shy to chitchat with the more sophisticated wives, had heard the shot and unthinkingly ran towards her husband.

"Bullets!" she blurted out fearfully, spilling her tangerine-colored Gold Spot onto her husband's tailored white suit. "Someone's shooting a gun down there!"

The jaunty mood at the party was ruined and the guests hastily made their way back to their gated estates in their imported cars with doors securely locked. Vimla had felt her husband's fury on the ride home, taking temporary refuge in the fact that he would not lose control in front of their driver. In the privacy of their bedroom, however, he had punched her in her face, the metal of his diamond ring cutting into her cheek.

After his death, Vimla retreated into the safety of his fortune and focused all her attention on her children. Her son, Harshal, unfortunately chose to emulate his father by developing cruel little habits. His personal favorite was to drown the purple sunbirds who nested in the greenery of their garden, snickering at their terrified fluttering until he felt their final, delightful shiver of surrender. After he had singlehandedly devastated the bird population in their garden, he casually began prowling the street for newer, bigger victims.

One morning, while Lovely was playing out by the driveway, Harshal crept out of the gated compound with his net. Just minutes later, he ran back inside with a stray puppy, locking himself inside the bungalow to evade the pup's ferocious mother. Vimla had watched in shock from a window, unable to move, as Lovely fled from the mother dog until two of the servants chased it away with a broom. Neither Vimla nor Lovely ever said a word to Harshal about his cruelty, but disgust had shone dully in their eyes. Thenceforth, Lovely refused to call Harshal *bhaiya,* the affectionate term for an elder brother, and boycotted the *Rakshabandan* ceremonies which celebrated the devotion between brothers and sisters.

Vimla chose not interfere in her children's silent feud, instead retreating into the cocoon of her bedroom or spending time next door with Maji. Over the years, the two women had forged a deep friendship, one further cemented after Maji's own husband, Omanandlal, had died. Though they shared similar fates as widows, Maji undeniably prevailed as the matriarch of her family while Vimla wilted into the background of hers, bullied by her son and daughter-in-law. Her remaining concerns in life were to find a suitable groom for Lovely and to encourage Himani to produce a grandchild.

"It's been two years now since they were married and still no sign of a baby," she lamented again.

"You've taken her to the Mahalaxmi temple, *nah?*" Maji inquired, certain that sincere prayers to the divine would be rewarded.

"Whattodo? She refuses to go."

"What about a lady doctor?"

"She refuses even that!" Vimla cried out, rapidly twisting her wrists back and forth to show her helplessness. "She even suggests that it's my son who needs to be checked out!"

"*Besharam!* Who does she think she is?"

"Whattodo? It's as if she doesn't want children. Everyone has started to talk now. Some even say it's because of that tamarind tree in the backyard, souring Himani's womb and all that. I want to get the tree removed but my son refuses to spend money on such a thing."

"Vimla dear," Maji said, leaning forward, "only God has the power to give and take, the rest—evil spirits inhabiting trees and such—is utter nonsense."

Savita strolled in, clicking her tongue in disagreement. "Auntieji," she said, speaking to Vimla. "Didn't you hear the story of the seven-months-pregnant woman who bought a *lassi* from a shop near the Matunga Cemetery?"

"Yes, it was in the newspaper yesterday," Vimla said, fear rising to her face. "She had a miscarriage immediately afterwards, didn't she?"

"She was a stupid woman," Savita clucked, as she strode away, "drinking milk products so near a place of death, opening her body to capricious spirits."

"Vimla," Maji said gravely, "Don't bow down to fear. Trust in God to unfold our destinies as they should be."

Pinky listened in to their conversation from behind the hallway door-frame, awed by Maji's conviction. Maji did not take nonsense from anyone, least of all irritating spirits from the otherworld. Ghosts, demons, *rakshas*, and the entire ill-bred lot—if they managed to scale the bungalow's iron gates—were immediately met with her imposing figure in the parlor.

The gods and goddesses of the Hindu pantheon, on the other hand, were another class of visitors altogether. Welcomed by Maji as VIPs, they had settled in the bungalow like demanding houseguests. Their statues—Krishna playing his flute along the riverbank, the elephant-headed Ganesh swinging his ample trunk, Saraswati dispensing wisdom from atop a lotus flower—spilled out of the puja room onto corner tables and behind glass cabinets where they surveyed the Mittal family's activities with rapt attention.

Maji took no unnecessary liberties with the gods and goddesses as they had a very unforgiving temperament when ignored. She carried sandalwood rosary beads wherever she went, squeezing in a twelve-bead lament as she made her slow, painful way to the bathroom, or a quick one-beader when the lanky *darjee* showed up at the door ready to encircle Savita's plump breasts with his measuring tape. Sometimes her supplications were quite lengthy, a full three times around the rosary beads, in fact, whenever she had her feet pressed by Kuntal. *Don't stop,* she would say, sighing with pleasure as Kuntal rubbed sesame oil in between her engorged toes. *I'm in the middle of my prayers.*

After her husband Omanandlal died, the gods and goddesses were the only authority Maji respected. Her reverence, however, did not stop her from bantering and bargaining with them on a daily basis. *O Lord Krishna, my son is such an idiot, going into business with that cheating Chatwani chap. Give him some sense,* nah? *I'll bring the Pan-*

ditji to do a full-day hawan *for you with the best sweets from Ghasitaram's shop.* Just like the Goddess Durga who maintained the harmony of the entire cosmos, Maji viewed herself as the power who kept her own little universe in balance.

✤ ✤ ✤

Pinky spotted the twins gathering inside their parents' bedroom and went to investigate. Dheer was sitting on the white bedspread blind-folded, reciting The Lone Ranger Creed. "'I believe,'" he said, "'that all things change but the truth, and that truth alone, lives on forever.'"

"You're just in time for the show *Kemosabe,*" Tufan said to Pinky as he uncorked a bottle of cologne his father had purchased from a small shop-cum-pharmacy near K. E. M. Hospital and waved it under his brother's nose.

Dheer possessed an uncanny olfactory ability, able to detect the most reticent odors and nuanced scents. With a mere sniff of the nose, he could recognize the components of each and every beauty aid that littered his mother's vanity, from the vast array of Indian *attars* in their tiny crystal bottles to Pears' "Pure as the Lotus" soaps and Max Factor perfumes.

"Old Spice!" he yelled now. Pinky clapped in appreciation.

"Genuine import or a local counterfeit?" Tufan asked, eyeing the bottle suspiciously.

Dheer crinkled his nose.

"A fake," he announced apologetically. "Probably bottled in Kalyan or Ulhasnagar."

"The Sindhi shopkeeper assured Papa that this is a genuine, smuggled item," Tufan frowned, recalling how he had even proffered a cotton-tipped toothpick saturated with the cologne for Jaginder's approval.

"If Papa couldn't tell," Dheer said, trying to be helpful, "then surely no one else will know."

"Papa's not going to wear some concoction of who-knows-what made by some bloody refugee!" Tufan said, defending his father's honor.

He discreetly tucked the white opaque phial under his kurta with plans to barter it to the neighborhood *raddiwallah,* an enterprising go-between who would transport the Old Spice bottle to where it could be resold. And then with a "Hi-Yo," he trotted away, blasting away an invisible posse of murderous outlaws.

Dheer guiltily shrugged his shoulders and turned to Pinky. "Let's find Gulu. He just came back from dropping Papa at work." He was hoping to convince him to drive them to Badshah Cold Drink House by Crawford Market for a refreshing potion of lime and orange juice mixed with salt, sugar, and pepper.

"Maji won't let me go," Pinky said, "not with my stomach today."

Dheer shrugged again and waddled out of the room.

० ० ०

Maji and Vimla were still in the parlor, discussing the annual influx of tourists from Saudi Arabia and the Gulf during the impending monsoon season.

"Live in the desert all year round and come here to indulge in our rains," Maji was saying resentfully. "Bathing only on Fridays and trying to cover their odors with their Arabian perfumery."

"The monsoons *do* renew India's colors," Vimla said wistfully, "the brown earth to emerald greens, the white sky to soft blues."

"And indulge in our girls, too," Maji continued, menacingly waving her cane in the air. "Now even some Parsi girls from Cusrow Baug are going to these Arabs to quietly compile money for their dowries."

"*Hai Ram!*" Vimla exclaimed, abruptly abandoning her reverie. "I don't believe it. Their community is such that they'll never let another Parsi starve. Still, *nah*, they all lost their jobs after the British left, whattodo?"

Is that why she keeps such a close eye on Lovely didi? Pinky wondered. Vimla often fretted about the changes she saw happening in Bombay since Independence, especially how modern girls insisted on being educated, some delaying marriage, a few entirely selfish ones even going on to have careers of their own. Sequestering Lovely was the only way Vimla knew of ensuring that her daughter remained uncorrupted by such wayward influences.

Maji, too, kept a close eye on Pinky, but in a protective, comforting way.

The difference, Pinky thought, lay in Maji's strength and Vimla Auntie's fear.

DEVILRY

Nimish was in an unusually chatty mood that afternoon, having just finagled Gulu to take him to the Parsi-owned Taraporevala's bookshop off Hornby Road. He was buying texts for a new class in English Literature at St. Xavier's College, one of the city's oldest and most revered institutions.

"I'm off," he called from the front door. He could barely contain the thrill of having a new set of books to cover upon his return home, crisply creasing each fold with the edge of his ruler until the paper's resistance deliciously gave way to defeat.

Gulu began to pull the Ambassador out of the driveway after flicking water to freshen up a string of jasmine flowers he had placed around a miniature statue of Lord Ganesh, the Remover of Obstacles, upon the dashboard. He obtained these flowers from a vendor who passed by the gate at first light, purchasing jasmine strings for the housemaids, too, and depositing them on the front verandah where, later, Parvati and Kuntal would leave a few coins in payment. He used to buy a solitary marigold blossom each day, too. But that was long ago.

"Can I come?" Pinky asked, opening the car door and jumping

in. "Maji's napping and I need a notebook for a project when school opens next week."

"Me, too!" yelled Dheer, waddling after them as fast as his legs could carry him.

"Me! Me!" Tufan shouted, not wanting to be left out.

The three of them climbed into the back seat.

"What's your project?" Nimish asked as Gulu pulled the car out of the driveway.

Pinky hesitated. "Ghosts."

"Ghosts?"

"*Ram! Ram!*" Gulu exclaimed as he slid the car onto the street and muttered a self-protective mantra. "What terrible things they make you learn in school."

"No fair!" Tufan yelled. "I never learned about them."

"But we got to see *Ben-Hur,*" Dheer said, as if the two were equivalent.

"Ghost stories, folktales—those things," Pinky said with an exaggerated shrug of her shoulders.

"Ah, I see." Nimish pursed his lips, one finger on the bridge of his spectacles as he shifted them back up his nose. "I wouldn't really bother with folktales," he began, "unless they are written down. Factual."

"Like what?"

"Like this," Nimish said, holding up the *Personal Narrative of a Pilgrimage to Al-Madinah & Meccah* and tapping the name on its cover, one Sir Richard F. Burton. "He came to India with the East India Company over a hundred years ago."

"Bor-ing," said Tufan.

"What does this have to do with ghosts," Gulu asked, "aside from the fact that the jackass is no better off than one himself?" He wanted to nip this bookish conversation in the bud. Nimish had a tendency to go off on complex tangents, keeping his audience jailed in tight cells of incomprehension until the end of his diatribes. Gulu, on the other hand, preferred more exciting, local topics: the latest film *Mughal-e-Azam,* with its voluptuous, dancing courtesans or the new neighbor with a sexual proclivity for big-bottomed men clad in tight polyester, for example.

"I think he's fascinating," Pinky said, sharply elbowing Tufan.

Nimish rewarded her with a smile. "He was Britain's greatest explorer.

He didn't just write about the people in the colonies but understood them, translated them for the world. Including us."

"He understood us?" Gulu asked with eyebrows raised, pointing a blackened fingernail at his loudly checkered shirt.

"I've been born too late to do what he did," Nimish continued. "Unfortunately, everyone's already been written about. But I want to travel like him, in disguise as an Arab, maybe even as an Englishman. Discover the dark underside of civilization, its perverse pulse. I want to understand what makes a society tick, what its collective dreams are, its yearnings."

At the mention of yearnings, Pinky grew flushed.

"You want to pretend you're English?" Gulu asked.

"I could pass."

"'Wheatish is not white,'" Tufan declared, borrowing one of his mother's favorite phrases.

"Pass-*wass!*" Gulu exclaimed. "Step one foot upon her Majesty's soil and you'll *fut-a-fut* find out how brown you really are."

"And the ghosts?" Pinky prodded.

"Burton wrote a book called *Tales of Hindu Devilry*," Nimish continued undeterred.

"Hindu devilry?" Pinky asked, wondering if Maji's priest, Panditji, knew of such terrifying matters.

The oily-headed, beady-eyed priest punctually made an appearance every Monday to dispense blessings and irrelevant advice, all the while keeping a sharp eye on the stack of rupees straining within Maji's enormous bosom. Pinky was quite certain that priests came into regular contact with ghosts and other such spirits but wondered if Panditji was interested in anything beyond calculating the exact number of sticky sweet *laddoos* needed at any given ceremony.

"What nonsense," Gulu said, dismissing everything Nimish had just said with a grand wave of his hand. "Christians like him are the real devils."

"It really wasn't about a devil," Nimish said, exasperated. "It was a translation of King Vikramaditya's ghost stories."

"Oh!" Gulu said, "I know all about those."

"Have you read the book?" Pinky asked.

"A long time back," Nimish said. "The king had to carry a corpse hanging from a mimosa tree all the way to the cremation *ghats*. And during his trip, the corpse was inhabited by Betaal, a demon who told him riddles, each containing an essence of human wisdom."

"Wisdom-*smisdom*, no need to read books for such things," Gulu said, clicking his tongue in disapproval. "Anything of value I learned during my childhood years at the train station."

Before Pinky could maneuver the conversation back on track, Gulu plunged into another one of his stories.

"You see," he began, "I was very little—maybe six, seven—when I first started shining shoes at Victoria Terminus. vt is like a heart—*di-dom, di-dom, di-dom*—you can feel it, *nah*? The very pulse of India. A hundred years ago the very first railway line in all of India was opened from vt."

"Bor-ing," Tufan said.

"I've heard this one before," Pinky began to protest. Usually she enjoyed listening to his tales but today she had more pressing matters on her mind.

"My friends Hari and Bambarkar and myself all worked for Big Uncle," Gulu continued, his voice brimming with drama and suspense. "He was so fat, I tell you, because he swallowed a tiger during his days in the military. When he opened his mouth, only roaring came out! But he provided us with a way to bring in a few *annas* a day for *roti* and *dal*. Sometimes even roasted *channa* in newspaper cones— still steaming, I tell you. We all felt very lucky on those days."

"Bor-ing."

The Ambassador wheezed to a stop at an intersection. Immediately a horde of vendors besieged the car, knocking insistently on the windows with their wares.

"*Jao! Jao!*" Gulu yelled, transferring his animosity toward Tufan onto them. "I earned my very own Cherry Blossom tin of polish in only two months," he said, glaring at the street beggars as if laziness were the sole reason for their impoverishment. "How I loved to caress the shiny metal with the red-red cherries on it. Each morning I even rubbed some on my nose to wake me up."

At this olfactory reference, Dheer perked up.

"One day Big Uncle was murdered," Gulu continued as he vigorously cut off a family of five piled atop a scooter. "A man with red, *paan*-chewing teeth took over. My friends Hari and Bambarkar *fut-a-fut* began working for Red Tooth, not even blinking an eye. But I stayed loyal to Big Uncle. He had been my protector after all. So Red Tooth beat me to a bloody pulp. I almost died right there on the platform." He exhaled dramatically, imagining dark burgundy curtains closing with a swish, the smell of *mirchee* popcorn crunching underfoot, the shouts of an appreciative audience as they cheered their youthful hero to his feet after his encounter with Red Tooth.

Nimish scrunched his nose, "Sounds like last month's film at Metro Cinema."

"You think I'm lying?" Gulu turned indignantly to Nimish. "See this scar above my eyebrow?"

All three boys peered into Gulu's face, unable to discern anything more sinister than a pitted patch of acne.

"But the demon," Pinky asked, "how did it get into the corpse under the mimosa tree?"

"These things happen," Gulu said, shaking his hand dismissively, "it's a common-enough occurrence."

"What rot," Nimish said. "It's all just superstitions. Even your brave King Vikramaditya was said to have been sired by a donkey."

"Have you no respect?" Gulu asked. "So Lord Ganesh has the head of an elephant. So King Vikramaditya was born in extraordinary circumstances. What difference does it make?"

"But the demon?"

"Pinky-*didi*," Gulu said with pronounced patience, "demons are floating spirits looking for a form to possess. Anything will do: a dead body, animals on the street, sometimes, I tell you, even this car's useless engine."

Nimish shook his head and buried his nose back in Burton's *Personal Narrative*.

Pinky's heart sank. Like Gulu's driving, a considerable percentage of his knowledge was improvised on the spot. Whether true, false, or irrelevant, Gulu strictly adhered to whatever came out of his mouth as if it had been a sacred verse from his tattered copy of the *Bhagavad Gita*. Despite his illiteracy, he carried the *Gita* with him at all times, citing passages to the beggars who tapped on his car windows. "*Doing your own duty imperfectly is better than doing another's well,*" he once quoted to the barber on the side of the street who had just inadvertently denuded the side of a client's head.

"Not to worry," Gulu continued, misreading her crestfallen expression. "Some can be quite friendly."

"And ghosts?" she asked. "Are they the same?"

"No, no, not at all," Gulu said. "Ghosts aren't interested in possessing. They're the spirits of people who died under bad circumstances like, you know, suicide, murder, that sort of thing. Perhaps they fell under a lorry brimming with bamboo or were flattened by a tree while hanging from the train during morning commute. Or perhaps they were not cremated properly because the family didn't have money for the required amount of wood. They come back to this world to correct their situation. Sometimes they come back to warn others."

"But how do you know what they want?" Pinky asked.

"You have to listen."

Pinky slunk back in the seat. This was not the answer she had hoped for.

"Not to worry," Gulu said comfortingly. "Some can be quite friendly. But you will be learning all of this soon enough for your school project, *nah*?"

※ ※ ※

The children decided to stop on the way back at the Empress Café along Colaba Causeway to have a cold drink and pick up a half dozen of their famed crumpets, one of Savita's favorite treats.

"Duke's Soda, Mangola, Koko-Cola," offered a bald waiter, wearing an ill-fitting red jacket and attempting a British accent as was required by the Anglophilic café owner.

Pinky decided upon a Gold Spot drink with a squeeze of fresh lime and a good measure of rock salt that, when sprinkled in, caused the soda to bubble venomously over the top. Dheer ordered toasted cakes in sweetened milk, and Nimish a coffee. Tufan selected Coca-Cola, wrapping his perspiring palm against the alluring hourglass-shaped bottle which, like the throat-burning drink, reminded him of the American film siren Marilyn Monroe.

Giving his bottle's narrow waist another squeeze, Tufan said, "Remember the vending machine at Metro Theater?"

Dheer nodded excitedly, mouth full of wet cake. "When the padres at school took us to *Ben-Hur*, we got to use it. You put the coin into a slot at the top and there is a rumbling noise. Then you push back the center slat and—*wah!*—one extra-cold Koko-Cola!"

A bus rattled to a stop nearby, looking as if it would rather have been stripped down and retired than goaded onwards. It choked and coughed up an array of noxious fumes; equally thick smoke shot from the radiator in front. The bus, an exact replica of the double-decker ones that clanged along the streets of London except for the acronym BEST—Bombay Electric Supply & Transport—stenciled on either side of the lower deck, was precariously tilted on its axles and dented in a thousand places, its red color barely visible under the grime and dust. Due to the increasing unrest between Maharastrians and Gujaratis over annexation of the city, the bus had been covered with wire mesh, giving it the appearance of a mobile jail complete with an armed police inspector riding at the door watching for hurled rocks and other signs of insurgency.

A conductor hopped out of the rear left side door, wielding his aluminum ticket box like a weapon. At once a mob rushed forward, strategically elbowing aside rival passengers in their rush to get on.

"I hate buses," Tufan said, "they stink."

"It's not so bad," Nimish said, "at least there's ventilation through the missing windows."

"They're teeming with Eve-teasers," Pinky declared, remembering the recent four-inch headline—"EVE-TEASER ARRESTED!"—in *The Evening News*, followed by a brief article detailing how the frotteur was caught offending a girl's modesty on an overcrowded BEST bus.

Bloody idiot, Jaginder had commented. *First the Romeo was thrashed by the passengers, then by the police. Now he'll rot in jail for six months.*

Unless he's from a good family, nah? Savita had asked, verifying that wealth and status would shield her youngest, if ever so misguided, from such humiliation.

Yes, yes, Jaginder had said, *for good families the disgrace of one's name in the papers is enough to satisfy the magistrate.*

Best thing to do when riding the bus, Parvati had cut in, *is to carry a knitting needle in one's bag. One swift jab at Romeo's privates and he'll never touch you again!*

"I think it's the women who are most dangerous," Dheer said. "When we went to *Ben-Hur* on the bus, a woman bummed me out of my seat!" He went on to describe how, with a mighty swing of her ample hips, she sent him flying into the aisle. When he had dared to protest, he received a neat whack from her overstuffed purse. The woman had been sporting a thick moustache and equally bushy ears and had plopped herself in the middle of the class of boys. *Always chasing after us girls,* she had bewailed as if she had been the object of their desire. And then unclicking her purse, she had coquettishly retrieved a handkerchief and daintily dabbed at her hirsute upper lip.

Nimish, Pinky, and Tufan burst out laughing.

The double-decker bus, reeking of stale urine and undigested fried lunch, now contemplated a full shutdown in front of the Empress Café while the enraged driver coaxed it back to life, with a solid beating by a rusted pipe. After the engine finally sputtered to ignite, the driver blared the bulb horn and veered onto the road where he overtook a contingent of Fiats and narrowly missed three lunching cows.

"I like to take the trams instead, green one if possible," Nimish added, "starting at Dhobi Talao all the way to King's Circle where the workers turn it around on ball bearings, more than an hour's journey."

"So long!" Tufan exclaimed, licking the curve of his Coca-Cola bottle.

"I get my reading done," he shrugged, "and sometimes meet friends on weekends to catch an English matinee."

"How can you concentrate?" Pinky asked. "That route takes you on Kalbadevi Road, the most crowded street in the whole city!"

"It's actually easier than at home . . . where there are distractions," Nimish said vaguely then abruptly called the waiter for another coffee.

Pinky stiffened, thinking about Lovely.

Suddenly, they heard the loud sound of drumming and shrilly voices filling the street.

"*Hijras!*"

A group of hermaphrodites, tall, with masculine features, but draped in flowing saris, danced down the road in their direction, one beating a *dholak* drum. Most of the pedestrians on the street gave them a wide berth, but a few bold men jeered at them from their open windows.

"*Arré chakkas*," they called, using the term meaning the sixth day of the week, the day the *hijras* typically came out in public, but also used abusively to taunt a cowardly or effeminate man.

"Go back to Koliwada," another shouted, referring to their settlement in the slums near Sion.

The *hijras* responded, some threatening to pull up their saris to display their missing genitalia, one even exhibiting a desiccated male organ imperiously propped up on a wooden splint in a sealed glass jar.

"Should we go?" Dheer asked, unsuccessfully trying to squeeze his entire body into the rickety chair as if to make himself invisible.

"They'll come after you," Tufan warned, "and steal your balls."

"No they won't!"

"Oh, that's right," Tufan said, double-checking the fly of his pants, "you don't have any."

Dheer shuddered. "Are they born like that?"

"Some," Nimish said, "others are castrated during adolescence by an insanitary knife and boiling oil. Or sometimes by pulling a strand of horsehair tighter and tighter each day until their things turn black and fall off."

Dheer crossed his legs. Tufan covered his privates with his Coca-Cola bottle.

"In Mogul times," Nimish continued in a whisper, "they guarded the emperor's harems, their position one of privilege. Many were even granted parcels of land. After the British drew up the Indian Penal Code in 1884, however, they were declared to be an offense."

"They're always at weddings," Pinky said.

"They make a living by playing on the dread and superstition that they evoke in others, especially at auspicious events," Nimish continued. "Even the police usually leave them unmolested, fearful of supernatural powers which stem from their ability to be both man and woman and to be neither."

The procession of singing *hijras* approached, sharply clapping their hands, drawing attention to their parade. They stopped in front of the Empress Café where the children sat, calling inside for the owner, a fat man known as Jolly, to come out.

"They have an arrangement with the local maternity wards and hospitals," Nimish explained. "They pay for the names of families where there has been a birth. They give blessings to the healthy ones and claim the unfortunate ones who entered the world with deformed or missing privates."

"I guess Jolly's just had a child then," Pinky said.

"Maybe he's abnormal," Tufan added hopefully.

The *hijras* dancing grew feverish, the din almost deafening as they sang and simultaneously hurled taunts at the local men from behind their *palloos.* "Oh Ma, we'll never be able to have children," they chanted. "So we've come to bless your child."

Just then Jolly appeared, his face looking as if he had a terrible skin disease but upon closer inspection the sores turned out to be globs of jam. He had just been taking a nap under a condiment shelf in the kitchen when a jar of marmalade fell off and broke open by his face. He stood now, glaring at the singing hermaphrodites, with an upraised broom in his hand. His wife, a tiny woman with dusty, flour-like skin, stood next to him with her newborn son in her arms. The *hijras* continued to dance, their undulating hands and bodies moving in suggestive ways while the leader demanded a thousand rupees. Despite this obvious attempt at robbery, the wife beamed, joyful that the *hijras* had come to announce the birth of her child to the world. She threw herself into bargaining with remarkable prowess.

The *hijra* leader brought his fee down to five hundred rupees.

"Go! Go!" Jolly shouted at them. "*Rundae key bachay,* sons of whores."

"*Arré* idiot!" his wife scolded him. "You want to insult the *hijras* during our happy occasion and bring their curses upon our heads?"

Jolly stormed inside.

Greatly pleased by the reprimand on their behalf, the leader immediately dropped his price to a hundred rupees. The wife pulled the required amount from her sari blouse and handed it to him.

"Show us the boy!" he then demanded.

The woman untied the triangular cotton diaper from the baby's hips, exposing his perfectly formed privates, his penis promptly releasing a firm stream of yellow liquid. The *hijras* clapped their hands in amusement, commenting on the workings of baby's organ, while passing the naked infant amongst themselves.

Nimish, Pinky, Dheer, and Tufan could not help but crane their necks for a better look, Tufan crestfallen when he realized that the baby would not be claimed by the *hijras*.

"He will be a great man," blessed one *hijra*.

"He will be prosperous," bestowed another.

"How lucky you are to have such a fair son," cooed a third.

"Please Ma," said the leader, tying a black thread around the baby's wrist to ward off the evil eye. "Give us a sari."

"Jolly!" the wife called out, beaming from the benedictions. "Bring one of the dowry saris."

The *hijras* beat their drum louder, singing, taunting, and dancing, until Jolly finally appeared and, muttering curses, threw an expensive wedding sari at them. Flashing him a smile, the *hijras* then politely thanked the wife and undulated down the street.

"Why must they see the baby like that?" Pinky asked.

"You have to see something with your own eyes to believe it," Nimish said, shrugging his shoulders as if the answer were obvious. "Otherwise there will always be doubt."

Dheer let out a loud burp, Tufan ordered another cola, and Nimish paid the bill.

Gulu drove up with the car. "Once I saw the *hijras* take away an unfortunate child," he said as they climbed in. "It was in the slums of Dharavi. The parents were devastated. There's no law to prevent the *hijras* from taking away these children. After all, they don't belong anywhere else."

DRINKING MOONBEAMS

S avita sat at her dressing table in the still of the night, holding the photo of her daughter to her eyes, and remembered that she had not seen her just after she was born. She had not known if it was a boy or a girl. She had not witnessed her umbilical cord being snipped. She had not heard her first cry. She had not held her bloodied, beating body against her chest. She had fallen unconscious just after her last push and had not woken up until Maji came in with the baby hours later, washed and tightly swaddled, ready to be fed.

I did not behold her coming into the world, Savita thought, beginning to weep, *and I did not behold her leaving it.*

She paused as the approaching storm rumbled in the sky. The thunder came in increasingly frequent intervals; the lightning imprinted the sky with phosphorescent bolts, yet the rains still did not come. The delay made her feel irritated, powerless. She wiped away her tears and tenderly tucked the photo back into the silver *bindi* box.

Jaginder had been so affectionate during Savita's pregnancy, convinced she carried a daughter after birthing three sons.

My raka, he had teased her, calling her a full-moon night as was prescribed by the prenatal scriptures, *our daughter will have the most princely dowry in all of Bombay—modern furniture, diamond jewelry, imported refrigerators*—sab kuch!

How delicious! Savita had smiled, feeling satisfied, indulgently contented with her life.

And we'll name her Chakori.

Chakori? Savita had been surprised at this unusual choice. *The mythological bird?*

Yes, Jaginder had said in a rare reflective moment, gazing affectionately upon her. *The most heavenly of birds.*

Who drinks moonbeams, Savita added, remembering the lore. It was at that moment that she finally fell in love with her husband.

Until then, their arrangement had been suitable. He was, after all, handsome with fair skin, of tallish frame, and just enough fat on him to appear imposing. He was dutiful, too, confidently taking responsibility for the family's shipbreaking business when his father Omanandlal passed away, giving Savita enough purse money to buy little treats of jewelry, and ensuring (thrice a week) that one son would be followed by another. Her worst fear was that she might have to wear a widow's white sari like her mother-in-law, Maji. As long as Jaginder was around, Savita would always be a leading contender amongst her friends for the Most-Number-One-First-Class-Life.

Or so she thought. When Lord Yama whisked away her newborn daughter, Savita was shocked. Not just at the irrefutability of her daughter's death, but that the tragedy had happened to *her,* in her world buffered by money and connections. She passed the mourning period alone while ancient superstitions effloresced in her mind. She called upon a tantrik who confirmed her belief that an evil influence had befallen their home and provided her with turmeric stones to hang above her children's beds.

She even decided to go on pilgrimage to Mehndipur, claiming that a witch had killed her baby with its evil eye. *Remember that female beggar that came to our gate, hahn?* she shouted at Jaginder, *Remember I was five months pregnant and the beggar would not be shooed away by Gulu until your mother gave her one of my old saris, hahn? Remember how Parvati swept up her footprints and burned them while you sat back and laughed? She was a witch, I'm telling you, she put a curse on my sari and killed my baby!*

Jaginder had unsuccessfully tried to reason with her, insisting that it had been a negligent accident. Maji chalked up the tragedy to fate. But Savita would not let herself be persuaded, declaring that the baby's ayah was to blame. *She's a witch! She's a witch!* she ranted, delving more and more into the world of secret charms and potent remedies, until her closest friends began politely to avoid her. *We'll give you some time, nah? Tell us when you're ready, okay?*

And then Jaginder underwent his metamorphosis, from butterfly into bug. He had been a strict vegetarian and teetotaler all his life, not even indulging in those alcohol-filled chocolates brought from abroad by visiting international friends. He had been refined, a true gentleman like his father, with never a rough word emerging from his mouth. He had been attentive, kind, and content in all areas of his life except for his longing for a daughter.

When she finally arrived, she had not lived long enough for them to have held a proper naming ceremony so she died without one. However, in Jaginder and Savita's hearts she was forever Chakori, their elusive little moon bird. After her sudden death, Savita had seen not grief in Jaginder's eyes, but confusion. As if the brevity of the baby's life had been an affront to his authority, to his uncanny ability to always make things go his way. Taking refuge in a bottle of Johnnie Walker Blue that had been tucked away in one of their locked metal cabinets, Jaginder lost his wings and cocooned himself, larvalike, in guilt, remorse, and blame.

He no longer wanted to make love with her, as if afraid of creating another little being who could be so suddenly lost. He was swayed by those ubiquitous billboards urging Use The Loop, and had insisted that Savita get fitted with the coil-shaped intrauterine device. *Didn't you hear,* Savita had retaliated, refusing such measures, *that it gives the husbands an electric shock?*

Parvati had suggested soaking rock salt in oil or orally taking the seeds of *sarshapa* soaked in a white rice-wash for birth control. Maji had even taken Savita to an Ayurvedic physician (after her son had desperately approached her to intercede) who prescribed a concoction of *japa* flowers and *tanduliyaka* roots for sterility. Savita had refused it all. *You don't want me to get pregnant?* she had fumed at Jaginder. *Then YOU drink haridra powder mixed with goat's urine every morning. It's supposed to be an excellent contraceptive for men.*

Defeated, Jaginder began to withdraw from Savita altogether, looking upon her with horror, as if she were to blame for what had happened to their daughter. He brooded in the privacy of their bedroom, anger turning his language sour. Nips soon led to swigs. Swigs to chugs. Chugs to whole nights spent away from her.

Savita wanted nothing more than to squash him.

Her mother, visiting from Goa, provided little relief from the grief that surrounded the Mittal household like June heat.

Chin up, darling, she had advised, delicately sipping her tea. *Really, you must get on with it.*

But Savita did not possess her mother's whimsical callousness, choosing instead to retreat into her own little world of darkness, vowing never to emerge again. And then came the news that her sister-in-law, Yamuna, had died somewhere near the Indo-Pak border and the household was thrown into mourning once more. Weeks later Maji returned with the infant Pinky, and her permanent addition to their family became a mocking reminder of Savita's own loss.

By then Savita had had enough of her self-imposed sequestration. She wiped the tears from her face, bought a stunning 22-carat gold jewelry set enameled with strutting peacocks, and invited her friends to lunch. She was all smiles. *What a lovely necklace. Kiss. Kiss. Jaginder bought it for me. So sweet he is, I tell you.* As if nothing had happened. Ten points for Savita.

What she kept suppressed inside her was fear. She did not believe that her daughter's death was a mere accident.

Wicked spirits were responsible.

So she ordered the bathroom door to be bolted at night, deathly afraid that whatever evil had killed her baby might still lurk within.

ॐ ॐ ॐ

Gulu disembarked in front of a dive that served only masala *cholay*, curried chickpeas, and fried bread and was known unofficially as Lucky Dhaba. Asha Bhosle and Kishore Kumar's popular playback duet, "*Yeh Raatein, Yeh Mausam,*" blared intermittently from inside, its reception entirely dependent on the fickle electrical services which most often shorted out during the oppressive hours of the premonsoon nights. He first approached the *paanwallah's* cart next to the eatery, hedged about by a group of men, some waiting for a *paan*, others lighting their cigarettes from a smoldering rope attached to the cart, most of them *gup-shupping*, catching up on the day's news. They gave Gulu a familiar nod.

"*Hahn-hahn*," one was saying, the tuft of hair on his shaven head declaring him to be of a high-born caste. "The whole of electricity in the city was gone except at the minister's daughter's wedding."

"These bastard officials never think twice before they loot and plunder."

"Can't digest their breakfast until they do."

"And the rest of the city was black as your face, not a single fan was working," one of the men said, slapping Gulu on the back.

"While rose petals lined the groom's path for ten kilometers!" Gulu added.

"You lying bastard," the men accused laughingly, their red mouths glowing, even as they exclaimed at this extravagance.

The *paanwallah*, a plump man with gleaming skin, kohl-rimmed eyes and a vertical *tilak* drawn from the arch of his nose all the way to his hairline, smoothed the chain of gold buttons on his kurta top. His fingers hovered over the moist red cloth in the steel dish that contained the *paan* leaves. He proceeded to snip the ends of the leaf, spreading it with lime before filling it with crushed betel-nut *supari* and cardamom, and a little tobacco. Folding the *paan* into a neat little packet, he pinned it with a clove.

Gulu placed it in the side of his mouth, his teeth crushing the first sweet-sour-pungent flavor from the leaves. Satisfied, he nodded his head and walked over to Lucky Dhaba to meet with his childhood friend, Hari, now known infamously throughout the city as Hari Bhai, Big-Brother Hari. They sat at a table outside, just under black clouds that were spread thickly across the sky.

"What's going on in the *chawl*, Bhai?" he asked, referring to the slums where Hari lived and operated his bootlegging empire.

"I tell you that *bhenchod* Renu seduced my neighbor's wife. We had to call in Tantrik Baba. He cracked his whip, saying he was going to set a spirit upon Renu, right into his *lungi* to make his organ malfunction. *Ha!* That *bhenchod* fell to the ground begging to be forgiven!"

Gulu laughed uneasily, and spat on the ground.

"What?" Hari asked. "Missing that whore of yours, Chinni?"

Gulu clicked his tongue. "Not her."

"Oh, the other one," Hari smirked. "That fishergirl."

"I was young back then, Bhai, very handsome. People used to tell me all the time, 'You should be in the pictures, Gulu,' they'd say. If only I'd tried, maybe my fate would have been different."

"Fate is fate," Hari said, pulling out a packet of *bidis* wrapped in newspaper and lighting one.

"Was it her fate to come to the bungalow, to make me fall in love, to disappear without a trace?" Gulu wondered aloud, his brow furrowing. Though they had both been employed by Maji, their worlds had rarely intersected. The ayah lived and worked inside the bungalow, Gulu on the outside. In all those years, they never communicated but for the single red-orange marigold flower he bought for her every morning, which she pinned into her hair. One thousand blooms. One thousand gestures of his love.

"Like a flame, *yaar*."

"I was going to marry her, Bhai. I was saving money. I kept telling myself another six months, now five, now four. And then—"

Gulu remembered Maji's low voice, her urgent call, *Take her to the train station; give her this money.*

"At first when I was driving to the station, all I could think was, *We're alone together!* How long had I been asking Lord Ganesh for this opportunity, I didn't even know. I just knew that I wanted her to marry me! I knew something was wrong, I knew she had been sent away. But I didn't want to ask. As long as I kept quiet, everything was the same. Like intermission at the cinema."

Hari grunted then ripped off a piece of greasy fried bread and dipped it into a plate of piping hot *cholay*.

"Then when I was at the station, she only told me that the baby drowned. I didn't know what to think, what to say. I don't know how we reached VT Station. I felt death clutching at my heart. I wanted to go back to yesterday, rewind the day. Like a film."

Gulu stuffed some bread into his mouth. He remembered her eyes. They had been red, red like those of the Goddess Kali. "All I saw was red. And suddenly I felt so afraid. I felt engulfed by her mouth, by her red tongue, by the bloodied words she had spoken. O Destroyer of the Universe! She had destroyed the baby's life, the family's life, my life, I shouted at her."

"It was an accident, *yaar*," Hari said, taking another bite. He had heard Gulu recount this story many times before but, like a good friend, patiently listened.

"The *palloo* slipped from her shoulder when she opened the door. The red disappeared and she became mine again. My beloved. I felt sick. The car was spinning. I no longer knew anything. 'Don't go!' I shouted. She tore the marigold from her hair and ran. I ran after her but she disappeared. It was like Goddess Bhoomdevi had opened up the earth and taken her in."

Gulu's eyes were running. He wiped them on a dirty handkerchief and heartily blew his nose.

"I beat my head against the steering wheel until it bled and then I beat it some more." And when he was finished, when his head was pounding and blood running down his temple, he had turned and seen the marigold, a burst of red-orange upon the blackness of the backseat.

"No woman is worth that much suffering," Hari said with a loud belch.

Gulu lit a *bidi* and took a long drag, nodding in agreement.

But silently he thought about that marigold flower, tenderly pressed between pages of newspaper and hidden under his cot. He had loved her. He had committed an unimaginable, unspeakable act to get her back the night she disappeared. He pined for her with an intensity that left scars upon his heart. He prayed only for one thing at night as he fell asleep: to see her once more.

Then, then, O Merciful Lord, he always ended his entreaty, *I will be content to die.*

What he did not know, what he would never know was that she had not loved him.

No, no, she had not, not at all.

For she had already given herself to someone else in the bungalow.

※ ※ ※

Jaginder piloted the Ambassador over the dark streets, sporadically lit by brilliant flashes from the sky, feeling more and more relaxed the further he got from his wife, his mother, the bungalow. Drinking dens peppered the Bombay coast at Mahim, Bandra, Pali Hill, Andheri, and right up to Versova, at least one surreptitiously nestled within each Christian fishing village. He had explored these *addas* in the thick of the night while Savita slept, thinking somehow that his shame was cloaked by the darkness. He was grateful that his dead father could not see how far he had sunk.

After his daughter's death and during the long years of prohibition, Jaginder had procured his own secret stash of Johnnie Walker and Chivas Regal. And, although his drinking was never openly discussed, Savita—ever conscious of status—carefully saw to it that the empty bottles of the most expensive brand, Royal Salut, were refilled with water, labels intact, and kept in the refrigerator. Others were sold off for decent prices to *raddiwallas* who, in turn, bartered them to boot-leggers. Jaginder had obtained a necessary permit from their family physician, Dr. M. M. Iyer, after a thick wad of rupees was stealthily slipped into the doctor's shiny briefcase. *Shall I declare you a confirmed alcoholic so you can have the maximum allotment?* the doctor had asked, grinning conspiratorially.

With the doctor's statement in hand, Jaginder was able to procure bottles of Indian Made Foreign Liquor from a legal wine shop. But the domestic brand tasted no better than the ones that had been brewed in the sewers by bootleggers with rotten oranges, coconut shavings, dark lumps of raw sugar, and large doses of *nausagar* to speed up fermenta-tion. Even for Jaginder's addiction, this concoction was too much.

He had fleetingly thought about frequenting the permit-rooms of the Wellington Turf Club or the Bombay Gymkhana where the Whites-only era had nostalgically, and somewhat reluctantly, faded into a grim acceptance of wealthy natives. But Jaginder did not want to risk dealing with the police subinspectors who stood stiffly inside these private clubs, one hand on a register to record the buyer's name, address, and number of pints and the other hand under his sleeve so that he could be persuaded to overlook the register. And besides, he didn't feel comfortable drinking in such an atmosphere because although visiting white sahibs were expected—indeed exhorted—to drink in order to maintain their auras of authority, Jaginder had no such excuse for his habit.

So he escaped to the *addas* in the middle of the night. He did not ask

Gulu to drive him there. For one thing, Gulu was off that night. And secondly, Maji had always counseled him, *You must always know how to make best use of your servants. Never subject them to your sudden whims.*

As he drove onwards, Jaginder's thoughts turned to his daughter. Last night, when he returned from the *adda,* Savita had been wide awake, waiting for him in a state of rage.

I'm done for, he had thought, throwing himself upon the bed in surrender. Let her yell at him, let her hit him, whatever it was, he deserved it. He knew that, even as he blamed Savita for their crippled relationship, he was at fault.

But instead of pouncing upon him, Savita spat out Pinky's name.

She's a thief! she screeched into his ear as the alcohol drummed in his temples and weighed down his eyelids.

Jaginder wanted nothing more than to fall into a pleasant, buzzing sleep. Oh, how nice it would be just to drift away.

She was in my bindi box just now! She found the photo—

Jaginder's eyes shot open. A dread filled his chest like smoke from a smoldering fire.

She knows?

I told her she was here because of our misfortune, our tragedy!

Jaginder groaned. They had agreed never to tell the children, except for Nimish who, though only four back then, understood that he was forbidden to speak of his dead sister. Now, now it was all in the open again. All these years of careful concealment, of trying to forget.

Why did you tell her it was our daughter? he yelled. *Why didn't you make up something?*

Because I can't take it anymore! Savita shouted back. *Pinky has a father. Why doesn't he raise her? Why haven't you done anything to send her back? Why do I have to live with this child, this girl, who is not my own?*

You have to let it go, Jaginder said. *Your anger's consuming you.*

My anger? Savita yelled. *And what about you? Disappearing every night. Not touching me anymore as if I'm a leper.*

She began to weep.

Jaginder closed his eyes again and, turning his back to her, forced himself to sleep.

FAMINE AMIDST SUDS

Parvati and Kuntal squatted across from each other, their knees splayed like wings, saris hitched up in between, darkly draping the topic of that morning's conversation.

"Humph! Thinks he's satisfying me with that bone-thin thing of his. No bigger than an okra!"

Parvati brought her index fingers to within three inches of each other.

Kuntal giggled.

"Expects me to slide around—Oh Kanj! Kanj!—like some sort of *sabzi* he's frying up!" Parvati picked up the paddle and began beating a desperate-looking shirt with vigor.

"That's not what you used to say."

"Humph. He was bigger back then. Everything shrinks with age *nah!*"

Parvati had married Cook Kanj soon after she and Kuntal joined Maji's household in the winter of 1943, four years prior to Pinky's arrival. Parvati had been fourteen, Kuntal a year younger; both had come all the way from the rural districts of Bengal in North India as refugees from a famine that wiped out three million people. Most of the dead were agricultural laborers like their parents. Neither Parvati nor Kuntal understood the decisions made by the English colonial government that led to famine conditions when there was enough grain harvest that year to feed all the people of Bengal. But it was a wartime economy and the British, already sensing their demise in India, firmly entrenched themselves by confiscating grain from the rural districts and destroying additional supplies that might fall into enemy Japanese hands. Provisions were transported to Calcutta, the capital of Bengal and a critical port for the imperial government, then out of India to other British colonies.

While Calcutta was buffered with grain and the city workers insulated from the inflationary impact of World War II, Indians in the outlying districts—the ones who had grown the rice—slowly starved to death. Parvati and Kuntal's parents heard rumors of food and relief kitchens in Calcutta and left their village in weather so hot that the air was sharp with the rot of freshly dead bodies. Entrusted to a neighbor, the girls had no choice but to wait and slowly starve. What little food was allotted to them slowly dwindled away as provisions were hoarded for family members. Parvati spent her days scavenging for edibles, collecting seeds and killing insects for nourishment. Whatever she found or could steal, she would share with Kuntal who had grown so weak that she could no longer stand. In this way, Parvati kept them alive. While Kuntal wasted away, Parvati's body stubbornly held onto its muscles and small deposits of fat on her chest and hips. She refused to let thoughts of death touch her. She would have escaped to Calcutta herself, following her parents, if only Kuntal had been stronger.

And then a contingent of village elders, three of them blind and the rest illiterate, appeared one day with a tattered copy of a British-owned newspaper, *The Statesman*, pointing to a grainy photo of emaciated bodies.

See dere, they cried out from mouths emptied of their teeth, *dey dead!*

And then they gave the girls, now orphans, leering looks that made Parvati realize that they must escape immediately. *If not to Calcutta, then Bombay,* Parvati decided, the *other* major colonial port. The City of Gold.

That night, after their neighbor had the opportunity to study the newspaper over a bottle of country brew, he yanked Parvati to his room.

You have no one else, he drunkenly reasoned, *so you're mine now.*

Through it all, Parvati clung to the thought of Bombay as her salvation and did not give up hope. Instead, as he lay asleep, she grabbed the small dagger that lay on top of his discarded lungi and plunged it into his heart as his eyes opened in shock. And then for good measure, she cut off his shrunken penis and tossed it out the window where it was speedily devoured by a fleet of rabid dogs.

As the night deepened into stillness, Parvati crawled out of his room and stole his remaining assets which included money, a gunny sack of rice, and a rusted bicycle. She barely noticed her bleeding wound as she cycled, with Kuntal strapped to the handlebars, to the station where she bartered her rice for two tickets to Bombay. On the train ride and in the weeks of homelessness that followed in Bombay, Parvati slowly nursed Kuntal to reasonable health. She made inquiries. She used the last of her money to buy fresh clothes for them. And then she knocked on bungalow doors.

Need maid? Need maid?

Door after door was slammed.

Cook Kanj, already in his midthirties, had answered Parvati's insistent knocking upon Maji's gate and—though annoyed at being awakened from his nap—was immediately taken by the look in her eyes. For despite the hunger that had wracked her body for months, Parvati's eyes glistened with conviction. He sat the girls down outside on the front verandah and, against his nature, gave them some food. When Maji woke up and saw Parvati energetically sweeping the driveway, she knew that she had found the help she had been praying for the last couple weeks ever since her previous housemaid had gotten married and left. Though they had no references, Maji was perceptive enough to sense that the girls had come from a good home and that, like Gulu many years before, all they needed was the possibility of a second life. *Two weeks*, she told them and crisply went about arranging their sleeping quarters.

The bungalow's two one-car garages sat like mouse ears in the rear. The first was occupied by Gulu and Cook Kanj. Maji briefly considered installing Parvati and Kuntal in the second garage, alongside the black Mercedes that took up most of the space, before settling on the back living room, the one which went unused except for formal company. Though she trusted Gulu and Kanj, they were men after all, and Maji did not want any scandals to erupt amongst the servants while she slept.

In his thirties, Cook Kanj had been quite handsome with his wavy hair and starched white shirts tucked into a *lungi* or, on a rare day, his one pair of trousers. He had kept his eye on the sisters from the moment they arrived, as if they were his personal wards. Parvati was brash and sharp. Kuntal shy and round. He lavished attention on them both, putting extra sugar into a tray of cashew *burfi*, offering mango *lassis* and lime sherbets on the sly, fattening them up a bit. And then, unexpectedly, Parvati's face began appearing to him at night, refusing to let him sleep. During the day, he surreptitiously glanced at her, falling more and more in love. Soon, his treats were only for her. *Why not?* he asked himself eventually.

Why not? Parvati thought when Cook Kanj suggested marriage, although the residue of her neighbor's crime involuntarily caused her to stiffen. Even so, she reasoned, Kanj had taken her in when others had slammed doors and cared for her with a protective tenderness reminiscent of her vanished father. He was like fried *paneer* cheese, gruff and crisp on the outside but soft and chewy on the inside. Upon learning of their impending nuptials, Maji gave her blessings and generously converted the second garage into their sleeping quarters.

"Good thing you never married. It's more work," Parvati now said to Kuntal, pushing a strand of loose hair away with the back of a sudsy hand. "At the end of the day, instead of letting me rest, he's grabbing this and that. I barely walk in and already he's loosening his *lungi*. Wanting me to touch his little okra. As if my hands have not been busy all day. Just wait, one day I'll go in with the clothes paddle, see what he does!"

"He loves you, *nah di*."

Kuntal was right. The years had not diminished Kanj's affection for his wife. And Parvati, for all her complaining, continued to throw flirtatious looks at him whenever she passed by the kitchen, even though he had begun to dry up like a lime left out in the torpid Bombay sun. She took great pleasure in inciting him, teasing him into desperation, and then taking her time to return to the garage at the end of the day.

"What love?" Parvati said dismissively. "I'm telling you, you're lucky."

Though they were sisters, Parvati was more of a mother to Kuntal. Having lost their parents, Parvati never had any intention of letting her sister disappear into marriage especially since she considered her an easy target for an unscrupulous man. Parvati's future with Cook Kanj was fixed in Maji's bungalow. But Kuntal, if she were to marry, might have to leave the household. Despite her own happy situation, Parvati continuously emphasized the dangers of men and the drudgery of marriage at every opportunity.

"The old fool can cook Moguli eggplant, *rasmalai*, the most extravagant dishes but can't even plant a proper seed in my womb," Parvati grumbled for effect.

Pinky's face appeared around the doorframe.

"*Hai-hai*, look who's been listening," Parvati said, her paddling unabated as she nodded with her chin in Pinky's direction.

"Need something Pinky-*di*?" Kuntal asked, rinsing off her hands.

Pinky shook her head as she walked into the bathroom and sat down on the wooden stool. "Can I take my bath?"

"You want us to leave now, right in the middle of laundry?" Parvati asked irritatedly.

"No, no, no!" Pinky said, "just that I can wash while you're here."

Parvati and Kuntal exchanged looks and shrugged.

Pinky began to undress. "Do you love Cook Kanj?"

"*Hai-hai*, what kind of a question is that?" Parvati readjusted her sari with her elbow. "I don't have to love him, he's my husband."

"Of course she loves him, Pinky-*di*," Kuntal said, clicking her tongue. "She's just saying that for my benefit."

"And why are you up so early?" Parvati asked.

"I couldn't sleep."

"Couldn't sleep?" Kuntal asked. "Is something wrong?"

"Maji doesn't believe me!" Pinky blurted out, tears already sprouting in her eyes.

"Doesn't believe you? About what?"

"A ghost! There's a ghost in here, in this bathroom!"

"Ghost?" Parvati put her paddle down and threw her sister a warning look. "Oh ho, that just means it's that time."

"Yes," Kuntal agreed. "You're thirteen after all."

"Any day now you will bleed from your *soo-soo*," Parvati pronounced matter-of-factly. "You'll have terrible pains in your belly. And you will smell and be banned from the kitchen. And the puja room too."

"My MCs?" Pinky asked. She had heard about monthly cycles from Lovely.

"It's not so bad, Pinky-*di*. All girls go through it."

"It *is* bad," Parvati interjected pointing an insinuating finger at Pinky.

"It just means you can have a baby."

"If your husband wields something more substantial than mine."

"But what does it have to do with ghosts?" Pinky asked.

"My cycles started just after we arrived in Bombay," Parvati continued. "I had terrible nightmares. I thought I saw my Baba but it was only a dream. Oh ho! What an attitude! He was displeased we'd left Bengal. But they were the ones who left us! They had no right to be angry with me!"

"That was long-ago Pinky-*di*," Kuntal said, soothingly.

"What happened to them?" Pinky asked.

Parvati slapped the paddle down and with a sigh, walked away.

Kuntal went back to the washing in silence.

Almost undetectably, the air grew chilled.

Pinky rinsed herself off, goose bumps rising on her body.

"Are you cold too?" she asked Kuntal.

Kuntal shook her head, reaching over to touch Pinky's forehead. "It's natural to feel a little chilled during your cycles, losing all that heat from your body, *nah*?" she said. "Quickly finish your bath now."

Pinky splashed her face with water and opened her eyes. She thought she saw a flash inside the bucket, a vibrant flash of black that strangely dazzled. Then, as she blinked there was a pulse of red and silver, two tinted milliseconds.

"Did you see that!" Pinky yelled.

Kuntal looked up. "See what?"

"Flashes inside the bucket!"

Kuntal squinted, peering inside, then shook her head apologetically.

Pinky began to dress herself, face downcast. "You believe me, don't you?"

"Your cycles must be arriving any day," Kuntal said kindly. "The first time it feels so strange . . ."

Parvati returned with a slim parcel wrapped in an old sari. She sat down on the wooden stool and slowly, almost reverently, unwrapped the yellow and red *bandhani* cloth.

"Oh *di*," Kuntal moaned when she realized what it was, "Pinky's too young, please."

"She wants to know what happened, so I'm going to show her."

The newspaper, *The Statesman,* was dated August 22, 1943. Inside its yellowed and blood-splattered cover was a full page of photos, mostly of emaciated women and children dying on city streets.

"See this photo?" Parvati pointed. In the coarse blacks and whites, a line of women stretched out, ribs protruding, faces pulled away. There was one shadowy man crouching against a cart in the corner. "Those are our parents on the end. There was a famine in our village so they went to Calcutta for food."

Pinky could not tear her eyes away from the blurry images, especially the one of their mother cloaked in a torn polka-dot sari.

"Did they find it?"

"What do you think?" Parvati asked, touching the snapshot. "It was all lies. There wasn't enough food in the city. They died right there on the street."

Kuntal began to softly weep, "Oh *di*, why did you keep that?"

"To remind me," Parvati said, carefully wrapping the newspaper back into the cloth. "To survive at all costs."

HUSBAND, HUSBAND-EATER

The statues in the *puja* room gleamed. Maji and Pinky took pinches of white rice powder in their fingers and drew mandalas upon the black marble altar. They placed a fresh flower garland upon the framed painting of Saraswati.

Maji began chanting a mantra: "*Yaa Kundendu tushaara haarad-havalaa.* May Goddess Saraswati, who is fair like the jasmine-colored moon . . . remove my ignorance."

After they had finished with the prayers, Maji sat back and sighed. "When I was young," she said, "there was a young Brahmin girl who came to live next door. She was thirteen, maybe fourteen, and was married to the neighbor's son."

She remembered that the girl loved eating alarmingly bright concoctions of crushed ice and fruit syrup that turned her tongue guava green and jackfruit yellow.

"A year later her husband died. I watched from the rooftop as two barber-caste women pulled her into the courtyard. This young girl was now a widow. They stripped off her jewelry and clothes. They wiped her forehead of vermillion and drew instead a vertical smear of funeral ash from the tip of her nose to her hairline. They shaved the hair from her head. They washed her body with cold water and wrapped it in a rough white sari. She was crouching the whole time, crying, crying. She looked up and saw me on the rooftop next door. I wanted to reach down and save her . . ."

Maji paused, pressing her eyes with her fingers as if to force impending tears back inside.

"Did you?" Pinky asked.

Maji gave a little laugh. "I was just a child myself. I ran to my parents but their grim faces told me not to interfere, that the *Laws of Manu* had dictated these rites. The poor child was given only one crude meal a day and she slowly grew emaciated. Her mother-in-law blamed her for the death, calling her *khasma nu khaniye*, husband-eater. She was not even referred to as a 'she' but an 'it,' as if she no longer possessed a gender. I passed fruit to her from a rope attached to my rooftop and she devoured it. But one day she was caught and sent away."

One tear now broke through and slid down Maji's cheeks.

Something hard and tight clenched in Pinky's chest. "What happened to her?"

"I don't know, *beti*, I don't know. Perhaps she was sent to the ashrams in Vrindavan or Varanasi to beg for her subsistence. After I was married, I asked your grandfather to take me there on pilgrimage. I searched every vacant face but I never saw her. Gandhiji made things a little better for widows but there is still no place for them in society. All those rituals they forced upon her—the funeral ash, the cutting of her hair—were to make her dead."

Maji dabbed at her eyes.

"I vowed then I would never allow that to happen to me. I would fight first, take my life even—"

"Maji!" Pinky was shocked.

"Forgive me, *beti*, I was young then and foolish to think such things. I wish my parents had had the courage to take that child into our home but they were afraid that her inauspicious shadow would fall upon me. I dreamt of that poor child last night. After all these years, I dreamt of her. How I wish I could remember her name."

* * *

At the breakfast table, Savita was complaining as usual to Jaginder. "There were mosquitoes hovering over my head last night on top of your snoring! I tell you, it's a conspiracy to keep me awake!"

It was true. Entire mosquito clans gathered in frenetic funnels over Savita's hair whenever she went out for her social engagements. Sometimes, a few devoted ones came home with her while the rest pressed forward on their feverish pilgrimage for other, equally perfumed buns. Kuntal sporadically unrolled her mat in Savita's room in order to rub away their detrimental effects and generally provide a sympathetic ear to her litany of ongoing afflictions.

Jaginder grunted.

"Oh, Parvati," Savita called out, spotting her in the hallway, "did the *darjee* drop off my Kanjeevaram sari for today?"

"Yes, it came this morning. I put it in your room," Parvati answered, making a quick escape. She found her sister cleaning the bathroom. "Oh ho! That Savita drives me crazy. Did you know that she and Jaginder had a big fight last night?"

"*Achha?*" Kuntal was busy arranging a cup of frayed toothbrushes and the dented tube of Kolynos Dental Cream upon the marble sink counter. The bathroom tiles gleamed.

"I knew it the moment he came back with the Ambassador. Not five minutes afterwards, I heard her screaming all the way from my quarters."

"Poor Savita-*di.*"

"What 'poor Savita'?" Parvati pointed a finger at Kuntal menacingly. "Have you ever seen her squatting down to do laundry even once, *hahn*? She doesn't have to lift a finger all day. Now she can't even lift her petticoat at night?"

罕 ⚶ ⚶

Cook Kanj was clattering breakfast dishes in the sink while, just outside the kitchen window, Gulu was loudly whistling as he readied the Mercedes for its afternoon outing. The twins were in various stages of undress, pretending to *deshum-deshum* each other like the heroes in their favorite movies. Jaginder Uncle stood restlessly in the hallway, resenting social obligations, especially those that had to do with his wife's family. Savita ran around the bungalow shouting orders, simultaneously cajoling and threatening the numerous members of the household while expertly trying on a sapphire and diamond-drop necklace.

"*Hai-hai,* Nimish. Do you call those shoes? At least have the decency to clean your spectacles."

"Dheer, are your ears working? I said cream kurta with the brown vest, not brown kurta with cream vest."

"Tufan, stop your whining-shmining! You're REQUIRED to go. You want me to tell your father?"

"Jaginder? JAGINDER? Where are you? Better get your youngest son in order, he's Eating-My-Head!"

Jaginder caught Tufan by the scruff of his neck as he streaked through the hallway in his underwear, delivering a blow that merely grazed the side of his head. Tufan deftly ducked—*deshum-deshum!*— and raced away. "You have exactly three bloody seconds to get dressed before I come after you!" Jaginder bellowed.

"Mummy, but I don't want to wear the cream kurta . . ." Dheer began to whine as he exited his room but stopped short when he saw his father standing in the hallway with upraised arm.

Nimish sidled past his father unconcernedly, eyes firmly in Sir Edwin Arnold's *India Revisited.* "'A drive next day about the cantonments and a walk through the native bazaars,'" he read out loud, "'serve to disclose how little India changes amidst all the alterations, embellishments and ameliorations which have come with the British reign. '"

"Don't think I won't give you a slap!" Jaginder roared at Nimish, vaguely aware that he might have been insulted.

"Jaginder? JAGINDER?" Savita called out.

He muttered under his breath as he trundled out of the hallway.

Heated words erupted from their bedroom followed by several high-pitched shrieks that sent the boys diving for cover. Pinky edged away from her hiding place and ran her grandmother's room. Maji was slowly donning a new white blouse that had been recently dropped off by the tailor. Her extra flesh hung around her. The blouse swelled, trying to hold back the two-fisted blows of her bosom. Fat puffed out at the end of the tightened sleeves as if it had just come up for air. Her enormous hips had just burst one entire seam of her petticoat. Parvati, who had been shaking out the nine yards of white, paisley-bordered sari, quickly unclipped a safety pin from her bra strap and, pinning it to the torn petticoat, restored order. Maji exhaled. "Why aren't you dressed yet, *beti*?"

"Oh, my head—" Pinky dropped onto the hard surface of Maji's bed. She felt exhausted.

"*Hai-hai*," Maji pressed her hand to Pinky's forehead. "Okay, lie down here. See how you feel when we're ready to go."

Pinky gratefully closed her eyes.

Jaginder was pacing in his bedroom feeling sorry for himself. He wanted nothing more than to escape to his office where he could give orders with impunity. The shipbreaking yards at Reti Bunder and the trading yards at Darukhana were like a worn-in pair of *chappals* that he could slip on without having to worry about washing his feet first.

Even the name Darukhana, referring to the gunpowder that the British used to store there after importing it via the main Alexandra Docks along the city's eastern coastline, felt potent, powerful. This despite the fact that the area, owned by the Bombay Port Trust, was packed with ramshackle corrugated-tin sheds housing merchants such as himself and hundreds of hovels where the impoverished workers, many migrants from Uttar Pradesh and Bihar, lived without proper sanitation. This, also despite the fact that the yard's impossibly narrow bylanes teemed with lorries and handcarts during the day and looters at night. Jaginder was not troubled by any of this, however, simply paying for access to one of the limited water taps and factoring the persistent thievery into his selling costs. In Darukhana, sitting at his desk with its constantly ringing black phone, Laloo scurrying nearby with notepad in hand, Jaginder felt important. In charge.

Social obligations coupled with Savita in her shimmering saris, however, made him feel acutely out of place. Jaginder coped with his discomfort by keeping his conversations to a minimum or to business-related topics, wary of Savita's unforgiving glare if he were to slip up. Now he stood dully as Savita ticked off a long list of instructions.

"And remember, don't say unnecessary things."

"I don't say unnecessary things."

"Remember at the Narayan's party," Savita huffed, "how you told my friend Mumta that Nimish wasn't interested in the shipeaking business."

"I was just telling the truth!" Jaginder yelled. A rush of blood shot through his body as if he were a wild animal suddenly ensnared.

"Truth?" Savita shouted at the image of her husband reflected in the mirror. "Since when has that been a priority? What will people say when they hear that Nimish is not interested in the family business?" She could hear Mumta gleefully repeating the tidbit to the rest of her friends, adding on irrelevant and inaccurate details for effect, so that Savita would slip behind in that week's tally for Most-Number-One-First-Class-Life.

"So what, it's just a matter of time before he'll have to accept his fate. Let him jiggle a few more brain cells in the meantime."

"You just don't understand," Savita said, piqued. There was no winning these fights, she had learned the hard way, when Jaginder pounced on her, reduced her to a quivering, tearful mess. Her best offense was to deny Jaginder the pleasure of the kill. Play dead. "That's all I have to say. End of discussion."

"I'm not done discussing," Jaginder roared. He was just getting started. He stretched his limbs, and cracked his neck in three places. Already, his stress began melting away, a solid showing of blood throbbed to his groin.

Savita remained silent, totally absorbed in the process of sticking a gem *bindi* to her forehead.

"And why do you care what your bloody friends think anyway?" Jaginder circled again. "Don't you have anything better to do?"

Savita deliberated on the *bindi*, then deciding against it, stuck it amongst the collection of red round ones that dotted the mirror like summer rash.

"Answer me!" Jaginder roared. But Savita remained silent. She had won this round, bloody hell.

Jaginder headed for the Mercedes that Gulu had tenderly polished and tucked back into the garage to keep it cool, and retrieved the aging Johnnie Walker from its trunk. On his way out, he noted the sparseness of Gulu's quarters. Aside from the jute cot on which he slept and a stray clothesline, the only other personal object was a poster advertising Cherry Blossom brand shoe polish with two kittens, one yellow, one slightly bluish, cozying up in a pair shiny black boots that hovered over the words *For Shoe Comfort.*

Jaginder studied the poster for a moment, briefly considering where Gulu disappeared to on his day off, once every two weeks, only to return late into the night usually singing a film tune as he swaggered into the gate. *Bloody low-caste inebriate,* Jaginder thought, curling his lip in disgust, *probably gets himself a whore on Falkland Road.*

"Sahib?"

"Oi, Gulu." Jaginder turned to face his driver who stood in the doorway. "Have a drink?"

"No Sahib, Maji's House Rules," Gulu said deferentially.

Jaginder shot him a look before taking a slug, deftly tucking the bottle back into the trunk.

Things were not always this way, he thought, now pacing the driveway, waiting for his family to get ready for the engagement luncheon at the Taj, the grandest hotel in all of Bombay. Built in 1903, the Taj offered Turkish baths, an electric laundry, and even a resident doctor. It was where he and Savita, many years back, had celebrated their engagement, overlooking the Gateway of India.

⚘ ⚘ ⚘

When he first had first seen her, she was so beautiful and vulnerable, like a tiny sunbird whose radiant plumage glittered as she flitted from person to person, the sunlight catching in her gems. He had declared that day, that come what may, he would protect her from harm.

Now look at us.

He was her fiercest predator.

When had things changed? Jaginder asked himself, knowing full well when they had. After their daughter's death, blame crept into their relationship like a scene from an American movie—cinematically, violently, and with special effects. They each were in thrall to it, hurting each other with abandon. And when the scene finally passed on to another, and the picture lost its initial thrill, they found that they were no longer even in the same theater. Jaginder sighed.

Savita walked onto the driveway, clicking an evening purse.

"You . . . look nice," he managed.

Savita's stride faltered for a fraction of a second, eyes dropping to the ground.

The rest of the family already stood assembled in the shade, each in their own world. Maji was worrying about Pinky's headaches which had started soon after her diarrhea troubles, and wondered if she should call Dr. M. M. Iyer to ply her with various tablets sealed in foil. Tufan stood by the car door, arms crossed belligerently, because Parvati had finally appeared in his room and, menacingly tying her *dupatta* back to free up her hands, forced clothes on him. Dheer was sulking in his cream-colored kurta with the brown vest. Nimish was still engrossed in *India Revisited.*

"Where's Pinky?" Tufan asked.

"Not well," Maji replied, "she'll be staying back."

A look of indignation arose in four pairs of eyes.

Unfair! Unfair! The twins shot each other looks of disbelief. Pinky always received special treatment from Maji.

What is she up to? Savita Auntie pondered icily as she dabbed at her lipstick.

Why didn't I think of that? Jaginder felt irritatingly one-upped by his niece. "Uh," he began suddenly, buoyed by the thought of escape, "I just remembered, I have to stop by the shipbreaking yards."

"Don't do this to me," Savita began, her voice betraying a tremor.

"It's close by to the Taj," Jaginder countered, "so I'll meet you there, what's the bloody problem?"

"Children, *chalo,* get in the car," Maji ordered.

"They'll be expecting you," Savita said, eyes hardening.

"So I'll be there for lunch," Jaginder roared as he paced in front of her. "You take care of the bloody chitchat!"

"Then go!" Savita yelled.

Quickly, Nimish came to Savita's side and, face darkened with anger at his father, gently settled her within the car.

Jaginder watched them pile into the Mercedes, Maji first in the backseat, followed by Savita. Dheer and Tufan squished in between. Gulu and Nimish in front.

He had won. Jaginder victoriously stretched his arms and let out a loud yawn to chase away the sudden sinking feeling. *Damn, damn, damn,* he thought. *I did it again.* Try as he might to be gentle with Savita, his anger at her bubbled up and turned him into an animal.

He quietly fetched the keys to the Ambassador and drove himself to the shipbreaking yards at Reti Bunder along the eastern coastline where sand once used to be dredged from the sea for building construction.

There was a buzz of activity when he pulled up in his shiny car. A chair, umbrella, and a cold drink were proffered. Jaginder gratefully took a seat and looked out upon his empire that he had inherited from his father and made even more successful with his sophisticated mind for business and money.

An end-of-life ship, weighing less than five-thousand deadweight tons and past its usefulness after twenty-five years on the open oceans, loomed before him, a hulking skeleton. A hive of sturdy fitters and cutters dismantled the ship as the heat soaked into the heavy, asbestos-laden steel plates, and stripped away each plate, nail, and screw with torch cutters and bare hands.

Semiskilled lifters, wearing only *dhotis* across their hips and scarves around their heads to protect themselves from the blaze of the sun, carted the metal scraps on their backs like ants on a carcass, their barefoot march synchronized to the rhythmic call of a singer-worker. Loaders conveyed the unwieldy cargo into mud-splattered lorries, garishly painted in reds and oranges, filling them with rusted metal to be resold, reused, recycled, and reincarnated into drainage pipes or perhaps, the frame of a new Ambassador car.

Most of the unskilled workers lived on the edges of the shipbreaking yards in shanties that stood unsteadily on stilts, amidst the graveyard of leaking barrels, open fires, and hazardous waste that possessed the coastline.

"Everything *theek-thak*, Boss-Sahib?"

Jaginder grunted his approval.

Yes, at least at work, everything was as it should be.

THE BRASS BUCKET

B ack at the bungalow, Pinky let sleep overtake her. The family had left and the housemaids went to the market soon afterwards. Cook Kanj resentfully arrived and placed a stainless steel plate of *moong dal* marinated in lime, soup with chunks of bright green *gia* squash, and steaming *roti* upon the dresser. Then, back in the kitchen, he quickly unrolled his mat for a much anticipated longer-than-usual nap. He calculated at least three hot, fly-filled hours before the family's noisy return.

Pinky woke sometime later and halfheartedly picked at the food. She cut across the parlor, stopping to dig her toes into the lush carpeting. It was strange, the hush of a room that usually burst with clamor and clatter. She stepped into the hallway where Cook Kanj's dry, raspy snores echoed off the walls.

The door to the bathroom was open and Pinky stood just outside it for a long time staring at the brass bucket, a *lota* hooked onto its rim. She noticed for the first time the water stains streaking from the pipe that encircled the room like a snake, and the patches of white lime that dusted the wall. The green-tiled room felt aged. A cracked wooden paddle rested on the pipe, warped and abandoned. A thin river of rheumy liquid lay in the joint where the wall met the floor, little dots of mold tenaciously adhering to its surface. Even with Kuntal's daily scrubbings, the bathroom never felt clean, never sparkled like the rest of the bungalow, as if no amount of detergents could wash away its internal decay or the burden of what it had witnessed long years ago.

Pinky pulled a small, hand-carved chair from the parlor and propped the door open.

"I'm sorry you died," she said, tentatively stepping inside the bathroom. She thought of the photo. Seeing the baby had cast some verifiable flesh onto the ghost's intangible presence, somehow making her more real, more human.

"I know what you look like," she said, edging nearer to the bucket. "Gulu says that ghosts come back to make things right."

She turned around; the door was still reassuringly open.

"Or to warn others," Pinky continued. "Is it Savita Auntie? Is she making you do this?"

Pinky peered into the bucket without touching it.

Nothing. It was completely empty.

"Why only me?" Pinky whispered.

Without warning, her head was thrust into the bucket.

It began to fill with water.

Pinky thrashed, unable to lift her head. Her breath turned frosty. The water drew closer and closer to her nostrils. She kicked her legs, turning her head from side to side, gasping. With horror, she realized that there was no one in the household to help, no one but the sleeping cook.

"Cook Kanj!" she screamed.

The susurration of the pipes as they gurgled and hissed was the only response.

Instinctively, she began to recite the Mrityunjaya Mantra, the life-giving prayer that Maji had taught her, saying, "It is powerful enough to conquer Death."

"*Om Tryambakam Yajaamahe . . .*" Pinky coughed as the water began filling her nose.

The bucket began to wobble back and forth. Pinky pushed at it with her arms.

"Sugandhim Pushti Vardhanam."

Suddenly it turned over and crashed to the floor, water flowing out of it like a river.

Pinky raced to the open door and across the parlor, throwing herself under the covers of Maji's bed. She remained there, shivering, until she heard the blessed sound of the Mercedes's engine turning into the gate.

※ ☆ ※

Lethargy crept into the limbs of the bungalow's returning inhabitants as they climbed the verandah steps. The engagement luncheon had been a success. Everyone had approved of the nuptial liaison between Savita's sister, Sunny, and her fiancé. Even Jaginder had taken a liking to his soon-to-be brother-in-law and was in an unusually good mood. Now, exhausted from an afternoon of socializing and the intense summer heat, the Mittal family gratefully gravitated towards the dining table where Cook Kanj, refreshed from his long nap, had laid out a light dinner of rice and dal.

He returned with a plateful of hot *papads*, spicy crackers made from *urad* and *moong* lentils, black pepper, and asafetida, that were toasted over an open flame before being served. The Lijjat Company *papads*, made by a handful of women in the slums of Bombay, were one of the few foods that Cook Kanj bought rather than made himself, grudgingly admitting that they tasted better than his own.

"*Baap re! Bahut garmi hai!* God, it's suffocating!" Savita exclaimed after eating, turning the ceiling fans on high.

Pinky padded in and wordlessly took a seat.

Tufan flapped his arms in a futile effort to ventilate his armpits where talc had long ago turned into sludge.

"The cuckoos haven't completed their flight from Africa," Nimish reported, scanning the newspaper. "When they finally arrive, the monsoons won't be far behind."

"Turn on the radio," Jaginder ordered. "Let's see what the bloody weatherman has to say."

"Pinky, *beti*, did you sleep?" Maji asked, listening as Lata Mangeshkar's love songs were replaced by an equally evocative weather report.

Pinky nodded.

Tufan eyed Pinky but refrained from rude commentary. He had spent the better part of the afternoon on his best behavior in an itchy and overstarched kurta. The effort had taken its toll. He wanted nothing more than to undress and fall into his bed.

"Good," said Maji, noticing with concern the pallor of Pinky's face, "then help Cook Kanj bring the chai."

Pinky walked to the kitchen where a pot of milk had begun to bubble on a black iron oven burner, releasing the scent of fresh ginger. She fetched the box of Brooke Bond Red Label Tea, glancing at the attractive family of four on its cover—mother, father, brother, sister— that were forever frozen in a happy moment with their milky glasses of steaming tea. She touched the picture of the mother and recalled the ancient tale of Savitri whose love for her husband Satvayan was so great that she won him back from death's immutable grasp. *Love isn't enough,* she decided.

Cook Kanj shook the black leaves into the frothing milk, adding crushed cardamom, cloves, a touch of cinnamon, and a good, long measure of sugar before stirring. He then poured the liquid back and forth, a full meter of distance in between the two pans, until the caramel-colored tea frothed on top before dispensing it into small glass tumblers that were arranged on a tray.

Seven hands reached out for the tumblers. As the hot liquid slid down their throats, the family members relaxed into their seats, letting out audible sighs. Nimish took his glass to his room, muttering something over his shoulder about having to get back to work.

"*Chalo,* that's over," Jaginder said, unbuttoning his top and vigorously scratching the thick pelt of hair that popped out from underneath.

"You liked Sunny's fiancé then?" Savita asked carefully.

"Yes," Jaginder said, the chai buoying his spirits, "it will be helpful to have a lawyer in the family. Bloody smart chap, too."

"I thought he was bor-ing," Tufan added, feeling resentful of the wasted afternoon.

Savita shot him a withering glare. "Go before I give you one slap."

Tufan tossed a handful of roasted fennel seeds into his mouth before gratefully taking off.

"Most importantly, the boy's from a good family," Maji said before draining her cup and, with Kuntal's help, slowly making her way to her bedroom. "Come soon, Pinky, I'll massage your scalp before bed."

"Coming Maji."

Jaginder let out a roaring burp followed by an equally impressive fart. "*Chalo*, I think we all should get an early night."

He and Savita rose from the table. Cook Kanj came out from the kitchen and picked up the dishes.

"What did you do while we were away?" Dheer asked. His cream-colored kurta was spotted with greenish stains. Unlike the rest of the Mittal men, he enjoyed nothing more than attending social engagements. There was bound to be an exciting assortment of foods, mainly fried—*pakoras*, samosas, *aloo tikkis*—that he could smother in mint chutney and eat to his stomach's content. He was bursting to tell Pinky about the luncheon's vast menu which he, as usual, had expertly sampled and memorized.

"I slept, what else?" Pinky said with an exaggerated shrug of her shoulders. Then, checking behind her to make sure no one was in earshot, she dropped her façade. Tears came to her eyes. "I need your help, *Kemosabe*."

"My help?" Dheer said, tossing a handful of candy into his mouth.

"Come," she said, pulling on Dheer's arm, "come with me."

"In here?" Dheer scanned the bathroom in disbelief, eyeballs darting back and forth, aware that they could get into serious trouble for being behind a closed door together. Suddenly, a disturbing thought came to his mind, causing him to involuntarily suck in his gut. *Oh my God, what's she going to show me?* "Ah, you, ah . . . well," he stuttered, carefully avoiding looking directly at her blouse but nonetheless noticing its delicate curves. "I don't think this is a good idea."

"I can't take this anymore!" Pinky began to sob softly.

Dheer turned a dull shade of red, backed himself against the door, and began sweating profusely. "Okay," he soothed, "there's no need to yell."

"I don't want to be the only one," Pinky said. "I want you to see it, too."

Certain that *it* was not a new type of chocolate bar, Dheer shook his head wildly and frantically unlatched the door.

"Please," Pinky motioned toward the bucket. "Just once, look inside once, and then you'll know."

At the words *look inside*, Dheer burst out into a fit of coughing. Flecks of brightly colored candy shell flew from of his mouth, decorating Pinky's blouse.

Pinky thumped him on his back.

Dheer could smell the coconut oil in her hair, the powder on her neck, the spicy clove scent of her skin. He felt faint.

And then, most unexpectedly, he was overcome by another odor. His eyes flew open. "Fenugreek!"

"The spice?" Pinky sniffed at the air but could not smell it.

"I hate the smell of it," Dheer confessed, grateful for the diversion.

"Why?"

He shrugged his shoulders, fighting the sudden tightness in his throat. A vague memory overcame him of when he had been a baby, happily playing next to his mother on her Jaipuri bedspread. He remembered how she held a glass tumbler in her hand filled with yellowish liquid, a tea of boiled fenugreek seeds, and how he had pulled on it and burnt his hand. For weeks afterwards, his skin reeked of acrid bitterness. "Boiled milk," he said, "I smell boiled milk now. And sugar."

"Maybe it's the chai from the kitchen."

"Now almonds."

"You're imagining things."

"Me?" Dheer looked at Pinky, unlatched the door, and stepped out, tears welling in his eyes. "Please don't do this. It's not . . . right."

"What are you talking about?" Pinky called after him but he had already fled to his room.

I'm utterly alone, Pinky thought, standing miserably in the hallway, *utterly alone.*

ELEMENTS OF DEATH

Pinky dreamt she was drowning. She felt herself being pushed down into water, down, down, down until her lungs began to burst. The only way out was to push her head further in, to stop thrashing, to trust that she would not die. But each time she grew afraid, each time she thrashed. Each time she startled awake just as she was about to pass out.

⚘ ⚜ ⚘

Cautiously, Pinky crept out of the bungalow, past the garage where Gulu slept, and into the dark garden. Almost immediately she was hit by a wall of heavy, premonsoon air that knocked her back. Her hair stuck to her face and neck where sweat congealed like glue. Threatening clouds now completely obscured the moon. An occasional bolt provided flashes of light, saturating the sky with electricity. Thunder rumbled menacingly.

The looming storm could be unleashed any moment, Pinky knew. She wiped the dampness from her face. Sweat poured from every crevice in her body and soaked her pajamas. Large bloodthirsty mosquitoes hovered in her face, undeterred by her swatting. Dense foliage swept the garden into darkness. Spiny shrubbery stuck into her back, curling ivy swung in her face, and shadows loomed in front of her, yet she continued to creep forward, the thickness of the garden closing in around her. Further and further she groped her way to the passageway.

She waited there, nestled in that suffocating greenery. Lightning tore through the sky and in that instant, she spotted Lovely sitting under the tamarind tree.

Pinky knew why she went there at night, to be away from her brother Harshal who, on the pretense of protecting her from corrupting influences, forbade her from going to friends' homes, watching movies, or even listening to the radio. On weekdays, he called from work to check that she had returned home immediately from SNDT Women's University. Vimla had been too fearful to intercede on Lovely's behalf. And Harshal's wife, Himani, was too busy protecting her own interests. So Lovely bided her time, suffering patiently, subjected to her brother's ruthless authority.

It was Harshal, not Lovely's unsuspecting mother, who would decide upon her appropriate groom, a weak-willed man that he could control with his money. And when that time came, Lovely would have to be prepared to do something drastic. And so she escaped to the tamarind tree at night to strengthen her resolve, to dare dream of another life.

"Lovely *didi*!" Pinky called, racing toward her.

A clap of thunder drowned out her voice. It was followed by a severe silence. A moment later, crickets began chirping, insects buzzed, leaves rustled.

"*Didi?*"

"Who's there?" came Lovely's terrified voice.

"It's me, Pinky."

"Pinky? What are you doing here?"

"I had to talk to you away from the bungalow," Pinky said, continuing to walk forward into blackness. Her fingers tingled. She held onto Lovely's voice as if it alone could protect her. An army of fine, little hairs along her arm rose up in unison.

Another bolt of lightning flashed and they ran to each other.

"Are you okay?" Lovely asked, clasping Pinky to her. "Did something happen?"

Pinky began to cry, inhaling the sweet fragrance of Lovely's skin, her clothes, her hair. "I know about the baby, *didi*. I know that she died. She died in the brass bucket in our bathroom!"

Lovely stiffened; a deep pain rose up in her chest. "Oh Pinky—"

"What happened that day, *didi*? How did it happen?"

Lovely sat upon the ground and pulled Pinky to her, holding both her hands. "The ayah was called to do something, and when she returned, she found the baby had drowned. It happened so fast."

"And then what?"

"The ayah was sent away. Panditji was called in right away to do a purification *puja*. Mummy took us over for that, myself and Harshal. She brought over some food while Cook Kanj transferred all the cooking stuff to our kitchen."

Though she had only been four, she remembered how Savita had thrown herself down beside the baby, wailing inconsolably. Lovely and Harshal had sat on a sofa in the parlor, holding the frightened twins, and watched silently as Parvati flung the ayah's bedding, her clothes, and her few personal belongings out of the bungalow with a sick sort of pleasure. Then she had lit a fire in the driveway and burnt everything that was even slightly flammable. Jaginder had crumpled beside Savita, begging her to stop crying.

"Maji took charge of everything. Her face was so pale and her hand shook as she dialed the phone. But she made all the arrangements."

Pinky tried to picture the devastating scene unfolding. Thunder boomed. And boomed again, closer this time. She began to shake, fighting the urge to sink to the ground. A blast of wind rustled the leaves, and the trees shivered in unison.

"I don't remember how long I sat there . . ."

Lovely fell silent.

I'll tell, she had whispered to her brother as they held the squirming twins. *I'll tell them what you did this morning.*

Harshal laughed. *You think Papa will believe you over me? He'll whip you for lying! And Mummy will cry and then he'll hit her, too. And it will be all your fault.*

Lovely had known he was right.

" . . . but a few hours later, Maji, Auntie and Uncle, and Panditji took the baby in the car and drove away. That's all. Mummy says that Maji was never the same after that. She had wanted a granddaughter so badly. She stopped socializing and all that, except for Mummy."

"It's all so terrible."

"I don't know," Lovely said, speaking very slowly. "She drowned, yes. But at least she's free."

Nimish crouched in the passageway, watching as a flash of light illuminated Lovely and Pinky together under the tamarind tree, holding each other close. He could not help but feel a sting of jealousy. If he were a girl, how easy it would be to talk with Lovely, to hold her hand, to lie next to her and look to the heavens.

When they were much younger—still children—they used to play together in the garden, and he would read her entire passages from books he found in the bungalow's library.

In unhealthy places a man should chew rhubarb, he once read in his most authoritative voice from *Nabobs*, a study on the habits of British colonials in India, *and stop his nose with linen dipped in vinegar.*

And vomit at the first sign of a chill, Lovely added, grabbing the book from him. Then they fell to the ground, throwing their arms around each other and laughing at their silliness.

It was Vimla who had come upon them like that and had put an end to their playing together.

As Nimish grew into adulthood, he expressed his adoration to Lovely from those same books, now scanning through them for a laden line or phrase that he could read out loud whenever Lovely came visiting. It was his way of secretly professing his love.

Pinky could not contain her shock. "How can you say that, *didi*?"

Lovely gave a strangled sort of laugh and squeezed Pinky's arm.

"There's nothing that can be done now Pinky. It happened so long ago."

"But," Pinky braced herself. She could not risk telling Lovely what was happening in the bathroom; she could not risk her disbelief, too. "But how does one die? What happens afterwards?"

"When Papa died, he was alive one moment and dead the next," Lovely said. "My friend Bodhi, who is a Buddhist, came over to comfort me. She sat with me and told me that a body actually dies in eight stages: earth to water, water to fire, fire to wind, wind to space, then flashes of light in the last four stages."

"Flashes of light?"

Lovely nodded. "In stage five, the thoughts of the mind dissolve into a flash of silver light that descends from the mind to the heart. Then a glowing red dewdrop ascends from the base of the spine to the heart. In the seventh stage, that of near-attainment, they merge together in a burst of blackness. And then comes the white light that ushers in the true dawn of death."

Pinky felt a wave of nausea rise up in her chest. She abruptly stood up. The air was so charged with the voltage of the gathering storms that she had trouble breathing.

"Are you okay?"

"I have to go," Pinky said flatly.

She had seen that intense light, those flashes of color. She had seen them exactly as Lovely had described.

Except in reverse.

She ran blindly.

She did not remember precisely where the passageway was in the connecting wall but she nonetheless ran with her arms in front of her, pounding the grass with her bare feet. She ran straight into the opening and, just as lightning illuminated the sky, crashed right into Nimish, noticing only in that split second, his horrified face. They went tumbling backwards, she sprawled on top of him. A thunderous din deafened their cries. Their arms caught in the vines; sharpened leaves cut their skin, their flesh was pierced by thorns. He pushed at her, trying to pry her away, but the passageway was so small and tight that there was little room to maneuver. She felt his sweaty flesh through the dampness of her thin pajamas, the weight of his legs entwined with hers. The sweet fragrance of the purple phlox was intoxicating.

"Pinky!" he whispered urgently. "Stop thrashing!"

He pulled away from her, groping for his spectacles that had been knocked away.

Pinky sat up, her heart pounding wildly. "There's a ghost!" she blurted out.

"What! What?" Nimish grabbed her arms firmly, his breathing hard and fast. "What are you talkintg about? Have you lost your mind?"

Pinky began to weep.

"Pinky—please," Nimish said, his voice softening even as he backed away.

They sat there in silence, listening to the crickets, the rumbling of the sky.

"Nimish *bhaiya*," Pinky whispered after a few minutes, "how do you talk to someone if you are afraid?"

He sighed, his aching heart out there in the darkness by the tamarind tree where Lovely sat alone.

"A story, you begin with a story."

THE GHOST

Pinky wandered into the kitchen in search of Cook Kanj as dawn cast its gray light. The bungalow's original kitchen and scullery had been dismantled in favor of a larger, brighter room with modern appliances, including a gas cooking table and an Electrolux refrigerator. Stainless-steel pots and pans lined the shelves and a brass basket hung from the ceiling to keep ants away from the fresh fruit. The three windows, two facing the driveway and the third the back garden, were covered with thin screens that diffused the sun's blazing afternoon rays.

A heap of green okra lay in a stainless-steel *thali*, their tips already having been snapped off during their inspection at Crawford Market. A plate of cucumbers, the top slice having been rubbed against the rest to defroth them of their bitterness, lay sliced and waiting to be peppered with rock salt. Onions, garlic, and ginger stood in separate piquant piles, freshly chopped and grated. A pan of oil simmered on the stove, black mustard seeds popping over the edge in sharp staccatos. Turmeric and chili powder stained the countertop in velvety blankets of yellow, orange, and red. Cook Kanj himself was squatting on the floor with a *thali* of pink lentils which he sifted through with brisk fingerwork, pulling out tiny rocks and sticks and other contaminants that he carefully inspected at close view before discarding into a pile on the kitchen floor.

Pinky watched intently, dreading the day she would be expected to know the rudiments of cooking.

Cooking skill is most essential in marriage, Maji had always stressed to her though she herself hadn't set foot inside the kitchen for two decades. As if to prove her point, she hauled Pinky there for a demonstration in deep frying which had quickly turned into a disaster.

Never mind, Maji had said afterwards, changing out of her oil-spattered sari. *Go watch Cook Kanj, I'll teach you how to make samosas later.*

Learning from Cook Kanj was a challenge, not only because he did not follow rules or recipes but also because he refused to teach. Instead, with hands flying and an occasional grunt, he transformed the heap of vegetables and spices on the counter into a mouth-watering feast, all without the least bit of instruction for Pinky's benefit. Nonetheless, he appreciated having her as his audience, imagining himself in a big kitchen, wielding his knife with quick strokes and throwing in spices with drama and flair while underlings watched in awe.

In his younger days, he had dreamt of one day working at the one of the ritzier restaurants like Bombelli's on the road from Churchgate Station to Marine Drive or Napoli's with its state-of-the-art jukebox. But life in Maji's bungalow had been good to him, enough so that he always repressed his unhatched plans for the future. Then, after Parvati arrived back in 1943, Cook Kanj gave up any thoughts of leaving and allowed himself to bake in the tandoor of married life. Even so, and though the Mittal family duly stuffed their stomachs at mealtimes, adding appreciative noises afterward, Cook Kanj felt that his talents went unnoticed. His resentment had turned him bitter, like the hard bumpy gourd that he sometimes stuffed with chilies and zealously shrank in the frying pan.

"Cook Kanj?"

Kanj grunted as he stood and poured the pink lentils into a bowl which he vigorously swirled under cold water.

"When do you mix milk, almonds, sugar cane, and fenugreek together?" Pinky asked, listing the ingredients Dheer had smelled in the bathroom.

Cook Kanj disliked questions about his cooking and showed his displeasure by ruthlessly throwing onions into the hot bubbling oil where they sputtered in protest. He then turned the gas on high before adding garlic and ginger, and stirred the contents with zeal.

"Please," Pinky pleaded.

Cook Kanj was not interested in anything that could not be fried, pickled, or masala-ed. Nevertheless, he sighed and, lowering the gas, allowed his mind to entertain Pinky's question. He had not mixed those ingredients together for over thirteen years. And then only for a few, short days. He sighed again. "Cereal."

"Cereal?"

"Milk-production cereal. I made it for your Savita Auntie after the birth of her babies."

After the drowning, he had shut down his kitchen as tradition dictated, having only made the cereal and the puja *halwa*. He had stashed away pots and pans and emptied out the fridge and pantry. He had shuttled urns of milk, baskets of majestic purple *brinjal*, trays of raw almonds nestled in their succulent green flesh, and even his entire set of Devidayal stainless steel cooking utensils to the neighbors, the Lawates. For the requisite three days, nothing could be cooked in this place of mourning. Their neighbor immediately hurried over with Ovaltine-thickened milk and fresh puris infused with sugar and crushed almonds. Parvati had gladly taken on the task of ridding the household of the ayah's belongings. Kuntal lit clay *diyas* in each room to lighten the baby's soul as it journeyed back to God, but more so to keep evil spirits from possessing her lifeless body. And Dr. M. M. Iyer had arrived that evening to administer a Coromine tranquilizer to Savita.

Cook Kanj returned his attention to the *thali* of okra, slicing the green fingerlike vegetables into small circles, their juicy interiors covering his knife in brownish slime. Pinky had more questions but judging from Cook Kanj's posture, his back squarely to her, she knew that he considered their conversation over.

Pinky paced the gloomy library, digging her toes into the balding carpet, fingering the intricately carved reliefs upon the teak furniture.

She touched the wide, iron base of the multiple-piped hookah which had corroded to a sickly greenish color, and sat upon a sofa that now sank dangerously in the middle, its heavy upholstery faded and torn. A white marble bust of Queen Victoria stood forlornly in one corner of the room, the tarnished brass plate proclaiming, Empress of India. Cobwebs looped and twisted within the chandelier. Stale curtains reeked of smoke and a bygone era.

Pinky marveled at the contrast between this forgotten room and the rest of the majestic bungalow which was meticulously kept up, down to the smallest silver inkwell displayed in the parlor. Her gaze fell upon a fourteenth-edition set of *Encyclopedia Britannica* that Maji had procured for Nimish from a book sale held at the US Information Center's library some years ago. Nimish had dived into it with zeal, scanning the texts for small, important details which he memorized with great care. Each new bit of information was like a rung on a ladder and, by god, he planned to keep on climbing, all the way to England if he could.

There were so many books in here, filling the shelves from floor to ceiling and looming over her as if she were insignificant, nothing. It was all here, stacks of the *Journal of Asiatic Society of Bengal* and the blue-bound *Rulers of India* series with volumes such as *Earl of Mayo, 1891* and *Lord Clive, 1900*. How did these men, Pinky wondered, compare to the great King Ashoka whose Wheel of Dharma graced the Indian flag, or Emperor Akbar who encouraged arts, literature, and religious tolerance?

Closing her eyes, she reached out and plucked a random book. All she needed was a story, one story that would make the ghost understand that she had not taken its place on purpose, that she was willing to share, that she should not be the one blamed.

She opened her eyes and read the title, *My Indian Mutiny Diary, 1860*, by war correspondent William Howard Russell. Printed inside was a letter addressed to him: *India is at present a blank, a blank I fear will remain unless you will fill it.*

A blank.

She understood at once that her story was not here, with these musty books but already inside her.

It was one of Maji's parables that had shaped her with its tale of strength, purpose, and enduring love.

Pinky stood outside the bathroom, her stomach clenching.

She knew she had to go in because no one believed her.

She heard Nimish reading out loud at the breakfast table from *A Passage to India*, his voice carrying down the hall. "Oh superstition is terrible, terrible! Oh, it is the greatest defect in our Indian character!"

She sighed and stepped inside.

"There was a princess," she said, hesitating before latching the door.

There's still time, to run away, to be safe.

She took a breath to calm her beating heart. The ancient Sanskrit play came to her lips.

"Her name was Ratnavali."

She stepped toward the bucket.

"Everyone thought she drowned."

Pinky slowly crouched upon the stool and cautiously peered into the bucket. There was a thin layer of clear water inside. She went on to describe how the princess had taken a ship to marry her future husband, a king of a distant land but en route, a violent storm sank the ship. Ratnavali was rescued and taken to the king's palace in rags where she was made a servant. Though no one recognized her, she knew the king was her betrothed, and quickly fell in love. The king happened upon her one day in the royal garden and was taken by her beauty. He arranged for them to meet clandestinely but his first wife, the queen, discovered them.

"Ashamed, the princess decided to end her life," Pinky continued. "She made a noose from a madhavi creeper and slipped it over her neck."

There was a sudden breeze in the room, a long rattling inhalation.

Pinky froze, the story vanishing from her head. She grasped for words, characters, any small detail that would bring it back.

The temperature dropped.

Run! Run! her head screamed.

But she held tight to the wooden stool, one hand clutching either side.

She could not run away again.

If there's something that frightens you, you must instead confront it, Maji had said. *You have that very strength inside you.*

Pinky took another deep breath, her exhalation visible in the frosted air, and held onto that image of the desolate princess—her head downcast, sari *palloo* covering her hair, the noose pulling upon soft flesh —thinking that this was her very last breath in this world.

"The king saved her," she said, remembering how he had gently put his arm around her and begged her never to leave him. The jealous queen, however, imprisoned Ratnavali in a cell that suddenly burst into flames. Thrice now, Ratavali thought her life had ended, first by water, second by earth, third by fire. Then as if by magic, the inferno spluttered out and she was recognized as the princess, the drowned princess.

The water began to flicker as if it were a dying flame.

A line of thick silvery smoke curled upwards.

Pinky gritted her teeth to stop them from chattering. "The king held Ratnavali to him at last. His queen. His queen!" she whispered. "Her rightful place at last."

She fell silent.

Shaking, she reached for the *lota*, dipped it into the water, and splashed her face.

She wiped away the moisture and blinked.

Two stormy eyes stared directly at her.

Pinky fell back off the stool, a thousand thoughts reeling through her head. *The flashes of light. Space to wind, wind to fire, fire to water. . . .* The ghost was coming back to life.

As if it were being sketched by an invisible hand, it began to take on the appearance of a girl with a slender nose, long eyelashes, and a sweet, silken mouth. It was tiny and naked except for a silvery mane that swirled around its lucent limbs like the celestial wings of a seraph.

Pinky put her hand out and, fingers trembling, tried to touch the ghost, the black pipes on the far wall faintly visible through its torso. It simply slipped right through her hands and bobbed in the bucket with tiny splashes, spraying water into the air.

It gestured to her now, *Come, come.*

Pinky shook her head, unable to speak. The ghost was beautiful, silvery, angelic.

Come.

The dim, hanging *handi* lamp swung wildly as the ghost placed its translucent miniature hands against Pinky's face, its eyes misting like rain clouds. Pinky's eyelids drooped, as she felt a pulsing coolness. She allowed herself to be pulled closer to the ghost, feeling at once a timeless bond with her. *She's my sister-cousin, my sister.* A strange love filled her chest, chasing away fear.

Without realizing it, her head now hung over the bucket, her body entirely enveloped in a vaporous fog as she was pulled more and more into the ghost's watery world. Slowly, almost imperceptibly, they crossed the boundary of the living and the dead, slipping into each other's realm of existence.

You were the one to call me back.

On the backs of her eyelids, Pinky saw flashes of images from the baby's brief days of life thirteen years ago. Faster and faster they flickered like a reel spinning off of its axis.

Mucus worked its way down baby Tufan's upper lip in two sluggish rivers.

Bangles shimmered as Savita unhooked her blouse, coaxing her barren breasts.

Bougainvillea blazed in the window, caught in a burning shaft of sunlight.

Pinky held her breath, afraid of missing anything. And then, as if the reel was coming to an end, the images slowed down and became distorted, like a waterlogged spool of recording tape. The black-and-white pictures struggled across Pinky's eyelids where they wobbled and bled together, no longer random but the mere vestiges of a story.

Piping encircled a flatly tiled room.

Colorless water flowed from a faucet into a dull metallic bucket.

A young face appeared, a tiny mole upon her cheek, the shiny embroidery on her bright sari palloo *sparkling like a firecracker.*

Her mouth moved in song.

Water fell from the lota, *a glistening stream.*

The face suddenly turned back towards the bathroom door as if a voice had called to her, momentarily disappearing from view.

And then—

Pinky jerked open her eyes, realizing that her entire head was submerged in the bucket. She thrashed, swallowing water in great gulps, her lungs bursting, a rattling deafening all around her. And then, just as she was about to black out, the pressure lifted and Pinky fell back, vomiting first, then gasping for air.

Once safely inside her bedroom, she curled up into a ball and wept, the ghost's final image searing her vision.

A disembodied hand appeared out of nowhere, pushing her down, down, down into the thick, glassy water.

A BLINDING VISION

M aji could no longer dismiss Pinky's recent behavior.
Just as Cook Kanj meticulously culled fresh purple *brinjal* from jute sacks at Crawford Market before currying them with onions, tomatoes, and spices, Maji called the household to her in order to collect, cut, and curry the disturbing information about her granddaughter's affliction.

"She is up all night snooping instead of sleeping," Savita jumped in.

"She'll be beginning her cycles soon," Parvati reported.

"She has no interest in cooking," Cook Kanj said testily.

"She's not learning proper things in convent school," Gulu commented.

"She's overwhelmed with schoolwork for next year," Nimish suggested.

"She needs specs," Kuntal offered.

"She's so sickly," Savita remarked and then discreetly motioned for Cook Kanj to add a sprinkling of crushed pistachios to her own drink.

Dheer simply shrugged, an embarrassed flush in his cheeks.

Tufan stood quietly, enjoying this game of finding fault with his cousin.

With all eyes upon her, Maji reclined upon her cushioned seat and fanned herself with a considerably outdated copy of *Filmindia*.

Perhaps I've not done enough, she thought. *Perhaps I've not been able to be both a mother and father to Pinky.*

Maji leaned back upon the dais and inspected a handful of *supari* from the silver tin on the table next to her. Yellowed coconut flakes swam in a sea of roasted fennel seeds, pink and white candies, and tiny little red balls of sugar. She carefully picked out the dark triangular pieces of betel nut and, between her molars, methodically chewed on their bitterness as she reflected upon her decision to take Pinky away from her father that fateful day. It had been the right thing to do, hadn't it?

She had stepped past Pinky's other grandmother without even a *namaste* and into the small, decaying flat in that desolate settlement of Hindu refugees. The walls were bare except for curling black wires that emerged from circular electrical outlets. An imprisoned wall fan peeked out from behind metal slats. An oval container of Yardley's talcum was displayed next to a tin wind-up car on a shelf near the *puja* table.

Yardley. Was it the very same talcum that Maji had slipped into Yamuna's overnight bag the day she departed Bombay as a new bride? She stared at that inanimate object that her daughter had once touched with her fingers, had once taken pleasure in sprinkling upon her skin. It was so unjust, Maji thought, that it remained here on the shelf when her daughter, her beloved daughter, was gone.

Pinky's father walked into the room, his eyes red and ringed with dark circles, and fell to Maji's feet weeping for forgiveness.

Is this the very same boy I fed sweets to with my own hand on their wedding day? Maji had asked herself, scarcely recognizing him.

And then Pinky whimpered in the next room.

That little cry stopped her heart. For a fleeting moment, she felt her daughter's presence. She knew then that Pinky belonged to her, that she would fight for her, and that she would win.

Taking her had not been an entirely unselfish act. It had been the only way for Maji to lift herself from the darkness: two deaths in two months, a daughter and a granddaughter. Pinky herself uncannily resembled Yamuna and this, this in itself gave Maji great comfort. She had been a gift from God, a way to right the wrongs of the past.

Maji sighed and tossed the magazine onto the floor, causing the household to snap to attention. The sluggish gathering of monsoon clouds on the shorelines had made her joints swell and ache more than usual. The ghost, Dr. Iyer had reasoned, could only be Pinky's imaginary playmate in a houseful of boys. *Children are inclined to such fanciful play*, he had added.

Yet Pinky needed to be away from the bungalow, this Maji knew.

"I'm taking Pinky to Mahabaleshwar," she said out loud.

Mahabaleshwar had been the summer capital of the British Raj in Bombay since 1828 when it was established by Governor John Malcolm as a European resort and sanatorium. As with most hill stations, Mahabaleshwar's air was noted for its restorative properties, natural beauty, and refreshing coolness. In the late summer just before the monsoons, the plateau was surrounded by a dense oxygen-rich fog. Even Mahabaleshwar's water was reputed to increase hemoglobin levels in the blood.

"Mahabaleshwar!" Savita said, eyes shining. "I went boating there once on Venna Lake!"

"They'll be all boarded up now for the monsoons," Nimish said. "You won't find a place to stay."

"I'll take care of that," Maji said. "If we go tonight, we'll reach there before the rains."

"I want to see Pratapgad Fort! That's where Shivaji slashed open Afzal Khan's guts with his steel talons and killed him!" Tufan shouted, reenacting this event by retracting his hand into a claw and sinking it into Dheer's fleshy belly.

"Oh the strawberries!" Savita cried out, slapping Tufan across the head. "What I wouldn't give for a Mahabaleshwari strawberry!"

"And their sesame *chikki* too," Dheer added.

"I'm taking Pinky," Maji said, her tone firm. "Just Pinky this time."

"It's not fair, you always do things for her!" Tufan whined.

"Just Pinky," Savita huffed before storming away, feeling once again that biting hardness in her heart. "Always just Pinky."

Maji made slow progress to the platform at Victoria Terminus, painfully leaning upon her cane and half-dragging her feet forward. The station, built during the imperial reign of England's Queen Victoria, rose from the ground like a grand cathedral. Its majestic carved stone and stained-glass exterior gave way, however, not to silent altars and slowly crucified gods but to the deafening roar of humanity in a hurry.

The expansive station interior swelled with the din of hundreds of thousands of people coming and going, punctuated by the clacking of trains. Pinky walked alongside her grandmother, holding her hand tightly as they made their way through the maze of stairways and platforms, weaving past the laborers carrying luggage atop their red-turbaned heads and past the blank-eyed beggars lifting and lowering their hands like mechanical dolls.

Just inside, a hand-painted board listed the train departures and arrivals: Punjab Mail to Agra in the north, Gitanjali Express to Calcutta in the east, and Kanniya Kumari Express to Cochin in the south. A train pulled in at the adjacent platform. Even before it had stopped, a ratty contingent of street boys slipped aboard and scurried to the pantry car in hopes of finding heated sandwiches, cellophaned sweets, or bottles of soda. A rush of bodies jostled at the compartment entrances with luggage, small children, and bulging parcels held balanced upon their heads.

At their platform, the smells of stale urine and the pungent grime of unwashed bodies infiltrated the sweet cardamom scent of tea steaming from round, clay *kullarhs* that were sold through iron-barred openings in the fuggy second-class compartments. While Maji and Pinky waited, Nimish and Gulu pressed themselves into the crowd, elbowing their way into a reserved compartment. They reappeared flush-faced a few moments later, successful in their bid to stow the luggage away under the seats and ensure that everything was in order. Pinky held two stainless-steel tiffins, each of the three stackable, enclosed sections had just been filled by Cook Kanj with something warm and aromatic. Potato-filled *parathas* lined the top, *karela sabzi* shrunken and tied like tiny green packages occupied the middle, and boiled potatoes accompanied by lemon and salt pickles in the bottom of the tiffin.

Half-leaning with one hand pressed on Pinky's head, Maji hobbled to their compartment and settled into her seat with a sigh. Nimish reached in from the window and grasped Pinky's hand.

"Here," he said, handing her *Sketches from My Past*. "I think, maybe, you might find it helpful." His eyes were soft, gentle.

Pinky clutched the book tightly to her chest, reigning in her emotions. Then she stuck her head out of the window, waving good-bye.

Closing her eyes for a moment, Pinky wiped away a dampness. When she opened them again, from the edge of her vision she caught sight of a woman in red climbing up from the tracks and onto the platform. Despite the fact that the wheels had already begun to creak forward, Pinky witnessed the action with a clarity so sharp it was as if everything was unfolding under the lens of a magnifying glass.

The mysterious woman walked through the crowd, past the *chai-wallah* squatting down to pour a cup of tea, past the piled luggage of a harried traveler who had missed the train, and past families leaning against their rolled-away bedding on the stone floor, playing cards and sipping chai. Her fiery red *palloo* with shiny metallic needlework along the edge, one end of which was tucked into her mouth to keep it from flying away, hovered in the air behind her like wildfire.

The woman strode past the red-coated, Nehru-capped porters betting on better tips from the first-class compartments and through a pile of debris that a sweeper had collected, leaving only a bit of residual dampness to mark her passing. And then seeing something, she stopped. Her sari *palloo* glowed brighter, almost blindingly bright.

Nimish and Gulu, unaware of the woman approaching them, turned to go.

The woman slowly raised her face towards the departing train, allowing the *palloo* to slip from her head. Pinky gasped. She knew that face. The woman's eyes caught Pinky's, boring into them with a gaze so heavy, so full of aching, that Pinky began to lose her balance, her nose skidding across the greasy glass window.

And then half-lowering her eyelids and smiling as if suddenly satiated, the mysterious woman pursued Nimish and Gulu, her fingers splayed as if to grab theirs from behind.

Slowly, almost hand in hand, the unlikely trio made their way back home.

BORDERS:
1960

~

*The face is what one cannot kill. It is what cannot become a
content, which your thought would embrace;
it is uncontainable, it leads you beyond.*
—EMMANUEL LEVINAS, *ETHICS AND INFINITY*

※ ※ ※

*Any human face is a claim on you, because you can't help
but understand the singularity of it, the courage and
loneliness of it. But this is truest of the face of an infant. I
consider that to be one kind of vision, as mystical as any.*
—MARILYNNE ROBINSON, *GILEAD*

AN INAUSPICIOUS SIGN

Pinky and Maji arrived in Mahabaleshwar at dawn.

The morning mist rose from the canyons, illuminating lush valleys of green and glistening waterfalls. The sky was a crystalline blue, the hue of the heavens.

They stayed in a vegetarian-only bungalow near the market, sharing a room that smelled faintly of Flit insecticide. Breakfast consisted of tea, toast, and gooseberry jam. After baths and a visit to the Krishna temple, known locally as Panchgana, Maji reclined in their room and snacked on *chana jor garam*, flattened flakes of black gram flavored with an abundance of red chilies and a drop of lime.

"Come," she said, patting the bed. "Come rest."

"I'm not tired," Pinky said, thinking of the mysterious woman at the train station. Who was she? And why had she followed Nimish and Gulu out of the station? She had not been a beggar of any sort, this Pinky knew instinctively. Yet there had been an unmistakable hunger in her face. A yearning. *Beware of inauspicious signs when you first start a journey*, Maji had always counseled, *for they are warnings given by none other than Lord Ganesh to remain at home.* But Pinky had not gotten off the train. She had ridden silently, falling into a restless sleep while in the adjacent bunk, Maji snored soundly.

Even now, Maji had already fallen asleep. Pinky pulled *Sketches* from her satchel and held it to her chest as if to recall the moment Nimish had grabbed her hand at the station and given it to her. She opened to one of the bookmarked pages: *Once when gazing up at stars, counting them one by one, Binda pointed to an especially bright star and said, "That is my mother"... and I understood then that the mother who is called away by God turns into a star and continues to keep an eye on her children from above.*

Pinky's throat constricted.

He understood her.

Even if he never would love her.

* * *

In the late afternoon, Maji and Pinky walked the grounds in the shade of the jamun trees. The oval berries had ripened from pink to a crimson black, ready for picking. Soon Pinky's tongue had turned a deep purple.

"Dried jamun's very good for the digestive system," Maji said, patting Pinky upon the head.

Pinky looked up at her grandmother. Her normally stern mouth had relaxed into a semblance of a smile. "The hills are good," she said with a sigh.

"Maji," Pinky said tentatively, "I saw a girl at the station in Bombay, I thought I recognized her."

"A school friend? You should spend more time with your friends."

"No, she was older, perhaps even married but I don't know her name. I could describe her to you."

"Hmm," Maji said, gazing up at the trees. "Did I ever tell you the tale of the monkey and the jamun tree?"

Pinky sighed. As with everything else about her, Maji's communication was highly regulated, consisting of a series of one-way transmissions: prayers to the gods, commands to the servants, reprimands to Savita, advice to Jaginder, and stories—whether from the Sanskrit epics or the *Panchatantra* animal fables—to Pinky and her cousins. And every ancient story had a lesson, a enigmatic relevance to their present-day life.

"A monkey lived in a jamun tree," Maji warmed up. "He was happy but had no friends –"

She gazed at Pinky to see if she was listening properly.

"Maji," Pinky interrupted, "how did you bring me back to Bombay? You never talk about it. I want to know."

Maji paused for a deep breath. "I heard you cry," she finally said, "the moment I arrived at your father's flat. You lay upon the bed, eyes shut, fists in tight balls, mouth wide open—" What she did not say was that Pinky's tiny face, the crevices around her neck, elbows, wrists, and knees were dotted with red pustules that oozed liquid. It was as if her entire body was weeping.

Maji had placed her palm upon Pinky's scalp and felt God's merciful presence in her. This child, this beautiful little child. She wanted nothing more than to cry.

What have you done to treat her skin? she had asked Pinky's father. There had been little money to spend on a doctor so instead, they had soaked her in a bucket with a drop of the disinfectant phenol.

Her sickness started just after Yamuna's passing, he said. At the mention of his wife's name, he began to weep once more.

"I massaged you then bathed you in boiled neem leaves," Maji said continuing along the path, overripe jamun fruit squelching underfoot.

She had gone into the tiny kitchen where she drew water from a clay vessel and washed her hands over the low sink. The fact that her daughter had never inhabited this cold, dark flat gave her some comfort. Nearby, a sack of coarse red wheat from America, cheaper than homegrown Indian *atta*, leaned against a wall. A half-empty jar of Kotogem vegetarian *ghee* stood on the counter. Maji opened a tightly lidded circular tin that lay next to the cook stove and took out a steel cup of turmeric. This she mixed with the last bit of chickpea flour in the household and a little water until it became a thick paste.

Pinky's father and his mother watched her in shock. Who was this woman who came into their home as if she owned it? With Yamuna's death, Maji's ties to them were tenuous, uncertain. Yet her willfulness left them speechless.

Pinky's cries filled the flat with a sense of urgency.

Maji sat upon the bed and removed Pinky's cloth nappie and top.

Then she held the naked baby to her bosom. Pinky stopped crying. Her eyes opened and she looked into the face of her grandmother.

I'm here now, Maji whispered. *There's no need to cry anymore.*

She placed Pinky upon a sheet and, dipping her fingers into the paste, began to gently rub the yellow substance onto her skin.

"Afterwards, I held you to me and we both fell asleep," Maji said.

"But how did you bring me back?" Pinky asked. "Didn't my Papa want me?"

Maji sighed.

She had stayed overnight, announcing the next morning that she was leaving and taking Pinky with her.

How dare you? Pinky's other grandmother had growled, summoning up the courage to challenge her. *We have been respectful because of your loss but this, this is outrageous.*

Maji remained calm. *The child needs proper care, care that she isn't getting here. I can give her that.*

She doesn't need anything from you! the old woman shouted, grabbing the baby and holding her tightly. *We'll never agree to such a thing.*

Pinky began to wail.

Stop, please! her father cried out. He had lost so much in the past weeks, his home, his business, his prosperity, his wife. How could he let his child go? Yet he knew that Maji would care for her, give her top schooling, marry her to a most suitable boy from a highly educated, wealthy family. Maji could give his child more than he ever could. She could secure Pinky's future. For her sake, how could he not let her go?

I entrusted my daughter to you, Maji said, her voice unwavering, *entrust yours to me.*

I won't be cheated of my grandchild!

She'll never be deprived of anything, Maji countered, her powerful presence radiating through the flat. And then, slowly as if laying out a trump card, she added, *I will help you, too. I can help you get settled. I will send money.*

Pinky's father fell silent, weighing this pact: his only child for much-needed money. Somehow, somehow it was not enough. He touched Pinky who looked so strikingly similar to Yamuna, her long eyelashed eyes, her slender nose.

Okay, his mother said shrewdly, handing Pinky over. *Pay off this factory now and give us ten thousand rupees every year always.*

No, Pinky's father said, ashamed that he had sunk so far, he—the son of one of the most esteemed businessmen in all of Lahore. *No! This is not right! This is not about money!*

He reached for his daughter.

You'll get remarried, you'll have other children, his mother said matter-of-factly. *This money, however, will not come twice.*

Maji gritted her teeth, the loss of her daughter so acute that it took her breath away. How easily she could be replaced in their hearts, in their home. *I'll wire the money as soon as I get back.*

And then, without so much as a glance, she turned and walked out into the daylight with Pinky, her *chappals* kicking up a cloud of dust that seemed to swirl around them, fusing them together, an unexpected wholeness within two shattered histories.

"Your Papa *did* want you, *beti,*" Maji said, breaking the long silence. "He wanted you very much but he knew that I could give you a better life. And so, for your sake, he let you go."

<hr />

That night, Pinky dreamed of plunging down the waterfall in Mahabaleshwar's lush canyons, the icy water roaring in her ears. In the next moment, she was boating in Venna Lake, Maji straining as she rowed them beyond the tourists, to the farthest edges. The water was murky, green plants swayed menacingly just underneath, the spiky leaves reaching out toward her. The boat rocked violently and Pinky fell. For a moment, there was no sound, just a long, lonely sensation of hollowness. Then she surfaced, gasping for air. She discovered that she was swimming in a brass bucket in the bungalow's bathroom, the ghost throwing rotting jamun fruit at her from above.

And then a hand pushed her downwards, so unexpectedly, so fast that Pinky did not have time to cry out. She struggled, staring up at the water's surface, just a few merciless centimeters above her. Just beyond it she recognized a face with a mole-flecked cheek, the face of the baby's ayah.

She woke up screaming.

"What is it?" Maji asked urgently, holding Pinky to her bosom.

"It was her," Pinky moaned.

"Wake up, you're dreaming!"

Pinky opened her eyes. Sweat dripped from her face, her heart pounded furiously in her chest. *It was the ayah*, she realized. *She was the woman at the train station!*

"Drink some water," Maji said gently, tipping a cup to her mouth.

Pinky threw herself against her grandmother, holding onto her tightly. "I don't want to go back! I don't ever want to go back!"

"Oh pho, *beti*, I knew that coming here would be good for you. But the monsoons will be arriving any day. Already the cottages and buildings are covered with *kulum* grass. Tomorrow, the whole area will be closed."

"I don't care!"

"You are growing fast now, becoming a young lady. Already there is marriage interest. You must learn to control your emotions."

"I don't want to get married!" Pinky blurted out. "I don't ever want to leave you!"

"Is that what this is all about?" Maji chuckled softy as if hit by a realization. "I was married at fourteen, just as the monsoons arrived. Your grandfather garlanded me as the first auspicious drops drim-drummed on my head. I knew then that Lord Ganesh had blessed our union. And your mother's wedding —"

Maji fell silent. "Times have changed now," she said in a strangled voice.

Pinky began to cry.

"Enough now," Maji soothed, reaching for a bottle of mustard oil. "You must be coming down with a cold from the chilly night air. Lie down and I'll rub some oil on you."

Pinky blew her nose. She had to find some way to reveal what she had seen at the train station, some way that her grandmother would believe her. "The baby, the one who drowned, will you tell me about her?"

Maji's face tightened as she continued applying oil in long, hard strokes along Pinky's neck and shoulder. "We do not speak of such things."

"But we speak of my mother, why not her too?"

"Why bring such sadness?" Maji sighed. "The past cannot be changed even if we desire it."

"But what happened to the ayah?"

"ENOUGH!" Maji shouted, heaving herself from the bed so that the bottle crashed to the ground. "Don't mention her to me, to anyone in the household. Do you understand? I've tolerated this nonsense about ghosts. I've brought you all the way here but I will not stand to have my ears, my home defiled by the mention of her."

"But, I saw—"

"UNDERSTAND?"

Shaking slightly, Maji propelled herself towards the door, then stopped and turned around. There were tears in her eyes. "Don't speak of this ever again," she said. "You are what is important to me. You. You. You. Why can't you see that?"

Pinky cast her face downwards. "I'm sorry," she whispered. "I promise."

Maji forced herself to walk away from Pinky into the dark night, a vision of her other granddaughter rising up in her head. After all these years, there was that ache in her chest that never went away, that one spot that was not powerful, but weak, not courageous, but fearful. It was a stain of India ink that long ago marked her heart but, just in the past four days, had threateningly begun to spread.

She remembered how she had driven down to the windswept ocean with Jaginder, their priest Panditji, and Savita clutching the dead baby.

According to the ancient Vedas, Panditji had informed them, *the baby's soul has not yet attained the worldly attachments that require a funeral pyre to burn away.*

And so their destination was not the cliffside crematorium atop Malabar Hill where Maji's own husband had been reduced to ash, but the Hindu burial grounds along the Arabian Sea.

As they had stood together just outside the grounds in a tight circle, they recited the ancient *shloka, Ram Nam Satya Hai, Satya Bol Gutya Hai*—Lord Rama's name is the truth, the truth is salvation.

Entwining the baby within the triangle of their arms, they had tenderly pressed velvety marigolds to her eyes and whispered their good-byes.

MONSOONS & MIRACLES

C ook Kanj was serving curry *chawal* the evening he found religion. Fried spinach-and-onions *pakoras* floated in a saffron-colored sea of chickpea flour, curds, and toasted *ajwain*. Normally, this dish— a family favorite—brought a hint of lightness to Cook Kanj's grim countenance. But not today. His frown only deepened, lips puckering as if having been accidentally scorched. He peered into the pot and cursed. The curry had turned out too watery. And no amount of heat had thickened it. Nor had adding extra flour. It was dinnertime and Cook Kanj was out of options. Although he was not overly religious, he prayed that moment for a miracle of sorts.

"Extra, extra sugar in tomorrow's puja *halwa*," he promised to the gods as he stood ladling watery curry onto stainless-steel plates. "Fine. Fine. Don't thicken my curry if you want to play those tricks. Just make them not notice, *nah?*" he beseeched silently as he slowly lowered the plate under Jaginder's nose.

Jaginder's eyebrows smashed together in a brief moment of surprised displeasure.

And then a monsoon cloud burst over Maji's bungalow.

Tufan and Dheer raced out to the driveway and stood there, arms outstretched, until their kurta pajamas turned translucent, accentuating Dheer's plump belly and revealing an army of moles marching across Tufan's backside. "*Jantar Mantar, kaam karantar, chhoo, chhoo, chhoo!*" they belted out as if they were magicians who had wondrously disappeared the heat, sweat, and sun.

Jaginder scampered to the verandah and jabbed a thick finger into the downpour. "Step one foot inside with your soggy bodies and I will give each of you two sound *chantas!*" he threatened in order to hide his sudden pang of jealousy at his sons' carefree elation. Once he had been able to stretch his arms to the sky and think the world belonged to him.

The earth and sky embraced with the ferocity of lovemaking. The wind moaned and whipped, clattering shutters, gusting through the open door, and causing leaves and dirt on the driveway to dance in wild waltzing steps. Savita glanced up at Jaginder and noticed, with a faint flush in her cheeks, an unusual tingling in her breasts. Could it be possible that she once again desired this man, this very same man who was currently prancing on the verandah, issuing orders and casting out threats with equal severity? Feeling disturbed by this thought more than by her sudden arousal, Savita quietly slipped out of her chair and fled to her room.

Nimish, too, felt heated: the courage that had tauntingly eluded him now mightily burst within him. The rains, of course, brought inescapable romance to the city. Lovely Lawate's shuttered window, behind which he could sometimes detect a faint light, beckoned with the intensity of a lover's gaze. Nimish adjusted his spectacles, muttering a quick "good night" to the vacated table before fleeing to his room.

"Gulu, the Ambassador," Jaginder's voice pierced through the thunderous roaring of the sky, the metallic pelting of water against rooftop.

"Sir?" Gulu appeared under a frightened umbrella that shrank back, shivering on its wiry frame.

"The Ambassador," Jaginder repeated, now swinging into action. "Don't worry, I'll drive it myself."

"Where are you going Papa?" Tufan squeaked as the Ambassador's headlights bore down on him.

"To pray," was all Jaginder said before plopping himself in the front seat and revving the engine. Gulu unlocked the green gates and reluctantly pushed them open, watching the Ambassador struggle its way onto the waterlogged street with all the apprehension of a father sending his daughter off on her wedding night.

Kanj and Parvati were nowhere to be seen, having cast aside their household duties and stolen away together under the inviting monsoon shadows. Only Kuntal remained, wet towels in hand. Nimish had slipped out the back door, emboldened by the pouring rains, cloaked by the darkened sky. Tentatively at first, then with heart beating in his chest, he crept to the wall that separated Maji's bungalow from the Lawates'. The rain pounded in his ears, blood rushed in his legs, desperation in his heart.

Just days before, he had been surreptitiously leafing though Sir Richard Burton's translation of the *Ananga Ranga*, an ancient text on sexuality between husband and wife. The text proclaimed that eating tamarind enhanced a woman's sexual enjoyment, a revelation that caused him to close the book's weathered pages with trembling fingers. Had his mother ever consumed tamarind? Nimish searched his memory for such an incident, but remembered that Savita diligently stayed away from all things sour, including tamarind chutney, saying that it corrupted her womb. And Maji? Her obese and masculine body draped in widow-white clothing was so far from anything remotely sexual that it made Nimish shudder to think of how his own father was conceived. But Lovely, Lovely sat under the tamarind tree and deliberately ate pod after pod in October and November when they were in full fruition. He could almost taste the sweet sourness that clung to her lips, painting them a saucy reddish-brown.

* * *

While Jaginder roared off in pursuit of salvation, Savita perched in front of her mirror, searching for answers. Right away she noticed two things.

Her eyes were glistening, the kohl lining smudged underneath like a bruise.

And, her sari blouse had grown visibly tighter.

She wiped her eyes, blaming the moisture in the air for the first

change. She could not understand the sudden shine in her eyes. It was
as if the rains had washed away the layers of hardness from her face,
the tiny wrinkles of resentment that spun out from her eyelashes. Savita
slid the sari *palloo* from over her shoulder and cast it to the floor. Her
blouse, sewn to perfection by the tailor only days ago, now cut into her
ribs. The sleeves held tightly past her elbows where they flared out with
silver embroidery. Six metal eyelets strained down the front. Savita carefully undid the clasps, taking in surprising gasps of air as the blouse was
released. Bra falling to the ground, she held her breasts in her hands.

Her nipples protruded outwards, pointing directly at the mirror.
Bluish veins rose under her skin like a map. For a moment, she became
acutely aware of the deafening noise of clouds bursting, the frantic
shiftings of the bungalow as it strained under the deluge, and her sons'
jubilant shouts. Suddenly remembering her husband, Savita's eyes
flickered to the door for a second, briefly hoping that it was latched.

And then, just before the electricity gave way, her mirror revealed
one more thing.

✿ ✿ ✿

Jaginder was nearly as good as his word. Soaked to the bone, he sat on
a wooden chair, eyes upon a wall. There upon a mantle shelf, covered
with a white crocheted cloth, Mother Mary and Jesus gazed from picture frames haloed by the ethereal glow issuing from brass candleholders.
A crude wooden crucifix hung, tilted slightly, on a nail above.

"*Channa* and peanuts too, man?"

Jaginder looked up. A fleshy woman wearing a floral knee-length
dress stood over him. Her hair was bobbed, face devoid of makeup.
A mole on her chin wavered at him with its three overgrown hairs.
Without waiting for a reply, she slapped down a full bottle of *daru*
along with a stained glass filled with ice and a bottle of Duke's soda.
"Yes," Jaginder grunted, handing her the cash.

The woman, the enterprising owner of this particular *auntie-ka-
adda*, snapped her pulpy fingers. Almost instantly, a young girl, her
pretty teenage daughter, appeared with a plate of *channa* roasted lentil
and peanuts. Jaginder stole a glance at her and placed another bill
on the table. A basket of fried fish and cigarettes appeared within
moments.

Now sitting with his drink in hand, Jaginder tried to remember how he had driven the Ambassador through the soggy streets, along the crashing coastline to the suburb of Bandra. He had barely been able to make out the clusters of stucco houses with their long sloping clay-tile roofs in the downpour. The palm trees nestled in between the homes swayed and snapped like ferocious guard dogs. He had driven by a cemetery littered with gravestones and cement crosses. One cross stood out in the front, obviously to mark the grave of a once-promi-nent Christian villager. Now all that remained were the initials I. N. R. I.—the inscription for Jesus of Nazareth King of the Jews that the Romans had put on Jesus's crucifixion cross—to hover above the villager's departed spirit for eternity.

How he had ended up at this particular *adda*, Jaginder couldn't recall. It was as if the Ambassador had led him there of its own accord. He could not stop himself from going; his fascination with the lower class people in the *adda* and their refreshing brew seemed to take away all his troubles. He berated himself for sinking so far, for trading away his honor and respectability, for sneaking off in the middle of the night or under the torrential wings of the monsoon because he was too shamed to own up to his habit.

He had ended up here at an *adda* in Bandra belonging to an intrepid middle-aged Christian woman known locally, and famously, as Rosie Auntie. Besides serving absolutely pure liquor, on which her honor depended, Rosie's *adda* provided a merry family setting with a religious backdrop that somehow made it all feel like God himself was joining in the fun.

"To the monsoons' arrival," Jaginder exhorted Jesus and then tossed back a long gulp. Rosie promptly arrived bearing another half-pint and fresh attitude. Then she sauntered over to the next table threaten-ingly. "No money, man, then out you go!" she yelled at the frightened patron.

The door opened; the rains gusted in with feverish intensity. A low cheer went through the crowd as a regular staggered in, squeezing water from his hat and theatrically slipping in the puddle it made. He was a thin man, with a large wormy mustache and a wave of hair that remained impossibly oiled in place despite the rains. Rosie ushered him to the nearest table where he was immediately absorbed into a round of cards as if his companions had simply been waiting for him to take his turn. A fresh plate of roasted peanuts was brought forth by the teenage daughter, Marie, who wore a pretty pink frock and a matching bow in her thick, black tresses. Her dark eyes sat quietly in her face, accentuated by long lashes and the beginnings of a loss of innocence.

"Peanuts? *Bas?*" the regular flirted with her. "What else can you give me?"

The girl left and returned with fried fish and her mother.

The regular scowled and ordered a round of drinks.

The rooftop began to leak over Jaginder's table. Palm trees thrashed above. Water from the road glistened on the floor like a snake. Little Marie raced back and forth to the tables, tray delicately balanced on her hip. The regular became louder and suddenly reached for her backside. A scream was followed by the sharp scrape of chairs being pulled back.

Jaginder watched fascinated, thinking *How lucky that guy is to be free with his emotions, to be out of control.* His life at the bungalow was so restricted, reserved, futile.

Rosie arrived at the scene, hips knocking back furniture that had not been pulled out of her path. "Shameless child!" she roared, expertly cuffing her daughter on the head. The girl fled the room, the tiny gold cross around her neck glinting in the candlelight.

"Sorry! Sorry! Sorry!" the regular pleaded and slurred, his hands waving like surrender flags above his head.

"Mr. Sorry again, eh man?" Rosie roared. "Hey Jonny! Hey idiot-son-of-mine!"

Jonny promptly arrived from the back room where he must have been lifting metal drums of brandy to pass the time. Sporting his best menacing grimace, he strode through the room, the purple crucifix on his arm flexing with pleasure.

"No need for *dadagiri* Jonny," said the regular's card partner, pumping his arms in front of him as if to slow down Jonny's formidable progress.

"No need! No need!" the regular screeched like a parrot. Though it was clear that he was a repeat offender, he appeared no less frightened by the spectacle of Rosie's bodybuilding son. Even his wormy mustache had shrunk under his nose as if to take shelter.

"OUT!" the son grunted in his best James Dean voice. He was wearing a tank top and knickers, below which stuck out two skinny legs like twigs giving him less the thuggy look he aspired to and more the appearance of a chocolate popsicle.

"No need! No need!" the regular pleaded again, his hand over his head as if to shield himself from invisible blows.

"Send him with Jigger, man," the Auntie gravely sentenced, nodding towards the door. Jigger was the *adda*'s resident taxi driver who gently shuttled customers home after the evenings grew long. The son lifted the regular by his neck. The man cowered and pleaded, though in all his time at Rosie's *adda* and despite all his offenses, not a hair on his body had ever been hurt. As drunk as he was, he knew that Rosie always took him back because he was, simply put, good for business. The other customers enjoyed the show, Jaginder included, alternately cheering him on to stand his ground and cajoling Jonny to beat him to a bloody pulp. Jonny half-dragged the man to the door where he tossed him onto the wet ground and dusted his hands as if having thrown out the garbage.

The regular allowed himself to be taken into the taxi by Jigger and, from the safety of its interior, flashed a wide grin at the customers peering out through the door. Meanwhile, inside the *adda*, the mood had grown cheery. "*Chalta hai*," the drunks bantered with each other as they ordered another round of drinks. "These things go on."

"The liquor went to the bastard's head," said the regular's friend, tucking his cards into his breast pocket. "He'll be back tomorrow with his long fingers."

Even Rosie seemed to have cracked a smile. In no time, Marie was back serving *channa* with a defiant tilt to her hips. Jonny had dissolved once more into the back room, recounting his exploits with unnecessary and unrealistic detail to his younger brother.

Jaginder sighed with a forgotten contentment. Throwing a handful of *sing-dana* in his mouth, he bravely invited himself into the card game.

The regular's friends shot each other looks but grunted in approval. Jaginder ordered a round of drinks, watching Marie from the corner of his eye. There was something about her, her vibrancy that starkly contrasted with Savita's chilly temperament and Maji's commanding self-control. *Yes*, he thought, *my daughter would have brought that same spirit to our home. Warmth. Vitality.*

He longed to touch her, to feel her carefree energy, her shining youth.

Marie came by their table and Jaginder watched as his hand moved from his drink toward her, toward her slender waist. To touch another woman, a unmarried girl, was sacrilegious, yet he knew he was going to do it. Something deep inside compelled him, a wish to punish himself for his child's death and his family's deterioration afterwards.

He reached out for both his salvation and his condemnation.

Rosie slapped his hand away. "Don't you have any shame!" she spat.

The *adda* fell silent, accusing eyes asking, *Who is this big-big person? Why does he want to trouble us?*

Jaginder recoiled as if it were his face that had been struck.

Oh God, what was I thinking?

Marie smiled demurely, thrilled to have caught the attention of such a wealthy Sahib.

Jonny grabbed Jaginder by the scruff of his neck and threw him out onto the street. "*Salam, Sahib!*" he said tauntingly before strutting back inside.

"She's young enough to be your daughter!" Rosie shouted from the doorway.

There was no humor, no show as there had been with the regular, merely a cold, sharp declaration that he was not welcome. He did not belong.

"I have no daughter, I have no daughter," Jaginder cried out, sprawled upon the wet pavement.

At last, at last, he wept for his loss.

✿ ✿ ✿

In the sudden darkness, Savita could not be sure of what she had seen in her mirror. Slowly, she lifted her finger and touched the wetness at her nipple. She brought her finger to her nose and smelled a familiar sweetness on it. A spiral of pain pushed urgently from inside her breasts. She held them again, shocked by their fullness. Bringing her finger to her mouth now, she let the taste from her finger settle into her mouth. And then she knew. A low cry filled the room as Savita collapsed onto her vanity. Unbelievably, more than thirteen years after the birth of her last child, her breasts had filled with milk.

≛ ≛ ≛

The monsoons brought life to the parched earth but also miracles to its yearning inhabitants. This year as the rains burst overhead, their promise proved even worthier. Dheer and Tufan danced in the offerings from the sky until Kuntal finally settled them in bed with a convenient stash of chocolate. Nimish remained outside, by the wall, waiting for Lovely to emerge.

Jaginder piloted the Ambassador through the standing water and spray, the wipers doing nothing more than agitating the flood gushing down his windshield. Water seeped into the car from below and through the open window, soaking his pants and shirt. The black clouds suddenly parted above, revealing a veiny and reddish moon, a reflection of his own bleary eyes. Anticipating the imminent return of his beloved Ambassador, Gulu awoke from a restless nap and peered through the gate for the familiar headlights.

The intense humidity had turned the match heads waxy and inert, leaving candles unlit and the bungalow dark. In the back garage, Cook Kanj and Parvati lay entangled on their bed, their bodies still urgently moving as lightning lashed above their head. Tomorrow morning, he would remember his promise and put extra sugar in the puja *halwa*. The deluge, after all, had arrived right as he served dinner. Untouched dishes and cold rice lay scattered on the table. Cook Kanj's watery curry had miraculously gone unnoticed.

So did another miracle of sorts.

Under the generous thundering of the rain-swept skies, a bolt remained unlocked past sunset, a forbidden door groaned open, a boundary was breeched.

The baby ghost ventured out of the bathroom for the first time— her silvery mane leaving a glistening trail of dew as fine and luminescent as moonlight.

RAIN-SWEPT
TAMARIND TREE

M aji and Pinky returned to find Bombay transformed.
From her perch on the front verandah, Pinky watched the
rains seduce the city like a duplicitous lover, bringing shouts of joy
and impromptu dancing in the streets, but also the unmistakable stink
of rotting sewage. That morning, on the day schools reopened for
the new school year, girls appeared in matching pink raincoats, boys
in khaki-colored ones, all sporting British gum-boots. Rain fell on
the scorched earth with a satisfying thud, accompanied by the joyous
singing of young women in the streets, clasping hands together and
turning round and round in wild circles as their long braids whipped
the damp air.

Just inside the bungalow, Maji stood alone, grateful for the moment
to remember her beloved husband, the times he would take her to see
a film, which he stubbornly referred to as *bioscopes* his whole life, the
two of them traveling to the theater in a covered horse carriage. They
had been young then, Omanandlal in his silk shirt with its four gold
buttons and she, sitting proudly by his side, head covered with her sari
palloo, a diamond stud flashing in her nose. Maji and Omanandlal

had been a handsome couple, arriving at the theater in the midst of the monsoons in their finest clothes.

The drumming of the rains never failed to deliver these precious memories, bringing with them a fullness for which she thirsted the rest of the year. It was as if she could fleetingly go back to that time of fullness, of Omanandlal, Yamuna, and the baby.

A parched city exhaled a collective sigh of relief even as the stormy dampness indiscriminately worked its way inside dwellings, from the chatai-mat huts in the slums to the ornate bungalows of the elite, such as the original Malabar Hill bungalows, The Beehive and The Wilderness, which were constructed in 1825 and later criticized for being most unsuited for the climate. Likewise, Maji's bungalow, The Jungle, was no match for the tropics with its oppressive humidity, intolerable heat, verdurous vegetation, and malarial insects. Even armed with a modern AC, proper electrical lines, and a new tile roof, The Jungle succumbed to the will of nature.

Now as the monsoons gathered in fury, unending rows of slick ants forged past the thick line of turmeric around the bungalow's interior perimeter that normally kept them at bay. Cockroaches climbed out of the toilet, seeking refuge. Ceiling fans whirled nonstop in futile attempts to dry the morning laundry that was now strung across rooms and hallways on impromptu clotheslines. Wall punkahs shorted out when water seeped into the wiring. Tufan flitted about in a constant state of undress, sneaking out into the pouring rain and jumping into the puddles until Parvati dragged him inside by his ear. Dheer prowled The Jungle as if on a hunt, attempting to locate an arid spot in which to stash his molding chocolate. Nimish strolled the hallways with a mossy copy of Thackeray's Vanity Fair in hand, reading over the thunderous din, "'Was there ever a battle won like Salamanca? Hey, Dobbin? But where was it he learnt his art? In India, my boy. The jungle is the school for a general, mark me that.'"

Savita remained bolted in her bedroom for long hours each day, naked from the waist up, staring at her lactating breasts. Jaginder spent so much time at Rosie's adda that the long-fingered regular invited him to a game of cards and promptly cheated him out of his wallet. Cook Kanj was locked in an unsuccessful battle against an array of sickly insects that infiltrated the kitchen from every spiraling crack and crevice. Kuntal strategically placed steel bowls under ceiling drips, the number of which increased with each passing hour. Parvati strung up jute laundry lines inside the bungalow now that clothes could not be dried outside. Gulu swept away the constant influx of water into the garage with a short-handled broom. Through it all, Maji maintained her usual stoic demeanor, ordering the floors to be wiped every hour and the toilets cleaned twice a day by the *bhangi*, willing the bungalow to survive the onslaught of yet another rainy season.

"Did you have a good trip?" Dheer asked Pinky as he fortified his school satchel with Gluco biscuits. It was the first week of school and he was still figuring out what provisions he required to make it through the day.

Pinky nodded, handing him packets of sugar-coated sesame *chikki* that she had brought from the hill station.

Dheer hesitated for a moment, then accepted the gift appreciatively. His mouth opened and closed as if he had something more to say but thought better of it. Swinging his satchel over his head, he waddled away. Pinky remained at home due to Maji's insistence and spent the glorious morning watching the rains whip at the windows and indulging in fried flour *muttees* dipped generously in mango pickle.

Later that afternoon, still putting off a bath, she retreated to Maji's room. Rows and rows of damp clothes hung overhead, fighting to shed their moisture. As she stared up at them lost in thought, she heard a rustling. Though her ceiling fan was off and the windows sealed, the clothes directly above her wavered. She sat up, remembering that strange feeling of love in her chest, that unexpected love for her ghostly cousin-sister.

A saffron sari shivered on the clothesline.

Could it be? The ghost had never left the bathroom before, needing water of some sort to survive. She had traveled through the pipes and occupied the bucket but never ventured into the rest of the bungalow. But now, now Pinky realized with sudden horror, jute lines were strung in every room, each hung with damp clothing, each a watery path of transit.

A cold draft whipped her face.

Pinky stood up on the bed and shook the sari with her free hand. It came away with a snap. Savita Auntie's blue *salvar* began to jiggle, the stiff cuff bottoms glittering with a scattering of sequins. Pinky swung her legs over the side of the bed and assessed the open door.

She began to run.

The clothes whipped at her, blinding her vision, impeding her progress. A towel wrapped around her face, sticking against it, suffocating her. Pinky grabbed at it, trying to pull it off. She fell to the ground. Behind her, the *salvar* jiggled again. The room filled with a rattling, a pulsing, a shining.

Just ahead, a pair of pants began to dance, the legs curling, reaching towards her with malevolence.

Pinky slapped them away but they coiled around her like a snake, tightening, tightening.

And then, just as hastily, they released her.

A mane of silvery hair abruptly fell out from the underside.

The pants continued to sway. Slowly, two tiny fists curled around the hem and two stormy eyes appeared upside down in one of the legs. Fury filled the room like a fog.

"You!" Pinky gasped.

The ghost stared at Pinky unmoving. It was as if she had come to take her in, to gauge her return, to restrategize.

"I know everything now," Pinky said, steadying her breathing. "The girl was your ayah, wasn't she?"

The ghost cocked her head, her hair coiling around it like a rain cloud.

"But it was an accident, right? There was no reason for her to drown you. That hand, the faceless hand you showed me, that's a mistake. It can't be anything else. I can't believe you."

The ghost's eyes churned. The jute lines began to shake, the clothes whipping back and forth, sending a spray of moisture into the air with each snap. The ghost held her hand out, palm up, and touched Pinky's cheek.

It was not a gesture of love but an icy, gelid touch, a burning freeze.

And then with a defiant flick of her flowing hair, she scurried back up the pants and vanished.

❉ ❉ ❉

Pinky's cheek turned blue and swollen like a bruise, its shape roughly resembling a handprint. She began to shiver uncontrollably, taking to her bed with a cough. The jute lines were removed from Maji's room and a floor heater installed to dry out the damp air. Despite this, the room remained steadfastly chilly.

Dr. M. M. Iyer was called in. "Could be a cold, could be the onset of pneumonia," he announced in his usual grave manner. "Only solution is rest." Nevertheless, in order to properly bill for his visit, he left a prescription in Maji's waiting hands.

"Take down the jute lines in the rest of the bungalow," Pinky pleaded with her grandmother, her voice weak.

"Nonsense," Maji said. "How will the laundry dry otherwise? Don't you worry about the damp air in here, I'll turn on the heater."

Pinky began to believe with a sick sort of feeling that she had been somehow duped. Her story of Ratnavali, she felt, had served as sustenance, bringing shape and features to the ghost's undefined body. But now it was strong enough to seek out its own sources of nourishment, traveling along the clotheslines and taking in the Mittal family's daily activities with the intensity of a starving child. Her world was bigger than the bathroom, bigger than Pinky. Bigger, Pinky thought with rising horror, than anything she had ever imagined.

Whenever the rains outside let up fleetingly, the inside of the bungalow remained under siege as if swallowed by a perpetual cloud. Underneath the orderliness that Maji so stringently enforced, an element of growing unease clung to dank walls and dampened spirits. The ghost moved fast, meticulously spreading her humid grip over the whole household and enveloping each member within a spreading tide of guilt as if each had had a role to play in the baby's death. Now, the initial joyful distractions that the downpour had brought were distorted, amplified, mutated by the ghost's increasing power.

Savita Auntie had been the first to experience the repercussions, exactly four days after the initial shock of discovering her breasts filled with milk. At first she took secret pleasure in their abundance. The feelings of emptiness and unworthiness that she had felt acutely for months after her daughter's death and in the long years since were instantly washed away by a forgotten fullness, a recaptured youth, an affirmation of her motherlinesss. She fussed over her boys with an eagerness that they had long since forgotten, tussling their hair affectionately and even sitting down to hear Nimish read an entire section from Lady Falkland's *Chow-chow: A Journal kept in India, Egypt, and Syria.* "'For after the heavy rains are over,'" Nimish began, "'the sky looks like a naughty child that has not quite recovered its good humor, when the least thing would bring back a flood of tears; and so the large gray clouds, tipped with white, seemed half inclined to weep.'"

"Maybe naughty *gora* children," Savita huffed at the comparison. "But you boys are much more resilient." When alone, she remembered the glorious swelling of her belly, the sheer awe of holding another life within oneself, and wanted nothing more than to become pregnant again. Although she and Jaginder had not been intimate in years, Savita downed a glass of aphrodisiacal saffron milk and seduced him the next night when he stumbled in from Rosie's *adda*. On the third day of the monsoons, Jaginder's mood had improved to such a degree that he took the entire family out for dinner at the Rendezvous Restaurant at the Taj Hotel and bought Savita an emerald drop necklace from their family jeweler. Savita was elated.

And then dusk fell into darkness on the fourth night. That evening Jaginder forsook the lure of Rosie's concoctions for his wife's even more bewitching brew. In their first years together as husband and wife, Jaginder—who had never set foot outside India—liked to think of himself as an explorer as was the fashion of the times, in the hallowed tradition of the East India Company chaps who ferreted their way into India and paved the way for Empire. He did not conquer land, per se, there was nothing left to conquer by the time he got around to it, not even a remote princedom. But, just as civilizable, just as exotic, lay his wife's virginal, luscious, mysterious landscape, draped in siren reds. Oh, how he felt when the naked shores of her body appeared in the horizon and when he first crashed upon them gun drawn, shedding blood, marking the territory as his own. A gateway was eventually erected in the harbor ensuring a smooth passage, but along with that came a resigned, bittered acceptance of his presence.

Simply put, the thrill was gone. And so following in the footsteps of the red-faced Brits, Jaginder had taken to drink. His daughter's death, of course, was a catalyst but sometimes he wondered if he had not been heading in that direction already, charging full tilt towards his own demise. There was nothing else to do in those unbearable times but to drown one's sorrows in a vodka gimlet and recall stories of the glory days when the sun never set. But now, now that many suns had set and Jaginder was lost in a cold, bleak, Londonish fog with Johnnie Walker as his only companion, he felt nostalgic for the inescapable heat of his wife's body, its heady sun-baked chaos, its crowds of colors and flavors, its untamed mangroves. How foolish he had been, he realized, to think he could live without her, for he was nothing without his jewel. His Savita.

Now, as they lay side by side on their bed, Jaginder felt an unfamiliar and extraordinary tenderness towards her, taking unusual care to caress the curve in her hips, to touch the softness of her lips, to take in the shine of her eyes before slowly, almost painfully so, fulfilling his pleasure. "This is all I ever wanted," he purred softly as he pressed his face into the sweet nutty smell emanating from her scalp.

"Jaggi," Savita whispered, her body glowing with an eagerness long since abandoned in the tediousness of their days together, "please don't let anything change this."

"I won't," he promised. And he meant it. Nothing, he vowed to himself, would take Savita away from him again, not his fears, not their past. Completely lost in their unexpected intimacy, he couldn't imagine anything different.

"Jaggi," Savita continued in an even more softer voice, "please, please stop this drinking. For my sake."

"I will," he promised. Savita's affection was a heady potion, one that gave him strength and vigor. And, most powerfully—hope.

Now, as their legs intertwined, Jaginder's hands took in Savita's slender neck, the sharp peak of her collarbone, the subtle rise in her chest. As his hands moved downwards, they grasped her breasts, caressing their lovely fullness. His tongue tasted the sweat pooled in between, moving outward until his mouth encircled her nipple. And then, as he began to gently suck, the baby ghost—hovering in a moist petticoat above—unleashed her vengeance.

Savita's breasts burst with milk.

Jaginder fell back, choking. Sweet, thick, raw milk stuck in his throat and began to freeze, to solidify. He could not get it out. He could not breathe.

Savita shot up, crossing her arms across her chest, reeling with confusion. Her breasts felt cold, like ice.

Swaying on his hands and knees, Jaginder had turned blue.

"Jaggi!" Savita screamed, thumping him on the back.

All at once, milk poured from his nose and mouth. He fell to the floor and sputtered. "What's wrong with you!"

Savita's eyes dropped. Her face closed. Her soul shut down. In the brief second it took to register Jaginder's implicit accusation, she realized that their recent gentleness towards each other had been too fragile to sustain.

"You!" she threw back before pulling the covers over her body. "*You* did this to me!"

"Me?" Jaginder struggled to his feet like a lion sniffing fresh prey. "They're *your* breasts."

"It won't stop!" Savita cried out in horror. Milk shot from her breasts as if in accusation that thirteen years earlier, it hadn't. She felt cold, alone, terrified.

Jaginder stared at her with increasing panic.

"I'll wake Maji," he said while wiping away the vestiges of milk that had spurted through his nostrils.

Even in the middle of the night, Maji had the presence of mind to know that something out of the ordinary was happening. "Don't call the doctor," she ordered. "No one outside this household shall know."

"What should we do?"

"Stay out of my room!" Savita wailed.

"Pray," Maji answered.

Visions of Jesus and Mary at Rosie's *adda* floated into Jaginder's head. "I'll do that," he said, relief drenching his concern. His mother would take care of things as she always did. Jaginder could escape.

Maji raised a disbelieving eyebrow at her son before turning her attention to her daughter-in-law.

Curled up in a ball, Savita refused all help and wept until exhaustion lulled her to sleep.

* * *

While his parents had been in the throes of lovemaking, Nimish crept from his room and out the side door. For the past three nights,

Lovely had not ventured through the rains to the tamarind tree. Undeterred, Nimish vowed to try again. An unexplainable urgency had gripped him, prodding him to finally approach Lovely and confess his love. "Confess or die," he whispered to himself as if someone had just uttered these words to his sleeping ear. Outside, the rains were harsh, unforgiving. They accompanied him now, a steady drum beat marking his resolute footsteps.

Lovely's window glowed dimly, the tamarind tree lashed and swayed in the deluge as if in warning. A longing like no other gripped Nimish, a wailing in his heart. Before he realized what he was doing, he raced to the outlying end of the garden and crawled through the small corridor in the wall, jasmine creepers brushing against his face, perfuming the air with an intense sweetness. Lovely's backyard opened before him, a tapestry of dark yearning hidden in the lush greenery.

And then Lovely appeared like an angel, tiptoeing though the mud and puddles in the direction not of the tamarind tree, but unexpectedly toward a side gate, a satchel strapped across her chest. Nimish's heart lifted, he held himself back from running to meet her.

"Lovely!"

Lovely stopped, frightened when she first saw the figure across the lawn.

"It's me, Nimish!"

"Nimish?"

She moved towards him, the monsoon's ferocious aria wailing all around her as the two met under the tree. Tentatively, Nimish grasped Lovely's forearm. His face was dark, full of longing. The rain had coated his spectacles, rendering them useless. He pulled them off, tucking them in his pocket. His dark eyes, long eyelashes thick with moisture, appeared to be weeping.

"Is everything okay?" Lovely asked, looking into Nimish's face.

"Yes, yes, yes," Nimish said, almost gasping for breath. *Confess or die.* A million times he had planned what he was going to say to Lovely, written it down on paper, changing words, phrases and then memorizing the whole thing, eating the paper itself so nothing remained. If he were a movie hero, the right declarations would spill out of his mouth, and then he would sweep Lovely into a song and dance before tearing away gloriously on his motor scooter, his beloved clinging breathlessly to his waist. Now, though, his carefully charted words escaped him as he held Lovely's forearm, the end of her sleeve sewed with tiny crystalline beads lying across his wrist like a soft embrace.

Rain pelted his face and dripped onto his kurta, glowing ghostly white in this darkest of nights. Words, actions, thoughts that were forbidden during the day, when the elders looked on with their disapproving eyes, when society's rules were rigorously imposed, were set free under the tamarind tree. Lovely found herself tenderly wiping the rain from Nimish's face with the end of her golden *dupatta*, the silken fabric that lay against her chest at last touching his cheek.

He looked down, unable to speak.

"Nimish? What is it?"

He gripped Lovely's arm, the heat from his hand penetrating her skin. "We grew up as brother and sister, but I never considered you my sister."

"No?"

"No," Nimish lifted his face to hers, determined. "Please, please don't tell me you see me as a brother. Save those words for someone else. Not me. Not me."

"Oh, Nimish," Lovely said, looking into his face with eyes that glistened. How many times had she and Nimish played when they were younger, running around in her backyard, even sitting under this very tree while the elders were napping, he fervently telling her about a book he had read while she cradled golden flowers in her palms, daydreaming of being somewhere, faraway from her family in another life, another time? But never, she realized, never away from Nimish. He was always there in her fantasies, standing with book in hand, a blush on his cheek, as he spun a story. As they grew, they spent less time together. Still, Nimish occasionally read from his books, the only way he knew to communicate with her, his absurd little quotes knitting them together. And his stories had taken her to other worlds, had given her what no one else could. Why had she never understood this before?

"Tell me something from your books," Lovely said. "Anything."

Nimish took a deep breath as one of his favorite poems came to mind. "'Pale hands, pink tipped, like Lotus buds that float, On those cool waters where we used to dwell,'" he recited softly from Laurence

Hope's "Pale Hands I Loved": "'I would have rather felt you round my throat, Crushing out life; than waving me farewell. '"

Lovely looked into his handsome face, noticing it as if for the first time. "No, Nimish," she finally said, "not a brother."

He swallowed his surprise as thunder swept through the sky. The fury of the rains filled his being with their desire, the pounding on the wet ground became the fervent pounding in his chest.

"Lovely," he began again, hoping for another promise, "please don't accept any of the proposals that Vimla Auntie brings over to discuss with Maji."

"No," she said truthfully, involuntarily glancing towards the bunglow's side gate as if something waited for her just beyond. "I never intended to." The last thing she wanted was to marry someone her mother or her brother had chosen, both of whom had turned a blind eye to her father's rages, even when he beat them. She had resolved to find love for herself, on her own terms. Maybe she would not marry at all. She had made a plan tonight, an ill-conceived one, perhaps, but deep inside, she knew that her time had run out. She touched the satchel by her hip. Her heart ached.

She pulled his hands to her face, and then—eyes closed—touched her forehead to his. Together they stood like that under the tamarind tree, the tree full of spirits, watching as their young hearts unfurled like blossoms in the dawn. *If not now, then someday, someday,* she silently prayed.

Nimish tilted Lovely's head back and pressed his lips to hers.

And then a branch whipped across Lovely's face, leaving a cut so fine that it appeared like a strand of misplaced hair.

"I must go," she said, recoiling as if having been stung. She pulled her *dupatta* across her shoulders, touching the blossoming line of red at her cheek, her fingertip wet with blood as her body tensed with an implacable darkness.

"Please don't," Nimish pleaded. "I'm sorry, I didn't mean to—"

But Lovely turned away from him and, in her uncertainty, ran not to the side gate but back into the bungalow. Nimish tried to catch the end of her *dupatta* in his hand, but the pattern of emerald leaves swam against his palm as the silken fabric slipped from his grasp.

* * *

That night other members of the Mittal household found themselves unexpectedly awake, too. Gulu, of course, had just coaxed the Ambassador out of the garage for Jaginder's nightly flight and was now drowsily changing into a dry *dhoti*. Cook Kanj and Parvati, stirred by the sound of the car's engine, languidly repossessed each other's bodies under the tinny drumming of water on their converted garage roof.

The ghost, meanwhile, noiselessly drifted from clothesline to clothesline, checking in on a sleeping Pinky and Kuntal first, and then making her way to the boys' room. Dheer snored in staccato bursts, and Tufan thrashed on his bed as if having a seizure. Nimish returned to the room, cheeks red, and changed into dry pajamas before lying down in bed, eyes turned upward as if in prayer. The ghost looked almost longingly down upon her three almost brothers, taking them in with hungry curiosity. Smiling now, she crept into the stiffness of a hanging shirt. The room grew chilled. Nimish reached for his cotton sheet.

Across the room, Dheer snored voraciously. And then suddenly, his mouth snapped shut, his nose ballooned out, and his eyes popped open. He pulled his knees into his chest and began to sniff the sheets. There was a nutty smell coming from them. *Almonds and hot milk*, Dheer thought, instantly feeling hungry. *And sugar cane.* He groaned with anticipation. But then another smell drifted into the mix. He glaumed at it with his fingers, vaguely remembering smelling this sweet-bitter combination once before. Rooting around under his pillow, he sniffed at the sheets with such intensity that he began to hyperventilate. His pajama top flapped up while his chunky buttocks glistened with sweat. The smell began to grow stronger. Dheer's nostrils flared, his mouth worked, his hands grasped, his mind whirred. *Fenugreek.*

Tufan woke with a start and found himself lying on his back, out of breath. Peering into the darkness, he could hear his brother's unusual panting and the sounds of sheets being pawed. Tufan smelled something too but not the same scent that his brother was searching out. His came from his own body. His eyes grew wide as he began to feel at his sheets, though with much more deliberation than his brother, his hand finally coming to rest at the wetness between his thighs. Feeling oddly satisfied, he quickly checked his penis which had shrunk to the size of a sickly caterpillar in the sudden chill of the pajama bottoms.

As the latter-born of the twins and hence the youngest of the brothers, Tufan had desperately wanted to grow up. To become a man and be taken seriously, like Nimish. Now, he felt with a rush of vigor, his time had come. He no longer had to wake up and coax his organ to fruition, it now did it on its own. Feeling smug, he brought his hand to his nose. But as he took in a deep inhalation of himself, he realized with horror that the smell emanating from it was not an indicator of his newfound manliness but a vestige of his childhood, a nightmare of micturition. Unbelievably, he had wet his bed.

Dheer began to gasp softly as the smell of bitter fenugreek clung to his nose, suffocating him with a wave of nausea. He knew this mix of bitter-sweet aromas from a long-repressed incident in the bathroom when he had not been able to avoid noticing Pinky's soft breasts pushing through her shirt, the powdery scent of her skin. Back then he had felt ashamed, angry, even aroused, and compensated by cutting off all communication with her. Now, as he struggled for breath and furiously rubbed his nose, he realized that he had been wrong. *Oh my god, it was something else!*

"Dheer?" Nimish pulled himself from his reverie. He was used to his brothers making all sorts of unnatural noises while they slept, Dheer even sometimes sleepwalked, but his gasping was starting to concern him. "Are you okay?"

Tufan lay absolutely still, terrified that his brothers might discover his accident. The urine began to work its pungent way up his spine.

"No, no, no." Dheer moaned, beginning to cry.

Nimish jumped out of bed and turned on the light. Water dripped from the clotheslines onto the floor, a diagonal of heavy rain, even though the laundry had been squeezed thoroughly and hung that morning.

"What's wrong!"

"I can't—breathe."

"Tufan! *Utho!* Go get Mummy and Papa!"

But neither the urgency in Nimish's voice nor the thought that Dheer might die propelled Tufan from his bed. He kept his eyes firmly shut, hoping against hope that Nimish would leave him alone.

"Tufan, you lazy idiot—wake up!" Nimish launched a book which hit him with a thud.

"You bloody—" Tufan jerked to sitting position.

"So—cold," Dheer moaned.

"It's the A. C., it must be stuck on high!" Nimish shouted, his breath frosting as he shut off the unit and wrapped a comforter around Dheer. "Calm down! Take in a slow breath."

Dheer moaned again. The smell was overpowering, thick, milky, bitter. His eyes rolled back in his head.

"GO!" Nimish yelled at his youngest brother.

Feeling as if Nimish was sufficiently distracted, Tufan jumped out of bed and raced to his wardrobe on his way out, pulling on a fresh kurta.

Running at full speed to his mother's room, he thudded across the dining hall, his footsteps echoing all the way down the east hallway to the puja room where Maji had retired after Savita refused her help.

"Oi," Maji called out, pulled from a trancelike prayer in shock. "Who's there?"

"Mummy! Mummy! Mummy!" Tufan raced into her room and called through the doorway. "Something's wrong with Dheer!"

Savita opened her eyes, hoping that the events earlier that evening had only been a nightmare. Then she realized that the front of her blouse was soaking, the milk no longer spurting but nonetheless leaking out. Her eyes dimmed.

"Mummy!"

With supreme effort, Savita focused on her son. "What now?" she called out, not wanting to open the door.

"Mummy, come! Dheer can't breathe!"

Savita snapped alert as if having been doused with cold water. *It's come for the rest of us at last,* she thought, *the evil spirit in the bathroom.* Holding one arm tightly against her chest, she flung open the door and ran to the boy's room, passing Maji and a freshly woken Kuntal on her way there.

Dheer had turned purple. Nimish was pounding him on his back as if to dislodge something from his throat.

"Dheer!" Savita shouted. Momentarily forgetting her own leaking breasts, she grabbed her son and began shaking him.

Tufan stood stiffly in the corner, eyeing his bed with fear. Awakened by Kuntal, Cook Kanj and Parvati raced into the room.

"Do something!" Savita wailed.

"Turn him upside down!" Maji ordered when she finally hobbled in.

It took three of them to hold Dheer up by his legs. Nimish continued to pound on his back.

The overpowering odor of boiled fenugreek, which only Dheer could smell, had worked its way under his cheekbones, grinding into his temples, making his head throb with such intensity that he finally threw up. Vomit, litres of it, poured from his mouth smelling of bitter fenugreek and curdled milk. The rest of the family gagged and covered their noses.

The ghost slinked up to the ceiling fan and draped herself against a slowly whirring blade. Her silvery hair glittered in the air behind her like sunlight through dissipating fog.

A few minutes later Dheer, changed into fresh pajamas, flopped back into bed, and promptly began snoring. Kuntal cleaned up the mess. Cook Kanj was already in the kitchen brewing up a pot of chai. Maji abruptly plopped down on Tufan's bed.

There in the yellowed light of the boys' room, a trinity of tightly held secrets was revealed.

Regaining her composure, Savita looked down to discover wide rings of wetness encircling her breasts. In the few seconds it took for her to clasp her arms across her chest and run out of the room, the other members of the household had noticed, too.

"Kuntal, go to her," Maji ordered with forced calmness. "See what can be done."

"I need to go back to sleep," Tufan squeaked in a futile attempt to dislodge Maji from his bed.

"Maji, what's wrong with Mummy?" Nimish rummaged on his desk table until he located his spectacles. Looping the wires around his ears, he surveyed the scene. A pile of sheets lay in the corner. Soaking wet clothes hung limply from the clothesline, strung diagonally across the room. The odor of vomit and sweat clung to the room.

"How did this happen?" Maji countered, pointing at Dheer whose chest now heaved thunderously with sleep.

"I don't know," Nimish guiltily pressed at the center of his spectacles. "I think he was choking on something."

Cook Kanj entered with the tea tray. As Maji reached for a cup, she suddenly became aware of a dampness spreading along her bottom. She shifted. "Eh?—*yeh, kya hai?*"

Tufan darted from the room and raced into the hallway before the second secret was revealed.

Parvati stuck her hand under Maji's enormous buttocks, feeling the bed. "It's wet."

Everyone looked up at the hanging clothes. Nimish glanced at his pile of rain-soaked clothes in the corner of the room and felt his heart clutch.

Parvati brought her hand away and curled her lips. "*Chee!* Not rain, *soo-soo!*"

"Tufan wet his bed?" Maji said, taking a deep inhalation. "Oi, get me off this bed and into a fresh sari."

Cook Kanj began collecting the chai cups while Parvati heaved Maji off the bed. No one spoke but every mind was churning with the unusual events of that evening, attempting to put it all together as if a puzzle: Dheer's vomit, Savita's soaked blouse, Tufan's wet bed—a trio of unrestrained bodily fluids.

"Everyone go to sleep now," Maji commanded as if everything could be ordered back to normalcy. She leaned heavily on Parvati's shoulders.

And then, so quietly that no one at first noticed, Pinky padded into the room. Having just arrived at the scene, she saw what the rest of the family had not: the baby ghost gleaming in the clothesline like a butterfly.

"Pinky baby, go to sleep now," Maji's voice became gentle.

But Pinky remained where she was, swaying with the effort to stand.

"Can't you all see?" she whispered, pointing to the ceiling fan.

The baby ghost lifted herself off the blade as if surprised. Pinky met her gaze. For a fugitive moment, each drowned in the eyes of the other.

"*Kya?*" Parvati asked looking up. "Another leak?"

"Pinky, baby, go to sleep now," Maji was firm. But even Nimish, now pushing back damp clothes to get a better look at the fan, noticed how his grandmother's voice faltered for the briefest instant. Cook Kanj set the tea tray down with an abrupt clang and crooked his lanky neck upwards.

"Can't you all see?" Pinky tried again. Though her face was pale and drawn, her eyes blazed with determination.

"I don't see anything," Nimish said.

"Pinky—go to bed!" Maji's voice was urgent.

"She's there right in the *punkah*."

"Who?" Parvati asked, shoulders straining from Maji's weight.

"The dead baby," Pinky said slowly, revealing the third and final secret of that night. "She's come back."

LIGHTNING AT
THE GREEN GATES

For an instant, Maji, Parvati, Kanj, and Nimish strained their eyes. And then Maji erupted into such a fury that the entire bungalow shook with her wrath. "This nonsense about ghosts again!" she boomed, gigantic jowls quivering while her hair lashed out behind her.

"A ghost?" Nimish threw up his hands. What his eyes couldn't see, his mind couldn't possibly fathom, even considering the unusual events of the evening.

Cook Kanj shook his head. "A good night disturbed for *this*?" he muttered, one hand cutting the air like a knife while the other deftly retrieved the tea tray.

"She's there! She's there!" Pinky yelled. She was not going to retreat, not now, not when the family's safety was at stake.

"See what happens when you indulge a child too much," Kanj muttered to his wife.

"Nimish, bring Pinky back to my room. NOW!" Maji commanded. "Come Parvati."

But Parvati did not move.

"I see it," she said firmly, still peering up at the ceiling fan.

Cook Kanj dropped the tea tray. A half-dozen steel cups flew into the air, splashing sweetened froth onto hanging laundry. Nimish dropped Pinky's arm and began to rip damp clothes from the jute cords. Maji's breathing became thick. The ghost now gathered herself into a dark cloud which thundered over the ceiling fan. The propeller began to whir with increasing speed, spraying frigid water everywhere and causing the yellow light in the center to short out.

"Get out now!" Maji ordered.

Whether she was shouting at the ghost or at the rest of them, Nimish did not stop to think as he grabbed Pinky and ran down the hallway. Cook Kanj and Parvati followed behind, half-dragging Maji. Unafraid, Nimish went back for Dheer who was still in a Kumbhakarna-like slumber on his bed. Not even the sudden downpour had roused him. They're gathered in the parlor, the only space in the bungalow, except for the puja room, free from impromptu clotheslines. In the sudden silence they waited, wondered, and wished for an explanation.

"Parvati, bring a blanket for Pinky," Maji said after shuffling into the room wearing a dry sari. "And Kanj, some chai."

Cook Kanj looked fearfully down the hallway where the kitchen light glowed weakly, casting a pale rectangle against a darkened wall. "*Hahn ji,*" he said tentatively. And then, watching his wife disappear down the hallway in search of a blanket, hips flaring as if to daring someone to accost her, Kanj hitched up his *lungi,* puffed out his concave chest as best he could, and marched off towards the kitchen.

"Maji?" Nimish began, his arm around Pinky. She felt its comforting weight and wanted nothing more than for this moment to last forever.

"Nimish," Maji said quietly, "there is some logical explanation. We must take care not to upset your mother."

Nimish nodded his head, recalling his mother's soaking blouse. She was in such a delicate state. And why? He struggled with this question, feeling a surge of anger at his father. *Where was he anyway, the drunkard?* Nimish was old enough to remember when things had been good between his parents, when his father inspired respect and awe, when his mother had been happy, just like she had been in the last few days. What an idiot he was to think that, somehow, things had miraculously changed. Something *was* different. But now, he realized with growing fear, it was not what he had hoped. There was a darkness spreading within the bungalow, something he could not even begin to grasp. "What's happening?"

Maji's face sagged, folds of flesh hung limply from her arms. After a long pause, eyes resting on Pinky, she confessed, "I don't know, *beta*, I don't know."

Parvati returned with the blanket and helped Maji get cleaned up.

"It's her ghost," Pinky said to Nimish, grateful that it was finally all in the open.

Nimish gave Pinky's shoulder a squeeze and fell into thought, attempting to make rational sense of the evening, to figure out the best course of action. Aside from Pinky's cough and the muffled clattering of Cook Kanj in the kitchen, the bungalow fell into an uneasy quiet.

⌘ ⌘ ⌘

Thankfully, Savita had missed the final drama in the boys' room. Earlier, Kuntal had tied a cotton *dupatta* around her chest until the pressure was strong enough to stop the swell of milk. Now Savita lay tearfully half-asleep on her belly, Kuntal on her side next to her, tenderly rubbing her head and neck.

"I have to get out of here," Savita wept, "before it's too late!"

"Don't say such things," Kuntal comforted.

"My boys," Savita reached for her arm as a fresh supply of tears rained across her face. "I have to save them!"

Her face grew fierce. "That brat, that Pinky, this is all her fault! She was the one to unbolt the bathroom door, wasn't that what Parvati said? It's in there, I know!"

"What's in there?"

"The evil spirit that killed my baby!"

Kuntal gasped.

"We must get out of here tonight!" Savita cried out.

"Let's wait for Jaginder Sahib to come back," Kuntal suggested. "He'll know what to do."

At the mention of her husband's name, Savita grew angry. "He cares only for his Johnnie Walker!"

"But Savita-*di*, all men are drunkards," Kuntal said, recalling one of Parvati's dire warnings about men, never mind that Cook Kanj was a teetotaler.

"*Bas!*" Savita cried, flinging the exquisite gold and diamond band from her finger, "I'm finished with him!"

♦ ◊ ❖

The ghost gracefully unfurled herself along a line of jute in the boys' room and hung upside-down, hair swaying beneath her, as she assessed her work. The room was a mess. Wet clothes torn from the clothesline now plastered the edges of the room, the floor and furniture glistened from the recent ceiling downpour, Tufan's bed filled the room with a sickly aroma. The ghost had not meant to take things so far that night, to reveal herself so soon. She would not have done so but for Pinky.

Pinky had pointed to her in accusation, revealed her presence to the rest of the family, before she was ready. The ghost shifted on the empty clothesline, drawing herself to the top of the armoire where a puddle of dusty water had collected, and reflected upon their fragile alliance. Everything had changed the moment Pinky ran out of the bathroom, refusing to see what the ghost had waited an eternity to reveal: the end of the reel, the last moments of the baby's life, the truth of her death. Abandoned in the bathroom, the ghost had made an abrupt decision: to forge ahead on her own. And then when Pinky had returned from Mahabaleshwar changed as if she had reestablished herself firmly on the side of the living, when she had said *I can't believe you*, the ghost was certain that she had made the right decision.

♦ ◊ ❖

Just outside the bungalow and wondering at all the commotion inside, Gulu stood at attention at the green gates and sucked on a *bidi* as if the inhaled smoke could somehow keep him warm as he waited for the Ambassador's return. Earlier than expected, his ears picked up the purr of the car's engine over the drone of the rain. Quickly, he swung open the gates. The headlights bore down on him for a freakish instant before the car came to a sliding stop in a spray of water. Soaking wet, Gulu opened the door, taking care to keep Jaginder under the umbrella as he walked him to the verandah.

"Oi, Gulu," Jaginder said jovially, "what to do? Responsibilities brought me home early tonight." It had not been obligations that had caused Jaginder to turn back on his way to Rosie's *adda* in the late hours of the night, satiating himself instead with a bottle tucked into the Ambassador's trunk, but a lingering sense of dread. He had abandoned his wife that night just as he did after their daughter died.

"Yes, Sahib," Gulu replied, steering the wobbling Jaginder by his elbow.

"I'm telling you, it's not easy having such responsibilities."

"I must take care of the car, Sahib," Gulu said, wiping his face with a damp cloth, before heading back into the downpour.

Jaginder grunted, remembering with sudden arousal how Savita had seduced him just the day before. Perhaps, he hoped, she would be better and willing again tonight. *And so what,* he thought generously, *if a little milk comes out, too.* Feeling oddly parched, Jaginder sauntered through the door and froze. "What's going on?"

Maji, Nimish, Parvati, Kanj, and Pinky sat in silence.

Is she dead? He pictured Savita prone in a spreading puddle of milk, panic beginning to work its way into his curly chest hair. He popped open the top two buttons on his kurta and began to rub vigorously.

"Where have you been, Papa?" Nimish confronted him, abandoning his usual caution.

"How dare you talk to me in that tone," Jaginder roared back, assessing his newest adversary. *My own bloody son, well, well. Finally, becoming a bloody man.* If he were not so drunk, he might have even patted Nimish on the back.

"Parvati, Kanj—" Maji began, moving her hand with a slight side-to-side motion. Kanj, getting the message, hastily stood up to leave. Parvati, however, took her own sweet time, watching the family drama as if it she had paid good money to see it.

"Where's Savita?" Jaginder asked, his face red with the effort of containing his emotions.

"Asleep. Exhausted."

He let out an audible sigh.

"What do you care about her?" Nimish shouted. "You're never here when we need you!"

"How dare—" Jaginder thundered. *Damn.* He had let his guard down too soon; he had no suitable retort ready. He was not going to let himself be shown up, however, not by his too-smart-for-his-own-good son. Leaping forward, he pounced upon Nimish.

But Nimish was too quick and Jaginder's momentum landed him on the sofa. *Damn. Damn. Damn.*

"Stop, both of you!" Maji ordered. Nimish abruptly sat, jaws feverishly clenching and unclenching in his slender face.

The ceiling suddenly sprung a new leak; a spattering of rainwater fell to the floor. Pinky sat on the sofa, watching Nimish with awe. Tufan sat nearby, jealous of his brother's daring.

"Jaginder, you're my oldest child, my only son. Your father and I have given you everything," Maji said, briefly engulfed by a torrent of longing for her dead husband. "And this is how you behave?"

"Ma!"

"You've been utterly irresponsible to your family and have shamed your father's name."

Jaginder's mouth worked furiously to form words that tauntingly eluded his grasp. If only he had not decided to finish off the bottle of Johnnie Walker. If only he had stopped when his head was pleasantly buzzing. Maji raised her hand to prevent him from embarrassing himself further. She glanced at Nimish, realizing that he, more than any other Mittal heir, embodied Omanandlal's unshakable sense of duty towards his family.

"Nimish," she said in her low, gravely voice. "It's time for you to step up."

"What!" Both Jaginder and Nimish were equally distressed by the news.

"Quiet!" Maji ordered. She reached back to her uncoiled hair and tied it into a hard knot. "I realized tonight that some changes have to be made. Changes that should have been made a long time ago." She sighed. "I have been too indulgent. I let things go too far."

"But—but," Nimish stammered, seeing his very life fading away into the brainless hell of managing his family's shipbreaking enterprise.

"I won't take this!" Jaginder bellowed. *So they bloody planned this,* he thought, feeling as if he had been dropped into a game of chess. *Nimish is a crafty son of a bitch after all.* Cracking his neck, a vague and badly thought-out plan took shape in his head.

"Don't you think that cunning Laloo finds your absences an unexpected windfall, eh?" Maji reasoned. "You've spread out the business too much and like a rat, he will find the holes."

"And you think Nimish will know what to do?" Jaginder bared his teeth and laughed.

Nimish felt the hot acid of rage rise up in him. He wanted nothing to do with his father's business. Yet the words seared him. "Me? What about you! Stealing away to drink as if we all don't know the sickening truth." *There*, it had been said, *the thing that was killing them all.* He was done pretending. Checkmate.

Pinky gasped. Tufan cheered. If his father was going down, he reasoned, better to cozy up to his brother.

"Get out of my house!" Jaginder ordered, spit foaming in the corners of his mouth as he landed a hard slap on Nimish's face.

Nimish reeled, his spectacles flew across the room. Dark bursts of red instantly bloomed on his pale cheek.

"It's true! It's true! I've seen you leave in the middle of the night!" Pinky yelled, facing off with her uncle. "I've seen you!"

"You!" Jaginder's fingers curled into a fist as he registered Pinky's outburst. "You ungrateful little —"

"*You* leave right now," Maji boomed, glaring at Jaginder.

Fighting the violent urge to leap at his mother and—*bloody hell*—wring Nimish and Pinky's necks, too, Jaginder slammed the door on his way out. "Gulu!" he barked into the rain, "Get me the Ambassador *fut-a-fut!*"

Gulu was in the garage, tenderly nursing the waterlogged Ambassador to health: drying off the seats with soft rags, picking out bits of leaves and grit that had lodged under the windshield and in the crevices of the dickey, checking the oil levels, and muttering words of comfort.

"Gulu!" Jaginder strode into the garage. "Are you bloody deaf?"

"Sahib?" Gulu took a step in front of the car as if to protect it from Jaginder's wrath.

"I'm taking the car out," Jaginder bellowed impatiently. "Go open the gates."

"But Sahib, I haven't dried the engine yet."

Jaginder plopped himself into the driver's seat and revved the motor threateningly. Gulu raced outside, just ahead of the car to open the gates.

The Ambassador roared away.

∇ ☆ ✤

In the other converted garage in the back of the bungalow, Cook Kanj held Parvati tightly. "Was there really a ghost?"

"There's always been something, something in the bathroom."

"Why didn't you say?"

"We weren't allowed to speak of such things. Savita grew afraid after the baby died and had the door bolted at night. Maji initially disallowed it but Savita refused to sleep at home and took the boys to the Taj Hotel until Maji agreed. And we learned to live with the strange noises in the pipes. Nothing ever happened before."

"Until now," Kanj said.

"Until now," Parvati said, "thirteen years later. A boundary was violated."

"We should leave before it's too late."

"Are you a man or boy?"

"But other strange things are happening. Haven't you noticed that my cooking is watery?"

"Of course I've noticed."

"You have?" Kanj's eyes grew wide. "Maji will sack me. Better to leave first."

Parvati clicked her tongue. "Ghost or no ghost, I'm not leaving."

"We can't live like this!"

"I'm not leaving," Parvati furled her eyebrows. "I told you, *nah*, my parents came to me as ghosts. Caused trouble. Flung me off my mat at night. I wasn't afraid then. I'm not afraid now."

"But my cooking."

"There's too much going on for anyone to notice."

Kanj looked downcast.

"Hey, hey," Parvati teasingly grabbed him by his chin. "Have *you* noticed that my cycle is late?"

"Late?" Kanj struggled to make sense of this. "It's never late, is it?"

"Never before."

And with that, Parvati pulled her husband under the cotton *rajai* and turned off the light.

In the sitting area, Maji's chest continued to heave after Jaginder's departure. *Oh Omanandlal,* she silently beseeched her dead husband, *how I wish you were here to rein in your son.* "*Chalo,* Pinky, come sleep in my bed," she finally said out loud. "Tufan, come from behind the door and help your brother get the extra *rojai* from my room. You can tuck yourselves up in the sofa for the night."

"I can't sleep!" Nimish declared. His cheeks were flushed, his newly bent spectacles smudged with too many emotions.

"You must try."

"But Papa?" Tufan squeaked from the doorway. Had Maji thrown out his father for good?

"Don't say your father's name in front of me," Maji ordered, growing angry. "Nimish will take care of the business. I will make the necessary arrangements tomorrow."

Nimish was overcome by a torrent of despair. *I can't let this happen. I won't let this happen.*

Tufan ran back and forth, ferreting out pillows and comforters, glad for the distraction.

Pinky helped Maji to her bed and sat down next to her. "Do you believe me now?"

Maji rested a warm palm against Pinky's face. But there were so many things crowding inside her head that she couldn't bring herself to answer.

It was after midnight when Jaginder made his way back to Bandra. Traffic was light, but as he passed the Mahalakshmi Temple near Breach Candy, he found his car struggling through a flooded corridor, where water levels rose dangerously above the car wheels. The Ambassador abruptly stalled. Cursing, Jaginder jumped out, one hand on the steering wheel, the other hand and shoulder against the doorframe, pushing the car off the road as best he could as he waded through the water. Three soaking-wet street urchins, ranging in age from six to ten, appeared from behind a shanty to push from the rear.

"*Jao*—go away!" Jaginder roared at them.

But feigning deafness, they pushed even harder.

"Hey, did your in-laws give you that car?" jeered a passing driver, tossing out a hackneyed insult, after rolling down his window and sticking his head full into the rain for effect. The street urchins hooted gleefully. A whole chorus of passing drivers joined in, alternately dispensing advice and making similar comments to pass the time. Some even ventured out of their cars, engines still running, to huddle around a moist pack of Wills Navy Cut cigarettes, pulling hard to get smoke into their lungs.

An enterprising vendor holding a wide, black umbrella and a basket of *channa* around his neck, appeared seemingly from thin air. A small, earthen pot beneath the basket burned wood, emitting white smoke that cloaked the vendor's face in a soft glow while giving the rain a distinctly woody smell that brought out even the most latent appetites. "*Channa jor garam!*" he called out, offering the spicy chickpeas in long, narrow cones of old newspaper. Only twenty-five *paisa* for a cone. The men bought a round, some disappearing to their cars momentarily to inch them forward in the street. The street urchins, sensing that they might not get paid for their work, became restless; the ten-year old grew threatening. Jaginder purchased cones for them and sent them on their way.

"Hey *vechi nakh*! Sell it off!" yelled a driver whose car crawled past the scene as he pointed at the stalled Ambassador.

"*Sala tu tari mai ne vechi nakh!* You bloody well sell off your mother!" retorted Jaginder. A chorus of boos and cheers resounded from passing motorists, lifting spirits all around. "What to do?" he asked the crowd, gesturing at his car.

The men yelled out suggestions, several graphically sexual and most entirely useless. And then, remembering waiting obligations, they dashed off to their cars after a last long drag on their cigarettes. One man, dressed in a tight shirt with a large collar and polyester pants, chewed his cigarette back and forth between his teeth. Slowly, he spat on the ground. "*Arré*, open the *bhenchod* hood."

Jaginder scowled before obediently opening the sister-fucking hood.

"I'm knowing of a mechanic," the man claimed while spitting a stream of red *paan* juice into a puddle. "Very good one, only two minutes nearby."

"Go then," Jaginder said, giving his reluctant assent, knowing that he had no other choice.

The man reappeared a half hour later. By then, a new crowd huddled over the Ambassador's soggy engine, peering in with the intensity of somebody watching *Kanoon* or some other blockbuster movie. The so-called mechanic, an impossibly thin man with protruding cheekbones, arrived with a rusted wrench and a stick, the end of which was alight with burning, oily rags. Hovering dangerously close to the petrol engine with his fireball, he expertly dried up all the electrical points. Jaginder jumped inside the car to try the engine. The men moved back as the Ambassador lurched violently and then hissed to a dead silence. The car would have to be towed.

The mechanic shrugged his shoulders, banging the engine with his wrench for good measure. Disappointed that the show was over so soon, the men reluctantly returned to their cars and their solitary lives. The mood grew dark. Another motorist jeered. The mechanic waved his torch around threateningly. Afraid that he might actually set his car on fire, Jaginder pulled several bills from his wallet. The first man spat thunderously onto the ground. Jaginder pulled out another ten and, with that, the two men vanished.

He was stranded.

❦ ❦ ❦

Gulu awoke with a start. Heart pounding, he gazed at the Cherry Blossom shoe polish poster hanging near his cot until he felt steady. The two kittens stared back at him forlornly, feet clad in shiny black boots. "*Tum bhee*—you too?" Gulu asked with forced lightness, fondly tapping their paper noses. He sat up, vigorously rubbing his face until it stung. Something was not right. His first thought was of Chinni, the prostitute on Falkland Road whom he visited on his off-days twice a month. They had a tenuous relationship, sometimes bordering on affectionate.

The last time Gulu visited, however, Chinni had pulled away from him. "I saw him! I saw him!" she had fumed, pressing her hands to her eyes.

"Who?" Gulu had asked roughly, the frantic bulge in his *dhoti* growing impatient.

"My long-lost son," Chinni had raged, ignoring both him and the bulge. "That *bhenchod* uncle of his brought him here, just a young boy he is. I will kill the bastard uncle the next time he comes." As if to prove her point, she had pulled out a nine-inch Rampuri knife from beneath her cot.

Had Chinni gone and done something foolish? Gulu wondered, feeling as if the garage walls were closing in on him. He jumped up, grabbed his tattered umbrella, and made his way to the front verandah. Seating himself on a stool, he strained his eyes for the Ambassador's headlights, deciding to sneak out after Jaginder's return, to check in on Chinni and make sure everything was okay. He ought to buy her another trinket, some colored glass bangles perhaps, the next time he visited.

An hour passed, maybe more, before Gulu heard the sound of an engine on the road. Still half-asleep against the wall, he made his way to the green gate, undoing the lock and chain. The gate swung open with a reluctant groan, piercing the rain's rhythmic drumming like a wounded dog. Wiping his eyes, he peered out onto the street. A faint light was visible at the end of the road. He began to feel relieved, almost elated. He locked the other gate and, pushing it open, took his position at the entrance—standing tall, despite the sparse protection of his umbrella, to welcome back his beloved car.

He waited. And then waited until he could bear it no longer. Peering out into the rain, he looked expectantly down the road. The light was still there, just beyond the edges of his visibility. He took a tentative step out onto the street, squinting his eyes and straining his ears to hear past the drumming of the rains on the hard ground.

"Jaginder Sahib?" he called out into the night.

A darkened figure appeared in front of the light and began to move towards the bungalow.

Even in the blackness, Gulu noticed two things:

The body was too slender to be Jaginder's.

And, it moved strangely unencumbered by the deluge.

Feeling frightened now, he closed one gate, firmly pressing its anchor into the ground. The figure seemed to stop as if registering the sound. And then it began to move faster, almost as if it were floating, the faint glow behind it casting eerie shadows along the road's rough edges. Gulu threw his umbrella down and pulled at the second gate. It was stuck. Water lashed his face with such force that he could barely see his hands shaking with feverish intensity right in front of his eyes. Thunder roared overhead, followed by an even more terrible noise. A low howl raced down the street, hitting his ears with an unearthly sound.

Throwing the full weight of his body against the gate, Gulu felt it suddenly give way and close with a fierce slam. The noise was matched only by another scream, that coming from his own lips, as his finger was caught against the metal and severed. As warm liquid gushed down his hand, the chain clanged to the ground. With his good hand he blindly groped the flooded concrete while his body continued to press against the gate. A rush of water carried his finger under the metal doorway and onto the street where it swirled frantically into an overflowing drain. Pressing his wounded hand against his armpit, he desperately wiped at his eyes, spotting the chain just beyond reach. Abandoning the gate for a split second, he lunged at the links as if for a lifeboat in a flood.

Turing around, he saw that he was too late. The gate had swung open. And in the split second of lightning that followed, he saw the flash of a flaming red sari *palloo*, a glint of metal, a beckoning of slender arms. A ghostly laugh from darkened lips.

"Avni!" he cried out as the chain once again slipped from his grasp and he fell, face forward, against the hard, wet earth.

PUDDLE OF
PINK GUM BOOTS

Lying next to her grandmother, Pinky had not been able to sleep, fearful of what the ghost might do next and searching her mind for a logical explanation for her drowning. *Was the ayah crazy? Is that what the ghost was trying to tell me?* Deciding to find the ghost after Maji's breathing slowed, Pinky halfheartedly listened to Gulu's movements outside, the moan of the opening gates, his voice calling out. And then came the terrifying scream followed immediately by racing footsteps.

"What! What!" Maji snapped awake as Pinky heaved her out of bed.

They watched the action from the verandah.

Cook Kanj rushed toward the front gate.

"He's fallen!" Nimish yelled out, having reached him first.

"Who's there?" Parvati called out to the darkness, retrieving the tattered umbrella from the driveway. A rusted edge of metal glinted in the moonlight, catching her eye. Pushing back curling ivy and jasmine blooms, she caught sight of a deteriorating brass plate inscribed with the words The Jungle and Christened in 1825. And just below that, a trail of perfectly formed footprints shimmered clearly on the street, despite the rushing water. Parvati leaned forward for a closer inspection, noticing six distinctive toes on the left footprint. She gasped, knowing without a doubt who had been responsible for Gulu's accident. All at once, as if they had been a mirage, the footprints vanished.

"Parvati!" Kanj called out, seeing his wife squatting by the gate, hand over her mouth. "*Tum theek ho?*"

Parvati swiftly stood and nodded, rushing away from the gate while glancing back at the thick foliage as if trying to detect something within the dripping leaves and tightly curled blooms. Only after she had reached the verandah, under the dim yellow bulb flickering hesitantly, did she turn her attention to Gulu. And then she let out a blood-curdling scream.

"His finger!" Nimish yelled, noticing the blood.

"Bring him inside!" Maji ordered as she called Parvati to obtain fresh towels, gauze, and her personal supply of aspirin. Cook Kanj ran to the kitchen, returning with a steel cup of turmeric paste, which he liberally applied to Gulu's stub as an antiseptic, and a cup of *nimbu-pani* which he poured into his gaping mouth. Gulu sputtered, coming to consciousness. "Outside," he moaned, trying to point with an intact finger.

"Where is he? Where is he?" Savita raced into the room, mistaking Gulu's comment as a reference to her returning husband. Peering out the window, she cursed at Jaginder and wildly waved her arms until Kuntal gently led her to a seat and began to massage her shoulders.

"The gate," Gulu moaned again.

"We have to leave!" Savita wailed, milk dripping down her blouse, making her feel dizzy, weak. "Get out before it's too late! Nimi, get my wrap and purse!"

"Mummy!"

"Do it!"

Nimish left the room. Dheer, fast asleep on the sofa was finally awakend by his stomach. Making no attempt to stifle a mammoth yawn, he stretched and plopped down next to Tufan who was huddled under a sheet.

"He must have stumbled in the rain," Maji declared, "and caught his finger."

"Gulu didn't slip." Parvati stood with her arms crossed. She had

had enough of the family's covering-up, especially now that the past had returned, leaving her damp footprints outside the gate like an evil omen. Glancing at ashen-faced Kuntal, however, Parvati bit her lip and decided against revealing the truth. *Kuntal mustn't know who came to the gate, not after what happened back then.* She recalled the purification ceremony they had done after the baby's death, blocking the ayah's spirit—alive or dead—from ever entering the bungalow. *We're safe from her as long as we stay in here.*

"Then what?" Nimish asked. "What happened out there?"

"It was the ghost," Parvati lied.

"Ghost?" Savita sat up.

"Ghost?" Tufan echoed, jumping off the couch as if he had just been bitten by one and dashed to his mother.

"Outside?" Pinky exclaimed incredulously. *Why? Why after all these years would she have left the bungalow?*

Maji shot Parvati a withering glare, "Bring some milk for the children."

Parvati reluctantly uncrossed her arms before walking off to the kitchen.

"Ghost?" Savita demanded. Suddenly it dawned on her that what lay behind that door was even more terrible than what she had thought all these years. "Dheer! Nimish!" she cried out. "Come here!"

Dheer sidled next to his mother. Nimish returned with her wrap and purse.

"Check the bathroom door!" she yelled at Parvati. "Make sure it's bolted!"

Pinky grabbed her pink gum boots and slipped out the door unnoticed in all the commotion.

"Was it the ghost?" Cook Kanj prodded Gulu as he crouched over him.

"A ghost?" Gulu looked confused. His face was pale. The cloth wrapped around his hand had sprouted red clusters of fresh blood.

"It's unbolted," Parvati said, returning with a tray of Horlick's Malted Milk.

"Biscuits too?" Dheer managed through his terror.

"She's already out," Parvati said. "I know it."

"She?" Savita gasped. Was it possible she had been wrong, that the presence in the bathroom was not the evil spirit that had killed her child but—

"Parvati!" Maji warned.

"No, tell me!"

"Pinky saw something," Maji said with a dismissive wave of her hand. "She's only a child."

Savita grasped at Parvati's sari *palloo*, "Who?"

"Your baby!"

Savita shrieked with such intensity that Dheer choked on his milk. Thick streams of bubbly liquid shot from his nostrils.

"Stop this nonsense!" Maji ordered.

"Where is she?" Savita shouted as she stood up, eyes wild. "Where is she? I want to see my little Chakori!"

"Mummy!" Tufan squeaked as Nimish forced his mother to sit down on the sofa.

"Savita, get a hold of yourself," Maji ordered. "She's dead."

"She's come back to me! I knew she would!"

"Mummy, you're not making sense," Nimish cried out, draping the wrap around her shoulders.

"Get a hold of yourself," Maji warned. "For your sons' sake."

"We're staying," Savita announced to Nimish, shrugging off the wrap. "My baby's come back to me."

Cook Kanj shook Gulu again, this time more vigorously. "Was it the ghost?"

Gulu's mind grasped to make sense of Kanj's question, of what had happened that night. In the fuzziness of his brain, he knew two things for certain:

Avni, the dead baby's ayah had returned.

And, he was not going to tell a soul.

"No," he said out loud. "I only . . . slipped."

"What did I tell you?" Maji boomed, exhaling loudly.

"Where's Pinky?" Dheer abruptly asked.

Everyone fell quiet and looked around.

"Pinky!" Maji yelled, straining forward on the dais. "Pinky!"

There was no response. Kuntal and Nimish were dispatched to check the east hallway but returned shaking their heads. Parvati and Kanj went together to check the rest of the bungalow and were equally unsuccessful. Maji's gigantic bosom began to heave as she lifted herself from the dais. "Pinky!" she called again.

"Maybe she went outside?" Nimish suggested.

"Outside?" Gulu asked, suddenly recalling his terrifying experience by the gates.

"Oh God no!" Parvati yelled, rushing to the door.

"Where is she?" Maji shouted, propelling herself at the front door, cane in hand. "Pinky! Come inside! Kanj, find her!"

Kanj took a tentative step onto the verandah.

"Pinky!" Maji frantically rushed to the gate, plowing him down in the process. Gulu and Parvati and Nimish were at her side, all four of them pushing open the gate.

The chain lay sunken in a pool of water.

Two pink gum boots lay overturned in a puddle just beyond.

But Pinky was nowhere to be seen.

CAPTIVE ON A
RAINY NIGHT

The Ambassador locked and abandoned on the side of the road, Jaginder hitched a ride through the stormy twilight, past Cumbala Hill, past his home in Malabar Hill, and all the way south to Churchgate Station on Churchgate Street. Just opposite the station was a small tea shop, the Asiatica, which contained a sprinkling of old men hunched over *The Evening News*; a flock of students clutching copies of Gorky, Chekhov, and Turgenev; and a scattering of newly married couples cautiously entering and exiting the closed-off, private cubicles known discreetly as "family rooms." Even at this time of the night, the Asiatica thrived with a friendly, relaxed energy.

Jaginder slowly walked past the tall marble-slab counter behind which the Irani owner, dressed in a thin white muslin pajama, sleeveless kurta top with a triangular neck, and the Zoroastrian *sadra* holy rope tied around his waist, perched on a high stool as he completed a transaction.

"One *peela hathi*, one yellow elephant," a young man said, pointing to a box of cigarettes labeled Honeydew with a picture of an elephant emblazoned on its front.

The owner reached over to extract the ten-pack and then, pulling out a drawer from under the slab, placed the change in one of six cup-like depressions—each containing a different denomination, from the tiny two-*paisa* coins to the large one rupee ones with King George's head in profile on the side.

Jaginder stood behind the counter, eyeing the cigarette display: the expensive Gold Flake and Capstan lay nestled together on the top, supported by rows of the cheaper Charminar, Honeydew, Scissors, Cavenders, Panamas. Cartons of Passing Show, sporting a dastardly toff in a top hat, lined the bottom. "One Gold Flake," he said, eyeing the faded poster behind the counter boasting *Will's Gold Flake: The Cigarette that made smoking popular.*

The owner extracted a single cigarette from a tin of fifty and handed it to him.

Jaginder found a vacant, round marble table and took a seat on a thin wooden chair that had *Made In Czechoslovakia* imprinted on its high back. Lighting his cigarette, he briefly wondered who would go to the trouble of importing these rickety chairs, of all things, from such a faraway Communist country. His gaze fell on one of the long vertical mirrors that were set into the wood-paneled wall. The top of the mirror declared: SORRY NO FIGHTING, NO SITTING LONG, NO TALKING LOUD, NO COMBING, NO SPITTING, NO DISCUSSING GAMBLING, NO WATER TO OUTSIDERS, NO ADDRESS INQUIRY, NO LEG ON CHAIR. Below that, the entire menu was scrawled in wet chalk: Tea – 10p, Coffee – 20p, Khari – 10p, Pastry – 25p, Brun maska – 50p, Omelet (single) – 50p, Omelet (double) – 90p, Coca-Cola, Gold Spot, Mangola, Ice Cream Soda, Soda – 25p.

"*Ek brun-maska aur* chai, *malai mar ke,*" Jaginder called out, ordering one of the popular Irani buttered buns that Rustom, the middle-aged owner, made on the premises until recently when his wife passed away. Now the buns and several other savories were delivered in a tin box by a cycler from Maqdoomia, a small entrepreneurial bakery located in Dharavi, Bombay's largest slum. Jaginder leafed through a scattering of newspapers that had been left on his table: the English-language *Times of India*, *Indian Express*, and *Free Press Journal*, the Parsi *Jaam-e-Jamshed*, and the *Blitz*, a weekly Communist tabloid. Inside the *Blitz*, his attention was captured by a the headline, "Gold

Bar Found After Sixteen Years!" *The American S. S. Fort Stikine explosion in the Bombay Docks in 1944,* the article stated, *is remembered not only by its devastation but for an ongoing mystery about one missing 28-pound bar of solid gold. The explosion created a wave so immense that it deposited the stern of a 4000-pound ship on the roof of a shed. The docks burnt away in an inferno. But the gold bar was never found. Oceanography experts stated that it had been carried away by an underwater current. Just yesterday, however, a man was caught trying to smuggle a gold bar with similar markings out of the country.*

Jaginder set the newspaper down and sighed, brooding on his own misfortunes. *How had things deteriorated so far?* He thought about Savita, her pained voice ordering him to leave her alone. His own son had humiliated him. Unbelievably, his mother had thrown him out of his own home. Jaginder gritted his teeth. He couldn't begin to fathom how to regain Savita's affections or his son's respect or his mother's good graces. The family business, however, was something that was still within his reach. He just required the proper legal documents to ensure that his mother could no longer interfere.

Jaginder recalled that his father, Omanandlal, was a respected elder of their community until the day he died. Men used to come from far and wide to seek his advice on business matters, and sometimes ladies accompanied them to discreetly inquire of Maji about a domestic matter. Jaginder had inherited this vast empire, the money and connections, the respect and awe. And he had carefully cultivated it so that he could pass it on to his own sons. Everything had gone according to plan. And then his daughter had died.

Rustom arrived with Jaginder's order: tea with a dash of cream made in a copper samovar and a hard, buttered bun.

"Caught in the rain?" he inquired, his friendly tone belying the vacant look on his face. Gone were his best days, when he and his fellow countrymen would gather over tea to reminisce about life in their old town of Fars. Now every bloody Irani owned his own tea shop. Gone also were the days when he served tea in pink cups for Christians and fellow Zoroastrians, flower-patterned ones for Hindus, and white ones for Muslims. Mahatma Gandhi had seen to that. Now Rustom was simply marking time; all his former friends seemed to be more innovative than himself. One sold four-tiered wedding cakes, another had managed to get his shop used as the backdrop for a popular Hindi film.

"Car stalled nearby," Jaginder replied.

"Ah," Rustom clucked sympathetically. His pajama bottoms had rolled under his plump belly, creasing at the crotch so that they lifted above his ankles, revealing hairy feet clad in *chappals.* "Bad time to drive, better to walk."

"I live too far to walk." Jaginder replied, fingering the bun.

"Ah," Rustom clucked again. "I'll on the fan—dry you up in no time."

As he walked away, he pointed upwards to the ceiling where a fan, a relic of the British days, with large ventilated armatures and extra long blades hung from a long, metal tube. The fan began to spin making a craak-craak-craak sound. Slowly it gathered speed until it sounded more like a helicopter, the loud whup-whup-whup threatening to blow away the newspapers with every rotation.

Jaginder began to shiver and waved his hand to get Rustom's attention. Behind the owner's head was a framed picture illuminated by a red bulb of a bearded Zoroaster, head wrapped in a white turban, gaze lifted heavenward in a striking resemblance to Jesus Christ. Above this was a picture of Mohammed Reza Pahlavi, the Shah of Iran, regal in his uniform decorated with an array of shiny medals, red ribbon across his chest, adorned by a sheath and sword, and cummerbund. His silver and black hair was neatly oiled behind his ears, his face occupied by tight, hard eyes and bushy eyebrows.

Rustom caught Jaginder's wave and gave him a large smile, his thin moustache briefly disappearing under his bulbous nose. "Dry already?" he called out to Jaginder, shutting off the switch.

"Yes, thank you," Jaginder answered back, pulling his coat tightly around his chest.

He brought the tea to his lips. *Tomorrow bloody morning,* he thought, *I will take control.* Even as he thought this, he knew that doing so was unforgivable, an irrevocable treachery. It was the worst sin, to betray one's mother. Yet, he couldn't simply acquiesce to Maji's wishes, step down from the helm of his company, let his position be usurped by a teenage son. He was trapped, like a wild animal in a hunter's merciless grip.

As the hot liquid seared his throat, he knew that he had no choice but to fight.

* * *

Earlier that evening back at the bungalow in chaos, Pinky had noiselessly made her way out to the green gates in search of the ghost. Unexpectedly, a young woman had stepped forward into the faint pool of light cast from the front verandah.

"Lovely *didi?*" Pinky edged back towards the bungalow, a chill working its way up her spine. "What's wrong?"

"Come!" Lovely beckoned, almost frantically.

Pinky stared at Lovely. She was dressed not in a cotton sleeping *salvar kameez* as she should have been at this time of the night but in a chiffon one, now soaked and badly ripped. Her silk *dupatta* clung tightly to her chest, accentuating the outline of her full breasts, the golden bird nestled invitingly in between them. Her thick tresses, usually tied back, cascaded down her back like a torn shawl; her normally bare lips were smudged with gloss, the color smeared across her chin like a lesion. A canvas satchel hung heavily at her hips. But something else struck Pinky as strange. Her voice was gritty and strained.

"Are you unwell *didi?*" Pinky asked. "Is everything okay with Auntie?"

"Please come!" Lovely urged, stepping toward Pinky, her eyes staring yet eerily unfocused.

A stray street dog sniffing the gutters for garbage backed away from her, growling with teeth bared.

"Come inside," Pinky said, starting to turn back to the bungalow.

"No," Lovely said as she took Pinky's arm and pulled her onto a red motorbike that was idling in the nearby darkness. "There's no turning back now."

Pinky's pink gum boots pitched into the air as Lovely gunned the throttle, landing in a puddle by the green gates. Lovely plunged the bike down the steep hill, away from the verandah's light glowing forlornly in a fog of flying insects, and towards the ocean.

"*Didi!*" Pinky shouted, clutching at Lovely's waist. "Where are we going?"

"To freedom," Lovely replied, as their homes on Malabar Hill dissolved into a glittering canopy reaching out as if to touch the stormy sky.

* * *

The door at the Asiatica flew open and a skinny fellow skidded in looking like a Spanish pirate.

"Inesh!" came a roar from the table of students, glad for the distraction from their tedious discussion of Russian authors.

"It's gone! She's gone!" the fellow called out to them, glancing at the door behind him as if he were being chased. Long hair tied into a ponytail, gold hoops dangling from both ears, flowing white shirt sailing on his thin chest, and low-waisted drainpipe trousers clinging to his legs, Inesh gripped one of the rickety chairs and spun it around before taking his seat. Placing his feet clad in pointed black shoes with Cuban heels on the edges of the chair, he leaned into the table and unsteadily lit a cigarette.

"What now Inesh?" joked one of his friends who sported an American-style crew cut. "Trying to *patao* another girl?"

"Hope he had better luck this time," said a fat-looking boy, cheeks stippled with pastry crust. "The last time you had to jump out the second-story window or risk being caught."

"That's nothing unusual," teased the crew-cut boy. "Inesh's always diving out the canteen window whenever Dean Patel comes to see who's bunking class!"

The table roared with laughter.

"Fools." Inesh blew a cloud of smoke directly at the fat boy. "I've been had."

"Again?" inquired Crew Cut. "Who's it this time?"

Inesh hesitated.

"Come on, *yaar*," Crew Cut teased him, "is it that Lovely girl?"

Inesh hung his head.

At the next table over, Jaginder ears perked up.

"Isn't she the beauty you brought here after she saved your life?" asked a third fellow, tight shirt unbuttoned halfway, revealing the barest of chests and a gold chain.

"Yes," Inesh said, thinking of his pride and joy, his ruby red Triumph

500cc that powered past the Rajdoot, Jawa, and Royal Enfield motor-bikes phut-phutting in his wake. He had acquired his bike by a stroke of fortune, buying it for 6,400 rupees off an airline pilot from England.

Only a week earlier Inesh, driving his Triumph through the rains, screeched to a halt when a frantic voice called for him to stop. And that is when he saw it, a downed electrical wire just inches from his throat. He turned to the voice that had saved his life, found it belonged to a goddess in gold, and could think of nothing to say but *Can I buy you tea?*

Lovely had refused, walking towards to SNDT Women's University campus without making eye contact, but he persisted.

Come, he had cajoled, *I'll take you on my motorbike, the only one of its kind in all of Bombay. I'll even teach you how to ride it!*

He saw her gaze fall upon his shiny bike. Tentatively, she reached out to stroke it. And then, eyes shining with possibility, she climbed up behind him, legs to one side, chastely holding onto his waist with one arm. He had driven to the Asiatica, his heart swelling with pride, while she laughed the whole way, lost in the exhilaration of that moment.

"I went to Malabar Hill tonight but—"

"Lost her to another suitor already, huh?" taunted the fat boy.

Crew Cut stood up and gyrated his hips, belting out the lyrics to the city's first rock-and-roll movie, *Dil Deke Dekho—Surrender Your Heart and See,* oblivious to the Irani owner's glares.

"Yo, Keki!" Rustom finally shouted at a scrawny waiter, and point-ing to his inventory of restrictions above the mirror said, "add NO DANCING to my list!"

"What Rustom *bhai*?" Crew Cut flashed him a look of innocence before sitting down and turning his attention back to his friends.

"No, not another suitor," Inesh said, his voice odd. "At least I don't think so."

"What happened, *yaar*?"

"I was waiting for her outside her bungalow," Inesh answered. "So I began practicing a poem, one of those in the *Gentleman's Guide to Wooing a Lady*. All very romantic, you know."

"Maybe she didn't like your poem," commented Fat Boy.

"She came outside all wild and crazy looking," continued Inesh, stubbing his cigarette out on Fat Boy's plate. "And the next thing I knew I woke up on the ground, both my motorcycle and Lovely gone!"

His friends broke out in resounding rolls of laughter. Fat Boy nearly choked on his hard bun.

Sitting on his stool behind the counter, Rustom felt he had been neglected for long enough. He abruptly shut off the fan above the students' table giving them the message to either order something immediately or leave.

"Rustom *bhai,* why are you offing the fan?" Inesh asked. Jaginder followed his eye to the nearby display of pastries, cakes, biscuits, potato wafers, buns, and *salli*—thin deep fried potato sticks—neatly arranged next to a bowl of Polson's butter.

"Some tea, coffee, ice cream?" Rustom asked, gesturing to the white and blue icebox with *Kwality* scrawled across the top and a grinning Arctic seal lounging just below.

"One strawberry and cashew biscuit," Inesh said forcing a wide smile, "and some chai."

"Chai all around." Crew Cut winked.

The ceiling fan wheezed back to life.

"She took your motorbike?" exclaimed the bare-chested boy.

"Yeah, right," chuckled Fat Boy. "As if a girl would know how to drive it!"

"I think somebody hit me," Inesh said, feeling his face for evidence of a blow. "I don't remember what happened. I looked all around, even climbed inside the gate, but she was gone. And my Triumph, too!"

"Don't worry, no one can hide a motorbike like yours for long." Crew Cut shook his head sympathetically, thumping Inesh on his back. "Best not to go after girls who already have suitors, *yaar.* Nothing but trouble."

"Instead of running away with me, she ran away with my bike!" Inesh cried out.

"Girls these days are too fickle," concluded Fat Boy before emptying an entire tin of Parry's toffees into his mouth.

"Excuse me," Jaginder said, walking over to their table. "By chance do you mean Lovely from Malabar Hill?"

"Yes," Inesh nodded, eying Jaginder with curiosity and suspicion.

"Lovely Lawate?" he asked by way of clarification. He could not possibly imagine his respectable neighbor's daughter riding a motor-bike. Girls simply did not do that.

Inesh nodded again.

"He could have snared any girl because of his bike," Crew Cut added. "It was his bad luck."

"You are lying," Jaginder said threateningly. "I know my neighbor's daughter. I knew her father when he was alive. Have you no shame?"

With that, he stormed out, forcing down the panic rising in his chest. *He's lying. Nothing but a bloody boy trying to impress his friends.* His neighbors, after all, had raised their daughter with the strict pro-tectiveness that he would have imposed upon his own daughter had she lived.

His own daughter.

In Jaginder's mind, his little moon-bird had become an embodi-ment of virtue. If only certain things had been preventable, his life would have unfurled in front of him as intended, like a lush Ori-ental carpet. No surprises, no detours. Just a thick tapestry of days and nights that at the end of his time on earth, he could roll up and proudly claim as his own.

❦ ❧ ❦

To everyone's surprise and relief, Police Inspector Pascal knocked on the bungalow's front door merely fifteen minutes after an urgent phone call was placed to the police station.

Inside, the occupants sat stiffly, fearfully. They had searched the bungalow inside and out. Yet, even as they searched, they knew that Pinky's abandoned boots signaled something sinister.

Pascal shuffled in wearing a long trench coat. He nodded curtly in Maji's direction, wiping his face with a handkerchief.

Kuntal took his black rubber coat and cap as Pascal slipped off his black gum boots and padded towards the couch in turmeric yellow socks. Cook Kanj appeared with a tray of tea and biscuits.

"No, no I'm fine," the inspector said waving away the cook with one hand while helping himself to tea with the other. "So, *kya hua?*"

"My granddaughter's missing." Maji's face was drawn and pale, her hands trembled.

"*Accha.*" Pascal fished in his shirt for a pen, pulling out candy wrappers, cigarettes, and a *paan* which he unceremoniously unwrapped and popped into his mouth. "Name? Age? Occupation?"

"Pinky Mittal. She's only thirteen."

"Have you called your neighbors?" the inspector asked. "Perhaps she wandered next door?"

"In the middle of the night, Inspector?" Savita asked shrilly, thoroughly unimpressed by the burly man who sat in front of her.

"Make the calls," Pascal ordered. "I have a feeling in my gut."

And a few too many free lunches, too, Savita thought cynically.

"I'll call Vimla Auntie," Nimish piped up, departing for the dining area.

"So." Pascal scribbled some notes on his pad. "What were the circumstances of her unfortunate disappearance?"

"Our driver slipped in the rain and cut his finger on the gate," Maji began, her bosom beginning to heave with emotion. "While we were tending to him, Pinky went outside. We didn't notice until . . . until it was too late."

Savita let out a dramatic sob.

"Was there anyone else by the gate?" Pascal asked.

"No," answered Parvati. "I went out when Gulu fell and saw no one."

"And where's this Gulu chap?"

Maji pointed to her driver, eyes closed, slumped against the sofa with his bandaged hand cradled to his chest.

Pascal raised a bristly eyebrow. "And why was he by the gate so late in the night?"

"He was expecting my son to come home," Maji answered.

"*Accha*. Your son. And where might he be?"

"At the office."

"So late at night?"

"Yes."

After a second cup of tea and more questioning, Pascal tucked his pad into his shirt pocket and sighed. "This is all most curious."

"'Curious?'" Savita cried. "That's all you can say?"

Nimish walked back into the room, ashen faced.

"Doesn't look like good news," Pascal inclined his head towards him.

"Lovely," Nimish managed to stammer.

"What is it, *beta?*" Savita turned in her seat to get a better look at her son.

"Did you talk . . . to . . . Vimla Auntie?" Maji asked, distress slicing her question into sharp fragments.

Nimish nodded forlornly. "Auntie is coming over just now with, with Harshal *bhaiya* and Himani *bhabhi.*"

"And Lovely?"

"She's missing!" Nimish cried as his hand involuntarily flew to his chest. *This is all my fault!* he told himself, remembering how Lovely had run from him, from his kiss.

"Lovely's like a sister to him," Savita explained to the inspector.

Vimla stumbled into the bungalow and fell into Maji's arms, wailing. Harshal looked shocked. He hobbled in and painfully lowered himself onto a sofa. A curious, blistering mark had sprouted upon his left cheek.

"Come, come," Maji comforted Vimla. "This is Inspector Pascal, one of Bombay's best."

"Mr. Lawate," Pascal began, looking at Harshal. "What happened?"

"Well," Harshal began, recalling Himani's hot body underneath him, the juicy flesh of her breasts and inner thighs. The night had begun in its usual manner with Harshal delicately rolling the sleeping Himani onto her back and parting her pliant legs. And then, with full erection, he had jolted her awake as he plunged into her body, taking intense pleasure at her startled little gasp. Afterward, while his wife was busy in the bathroom where she always vanished postcoitally for extended periods of time, Harshal had tossed in bed, unable to fall back into a satiated sleep as usual. The air around him felt thick, sticky with desire.

Heaving himself out of bed, he had wandered to his window and saw something that shocked and enraged him.

"Well," Harshal began again, gritting his teeth as he purposely concealed two incidents surrounding Lovely's disappearance:

Nimish and Lovely's tryst under the tamarind tree.

And his own encounter with his sister just afterwards.

"Naturally, we were all sleeping," he said, remembering the feel of his hands around Lovely's silken neck, her muffled cry. "I woke my mother after the phone call and discovered that my sister was missing."

"Was there anything unusual in her room?" Pascal said. "Signs of a forced entry?"

"No," Harshal said, realizing with a panic now that he'd have to get back to her room before his mother and wife. He had to get rid of the blood.

"Sounds like she had a secret rendezvous." Pascal winked.

Nimish sank into the sofa and earnestly wiped his spectacles. *If anything happens to her, I'll never forgive myself.*

"How dare you suggest such things," Vimla said in shock.

"Then why wasn't Lovely in her pajamas in the middle of the night?" Harshal asked, clenching his teeth as if fighting off an invisible pain. His bowels feeling as if they had swollen inside, pressing against his anus with unbelievable force.

Pascal laughed gruffly. "I wouldn't worry, she'll probably show up in an hour or two with flushed cheeks. These things happen when there's no father to enforce discipline. My advice is to find her a suitable boy before her reputation is spoilt."

"My Lovely's a good girl!"

"Don't worry, I will do the needful," Harshal nodded. He felt afraid though. Afraid of what his sister had done, afraid of what she would do if she returned.

"But Pinky," Maji asked, all at once feeling furious at Lovely, "surely Pinky was not involved in *this*."

Vimla loosened her grip on Maji's hand, offended by her insinuation.

"The two disappearances are linked," Pascal said, standing up and brushing biscuit crumbs from his lap. "Please call the station if you have any further information. In the meantime, stay at home. Keep a close eye on the children."

After he left, rain pellets and a fine mist dusted the bungalow's front door where unspoken accusations began to fester, working their way into Maji and Vimla's hearts. A tiny fissure, finer than the wispy strands on a newborn's head, had opened up deep within the layers of their lifelong friendship.

THE CALIGINOUS OCEAN

A n unbearable silence filled the parlor.
      "You stay," Harshal said, slipping his feet back into his wet *chap-pals*. "I'm going back."

"We'll all go back," Vimla said, releasing Maji's hand and leaving without a word to her.

Feeling the helpless eyes of her family on her face, Maji held back tears that gathered like monsoon clouds behind her swollen eyelids. No one wanted to sleep; activity of any kind, anything to occupy their minds, was the only way to bring relief. "Kanj, make the puja *halwa*," she finally said, "and some flatcakes. It's going to be a long night."

Cook Kanj trundled off to the kitchen.

"Parvati, Kuntal, the boys' room needs cleaning."

"What if the ghost's still there?" Kuntal asked.

"Let it make trouble," Parvati said menacingly, and grabbing Kuntal's hand, strutted down the hall.

"I'm coming with you," Savita said to them.

"To clean?" Parvati raised a disbelieving eyebrow.

"To see *her*," Savita huffed.

"Savita, don't," Maji said.

"I'm going to find my little moon-bird," Savita said, "and nobody will stop me."

Nimish stood to walk with her.

"Nimish!" Maji called out. "Leave her be. You and your brothers go get the *gaddhas* from the living room to unroll on the floor. We can all rest here tonight."

Then, taking a deep breath, Maji pinched the fold of skin between her eyebrows. "Gulu, *utho.*"

Gulu groggily lifted himself off his mat where, despite the flurry of activity, he had begun to doze. He suddenly jumped to attention, the loss of blood making him dizzy. "Maji, please forgive me for all this—"

"Tell me," Maji said hopefully, "was there anything more? Anything we didn't tell the inspector?"

"No, I—I slipped while closing the gate."

"That's all?"

"Yes."

"There's something you're not telling me."

"That's all I remember."

"Did you see someone outside the gate?" Maji leaned forward, "Pinky's missing. Do you understand the seriousness of this?"

Gulu's face contracted, uneven teeth bit into his bottom lip. *Oh God,* he thought of the ghostly laugh, the reddened lips, *would she really harm Pinky?*

"Do you understand?"

Gulu felt the heat from Maji's stare, felt his body jerk into place as if being pulled by an invisible string. Maji was his benefactor, the one who had taken him in, given him a second life. Try as he might, he could not lie to her. "I saw . . . something."

"Tell me!" Maji yelled, waving her cane at him.

Shrinking back onto the floor, Gulu recounted the details: the moan of the gate, the shrouded figure in the street.

"Was it Lovely?"

"I don't think so but I didn't see her face."

"Then how do you know it was a woman?"

"I heard her voice."

"What did she say?"

"She beckoned to me," Gulu recalled her slender arms, the flash of her scarf, "but then I fell."

"Don't play games with me," Maji boomed. "Who was she?"

Gulu lifted his face so his eyes met hers. *If only I could see her alone, find her before anyone else, make everything okay.* His finger throbbed, blood pushing at the flimsy cloth bandage, saturating it with every heartbeat.

"Please," he pleaded.

"WHO WAS SHE?"

Tears slid across Gulu's face. He dropped to his knees and covered his face, uttering the name that had not been heard inside the bungalow's walls for over thirteen years.

✿ ✿ ✿

"Freedom?" Pinky shouted, the dampness in her clothes was making her skin pucker in the crevices under her arms and where her underwear's elastic clutched at her bottom. Her thin cotton pajamas had been soaked by the drenching rains. She realized that she was shivering, however, only after they had hit the glittering curve of Marine Drive, its Queen's Necklace of streetlights illuminating the bay's plunging neckline. The Arabian Sea crashed against the shore sending spray forty feet into the air. "What are you talking about?"

Lovely remained silent, her vacant eyes staring straight ahead, her knuckles white against the handlebars.

"Turn back!" Pinky cried out. Silently, she recollected that she had known Lovely almost her whole life. Surely, there was a reason for this madness, a reason why Lovely couldn't tell her more. *Is she running away from home?* Pinky couldn't shake the feeling that something utterly destructive possessed Lovely. She held onto her waist for dear life, straining her eyes at the passing sights, beacons by which she hoped to guide them back home.

They turned onto Churchgate Street, a main boulevard with high-rise commercial buildings in soiled grays and browns topped by equally doleful residential flats. Piles of wet debris cluttered the corners of the sidewalk, paved with little squares of saffron-colored brick which glimmered under the incessant pelting of the rains. A deteriorating wall was covered in peeling movie posters. An advertisement for a nearby undertaker proclaiming WE CAN SEND DEAD BODY ANYWHERE ANYHOW ANYTIME had been hastily pasted over top. Another poster warned "The Cemetries Are Full. A Driver Lived in Haste Died With Speed." And yet another read *Hindi-Chini Bhai-Bhai*, promoting India and China's fraternal relations in celebration of Premier Zhou En Lai's visit to Delhi several months back.

Rains gushed near an overburdened gutter, spraying dirtied water into the air. Across the divider with its black curving separators, Pinky spotted a solitary figure, a man walking quickly in the other direction, head hidden under a black umbrella, and considered calling out to him. *But what would that accomplish?*

Lovely gunned the accelerator and they reached Flora Fountain, Bombay's central hub, named after the Roman goddess of abundance. From there, they continued southward, curving past a black stone statue of King George dubbed Kala Ghoda, the Sir David Sasson Library where Nimish spent much of his time, and the Rhythm House which, because of restrictive copyright laws, did not stock Tony Bennet or Elvis.

The Triumph slowed as they entered Wellington Circle, approaching the fully air-conditioned Regal Cinema, the name crawling boldly along the building's cement edging. The theater was showing *Mughal-e-Azam*, the tragic love story of Prince Salim and the beautiful Anarkali, who was buried alive by the Moghul emperor. Anarkali was played by none other than the famed actress Madhubala, whose magazine photo Pinky had tucked into her teak chest as a proxy for her mother. Now upon an immense movie hoarding, Madhubala's anguished face rose up against a backdrop of a sixteenth-century battle scene—eyes closed, head thrown back, mouth parted in unutterable sorrow.

"Mummy!" Pinky cried out.

When Savita had seen *Mughal-e-Azam* with her friends she had wept for days after. *Fate can be so cruel,* she had lamented, braced against Nimish's shoulders. *How can anyone stand in the way of such love?* The movie was such a phenomenal hit that *Filmfare* ran a story about a taxi driver who had paid to see it over a hundred times. *Can you imagine working so bloody hard to spend your money in such a way?* Jaginder Uncle had commented. The whole family had tittered over such foolishness.

"Stop! Please just stop!" Pinky screamed, pressing herself against Lovely's back and trying to reach up to the handlebars.

"Don't stop me," Lovely warned, easing onto Colaba Causeway, heading directly for the tip of Bombay, passing the Empress on the right, the café where not so long ago Pinky had sat with her cousins and watched the *hijras*. The left side of the street was crammed with shops selling smuggled goods such as Gillette shaving cream and other luxury items, now all closed, barred against looters and the torrential rains. Beyond that, rising out of chilly Bombay Harbour, stood the yellow basalt Gateway of India built in 1911 to signify the enduring nature of British rule. Lovely steered them past the Esplanade, a row of three-story buildings where affluent Parsi families resided, and then beyond the BEST bus depot to Cusrow Baug.

Pinky frantically tried to piece together a plan. *She's running away, she's taking me. As soon she stops the bike, I'll jump off.* They sped by a small petrol pump, veering off the causeway and onto a quiet tree-lined lane edged by a cluster of old buildings with high wood-beamed ceilings. Maji's first cousin Uddhav Uncle lived in the last building called Dar-ul-Khalil, Pinky suddenly remembered with a flash of hope. He was a widower who intermittently rented out the small, six-by-eight-foot cubicle in his flat to docking sailors. Pinky caught a glimpse of the fierce Afghani Pathan who guarded the building at night, his longs legs sticking out of the *kholi* under the wooden staircase where he slept, undisturbed by the rains.

Bhenchod *loan shark*, Uddhav Uncle had called the Afghani, originally from Kabul, his mouth curling in disgust. *When he's not charging impoverished mill workers twenty-five percent monthly interest, he's bartering with the sailors for tins of Dunhills or State Express 555 or for those* bhenchod *Yashica gadgets.*

His type is unpredictable, Maji had declared.

And bloodthirsty, too, Uddhav Uncle added. *The bastard carries a six-inch knife.*

Pinky's heart sank as they cut across Wodehouse Road and ended at the Koli fishing community, situated on a rectangular bay, catercorner to Nariman Point. They were engulfed in the stench of rotting fish. Pinky began to gag, holding her pajama top to her nose as if the flimsy cotton, now completely soaked, could filter out the saturating odor.

Beyond, near the sands, clusters of small homes huddled together to protect themselves from the chilly ocean winds. A sole coconut tree rose up into the darkness.

Lovely stopped the bike and, tightly gripping Pinky's hand, pulled her down to the shore.

"Come," she commanded again in that strange, gritty voice so unlike her own.

"No!" Pinky shouted, taking in the caliginous ocean sprawling to infinity as she pulled from Lovely's hold. "I'm not going anywhere! Not until you tell me what is happened!"

"You're shivering," was Lovely's response. "Here take my *dupatta.*"

"But it's wet," Pinky said, nonetheless reaching for the exquisite silk. As she touched it, she felt an energy pass from Lovely to her, a mystifying heat, a radiance that numbed her resistance. Lovely walked ahead, the *dupatta* tied to her waist, Pinky behind, holding onto it as if for dear life. Despite her terror, she did not want to be left alone in the strange darkness. They walked past a darkened hut on the outskirts of the village, circumvented the village itself, and finally stopped near the jetty where a dilapidated trawler swayed with the current and small wooden canoes lay overturned in the sand.

Lovely pushed a craft into the foaming waters of the Arabian Sea, Pinky climbed in across from her, continuing to clutch at the *dupatta,* allowing it to overwhelm her reason and resolution with its eerie, satiating heat. *Lovely's like a sister,* she told herself. *She won't harm me. She'll take me home afterward.* The rains grew heavier; a heavy fog rose up over the stormy waters. Only Pinky and Lovely's heads bobbed above the surface, like dolphins coming up for air. Stormy waves crashed around them but the small patch of water surrounding the canoe remained strangely calm as if it were welcoming Lovely within it, like a mother opening her arms to a beloved child. The tiniest blush of pink colored the horizon.

From the canoe, Pinky could see a fisherman stepping out of his home. She could just make out his white *tikkona,* a checked bandana-like cloth twisted like a rope and pulled back tightly, and his T-shirt with dark stripes. A white cloth covered his head. He turned as if to look at them, hand pressed perpendicularly to his forehead, and then disappeared into his hut.

A sudden rush of wind whipped the silk *dupatta* from Lovely's waist and Pinky's fingers. It caught on the back of the boat, trailing along in the water like the tail of a mythical beast, gold and glittering. Pinky spasmed as if abruptly waking up. All at once, she was shocked by the iciness of her damp clothes, the bite of the ocean's spray, the sheer horror of her situation. *Oh my god, how did we get here? In the middle of the ocean?* Lovely's seemingly innocent words at Hanging Gardens came flooding back to her. *She drowned, yes,* Lovely had said about the dead baby. *But at least she's free.*

"*Didi!*" Pinky screamed. "Take us back!"

But Lovely continued to row them past the rectangular inlet and into the bay, where the stillness inside her grew more and more powerful, nourished by the depthless ocean, the water surrounding them in all directions.

"We can still make it back!" Pinky yelled, thinking, *She's going to drown us! We're going to die!* Was that Lord Yama, God of Death, right now canoeing towards them waiting to pluck their souls? "What happened! Why are you doing this! Tell me!"

Lovely rowed faster and faster. Pinky noticed a trail of wetness running down her leg, glistening.

"What's that!" she shouted, pointing. "Where's it coming from?"

Lovely stopped rowing, her eyes sunken. And then, slowly, with fingers splayed, she grabbed at it.

"Oh my god!" Pinky yelled, seeing Lovely's hand smeared with blood. "We need to get you to the hospital!"

She tried to force the oars from Lovely's hands but found them locked in a deathlike grip. Whatever terrible accident had happened to Lovely, Pinky had to make her realize the consequences of what she was about to do. "Everything can be made right!"

Lovely remained unmoved, methodically rowing without responding.

"*Didi!* Don't do this!" Pinky screamed, saying the only thing left to give Lovely hope, to save them both. "Nimish loves you! Not me, not any other girl. Only you! Don't you see? Whatever happened tonight, he'll marry you! He loves you!"

Just like one of Lord Rama's piercing arrows of passion, Pinky's words hit their mark. It had been Nimish's confession of love that had first unlocked Lovely's guarded heart with wonderment and possibility.

Now again, his name, the promise of his love traveled deep to her core where her spirit lay trapped by something terrifying, powerful, dark. It was too late for her to save herself from what had transpired after she fled the tamarind tree, but the love Nimish kindled in her heart was just enough to break free from the hard, lifeless, unyielding presence within her. For the briefest of moments, her rowing faltered; her face softened; her eyes grew clear.

"Tell him to come to me," she managed, her strangled voice barely audible. "I'll wait as long as I can but I can never go back."

And then, all at once, her body grew strangely translucent. An eerie wailing rose up from the bowels of the boat, and the ocean crashed against it. Pinky held on tightly; at any moment, she could be thrown into the swirling sea. She cried out, not wanting to die in the merciless ocean, not wanting to be taken away from Maji and Nimish. She called upon Matsya, Lord Vishnu's colossal fish avatar who saved Manu, the forefather of humanity, from the primordial flood that devastated the earth. *Send me your conch-shell boat, too!*

And then, scanning the infinite water all around her, she suddenly recalled the drought that had orphaned Parvati and Kuntal. She remembered the press photo of their emaciated parents, the newspaper itself tenderly wrapped in a yellow and red *bandhani* cloth for safekeeping. *To remind me,* Parvati had said that long-ago day in the bathroom, *to survive at all costs.*

Pinky's eyes fell on a half-broken oar resting inside the boat.

"Lovely *didi*, please, let's go back!" she called into the deafening din.

"You want to know who drowned the baby?" Lovely shouted. Her soaked clothes pulled tightly against her slender body, revealing taught, youthful muscles underneath.

"No!" Pinky cried out, "no! no! no!"

"All this time I've been waiting, watching over you," Lovely said. "Don't be afraid. I will set you free."

Lovely leaned in, her hand grasping Pinky's arm, the other hand pressing at her heart.

"No!" Pinky screamed.

The ocean boiled over into the small boat, tossing it like a toy. Pinky felt something beginning to enter her body, a deadly tightness grasping at her chest. With all the strength left inside her, she lunged

sideways at the oar and swung it. A terrifying shriek radiated from
Lovely's mouth as she fell overboard, the heavy contents of her satchel
dragging her downward. A torrent of water crashed against the boat,
slamming Pinky against the side.

Lovely's hand surged from the dark water, clawing at the air.

Pinky reached out—precariously, dangerously—to grasp it.

CHALICE OF DESIRE

Maji spat on the floor of her parlor, something she had never done before. But the ayah's name had lodged deep in her throat, causing it to tighten and constrict in fury. To inflame and swell with horror. She unwillingly remembered that drowning day, making her rounds around the bungalow, pausing before her bathroom door where the laundry was done back then. *She's a witch!* she heard Parvati say, the accusation piercing like one of Lord Rama's arrows. At that time, Maji had frowned, thinking it no more than irreverent, mindless banter between maids. But now, now the first seeds of doubt began to blossom.

"You saw her?" She gripped a bolster and held it to her abdomen.

"Yes!" Gulu cried out, still crumpled on the floor. In a disjointed narrative, the retold the details for Maji, the glow of the headlights, the gate swinging open on its own, his confrontation. "It was like she was a spirit! A demon like in King Vikramaditya!"

"There's no such thing," Maji said, the statement coming out more like a question, for she herself was no longer sure, the foundations of her belief having been shaken. The drowning had haunted her for so many years. Now the ayah had come back, her purpose seemingly clear. Maji fell into silence.

Gulu dropped his eyes.

Maji's face suddenly hardened. "I won't let her take my granddaughter."

A sharp honking outside pierced their thoughts. The two of them looked towards the door with anticipation.

"Jaginder?" Savita, appearing with a glass of warm water which she sipped almost hesitantly, her hair disheveled, manner confused, halted. As angry as she was with him, his bulky presence would be a comfort to her, especially after the terrifying events of the evening. The ghost had not shown herself in the boys' room while Parvati and Kuntal were cleaning in there, despite Savita's tearful appeals. *Please come to me,* she had begged. *Please let me see you, hold you. Just once.* But there had been nothing, no sign of recognition. *Let her be,* Parvati had finally told her, wet rag in hand, *the ghost will show herself when she wants to.*

"No, Mummy," Nimish said, dragging a dense mattress into the room with his brothers. "It must be the taxi."

"Go now." Maji waved Gulu towards the door. She had made arrangements with Bombay Hospital. "They'll take care of your finger."

"Maji," Gulu said, noticing how his entire arm was now throbbing. "I must stay here, in case . . . in case she returns."

"Who returns?" Savita asked.

Maji looked at her daughter-in-law and sighed deeply. "Avni," she finally said, her voice barely audible.

Savita dropped her glass. "She's come back?"

"Yes."

Kuntal let out a gasp, holding herself back from racing to the door to see if it were true. She remembered the last time she had talked with Avni, offering to bathe the baby herself that morning. They had fought. She remembered Avni's angry voice, gritty, as if it held the sandy beaches of her youth.

"Why is she back?" Savita shrieked.

The taxi blared impatiently.

"Go now," Maji ordered Gulu, dismissing him with a wave.

"She wants to kill all my children!" Savita began to sob. Unwillingly, she remembered how Avni managed all three of her boys with amazing skill and patience, especially little Tufan whose terrible colic drove her mad. But as time passed, Savita had fresh brass-and-thread amulets tied on the boy's upper arms each month to ward off Avni's growing hold on them. *If someone else could manage the boys as well as she does,* she had said helplessly to Kuntal from the privacy of her room, *I would find another ayah fut-a-fut. A simple girl like you.*

Dheer and Tufan shrank under a comforter. Nimish put his arm around his mother and led her to a chair. "She can't do anything to us anymore, Mummy."

"She's a witch," Savita wept, "a witch! Don't you know that witches take the corpses of babies, *hahn*? Because babies have no knowledge of right and wrong. She killed my baby and is forcing her to do wicked deeds!"

"Stop, Mummy!" Nimish held his mother tightly. "Please stop!"

"It all makes sense," Savita wailed. "The ayah returning, my baby coming back as a ghost."

The honking cut through the night.

"Go now!" Maji ordered Gulu again.

"She's not a witch," Gulu said quietly, standing at the doorway. And then, he vanished into the rain.

For a moment, no one uttered anything, the bitter night now having taken three away from their household. The remaining family members drew close as if to protect themselves from disappearing, too.

"Maji," Nimish finally spoke, fighting to restrain the of emotion in his voice. "What happened to the ayah?"

Maji clenched her jaw, not wanting to open up the past, that terrible day the baby drowned.

"Tell us!" Savita cut in.

"I sent her away."

"You sent her away?" Nimish asked incredulously.

"You told us she was in jail!" Savita yelled.

"What happened that day was terrible," Maji replied, her voice was tired, worn away. "But I simply could not send that girl to jail."

"How can you say that?" Savita said, pointing an insolent finger at Maji before using it to dial a number on the phone. "If she were in jail, then Pinky would never have been taken."

The blow landed hard.

"Put the phone down!" Maji shouted. Her voice wavered on the last syllable, the only indication that she had been wounded by Savita's remark.

"Inspector Pascal, please," Savita said, perilously disobeying.

"Savita!" Maji yelled in fury, attempting to propel her gigantic body towards her.

"Give him this message when he arrives," Savita said undeterred, her voice clear and crisp. "The perpetrator's name is Avni Chachar, originally from the Colaba fishing village. She was our ayah thirteen —"

Maji depressed the white plastic button and grabbed the phone from Savita, glaring at her with such intensity that Savita at last gave in.

"He's not to be trusted," Maji hissed and then began dialing her priest. When Maji was in too much pain to go to the temple herself, she phoned the priest on his direct line, a small perk from the temple to reward generous devotion through the years.

The phone rang and rang. Maji counted silently in her head *seventeen, eighteen, nineteen,* determined to let it ring until it was answered. Finally, she heard a click and an angry grumble.

"Panditji."

Even woken from a deep sleep, the priest immediately recognized Maji's low voice. He assisted the clientele living in Malabar Hill, the most exclusive area within the city's boundaries. His good fortune was more than apparent in the tiered folds of flesh that spilled over the edge of his *dhoti,* kept in check only by the thin sacred thread that strained across his chest. He cursed quietly, then vigorously rubbed his bald head with his free hand to bring circulation to his brain and civility to his tongue. "Maji," he said in his sickly sweet voice. "*Subkuch theek hai?*"

"No, Panditji. Nothing's okay. Please come."

"Now?" The priest checked his stainless-steel Swiss Favre-Leuba wristwatch, given to him by another of his wealthy clients a few years back. *Two in the morning. Who does she think she is, this crazy woman always making requests? As if I don't have even more esteemed clients to attend to. Tomorrow morning, in fact, I have a Mercedes-car hawan. And I need my rest if I am to function properly. I'm going to tell these Mittal-fittal people no. Absolutely no-no-no!* He indignantly puffed out his bloated belly.

"Panditji," Maji pressed. "You'll come, won't you? I'll make a most generous offering."

"Of course, of course," Panditji heard himself say. "Always I am at the service of my most devout families."

Maji replaced the receiver and momentarily examined her thick fingers, the joints swollen, the nails yellowed. She could hardly believe what she was about to do. Glancing at Savita, she hesitated. Savita braced herself in her chair, ready for Maji's chastisement. Over the years, they had exchanged many heated words but never before had Savita so openly defied her mother-in-law. She took comfort in the fact that Jaginder wasn't around to take his mother's side.

"Do you remember," Maji started and then paused.

Savita looked up. Desperation, not anger, etched Maji's face.

"Do you remember the tantrik you called after the drowning?"

"The tantrik?" Savita asked, bringing her hand to cover her mouth as if to contain a foul word. "But . . . but you were so upset when he arrived, you didn't even allow him into the house."

Back then, Maji would not let her bungalow be defiled by black magic. But now, now things were different. Pinky was in the hands of the ayah who possessed some sort of supernatural powers. *Pinky, Pinky, Pinky*, Maji silently intoned. She would do anything to bring her granddaughter back. Even bow down to the murky underworld of superstition and demonry. "That was then—"

"Maji? A tantrik? Are you sure?" Nimish asked in shock.

"Parvati knows how to find him," Savita said, apprehension creeping under her skin. Much as she wanted Maji to give legitimacy to her superstitions, Savita felt that as she finally did so, the very structure of the bungalow was crumbling.

"Oi! Parvati!" Maji boomed, throwing her head back for full volume.

Parvati and Kuntal hurried in from the boys' room, wet rags in their hands. Cook Kanj, alone in the kitchen preparing breakfast, rushed in as if something else terrible had just occurred.

"I need you to find a tantrik for me."

"A tantrik?" Parvati asked, checking to make sure she heard correctly.

"Yes."

Parvati paused. She had gone to see one long time ago, Gulu had taken her, when she and Kanj had first married and weren't able to get pregnant. *A year will come when you have long given up hope, a year with such heavy-heavy rains that will finally wash away the past. Then only you will be with child,* he had said and then had her drink a bubbling crimson liquid that made her bleed for days after. So much time had passed since then that Parvati had deemed him a fake. Yet, yet—Parvati touched her belly, her period was almost five days late. *Could it be?* "I can find him for you."

"Bring him now."

"I'll take the car. Kanj can drive."

Cook Kanj nearly fainted. He hadn't driven since he was a boy. And now his wife wanted him to take her to the back alleys of Bombay to find this fearsome creature? He remembered when Gulu had taken Parvati to see him. Kanj had begged her not to drink the concoction of goat's blood with something equally repulsive mixed in. When she bled afterward and grew so weak that she took to her bed for a month, Kanj pulled out one of Maji's kitchen knives, threatening to gut the tantrik like a fish. It was his fear of returning to those impossibly narrow lanes pullulating with filth and despair that had kept him enclosed within the lush safety of the bungalow's green gates.

"Par-vati." Cook Kanj said deliberately as to remind her of what the tantrik had done to her.

But paying no attention, she tossed her braid and went to fetch an umbrella. On her way back, she pulled Kuntal into a corner.

"Promise me," she whispered to her, holding Kuntal's shoulders, "promise me, no matter what happens, no matter what, you won't step outside the bungalow."

"She's out there," Kuntal said, her breathing heavy. "She's come back!"

"Don't go out!"

"Maji," Cook Kanj was attempting to cajole her in the parlor, "wouldn't it be better to enlist Panditji instead?"

"He'll come, too. I must go pray."

Kuntal helped Maji to her feet, escorting her to the puja room. Cook Kanj brought the puja *halwa,* fresh water, and *tulsi* leaves.

And then he and Parvati left in search of the Tantrik of Dharavi Slum.

* * *

Kuntal excused herself momentarily and retreated to the closed-off living room just to the rear of the dining area.

When she and Parvati first arrived at the bungalow as young girls, the living room had been the only place Maji could think of to put them. The storage pantry and kitchen were not proper and the two outside garages were already occupied, one by a car, the other by Gulu and Kanj. And so, the very same social convention that held them down opened the doors to the grandest room in the bungalow, a room that was strictly off-limits to the children and used so rarely that the two house maids claimed it as their own.

When Parvati married Kanj, she moved to one of the outside garages that Maji had converted into a living quarters complete with an outdoor toilet. Even so, it was an adjustment for her, one that she complained about regularly. *Maharani Kuntal,* she teased, *hope you rested nicely in your lavish quarters while your poor sister lay wide awake in a creaking cot with a husband who snores so loudly that even the street dogs can't sleep.*

The exquisite room was decorated with heavily embroidered brocade-covered furniture in greens and golds. Giant bolsters in matching fabric reclined against the far wall where a clean, white sheet was tightly spread on the ground. Farther back, three carpeted steps led to an alcove with dark teak chairs and a low table. The alcove was stunning, covered from floor to ceiling in intricate scenes of sapphire-toned peacocks and amber-tinted elephants, emerald-clad sages and ruby-colored jasmine painted upon a lavish silver background. Colored mica glasswork panes, cut precisely with a diamond-tip stylus, were inset into each panel, glowing with scarlet-tinged light.

Standing beneath its majestic arched ceiling, the diffused hues falling upon her, Kuntal felt as if she were inside a palace. It was here, to the side of the low table, that she unrolled her mattress each night for sleep. Her few possessions—several of Savita's cast-off cotton saris, some silver jewelry, and a miniature toy kitchen set—were discreetly tucked into the lowest drawer of a carved wooden cabinet.

On certain nights, when Kuntal was not so tired that she fell onto her mattress with eyes already shut, she sat upon one of the teak chairs or reclined against one of the plush bolsters, allowing the darkness of the room to envelop her. Then, with bangled arm outstretched, she

imagined that she was indeed a *maharani*, listening to concert musi-
cians—their sitars, tabla drums, and *shenai* droning in the background
while a beautiful vassal offered her mango sherbet in a golden, gem-
encrusted chalice. *Bring the dancing girls*, she commanded, diamond
rings flashing on her fingers. This recurring fantasy was her one escape
from her circumscribed life. And because of it, she desired nothing else
beyond the bungalow's green gates, a world that remained terrifying,
reminding her of the days when she and Parvati had been on the run.

Tonight, however, Kuntal had no fantasies to indulge in. Instead, as
the family was gathered in the sitting area waiting for the Panditji and the
tantrik to arrive, she sat locked in the living room, letting pained thoughts
about Avni wash over her for the first time in many years.

The morning the baby died, Parvati had awakened in a rage with
Avni. *She's a witch! She's coming between us!* she fumed to Kuntal, beating the laundry with exceptional vengeance. *You used to tell me everything. Now you're hiding something from me. What is it?*

Unwillingly, Kuntal thought of the rough feel of Avni's tresses that
covered her face like a shawl in the mornings.

Parvati, suddenly noticing the demure tilt of her sister's face, began
to sputter, *Did she? Did you?*

Kuntal shook her head in shock. *No! No! No! It's just that I was so
alone. She brings me happiness. Isn't that enough for you?*

Parvati stared back, eyes hardening with hate. After an intermi-
nable silence, she held up a tiny remnant of the brown soap used for
washing the clothes and muttered, *I must fetch a new bar from the
storage room.*

After the ayah's sudden departure, Kuntal had been inconsolable,
hiding her grief behind the living room's intricately etched glass doors.
Once inside, she pulled out the miniature kitchen set, Avni's sole gift
to her, pressing the diminutive tandoori oven to her eyes until she felt
they were afire from the pressure.

She did not relent until the unnamable, unspeakable feeling that
Avni had ignited within her had burnt away into ash.

※ ※ ※

Though tiny and without an AC vent, the puja room always remained
refreshingly cool, as if it had an open window to the heavens. Maji

sat on the wooden bench in front of the altar and dropped her head
into her hands in sheer exhaustion, wanting nothing more than to lie
down and sleep. It was only in the space of this little room that she
could let the sternness leave her face, the strength leave her limbs.

Out there in the rest of the bungalow, she was the supreme power.
In here, though, she was the supplicant, the powerless one. It was
a transition Maji made daily, easily, for running the household had
become a juggernaut, slowly trampling the little health she had left.
The puja room was her sanctuary, the only place aside from her early
morning rounds, that she was left undisturbed. And now, hidden from
the eyes of her family, she let the full weight of Pinky's disappearance
descend on her, distending her chest with a terrible ache. Her granddaughter was out there somewhere, cold and terror-stricken. Gazing
at the altar in front of her, Maji did not allow herself to think that
Pinky might be dead.

Small silver figurines of Lord Krishna, flute at his lips, and his consort Radha stood stiffly on a carved silver swing. Maji lifted them,
removing their silk outfits—golden *lungi* for Krishna, golden sari for
Radha, and placed the deities in a silver urn of water with three fragrant *tulsi* leaves floating atop. She slowly bathed and redressed them,
mind completely focused on this sacred act, and returned them to the
swing's silk cushion. She dipped her ring finger in a small cup of red
paste and pressed it to Krishna and Radha's foreheads, leaving a mark
on each. She repeated this step, placing *tilaks* on the framed color
images of the other gods: Ganesh, Ram, Sita, Lakshman, Hanuman,
Shiva, and tiger-riding Durga, the warrior goddess known to be especially attentive to her devotees.

In the corner of the altar, resting atop the red embroidered cloth,
sat two glass jars. The first held cotton balls and the second contained
ghee. A spoon was submerged in the yellow waxy-looking butter. Maji
pulled at a cotton ball, twisting a thread between her forefinger and
thumb until she had fashioned a wick. She set the wick within the
concave center of a silver *diya* and pressed it against the indentation
at the lip. After spooning in the ghee, she took a match and lit the
wick. In the light's flickering halo, the gods began to dance. Several
incense sticks stood in a holder, fanned out like a peacock's tail, releasing their sandalwood scent from minuscule swirls of smoke. Maji rang

a small silver bell to engage the gods' attentions. Then grasping the long handle of the *diya* with her right hand, and placing her left hand underneath, she began to move it in a circular path, carving the Sanskrit letter *Om* in the air while chanting prayers. *"Om Jaye Jagdish Hare . . ." With Your Grace the evils of the worshipper vanish.* It was a prayer that never failed to bring her peace and comfort.

Afterward, she cracked a coconut as an offering. She spooned Krishna and Radha's bath water into her palm and drank it, shaking excess drops onto the top of her head to bring divine blessings. Again, she stretched out her palm and put a handful of *prasad* in it: golden raisins, almonds, and *halwa*. After she finished chewing, and pressed the heat from the *diya* to her eyes, there was nothing more to be done. Yet Maji continued to sit silently in front of the altar. "O most-compassionate Lord," she finally spoke. "I know that the past cannot be undone. Yet why now, why has Pinky been taken? If my actions are somehow responsible for this, please be merciful with this old woman sitting before you."

Tears began to drip from her weathered face and onto her white cotton sari. She placed her open palms on either side of the silver swing, and gazed at Radha and Krishna. Their expressions remained steely, the scarlet *tilaks* had bled from their foreheads across their silver faces, looking like open wounds.

"Take whatever you want, take my life even," Maji begged, "but please—please bring my Pinky back safe."

࿐ ࿐ ࿐

Panditji arrived in the temple's private car, a luxurious Chevy Impala with wide wings and tinted a saffron color by a devotee who painted movie posters for a living. The devotee had also painted the likeness of Lord Ganesh on the rear, thinking that the deity would force other, mostly Hindu, drivers to keep a respectful distance. His talents, however, far exceeded his vision and the portrait of Ganesh had been so realistic—a huge belly spreading across the swept-back rear fenders and an elephantine trunk that curled around the chrome-rimmed, rear-mounted spare—that at least a half dozen drivers banged into the car each day to make impromptu offerings.

Panditji's assistant, a young, attractive boy with a thick mop of hair, lugged the priest's apparatus to the parlor: an iron *kund* for the sacred fire, flat sticks of wood, a stainless steel urn of *ghee*, camphor dots, and puja *samagri*, a fragrant potpourri that consisted of lotus seed, honey, sugar, turmeric, bright-red *sindoor* powder, and other dried flowers and spices. The young boy placed a thick cherry-colored cushion on the ground. Panditji plopped down on it and then, crossing his legs lotus-style, vigorously rocked back and forth until his buttocks had spread out across the breadth of the cushion. As his assistant set up the *kund* with the wood and camphor, the priest closed his eyes and pondered on several matters that had been troubling him on the ride over:

Why was he required to do this *hawan* in the middle of the night?

And, how much could he expect to be paid for such a house call?

He quickly finished off a glass of boiled buffalo milk sweetened with a chunk of musky-flavored raw sugar.

"Oi," he called to the boy with a milky belch, "is everything ready?"

"Yes, Panditji."

The priest reluctantly opened his eyes, acknowledging Maji and her family seated around the iron *kund* on white sheets. With more enthusiasm, he noted the *thali* of coconuts, bananas, and honey that had been placed by his side. A small fire lashed out of the iron vessel, smoke rising to the heavens. "What seems to be the trouble?" he asked in his high-pitched voice, eyes gazing upward as if he already knew the answer.

"Pinky's been abducted," Maji answered, her voice stumbling.

"And Lovely, too," Nimish added.

"By the children's ayah from many years ago," Savita added. "She's a witch!"

"Oh-ho," the priest said, not looking at all concerned. "Bombay's going to the dogs only. All these uneducateds thinking they can blackmail their way into the upper castes."

"Blackmail?" Nimish asked, feeling strangely relieved. *Yes*, it must be blackmail, he silently reasoned, *the ayah could not be capable of anything worse.*

"There's something more," Maji said reluctantly.

"Yes?"

"A ghost."

"Ghost?" the priest's voice cracked. He shifted uncomfortably, fingering the sacred thread across his chest as if it alone would protect him.

"My daughter's come back to me!" Savita wailed, keeping her arms crossed tightly around her chest where milk continued to drip.

"Make her go away!" Tufan squeaked, holding desperately to his jute-rope gun.

"Make her stay!" Savita shouted, slapping Tufan across his head.

"I will make the necessary requests; the rest is God's will," Panditji said, wondering if the Mittal family had all suddenly gone mad, stark raving mad. These things certainly happen. He had seen carefully veneered families simply crack open after years and generations of dysfunction, running to him for a magic balm. He kept these family secrets tucked inside his Buddha-like belly, each a delectable sweet duly consumed, regurgitated, and enjoyed once more. Every secret, after all, came with a side of forever-indebtedness, a chutney of money and gifts that silenced his tongue. Now, adjusting the sacred thread around his fleshy belly, he began chanting while ladling *ghee* into the fire and brutally ripping off flower petals, indiscriminately tossing them in.

"*Swaha*," he incanted at the end of a phrase, grandly lifting his flattened palm from the fire to the sky.

On cue, the family threw in a handful of dried flower petals and camphor *samagri*, causing the flame to crackle and brighten. Panditji droned mantras for more than an hour, occasionally yawning and scratching his armpits. His mind flitted back to his childhood, when he was known simply as Chotu Motu, little fat one, and when he used to watch his own father perform the very same rituals, three strands of white thread tied over his left shoulder and lines of white ash smeared on his forehead, arms, and chest, markings that denoted him as twice-born. Panditji's thoughts then moved into a pleasant comparison of Maji and Savita's breasts, giving Maji's points for sheer enormousness but choosing Savita's tautly plump ones in the end. He imagined slipping his hand down into her cleavage, rubbing some red, powdery *sindoor* onto her nipples, and then giving each breast an obliging little toot on his way out.

"*Swaha*," he incanted again.

Dheer and Tufan had fallen asleep, heads lolling against one of the sofas. Maji began to worry that the tantrik would arrive before Panditji left, and signaled Kuntal to retrieve the breakfast that Cook Kanj had prepared. Noticing Maji's restlessness, Panditji cut short his prayers and waved his hand over the *thali* of vermicelli noodles cooked with almonds and milk as a way of blessing. Kuntal served the food. Forsaking utensils, the priest stuffed fingerfuls into his mouth, swaying with pleasure. Maji discreetly motioned to Panditji's assistant to begin packing up the puja apparatus.

"What's the rush?" Panditji asked. He preferred to remain seated in front of the *kund*, the accruements of the *hawan* surrounding him like faithful servants. After the meal was completed, Maji pressed a thick red envelope into Panditji's hand. The priest pushed it away from him as if it were polluted, but not before testing its thickness. Maji had been generous. Satisfied, he let out a low burp. "The gods have always been pleased with your devotion."

"And Pinky?" Maji asked, hoping that her piety alone would guarantee her granddaughter's safe return.

"In God's hands."

"And the ghost?" Savita inquired.

"*Bhoot-fhoot*," he replied, waving her away as if he couldn't be bothered. "I tell you, Bombay's going to the dogs."

With that, Panditji plopped himself into the saffron Impala and sped away.

SLUMS & SEWERS

P arvati and Kanj drove down the dreaded Mahim-Sion Road that roughly served as the border of the top of the triangular area known as Dharavi, Bombay's largest slum. This stretch of garbage-encrusted road was usually traversed by people on over crowded, single-decker buses, people who were willing to wait a full hour for a space, some even bypassing the dangerous road altogether on a train, rather than having to traverse the road on foot, bike, scooter or even by car.

Before crossing over the Western Railway Line which bordered the seaside edge of Dharavi, Kanj stopped and parked the Ambassador near Mahim Station. "I'm turning around," he said, clinging to the steering wheel as if wanting to make a quick getaway. "We'll be killed."

"*Lakhs* of people live here without being killed."

"We're outsiders, Parvati. This is not our home."

"We *must* find the tantrik."

"Why? Why should we put ourselves at risk for *them*?"

"Because Maji took me in when no one else would."

"So what?" Kanj hissed. "You're still just a servant. One mistake and she'll get rid of you just as she did Avni."

Mahim Crossing was just ahead, which led past the railroad tracks and onto Dharavi Main Road, a rough pathway that had been constructed by the slum's residents by placing rocks on the marshy ground. Now the road consisted of sluggish mud that stank of urine and feces. Yet this smell was nothing like that of the tanneries, nestled beyond Mahim Station, which permeated the air with acrid sulfur and rotting meat. Ghostly balls of wool fluff littered the path, visible only by the light of Parvati's lantern.

The slum sprawled out before them, a densely packed collection of corrugated-tin hovels with bamboo-strip *chatai* mats as walls, each covered with plastic tarps to ward off the monsoons. The settlement in front of them had no electricity, bathing Parvati and Kanj in total darkness but for the dim light glowing inside the dwellings. Shanties had sprung up at random, with empty jute lines out front. An overstuffed gunny sack reading 53 Grade lay just outside one hovel, near an overturned bucket and a faded advertisement for British Petroleum motor oil. A ladder, uneven crossbars straining across its width, leaned up against a second story, precariously perched on steel rods, one side supported by a haphazard brick wall with curling wires hanging down. One of the wires had been fashioned into a clothesline from which a tiny pair of yellow shorts hung, forgotten. A rubber tire had been scavenged and placed on top of the second story, on a torn blue tarp, waiting to become useful.

"We have a good life, plentiful food, shelter, our own toilet in the best neighborhood in the city," Parvati said. "Do you want to risk that by refusing Maji?"

"Do *you* want to be skewered like seekh-kabobs by these *goondas*?"

"There," Parvati said, pointing to a low fence that surrounded an ancient-looking cross. "Let's go there."

"*Hatao!*"

A group of men, cloaked in woolen shawls and plastic bags, approached smoking Shivaji *bidis*. They wore loose knickers and shirts. One was visibly afflicted with elephantiasis; his acutely swollen leg was thick and leathery, the skin pebbly in appearance, the foot unrecognizable altogether. "Looking for something?"

"Hari Bhai," Parvati said sharply as Kanj considered the dagger the leader was flashing. *Entirely inappropriate for slicing,* he decided, growing faint, *but perfect for gutting.*

The leader, short and stocky, with cruel eyes and the white patches of advanced vitiligo upon his face, took a step back. Hari Bhai's name sent chills down his back. "And what business do you have with him?"

"Tell him Gulu from VT sent us."

The vitiligo-afflicted man fished a piece of fried onion from his teeth then spat on the ground as if to frighten the visitors with his horrible hygiene. "We'll be back."

They left Parvati and Kanj shivering near a broken charpoy, supervised at a distance by the elephantiasis sufferer, who rested the swollen folds of flesh that composed his foot upon a brick.

"This is your grand plan?" Kanj hissed, squatting to make himself more comfortable. "All the time in the car you tell me '*trust me trust me*,' and now we're surrounded by criminals. This is all you have to say?"

"Hari Bhai and Gulu are childhood friends," Parvati whispered while surreptitiously wiping her brow with the end of her sari *palloo*. "They shined shoes at Victoria Terminus together. He helped Gulu find the tantrik years ago. Don't you remember?"

"I don't remember anything but the foul liquid he cooked up and made you drink, *cheel*."

It was true, Hari Bhai and Gulu went a long way back but Hari Bhai went even further. He was a descendant of the original Koli inhabitants of Dharavi, when it was not a sprawling slum but a fishing community along the Mithi River and its offspring, the Mahim Creek, both flowing into the Arabian Sea. As the youngest child of seven, he was not needed to work at the dam built across the creek where fish, mainly crab and shellfish, were trapped during high tide and caught in the fishermen's nets at low tide. Over time, the river and creek had become intensely polluted by the tanneries and other industries that flourished within Dharavi's boundaries, and the fish began to reek of kerosene. The continual governmental land reclamations, transforming the muddy swamp lands along the Mahim–Bandra stretch into inhabitable space, had finally forced the sea to recede, leaving an entire community deprived of its ancient means of sustenance.

Hari Bhai, known back then simply as Hari, had drifted along the railroad tracks, unsupervised for most of the day, finally finding suitable work at VT train station. He had banded together with other outcast boys, Gulu included, and began to shine shoes under the mentorship of Big Uncle. When Big Uncle was killed by his rival Red Tooth, Gulu ran away, devastated, but Hari had shifted his loyalties easily, even rising to the role of Red Tooth's right-hand man. In time, Hari murdered Red Tooth over a money dispute and had become a fugitive, not from the law but from Red Tooth's men who were intent on a revenge killing. Dharavi, with its dense labyrinth of shanties and over fifteen thousand people per square acre, beckoned as the ideal hiding place. And so Hari returned to his *zopadpatti*, back to the Koliwada district of Dharavi with its Ganesh Mandir temple and the two-hundred-year-old Khamba Deo shrine, to reclaim his destiny.

"Come."

Hari Bhai's men were back, their attitude more hospitable.

"Where are you taking us?" Parvati demanded.

"No questions," the leader warned, touching a patch of discolored skin upon his chin as if it would bring good luck, "*Bhaiya* doesn't like questions."

They were led through the shanties, the road awash in sewage and rainwater. A disheveled woman with a large nose ring squatted on the road, muttering to herself as she rubbed ash onto a cooking vessel in the middle of the night. A rubbery breast fell out of her dark, blouse-less sari when she leaned over. As Parvati and Kanj continued to walk, the path widened a bit, the homes grew progressively better, and the smell of the communal toilets became less pervasive. Now they passed a section with low-rise, narrow structures each consisting of eleven rooms, all facing toward the road. The buildings had proper tile roofs, cement front porches, and small open drains. One of them boasted a hand-painted sign reading Lijjat Papad with a drawing of a fair-complexioned, feminine hand, wrist adorned with two green bangles, holding a lotus flower aloft.

"*Lijjat papads!*" Kanj exclaimed with surprise, despite his trepidation. "Here in Dharavi?"

The men laughed. "You won't live here but you'll eat from our homes."

Kanj became indignant.

"*Hahn, hahn,*" one of the men, sporting a wide moustache, nodded proudly, "My wife's a *sanchalika*, head of the local branch at our home, over there—where the sign is. Still small-small business it is—making *papads* for you people to eat—only started last year, but already very profitable."

"She makes more money than him!" teased one of the men wearing a sleeveless *banain* undershirt which accentuated his thick arm muscles.

"That's why *we* were finally able to rent a proper home *yaar.*" The mustached man waved him away.

"But you can no longer beat her now, *hahn bhai?*" the undershirt-man jeered, holding his open palm threateningly in the air.

"My wife's under my control only," the mustached man replied in a slow, smoldering tone, lest his manhood be doubted by the two strangers they were escorting.

"Yes, yes," the vitiligo-afflicted leader said placatingly in order to ward off any potential fighting. "Hari Bhai says that rolling *papads* is good work for our wives and sisters."

"*My* wife," continued the mustached man, now proudly puffed up at the mention of Hari Bhai's approval, "rolls out three kilograms of *papads* every morning. She goes to Bandra before dawn to collect the wet dough."

"While we men travel to Bandra each night with our own *wet goods,*" the undershirt-man laughed insinuatingly.

The other men guffawed.

By then, they had reached a relatively impressive two-story home that sat opposite the fenced-in cross belonging to a Christian family that unofficially governed the Koli community of Koliwada, situated in the northwestern section of Dharavi. Hari Bhai used their residence for all of his public audiences.

Parvati and Kanj were taken into the main room where Hari Bhai sat, sipping a cup of tea. His face was handsome, jaw strong, hair gelled back, eyes shaded even though the interior was dark. "Come, come," he said invitingly, snapping his finger at the servant to bring some more chai. "So you are friends of Gulu?"

"Yes," Parvati and Kanj both said, remaining standing.

"He's like a brother to me," Hari said reassuringly. "Sit, sit."

They sat.

"What can I do for you?"

"We need Tantrik Baba."

Hari Bhai smiled and leaned forward intently, pulling his sunglasses down to take a better look at his guests. An ugly scar ran up from the top of his eyelid through his bushy eyebrow.

For a freakish moment, Kanj thought that he and Parvati were going to be murdered. *I'll beg,* he decided, *cook them first-class* aloo tikkis *in exchange for our lives.*

But then Hari sat back languidly and snapped his fingers at the mustached man, "*Jao, usko bulao.*"

Parvati nodded her thanks. Kanj tried to keep his knees from shaking.

Hari Bhai let his gaze linger on Parvati's body, tightly clad in a mango-colored sari. "So sister," he said, his words slow and deliberate, "you need the tantrik."

۞ ۞ ۞

It had been Hari's relationship with the tantrik that had fueled his mythical rise to power. With his help, Hari had taken control over Koliwada unchallenged, even by the extremely violent slumlords like Vardraja Mudaliar whose ruthless influence was felt all over Dharavi, including the Zone III precinct of the Bombay police. Hari's growing business enterprise tapped into an ancient Koli tradition, the only one remaining after the Mahim Creek had dried up and deprived his community of their ancient ways of fishing. Hari coined his famous slogan. *Mahasagar nahi? Navsagar chali!* No ocean? Go alcohol!

According to ancient traditions, Koli communities all over Bombay had always distilled alcohol from various fruits including jamun, guava, orange, apple, and the sweet brown *chikoo*—whose stems additionally provided milky latex for chewing gum. The famous Dharavi Koliwada Country, brewed right in Koliwada, was the most potent because of its special saltwater infusion. When the Chief Minister of Bombay, Morarji Desai, imposed Prohibition in 1954, the Kolis' distilleries were forced underground. Hari rallied his community by accusing Desai of *country-bandi* instead of *daru-bandi,* banning their homemade country-made liquor while, at the very same time, selling his own version of legal alcohol in bottles labeled Indian Made Foreign Liquor.

Then, enterprisingly, he took advantage of the open spaces Dharavi had to offer—the unreclaimed swamps and the illegal dumping sites—to bury hundreds of barrels of the sugary liquid for fermentation. Sometimes he stored them in the sewers of nearby neighborhoods such as Sion, where school boys would dare each other to lift the heavy cast-iron sewer grates for a better look. After the alcohol was distilled, up to fifteen liters were stored in a tire tube which could be easily carried around the worker's neck, leaving his hands free to help him wade through the marshlands. Hari had procured a fleet of huge, black American cars—Plymouths, Chryslers, Dodges—to drive his homemade liquor from there all over the city, the best stuff going to the *addas* along the coast, including to Rosie's in Bandra.

Hari was seen as a savior by the Kolis, a Robin Hood of sorts, flouting the law while at the same time maintaining a certain degree of moral integrity by refusing to partake more dubious practices such as adding battery acid to his brews. His fellow Kolis began to call him *Bhai*—Big Brother—for Hari ensured each and every male Koli member of his community a steady job in his business empire and a salary of two-hundred rupees a month. In return, his people were remarkably loyal, obeying him blindly when he asked them to vote for a particular politician or later, when they became foot soldiers of the Samyukta Maharashtra Samiti.

❀ ❀ ❀

In the darkened room, holding her cup of tea, Parvati related the story of the baby's drowning and the ghost's sudden appearance in the bungalow. The men nodded solemnly. The haunted lanes of Dharavi teemed with wailing ghosts, vengeful spirits, and restless souls.

"Yes," Hari Bhai said afterward, surprisingly moved by their tale. "Tantrik Baba will help."

THE TANTRIK

The tantrik had been meditating when one of Hari Bhai's men summoned him. Irritated by the interruption, he commanded his favored spirit, a perverted ghost named Frooty who liked nothing better than to slip into a loosened *lungi* and give the unsuspecting organs a blood-constricting twist, to visit the mustached man that night.

The tantrik and Hari had an uneasy relationship, one bound by an unbreakable promise, but ultimately, weakened by differing philosophies. Even so, they upheld their solemn vow to each other, taken when they were mere boys. The tantrik continued to tie protective amulets on Hari's wrist, warding away potential rivals and police alike. And Hari took care of the tantrik's family, even some years later, after the tanneries were relocated securing them a top flat in Diamond Apartments, Dharavi's first high-rise building built overlooking Mahim Station. And, though the tantrik refused all association with Hari's ring of corruption and crime, he had not been able to refuse his gift of a transistor radio. For in his spare time, the tantrik had become terribly addicted to the government-owned broadcast *Akaashvani* and its continuous emission of the most depressing Hindustani classical music.

Destiny had brought the tantrik and Hari together. Dharavi's dense mass of humanity served as a veritable wall that separated their neighborhoods, located on opposite ends of the triangular community. The tantrik grew up near the Central Railway Line that formed the slum's eastern border, while Hari was firmly ensconced in Dharavi's northwestern pocket. And while Hari traced his ancestry back to the original Koli inhabitants of Bombay, the tantrik descended from the Konchikori community of traveling magicians and performers originally from Sholapur, a city known primarily for its textiles, located on the outskirts of what until recently had been known as Bombay State.

The tantrik's special powers first manifested at age four when he cured his sister by putting his hand to her feverish head. After her miraculous recovery, word spread quickly and the tantrik spent entire days sitting on a charpoy administering to every sick, ill, or desperate person who came to his doorstep. But he quickly grew resentful of missed time with his friends. So, for a stretch, instead of curing them, the tantrik inflicted his supplicants with relatively harmless ailments such as diarrhea, impotence, and massive hair growth.

"Stay away from him," the neighbors began warning each other. "Otherwise you'll be running to the latrine ten-twelve times a day, your motions coming out with such force that even the rats run for cover."

"*Hahn*," said another, "and what hope does poor Dhondya have of finding a wife now? Not even the five-rupee whores on Falkland Road are able to restore his manliness."

"And what about me?" complained a third whose lion's mane of hair growing from his ears much later earned him a coveted spot in the *Guinness Book of World Records*. "I simply asked him to help me secure a proper dowry for my daughter."

The tantrik's family became veritable outcasts and no amount of ear-pulling, cheek-slapping, or general physical torments by his parents could convince him to change his ways. Only when his father threatened to uproot his family and return to his itinerant street-performing ways did the tantrik attempt to cure again.

He went into seclusion for a year, dutifully practicing *sadhana* in the dark hours of the night, staying up to recite mantras or visiting Matunga Cemetery in order to learn how to tame the most powerful spirits. Each night between midnight and two, he exhumed a corpse buried less than three days, one that would still have its spirit lingering nearby, and bathed it in thirteen liters of milk. After the contaminated milk curdled while being heated, he rolled the curds infused with sugar, *ghee*, and wheat flour into small balls which he placed at the corpse's head and feet. Finally, using a special mantra, he cajoled the spirit back into the body, and—once there—brought it firmly under his control.

During the day, the tantrik refused all food, drinking only a bit of *nimbu-pani* to survive. His neighbors began to approach his hovel again, excitedly keeping track of his progress and even placing ten-*paisa* bets on whether or not he would survive the grueling routine. He *did* survive, emerging from his self-imposed exile more powerful than ever, and was henceforth known as the Tantrik Baba of Dharavi. While Hari continued expanding his empire across the city's vast perimeters, ensnaring politicians, police, and the privileged within its intoxicating net, the tantrik continued to mainly serve those in the heart of Bombay, the people of Dharavi Slum.

✳ ✳ ✳

Just before dawn, the tantrik stepped onto Maji's front verandah, stopping to pluck a jasmine bud and indulge in its divine fragrance, one unadulterated by the sickening smells that normally assaulted his nose in Dharavi. And then, as if trying to hold onto the aroma, he proceeded to eat an entire vine.

Maji and Savita shrank back. The tantrik was a fearsome-looking man covered head to toe in white ash, naked except for a small loincloth and brass bells around his ankles. His matted hair was coiled into a huge bun that rested slightly askew on the top of his head, a thick beard fell from his face to midchest, where a rosary of 108 conch shells dangled. His body was powerful, eyes blazing scarlet. He carried a peacock-feather fan and a bullwhip.

He arrived with his son who set up the items required for the puja including rice, curds, sandalwood paste, *ghee*, incense, and water for washing the tantrik's feet.

"The natural order in this household has been violated," the tantrik announced after the necessary preparations for the puja had been made. His voice came out in a low echoing moan, as if he were speaking from an underground tomb. His gaze lingered momentarily on Maji. "Your household will never find peace unless the path designated by nature is redressed."

The tantrik stood up suddenly and wandered inside the bungalow, tapping the walls and swatting the air with his fan, demanding, *"Tu kidar se aayi hai?* Where have you come from?"

The rest of the household followed him at a distance, walking from the parlor up to the dining area, down the east hallway where Jaginder and Maji's rooms lay, back across to the west hallway past the boys' bedroom. The tantrik stopped just outside the bathroom and, for a moment, inwardly lamented. Too often he was called upon by desperate or greedy people to enact some sort of revenge. In those cases he would put on a show, cracking his whip, letting out blood-curdling screams, eventually making a spirit speak out of an unsuspecting person's mouth, declaring that it had traveled all the way from the cemetery to make trouble. This spectacle was usually enough to frighten the guilty charlatan into confessing to having stolen goods or whatever his crime might have been. But on occasion, the tantrik's services were actually needed to reweave the cosmos, to restore the natural order that had been overset by ignorance, desire, attachment, or greed. And that is when he tapped into his cosmic powers.

As soon as he had entered Maji's bungalow, the tantrik immediately felt the ghost. Her pain, anger, and silent accusations dripped from the cracks in the roofing and bubbled from crevices along the baseboard.

He stepped inside the hallway bathroom.

The ghost unfurled itself from the ceiling, invisible to all but the tantrik and Parvati. Almost humanlike now, she was more powerful than ever. She vowed to make them pay, her entire family, for their crimes, for allowing her to die.

"Tu kidar se aaya hai?" the tantrik repeated more vehemently, looking directly at her.

"Where is she?" Savita cried out, shivering. "Where is she?"

"Over there!" Parvati pointed.

Cook Kanj threateningly waved a frying pan in the air.

The ghost opened her mouth, expelling a secret language that, like waves upon the ocean, crashed upon the tantrik's ears. The ceiling began to drip as if it were raining inside.

The tantrik chanted, "*Shiva Shakti Shiva Shakti . . .*" calling out to the male and female forces of the universe. He began to sweat; white ash trickled from his face. The ghost approached him, her diaphanous silver mane twisting with fury behind her. The black pipes that encircled the bathroom wall began to shudder, blasts of water erupting at random.

Savita clung to her boys, Maji rested heavily on Kuntal's shoulders. They stood frozen in the hallway, sodden laundry whipping at them as if being blown by a powerful wind.

The tantrik's son whispered cryptically, "Tantrik Baba seeks the unification of the polarities of the world, consciousness and energy. Only then will illumination be possible."

Nimish opened his mouth to respond but Savita swiftly pinched his arm.

The ghost swirled around the tantrik's head, her arms moving in slow-motion like a silken cloth fluttering underwater. The tantrik held firm, matching his powers with hers. Rain pelted the room; the naked bulb swung wildly. Frost crept over the tantrik's naked body, slowly, slowly encasing him in ice.

"*Ye bahut zordar atama hai,* this is a very strong spirit," he gasped, falling back. "She will not go."

"I knew it!" Savita blurted out. "She's come back to me!"

"She's always been here," the tantrik said. "An astral alignment brought her out."

"What alignment?" Maji asked.

"A violation of a boundary or possession by a girl—"

"Pinky!" Savita shrieked. "I knew it!"

"Girls have certain unconscious powers at transitory times in their lives, power to commune with the otherworld—"

"Divine or demonic?" Parvati asked.

"Either," the tantrik's fiery eyes rested on her. "She died before her time. She is angry."

"But what can be done?" Nimish asked. They had all suffered after her death, the pain of loss, Savita's dark descent into superstition and fear, Jaginder's retreat into alcoholism, Nimish's own unassuaged guilt.

"*Shiva Shakti*," the tantrik intoned. "The universe must be brought into balance. What you have given will be given; what you have taken will be taken."

"But my little moon-bird!" Savita cut in feeling once again the dark pain in her chest. "Is there no way to end her suffering?"

"There are two ways," the tantrik held up his flattened palms in the air. "Allow her to stay here, replace her pain with its cosmic counterpart. And one day she will leave on her own."

"Just like our Mama and Baba's ghosts," Parvati whispered to Kuntal.

"And the other?" Nimish asked.

The tantrik dropped one of his hands, the other remained firmly in the air, five fingers tautly splayed to represent the elements of visible life: earth, water, fire, sky, and wind. "Invisibles are only made of fire, sky, and wind. They seek water and earth in order to inhabit the world as we do."

He waggled his thumb. "What once killed the ghost now sustains her. She is bound within the walls of this bungalow. Her life and death are once again at your mercy."

The tantrik fell into a meditative trance.

The show was over.

DEATH &
DISINHERITANCE

A ray of early morning sun broke through the clouds.

Jaginder hailed a taxi from a hotel near the Asiatica to Darukhana, the gritty industrial area where his office was located. Usually he never arrived before midmorning. By then the grounds were already pullulating with workers sorting through remnants of ships broken at the yard, and his assistants were buzzing around the office, negotiating deals, and recording accounts in their ledgers. Today, the *godown*, where the wares were stocked, was eerily quiet. Two refrigerators rusted in the muck; large steel pipes glinted from overnight rain.

Jaginder climbed the steps onto the raised, open platform and went into his office. A locked storage facility lined one end, containing round bolsters to lean against and thick mats that were unrolled onto the floor by the company servant at the start of each day. Opening the storage door, Jaginder maneuvered one of the heavy mats onto the vinyl-covered floor and covered it with a white sheet.

Sweating now, he pulled out his small, wooden floor desk and placed it in its usual position, by the entrance, next to the black phone that only needed to be plugged in. His ruby-colored ledgers lay neatly in a stack in one cabinet. Sitting cross-legged on the floor in front of his desk, Jaginder opened the top ledger. The cover lifted from the bottom, thin pages folding out like an accordion. He blankly stared at the accounts, all recorded in the cryptic Lunday script used in their family to notate financial transactions.

Sluggishly, he uncorked the inkpot resting on the flat backboard of his slanting desk and dipped the quill into its dark depths. Usually he used an imported Schaeffer pen, kept tucked in his shirt pocket. But he didn't have his pen with him and was too tired to try to locate one within the cabinets. Jaginder checked his watch, wishing for a cup of hot chai. The servant was already fifteen minutes late. *So this is what bloody happens when I'm not here.*

He turned to a blank page. Quill hovering over the sheet, he hesitantly began drawing a Ganesha, a symbol he formed at the start of every new account or transaction to signify an auspicious beginning. There was nothing favorable about what he was going to do, yet out of habit, he completed the symbol and put his pen down. Outside, he heard the scurrying of feet. The company servant, wearing a white undershirt, cotton *lungi*, and wool shawl, was bounding up the stairs loudly whistling the tune to *"Prem Jogan ke Sundari Pio Chali"* and gyrating his hips as if he were a Moghul prince with hoards of courtesans at his feet.

"Sahib!" he screeched, almost dropping his cup of chai as he rushed to fold his hands in greeting.

"You're late," Jaginder said, annoyance scrawled upon his face.

"*Hahn-ji,* Sahib-*ji,*" the servant stammered, sweat beads popping up on his bald head. "Bus was late. Road was being bad due to monsoon."

"Bring me some tea."

The servant scampered away in search of the resident chaiwallah, his tea and tune both forgotten in the rush to execute his orders.

Jaginder stared outside. Just below, workers had begun to arrive at the *godown,* moving iron fragments, the *thoka-thaki* sound of their hammering filling the air with a sad, hollow rhythm. When he was a little boy, he had often accompanied his father, Omanandlal, to this very same place. Taking the train from their bungalow to nearby Reay Road Station, his favorite time to visit was Diwali and New Years when the Gujarati businessmen in the area cheerily called out *"Sal*

Mubarak!" and when Omanandlal kept stainless-steel trays of pistachios, almonds, cashews, cardamom pods, and golden raisins to offer to all those who visited.

For hours, Jaginder had sat by his father, watching him check his account books, learning how to conduct business transactions, manage his underlings, and interact with clients. He imagined himself sitting in his father's place; every action he undertook was done with full consciousness that—one day—he would. Sometimes he had stayed there until the end of the day, arriving home with his father who would slip the *bathuee* off his shoulders before even washing his hands, handing Jaginder the heavy cotton vest with large pockets in the front, filled with rupees, to be stashed in one of Maji's locked metal cabinets.

Omanandlal had been a simple man, always dressed elegantly, clean-shaven but for the small, neat moustache that represented honor and manhood for men of his class. He never lost his temper, never walked too fast, never berated his workers, and never let an impoverished man leave his door empty-handed. He had painstakingly learned to read and write in English, keeping his Hindi–English dictionary by his side and signing his checks in laborious cursive writing, the belly of his broad-tipped Parker pen filled with India ink. Jaginder always wished he could have been like his father, but the time of Indian honor and chivalry had quickly passed in favor of the new reigning empire of bureaucracy, coercion, and corruption. What choice did he have but to keep up with the times?

In a rare sentimental act, Jaginder had preserved his father's office after Omanandlal's passing, rather than modernizing it like many of his colleagues had done by installing permanent walls, desks with chairs and such. Sitting cross-legged on the thick mattress, his father's old desk in front of him, Jaginder felt the comforting weight of Omanandlal's legacy. Though irritatingly Nimish had never shown any inclination for shipbreaking, Jaginder had always assumed that his son would take over the trade after college. He imagined them sitting side by side, he teaching Nimish the ins and outs of daily affairs until Jaginder was ready to retire. And then, he imagined, he would still visit his office each morning to socialize, but he would also be free to spend his afternoons walking along the exclusive shores of Juhu Beach. What Maji was trying to do was an

insult to the natural order of things. How could he be passed over?
And in favor of a mere boy?

The company servant returned, a cup of scalding chai cradled in
his hands. He placed it beside Jaginder on a small table and brought
a tray of Parle-G biscuits to accompany it. Then he scampered to
the storage area, pulling out mats, sheets, and bolsters, setting up the
office for the day as unobtrusively as he could. Jaginder could not concentrate upon his task. He wrote, *Be Known To All Men This Indenture
Of Will Executed On The Fourteenth Day Of June 1960 By Mr. Jaginder Omanandlal Mittal* . . . and put his quill down. Unwillingly, he
remembered the first and only time he had held the infant Nimish in
his arms. His child had been impossibly small, heat emanating from
his fuzzy head as if it were a furnace. *Don't drop him! Aiiee, you'll break
his neck!* Savita had cried out. Jaginder grew so afraid, felt so clumsy,
that he never picked up his son again until he had grown into an
unbreakable toddler. By then, though, Nimish squeezed uncomfortably from his father's big arms, racing instead into the soft ones of
his mother. *No*, Jaginder thought, *Nimish never really cared for me.* He
picked up his quill and dipped it in the ink.

Just then his assistant, Laloo, scurried in with the morning's newspaper tucked into his armpit.

"You're here, Jaginder-ji?" Laloo's whiskery moustache and thick
hair were slicked back; the oil had saturated the collar of his polyester
shirt. His tone was unusually reserved.

"Yes. Important business."

"Important?"

Laloo squatted down by the floor desk, trying to surreptitiously
decipher the curling Lunday script in the ledger book as he fingered
his moustache. Jaginder snapped the cover of the book shut.

"*Kya hai?*" Laloo squeaked. "Did something more happen?"

"Something more?"

"Since last night," Laloo stammered, buckteeth nibbling furiously
upon his lower lip.

Jaginder rocked back, shame and anger dueling in his chest. What
did Laloo know about last night? So much had happened in the
course of several hours that Jaginder had trouble keeping track. It had
all started with Savita's breasts. From there he left for Rosie's *adda*,

then returned to the bungalow where he fought with Nimish and his mother. Then he left again. The Ambassador had broken down and he'd ended up at the Asiatica.

Could Laloo have spotted me somewhere? Jaginder had a severe dislike for his assistant. But Laloo's father had spent his life working for Omanandlal as a *babu*, a clerk, whose only qualifications were that he knew English and could use a typewriter. At one point the entire business had depended on Laloo's father's ability to fill in English-language forms for banks and government offices. Because of this, Jaginder felt a sense of obligation to retain Laloo, despite the fact that he was an idiot.

"What are you insinuating?" Jaginder shouted.

Just then, the company servant who had been listening to the conversation while setting up the office, discreetly plugged in the phone by Jaginder's desk. Immediately it began to ring.

"Jaginder Mittal," Jaginder answered without missing a beat.

"Ah. Your mother did say you would be at the office though I've been trying to reach you there for the last several hours."

"Who are you?" Jaginder felt the heat rise in his chest. *Had Maji already contacted the lawyer?*

"Inspector Pascal from the police—"

"Police? What do you want from me?"

"Where were you last night?"

"That's none of your bloody business!" Jaginder shouted, keenly aware that Laloo and the company servant were both intently listening in.

"It's in your best interest to cooperate considering what happened."

"What happened is my bloody business," Jaginder repeated. "I do not care to discuss this further. Good day, Sub-Inspector." Jaginder slammed the phone back in the cradle and ripped out the cord. "*Ye kya* bloody *tamasha hai?*" he shouted at Laloo and the servant who were both staring at him with mouths hanging open.

The company servant scurried about, desperately searching for something to make him appear busy. Laloo simply extracted the morning paper from his sweaty armpit and placed it on Jaginder's desk. "You've seen this already, I assume," he said lugubriously, inwardly thrilled to have one-upped his boss.

"Seen what?" Jaginder stood up and unfolded the *Free Press Journal.*

Laloo pointed to a headline with a sharp, dirty fingernail: "Daughters of Prominent Bombay Families Missing." The article went on to read, *Pinky Mittal, age 13, youngest daughter of Jaginder and Savita Mittal disappeared from her family home in Malabar Hill at approximately one in the morning. At approximately the same time, their neighbor Lovely Lawate, age 17, only daughter of Mrs. Vimla Lawate also disappeared. The two cases appear to be connected.* Further down was an article detailing a missing motorbike, a ruby red Triumph 500cc, the only one of its kind in all of Bombay.

"This is a bloody joke," Jaginder said, smashing the back of his hand against the paper, recalling the college boys' conversation at the Asiatica.

Desperately trying to hide his excitement at being involved, however tangentially, in this unfolding drama, Laloo rocked from leg to leg like an overanxious child.

"Call me a taxi," Jaginder roared at the company servant.

"I'm very sorry," Laloo said gravely, though he was not in the least.

"She's not my daughter," Jaginder retorted. Even so, he tucked the newspaper under his arm as he walked out onto the unpaved street, impatiently waiting for a taxi to take him home.

❦

Along with the newspapers, including the *Free Press Journal,* a stream of relatives and friends arrived at Maji's green gates, each hoping to be the first on the scene to express concern about Pinky's abduction. Relatives far and wide all appeared wearing muted colors almost as if in mourning, keeping their eyes open, their alarm tucked behind their ears, as Savita revealed that their ex-ayah was the culprit.

They packed into the bungalow like overlapping squares of *burfi* in a box of sweets, sweaty bodies sticking against each other, silver-embroidered *dupattas* drooping in the morning humidity. The only one undisturbed by the commotion was the baby ghost who, in her almost humanlike state, now required regular periods of rest. Wearied from her nightly activities, she had curled up in the bathroom pipes and fallen asleep with a tiny thumb in her mouth. The bathroom door was bolted, the jute lines taken down.

The rains had finally ceased sometime during the night though the sky remained dark. The back living room, which was rarely used except by Kuntal as her sleeping quarters, was finally thrown open. A contingent of bitter men, most of whom had been dragged out of their beds much earlier than they preferred on a Sunday morning, oozed into the room's stale air seeking relief from the heat, congestion, and their furtive memories of the ayah.

"She was too pretty for her own good," a middle-aged man commented, recollecting her fitted *choli* blouses, the gold embroidery along the neckline hypnotizingly brilliant.

"Her type was meant for prostituting, nothing else," said Maji's cousin, Uddhav Uncle, resentfully. He remembered nonchalantly leaning against a doorframe as he had seen Raj Kapoor do in the movies, throwing a suggestive look at Avni's sari-clad hips. She had simply walked past him as if he didn't exist.

"How do you know about such things *bhai*?" asked another teasingly, slapping him roughly on the back. "We better get you remarried, with a proper wife to take care of your needs."

Other men smoked on the verandah, stealing smug glances at the have-nots—the unrelated curiosity-seekers, the beggars, and a throng of three-legged dogs—that congregated on the other side of the chained gate. Parvati stood guard, brandishing a large umbrella which she swung with great vigor at anyone who attempted to scale the gate for a peek.

Their neighbor, Vimla Lawate, had unobtrusively brought over her personal cook who worked alongside Cook Kanj, boiling pots of chai and preparing lunch for the crowd. After her initial appearance, Savita had barricaded herself in her room trying to stem the flow of milk from her breasts, Kuntal comforting her. Seeking relief from the crowds, Dheer and Tufan knocked on their mother's door and quickly fell asleep inside. Nimish remained at his grandmother's side in the parlor, directing traffic, answering questions on behalf of the family, slipping temporarily into the position of head of the household. It was a burden he accepted with intelligence and grace. Maji, slumped upon her dais with a cup of chai, noted this with pride.

There had been no time that morning for her to reflect upon either Panditji's or the tantrik's words. For the first time since the death of

her husband, Maji had forgone her morning rounds. Instead, she had
to become an unwilling hostess: accepting the well-wishes of her relations while ignoring their unspoken accusations and the glint in their
eyes. *Is this the end of Maji, the downfall of the Mittal family?*

Maji grasped her forehead in an effort to stem the rising pain in her
head. The bungalow swelled with the intensity of the people packed
between its damp walls, each pressing for a bit of space, each vying to
show that he or she had been the closest to Pinky and so, by corollary,
was the most affected by her disappearance. The din—shuffling legs,
uncomfortable coughs, restrained conversations, chai cups clinking
against saucers, an occasional fart—grew more insistent, as if in expectation of something happening, as if in anticipation of relief. A phalanx of
ladies gathered along the long sofas, whispering away, each clutching
a teacup to her bosom as if a thief were loose in the bungalow.

"Abducted, can you believe?" said one wearing glasses with plastic
frames so large that her brightly lipsticked mouth was the only other
visible feature on her face.

"In my day, ayahs did as they were told, *hai-hai*. Nobody beats their
servants anymore," reflected an elderly auntie with a sharp tongue,
drifting into comforting nostalgia.

"I knew the ayah was a bad seed from the moment I saw her. *Hahn*,
don't you remember how I tried to convince Maji but she didn't listen,
and now look, utter chaos," said a third, a no-nonsense woman with
a gibbous protrusion on the tip of her nose.

"She had six toes on her left foot," Parvati interjected, appearing
with a pot of tea. "Chai anyone?"

The ladies on the couch drew back with a sharp breath.

"She was a witch, I'm telling you," the big-glasses auntie reflected,
latching onto this tidbit of information as if she had known it all
along.

"In my day such unnaturals lived in the villages only," clucked the
nostalgic one. "Nowadays, they think nothing of moving into your
very home."

"Maji must go on pilgrimage to Mehndipur, seek Lord Balaji's
mercy. Otherwise, utter chaos," said the third, clicking her purse snap
as if she were about to leave, though she secretly hoped that the drama
would stretch on for the better part of the week.

"Only a tantrik can get rid of such corruption, I'm telling you," warned Big Glasses, pursing her lips and peering around the room as if to spot the evil eye.

"*Tantrik-mantrik*," said the nostalgic auntie, delicately biting into a diamond of *besan burfi*. "In my day, a proper thrashing would have sufficed."

* * *

Jaginder stepped into the bungalow, still wearing his kurta from the night before, now wrinkled, stained with dried bits of mud, and smelling faintly of smoke and stale liquor. Conversations died out as every eye in the bungalow focused on him: *Look at the poor fellow, must have been out the whole night searching for Pinky.*

Maji felt the quiet awe that now surrounded Jaginder. How easy it had been to cover up his drinking all these years, the disintegration of his relationship with Savita, the loss of respect from his sons. These secrets, like others, had circulated safely only from Mittal ear to servant ear and back again, connecting the household in a web of complicity. Maji glanced towards Nimish, who struggled to contain his rage, and touched him softly on the arm.

Jaginder stood frozen, resentful of the meddlesome crowd and Maji and Nimish's tight alliance. He puffed out his chest, ready to blindly attack, to do anything to save his reputation, his good name in the community. As he looked at his mother, however, he noticed a sadness in her eyes, the small bald patches at her temples, the tremor of her hands. And it suddenly struck him that his mother was an old woman, worn from having to be so strong all these years, to single-handedly hold the family together. And he realized that, somewhere along the way, he had failed her. After his daughter drowned, he had allowed himself to do the very same—but in an endless river of indulgence, irresponsibility, and inebriation. And he had foolishly thought that his family would not notice.

But last night had been different. The fragile tenderness he and Savita shared had finally been crushed. Nimish had torn open the thin veil concealing his father's secret. And Maji had thrown him out, staking the family's future on his son. Jaginder thought of his aborted efforts to disinherit Nimish, and shame and sorrow flooded his chest as it had back at Rosie's *adda*. He wanted another chance to win their love, their respect. He couldn't imagine living apart from his family. He suddenly felt weak, as if every muscle in his body was straining to maintain a facade. As he stood there in front of his mother and son, he wanted to surrender, to accept responsibility at last for his misdeeds. But all of his relations were packed into the bungalow, as if in a courtroom, watching, waiting to render their verdict. It was too much humiliation for him to bear. He remained defiant.

"You didn't find her?" a relative finally asked as a murmur passed through the crowd.

Jaginder shook his head.

Slowly, Maji extended her hand towards her son. She had noticed Jaginder's hesitation, the slight slump of his shoulders. He was asking for her mercy, even as he stood before her. Jaginder knew better than anyone that Maji would never risk tarnishing the family's name by publicly shaming him. Yet, he had come back upon hearing the news of Pinky's disappearance. He had come back.

"Come, *beta*," she said. "We were worried."

Jaginder stood stiffly, trying to swallow his surprise at the gentleness in his mother's voice. She had not used that endearment—*beta*—since before he was married. If the bungalow had not been packed with spectators, he would have fallen at her feet and wept.

Outside the clouds abruptly burst with a terrible roar; rain pelted the rooftop and drenched the interior in gloomy darkness. Lamps were switched on and windows closed. The water pipes began to rattle and whoosh. Clutching purses tightly, ladies furtively looked around the bungalow. A leak sprung in the ceiling and then another, and a third. Water dripped rhythmically, ominously, upon the guests below.

Nimish caught Maji's eye.

"Parvati, get some buckets," Maji ordered, trying to hide her rising horror. From somewhere in the back hallway came a tinny noise.

"Eh? What's that ringing?" one of the guests asked.

"I'll go check," Nimish said.

"No," Maji said. "stay here."

The bungalow creaked under the monsoon's weight. Water began to flood from the hallway.

There were shouts and a general shuffling towards the door.

"Must be a burst pipe," Maji said, turning to Jaginder.

"Bloody hell," was all Jaginder could manage to say, peeling off his socks.

Nimish edged into the shadowy hallway, his feet splashing through icy puddles.

"The roads are going to flood!" Parvati shouted, pointing outside.

The electricity shorted out, casting the room into darkness. Everyone froze.

In the blackened hallway, Nimish stood motionless, his fingers stretching toward the bathroom door. Slowly he reached out, feeling for the bolt.

It was unlocked.

The door blew open, knocking him off his feet. An icy chill shot past him. In the parlor, someone screamed. The lights flickered on and off, alternately revealing and concealing a scene of pandemonium. Ladies dove aggressively into the pile of *chappals*, retrieving shoes. Men searched in vain for misplaced wives. Savita and Kuntal came rushing out of the bedroom with the twins. People jostled at the door. Somewhere in the confusion, a breast was grabbed.

Thunder ripped across the sky.

"Get out!" one of the guests yelled, joining the stampede of people racing down the driveway and out past the gates. "The roof's caving in!"

"The children!" Maji yelled.

"Oh my God!" Savita cried out.

"Here! Over here!" Jaginder shouted, fighting his way upstream to his wife.

And then, as the last guest fled from the bungalow, the power abruptly returned.

Maji stood in the middle of a pool of rainwater, eyeing the solid roof above her.

Jaginder straightened his kurta, throwing dirty looks at his fleeing relations. "Bloody cowards! Afraid of a sprinkling of rainwater!"

"It's just a leak," Maji said, her chest heaving.

Sure enough, in the right light, the water appeared to be originating from a gap in the roof.

"Nimi!" Savita called out in a shrill voice, "where's Nimish?"

"I'm here, Mummy." He appeared, limping slightly, and regarded his mother's pale face. "The door was bolted." He lied for the first time to Savita's face. "Everything's okay, I checked."

࿔

In the stillness of the puja room, Maji began to think. This terrible monsoon night had left her household, her beliefs, her very core battered and bruised. She did not know how much longer she could hold things together. Now all her relations would be gossiping about the bungalow's terrible state of disrepair, making up stories about how they were almost crushed to death by a collapsing roof. And to make matters worse, Savita's socialite parents would arrive any day from Goa, where they owned a second home on Colva Beach.

Maji pushed these thoughts aside and briefly reflected upon Jaginder. This terrible night had finally brought him to his senses. She pondered the tantrik's cryptic words: *What you have given will be given; what you have taken will be taken.* Maji had implored the gods to give Pinky back. *Take what you want,* she had begged. The entire night, it seemed, had been like a scale, deadened with the heaviness of loss. Perhaps now with Panditji's prayers and the tantrik's puja, the balance might swing the other way. Certainly, Jaginder's repentant return was an auspicious sign. Eyes closed in front of the gods, Maji indulged in a moment of gratitude.

But then she remembered: the ghost was bound within the walls of the bungalow. *What once killed the ghost now sustains her life.* Maji shifted painfully in front of the altar and opened her eyes. The ghost was at her mercy. As powerful as it had become, Maji was more powerful. She had the ultimate weapon.

"Water," she said out loud.

The baby had drowned in a bucket of water. And now, Maji realized, by denying the ghost this substance, she could kill it.

FISHING VILLAGE

Pinky opened her eyes. She was lying on a sort of cot, covered by a rough blanket. Her head throbbed, her body felt as if it were on fire yet her fingertips were blue. "Maji?" she called out in fright. A sharp pain stabbed her in the side of her chest.

Immediately, a woman appeared and squatted by her side. A tattoo was etched onto her forearm. She wore a green cotton sari pulled back between her legs with a faded turquoise blouse. Her hair was pulled back in a bun encircled by a jasmine wreath. A chunky silver necklace fell across her chest. Her face was dark, like chocolate, and deeply marked with wrinkles as if by a troubled life. She was not old but her countenance was weary. Gently, she spooned water into Pinky's mouth and replaced the cloth covering her forehead with a cool one.

"Lovely?"

The woman shook her head, "You can call me Janibai Auntie."

"Lovely *didi*? Is she here too?"

"I'm sorry," Janibai said. "Only you. Was she with you?"

"No," Pinky lied, suddenly aware of her strange surroundings.

"Rest now," Janibai said, standing up and looking out the door.

Pinky heard voices outside speaking in a dialect that she did not understand but recognized from her outings to Crawford Market as Konkani, the language of the fisherpeople. A youthful man dressed in a *tikkona* with one end tied like a rope between his thighs, revealing tight, muscular legs, and a striped T-shirt, entered the small hut and began shouting. He and Janibai exchanged heated words, all the while alternately pointing to Pinky and to some unknown object that lay outside the palm-leaf walls of the hut. Pinky looked out the open door and saw a rectangle of golden sand glittering in the morning sun. A cluster of small, dark faces peered in, chattering excitedly. The skin of Pinky's face felt tight, her throat was parched and breathing labored. She closed her eyes, allowing sleep to finally overcome her.

Suddenly, the prattling children fell quiet and a burly man burst in, carrying a glistening black rubber raincoat over his arm, pants tucked into black rubber boots. "Janibai Chachar?"

Janibai nodded her head.

"I'm Inspector Pascal of the police and I'm looking for your daughter, Avni Chachar," he said in a voice that demanded rather than inquired. A Smith & Wesson . 38 hung from the webbing holster at his hip.

Janibai drew back sharply and shook her head.

"No? What do you mean by no?"

The fisherman stepped forward. "Her daughter's not here, sir."

"Where is she?" Pascal's brow thickened.

"She died thirteen years ago, sir."

"And who are you?"

"Her nephew, sir," he said, pointing at Janibai.

The inspector paused for a minute. Outside, the children began shouting again. A thin, balding man wearing khaki shorts and a matching *topi* was running down the sand. When he reached the open door, he tapped it halfheartedly before standing at attention in the doorway. The triangle of small faces reappeared, intently watching the action.

"Ah," Pascal said with as much disdain as he could muster. "Assistant Police Sub-Inspector Bambarkar to the rescue, I see."

"Yes, sir, Inspector Pascal, sir," Bambarkar said, surreptitiously gripping the doorframe with one hand to keep from being blown over by the strong ocean winds.

Pascal refocused his attention on Janibai. "Your daughter was spotted at Malabar Hill last night."

"How can that be possible, sir?" the nephew asked disbelievingly.

The inspector shot him a glare perfected during his years in the police service, one that immediately reminded the recipient that he could be thrashed at will. As if on cue, A. S. I. Bambarkar pulled out a long bamboo stick and, bracing himself against the door, began to slap it on the palm of his hand.

"I'm not mistaken," Pascal stated deliberately.

Janibai crossed her arms, unfazed by the inspector's implicit threat. "You did not see my daughter, I'm sure of it."

"Where's your proof?" Pascal demanded.

"I saw her die with my own eyes."

"How?"

"She threw herself in front of a commuter train at Masjid Station."

"Suicide?" Pascal said.

"She was distraught," Janibai said. "She didn't make sense, talked about the midwife and a sacrifice. Her sari was wet, her mouth crusted red."

"And what were you doing there?" Pascal asked. "The fish markets are at Khar-Danda, Citylight, Dadar, and Crawford."

"I've always sold at VT," Janibai answered. Believing that Victoria Terminus Station had been built upon the ruins of Ekuira's original shrine, she went to VT to not only sell her fish, but to pay homage to her patron goddess.

"Very suspicious," Pascal grunted, then began to circle the small room, his eyes taking in a pile of baskets in need of repair, lingering hungrily over the savory pot of fish fried in peanut oil with tomato, onion, and *kala* masala, the plate of rice and curry, the hot *bhakri* bread.

He peered into the cot, at the small body huddled under the covers. Shouting with surprise, he dropped his raincoat and pulled back the blanket.

"It's the missing girl!" he yelled, accusingly at Janibai and her nephew. "She looks exactly like her photo!"

Pinky's eyes briefly fluttered opened.

"We don't know her name," the nephew said. "I found her on a boat at sea early this morning."

"You found her in a boat on the ocean?" Pascal asked. "During the monsoons?"

"I don't know how she got there, sir," the nephew said, not revealing that he was almost certain he had seen two people in the canoe, that the boat had overturned as he approached. "I saw the boat bobbing on the waters early this morning when it was still very dark. I found the little girl in it, unconscious."

"Very nice story, you must sell it to the picture-*wallahs*," Pascal said magnanimously as he rubbed the handle of his Smith & Wesson. "Now let me tell you what really happened. Your cousin Avni paid Pinky's neighbor to abduct her. Avni planned to hide her here until the Mittal family paid her a big sum of money. I know how your type works."

"A big sum of money?" Janibai asked, shocked. "Why would anyone do that?"

"I told you sir, I don't know who this little girl is," the nephew insisted. "I never saw her before this morning."

"Her name's Pinky Mittal and she disappeared late last night from the home of Jaginder Mittal of Mittal Shipbreaking Enterprises, Ltd of Malabar Hill," the inspector said, in a mixture of fury and elation.

Janibai gasped, immediately recognizing the name. *My daughter's former employer!*

"Aha!" Pascal said, raising a thick finger at her. "So you *were* lying!" "Tell me," he said, "was there anything else in or around the boat?"

There was a long pause. Pascal frowned. Bambarkar scowled. The children outside chattered. "Either you cooperate or I will search this place myself."

"Get it, Auntie," the nephew said to Janibai in their Konkani dialect.

Janibai reluctantly retrieved a small bundle wrapped in paper from the corner of the room. A damp and badly torn golden *dupatta* lay inside, embroidered in a pattern of cascading emerald leaves. A label at one end read Sweetie Fashions, one of the exclusive shops along the Colaba Causeway.

"You were stealing the girl's *dupatta*, too?" Pascal thundered. Collecting himself and his raincoat, he barked at Bambarkar to load Pinky into his jeep. The officer lifted Pinky from the cot, his pencil-thin legs shaking with the effort.

"I'm taking her to the hospital," Pascal announced benevolently. "Her family will be most relieved that I've rescued her. I myself will be back in a few hours. In the meantime, A. S. I. Bambarkar will stay here to keep an eye out for your daughter, Avni. Either she turns herself in or you will both find yourselves in jail by sunset tomorrow."

"I will do the needful, sir," Bambarkar said, eagerly anticipating being the sole officer in charge, commanding respect with a tap of his bamboo *lathi*. Pleasure dotted his sweaty face.

Waking up, Pinky began to cough.

Pascal began to interrogate her. "Tell me, little girl, what's your full name?"

Pinky stared vacantly.

"Never mind, I know who you are." He paused to take a deep breath and puffed his chest out with satisfaction before lifting Pinky's face by her chin. "Can you tell me what happened last night?"

Pinky was burning with fever, her body shook with chills, but even so, she refused to speak to the burly police officer whom she instinctively mistrusted. All at once she noticed the *dupatta* that Pascal had tucked under his arm. "Give me that!" she said.

"Is it yours?" Pascal asked, shaking the *dupatta* at her. "Or, perhaps, Lovely Lawate's?"

Pinky could not contain her surprise. *What do they know?* she wondered.

"She took you from your home, didn't she? Didn't she?" Pascal shot Bambarkar a look that seemed to say, *Watch you bloody fool, watch how I solve two cases at one blow.* The assistant sub-inspector tried to look impressed. "Where is she?" Pascal asked. "I have a feeling in my gut that Lovely and Avni were together last night, too."

Pinky pressed her lips together, struggling to contain her emotions.

"Start by telling me what happened to Lovely after you both reached Colaba."

Why did Lovely didi want to drown me? Pinky asked herself as the blurred events of the previous night unspooled in her head. All at once and with diamond-sharp clarity, she remembered Lovely's terrifying voice, the crushing heat in her chest as if something were entering her body, and the sickening whack of the oar.

"Listen, little girl, tell me what happened to Lovely or I'll put your Maji in jail."

"You can't do that!"

Pascal began to laugh. "Oh, I can, I can. I can do whatever I want. Imagine that, your fat grandmother rotting in an overcrowded cell, surrounded by *chors* and *dakus*, lowlife criminals."

I won't let him take Maji. Never-ever-ever.

"TELL ME!"

Bambarkar gave her a firm, little shake for good measure.

Pinky coughed a phlegmy mass at his face. *I won't let Maji go to jail because of me,* she thought. *I did it all, befriended the ghost and . . . and Lovely.* She hid her face in her hands.

But her words, rang clear.

"I killed her."

WATER-ELIMINATION PLAN

From the emergency room of Bombay Hospital, a ward boy was dispatched with a small notebook to be delivered to Dr. M. M. Iyer who was at the hospital canteen eating an onion omelet. The Goanese mess contractor hovered nearby, looking for signs of gastronomic satisfaction. The notebook contained the message, *Child with high fever admitted* with the additional clarification *Jaginder Mittal Family.*

He signed the note, marking the time as 9 a.m. The ward boy departed. Normally, the doctor would have taken the full half hour allotted before showing up at the ward, perhaps topping off the omelet with a serving of *idli-sambar*, perhaps even escaping outside for a quick smoke. But today, expecting that Maji or at the very least Jaginder would be impatiently waiting for him, Dr. Iyer pushed his dish aside and, grabbing his white coat, headed for the pediatric ward.

He was careful to have his coat on before entering, lest he be caught by the eagle-eyed, iron-fisted head of the hospital, Dean Bobby Bansal, and fined twenty-five rupees. Just last night, the Dean caught one of the residents smoking in the surgical ward and promptly threw him out of the hospital, refusing to accept payment from his family for his reinstatement. Dr. Iyer paused outside the door, slicking back his hair, adjusting the stethoscope around his neck, patting a percussion hammer and notebook in his bottom pocket while pulling a pen out of his top one.

Pinky had arrived before him, pushed on a trolley with small, squeaky wheels.

"Your patient, Doctor Sa'ab," said the head nurse, a Keralite Christian by the name of Mary. She wore a white dress uniform and an all-white cap to differentiate herself from the white-and-blue-cap-wearing junior nurses. Her dark hair was neatly clipped in a bun in the back of her head. Having never married, Mary continued to live in the nurses' dorm behind the hospital where no men—whether boyfriends, doctors, or even family members—were allowed.

Pinky lay in the far end of a greenish room with one sole black-grilled window where entire clans of thick-bodied flies buzzed excitedly, drawn to the smell of urine and disinfectant that emanated from the opened window. An indolent ceiling fan lethargically stirred germs from one cot to its neighbor and back. Mary drew a dingy cloth curtain around Pinky.

"Ah, yes," said Dr. M. M. Iyer, examining Pinky's chart. Graphs indicated elevated temperature, elevated pulse, and a normal blood pressure. So far, there was no record of bowel movements or urine output. Other information such as the greenish discharge from Pinky's coughing was noted on a separate page. "Pneumonia," he stated, noting his diagnosis on the chart before handing it to Nurse Mary who hung it on the end of the bed. "Start her on penicillin."

"Yes, Doctor Sa'ab."

Then, surprised, he pushed back the curtain and looked around him as if he had misplaced something. "Where's her family?"

"She was brought in by the police," Mary reported in a crisp whisper.

"Police?" Dr. Iyer was intrigued. "The circumstances being?"

"Unknown."

"Has her family been notified?"

"Yes, Doctorji."

Dr. Iyer hesitated. He wanted to be present when Pinky's family arrived so he busied himself checking Pinky's heartbeat and lungs, hoping she might wake up. After checking on several of his other young patients, he took a seat at the nurse's desk where the doctors usually retired after their rounds to write out their notes.

The ward boy reappeared with another notebook for him, paging him to the Administration Ward.

"Inspector Pascal, summoning me?" Dr. Iyer muttered to himself, beginning to sweat. "Mary, send me a message at Administration as soon as the Mittal family arrives." Then shaking his head in disbelief, he rushed away, just missing Maji and Nimish.

"Where's my Pinky?"

Nurse Mary pointed to one of the rooms.

Tears that had been held back all night now rolled down Maji's face as she crossed the room and stood by her granddaughter, afraid she might collapse from relief. "*Beti*," she said softly, pressing Pinky's hand.

Pinky opened her feverish eyes. Maji slid against the cot, simultaneously thanking the gods for her safe return and imploring them for her recovery.

"Inspector Pascal said that he found you in Colaba," Nimish said. "Is it true?"

"Let her rest," Maji ordered sharply.

"Her *dupatta*," Pinky whispered sharply, tugging at Maji's sari, "get it back."

"Her *dupatta*?" Nimish asked anxiously. "Where's Lovely?"

"Don't talk," Maji said, glancing around. "Others can hear."

Dr. Iyer walked briskly into the pediatric ward, Pascal at his heels. "She has a severe case of pneumonia."

"Pneumonia?" Maji asked.

"We must keep her here," the doctor said.

"For how long?"

"She's under house arrest," Pascal interjected.

"Please, Inspector," Dr. Iyer said coldly, knowing that within the confines of the hospital he commanded even the inspector's compliance, "the child's very sick. Arresting her isn't necessary."

Maji stepped in front of the inspector, blocking his access to Pinky's bed, "What's this nonsense? Nimish, please, go find me some tea."

Nimish hesitated but Maji's glare sent him reluctantly out of the ward.

"Doctorji, please give us a moment," Maji added, dispatching Dr. Iyer, on his way too.

"Now Inspector," Maji said. "You're not telling me that my grand-daughter's responsible for anything that happened last night?"

"I'm very sorry," Pascal said. "But this morning she confessed to killing Lovely Lawate."

ॐ ॐ ॐ

Back at the bungalow, Jaginder sat on the sofa, restlessly scanning the newspapers. Dheer and Tufan slept in the parlor. Savita remained locked behind her bedroom door, not joining in even when she heard the telephone call and the boys' shouts of joy that Pinky had been found. *What about* my *daughter?* she asked herself, untying the cloth that bound her chest. She had had the strangest dreams when she finally fell asleep that night after the tantrik left. She had been lying naked upon her bedspread singing the lullaby, "*Soja baby, soja, lal palang per soja.* Sleep baby, sleep on a red bed, mummy and papa are coming."

And then her baby girl had reached for her, had crawled upon her chest and begun to nurse, sucking and sucking until there was nothing left. In the dream, Savita had tried to hold her but her breasts had turned into long drain pipes, the baby suckling at the very end of them. *Mummy's coming!* she cried, trying to push her breasts away to reach for her child. She had woken exhausted, her nipples sore and cracked, breasts once again full of milk.

If I were to die, she reflected, *I can leave all this pain behind and be with my baby girl.* For a moment, she relished the thought of haunting her mother-in-law and husband from the otherworld, her vengeful spirit spiting their authority, upsetting the bolsters on Maji's dais and lurking in Jaginder's bottles of Royal Salut. But then she thought of her sons, her much-anticipated luncheon with the wife of a motor scooter tycoon, her jewels. How could she leave all that behind?

Kuntal arrived with a plate of food. "You must eat and drink," she implored, attempting to put a piece of bread, slick with Polson butter, into Savita's mouth.

Savita began to weep, placing her cheek against an open page of the latest romance novel that Kuntal had thoughtfully procured from the local library. "Why won't she come to me? Why can't I see her?"

Kuntal stroked Savita's thick hair, gently wiping away her tears.

Then they heard a knock at the door. Savita sat up and blew her nose.

Jaginder entered cautiously, motioning for Kuntal to leave. "Pinky's recovering now. You'll be better soon, too."

"Better?" Savita asked in a soft, menacing voice. She began to tear at the eyelets on her soaking blouse until her breasts lay exposed, still dripping white liquid. She held them in her hands. "*These* are not better."

Jaginder looked away, a flush of shame in his cheeks.

"Can't you look at me anymore?"

"Savita, please."

"Please what?" she flopped on her back. "Go, just go."

"I'm sorry—"

"Do you know what happened?" Savita halted and took in a long breath. Her erect nipples pointed accusingly at the clothesline above. "A ghost!"

"Ghost?"

"Our daughter!"

"Our little Chakori?" Jaginder was shocked. "You're starting to imagine things. You need some proper rest."

He walked over to the bed and tried to relatch her blouse.

Savita angrily pushed his hands away. "Go ask your mother if you don't believe me. She was the one who called for a tantrik to come here last night. She knew all these years that the ayah deliberately drowned Chakori and she kept it a secret. And now that terrible witch has come back to kill our sons. Dheer almost died last night!"

"What the bloody hell are you talking about?" Jaginder asked, fear rising up, clutching at his throat. *Oh God! Oh God!*

"Go!" Savita shouted, throwing the romance novel at him. "Leave me alone!"

Jaginder clenched and unclenched his fists, then turned and closed the door behind him. Outside, the Ambassador was gone, Gulu had taken it to drive Maji and Nimish to the hospital. But the black Mercedes remained in the garage. Jaginder popped open the truck and reached for a bottle of Blue Label that was stashed there. He poured the liquid down his throat until he began to gag. Then he threw the bottle against the wall, splattering Gulu's sparse room and his Cherry

Blossom poster with whiskey and bits of glass. He took the broken bottle and, with steely deliberation, slashed at his arm. But the searing pain of the jagged glass was nothing, nothing compared to the anguish in his heart.

⁕ ⁕ ⁕

"That's utter nonsense," Maji said to Inspector Pascal, even as she felt the crushing weight of those words: *killing Lovely Lawate.*

"Apparently Miss Lawate took Pinky just before your phone call to my precinct last night. From there, they proceeded directly to Colaba. There may have been a third person, someone with a vehicle. It's my belief that they then met up with your previous ayah, Avni Chachar. As I already told you on the phone, I found Pinky at Janibai Chachar's home in Colaba. In my opinion, Miss Lawate was trying to run away with a boy, using Pinky to cover her tracks. Avni was in on it for the money. I'm talking blackmail of course."

Maji was so shocked by the inspector's theory that, for a moment, she could not speak. "Am I hearing you correctly, Mr. Inspector? I've known Lovely since she was a baby. She would never harm anyone, especially my Pinky." Silently, she thought, *Avni? Has she really come back?*

"I'm still piecing the facts together."

"And what facts are these?"

"Janibai Chachar's hut. Pinky's confession."

"Pinky's confession?" Maji retorted. "Is this how you operate? Forcing a gravely ill child to talk? Believing her delirious rantings? I suggest you try to find Lovely."

"My men are fanned out all over Bombay. If she's alive, she and her lover," he paused to let the scandalous word sink in, "will most certainly try to leave the city."

"And what about this Avni Chachar?"

"She must have been displeased to have lost her job, so much so that she became vengeful."

Maji recoiled. "I want my granddaughter's name removed from your files. If you harm her in the slightest way, you will have me to contend with. I think you understand me, Inspector Pascal."

Pascal ground his teeth. He knew that Maji had powerful allies in business and government who could make trouble for him if he proceeded against her granddaughter. And besides, he really did not believe Pinky's confession and neither would any judge with half a brain. It was a cover-up for something. "Your granddaughter *is* involved."

"I want her uninvolved," Maji said, her voice like the steel her family had bought and sold for generations. "You found her ill but untouched and brought her to the hospital. That's your new story. I'll do whatever it takes."

Pascal slowly raised an eyebrow, a question, a confirmation.

"Whatever it takes. And not a word of this to Lovely's family."

"Agreed."

"And I'll send my son to retrieve Lovely's *dupatta* this afternoon."

Pascal looked surprised.

"You will be paid for it, of course, and well paid," Maji said.

"Just outside Churchgate Station then," the Inspector sighed resignedly. "There's a restaurant, the Asiatica. Five p.m."

After Pascal left, Nimish arrived with the tea. "Why's she under arrest?"

"For her own safety, *beta*," Maji replied. "They have not found the ayah yet."

She didn't add that it would be best to keep Pinky in the hospital until the baby ghost had been dealt with.

"And Lovely? Did they find her?"

"No, *beta*," Maji said, struggling to contain her confusion and sorrow. "Not yet."

Pinky kept her eyes closed during the conversation, pretending to sleep but digesting every word, every lie, every concealment. And though she was immensely grateful to Maji for keeping her out of Pascal's clutches, she could not understand why her grandmother had sacrificed Lovely in the process. Nimish was her only hope now. *He'll find Lovely. If she's alive, he'll find her. He needs to know the truth.* She opened her eyes, "Nimish—"

"You're awake," Maji said, pressing her hand gently. "Don't talk to anyone. Pretend you're asleep if that Pascal tries to question you again. Don't say another word."

"But Lovely—"

"Not another word!" Maji commanded. "It's not safe to talk here, you never know who may be listening."

Nimish turned to give Pinky a look that said, *I'll be back.*

His eyes were resolute, his love painfully exposed.

Pinky had to return to the bungalow, to Nimish, before it was too late. *Tell him to come to me,* Lovely had said in the boat, *I'll wait as long as I can but I can never go back.* Pinky forced herself to sit up. She had to get out of the hospital. If Nimish did not come back that night, she decided, she would find a way out on her own.

❀ ❦ ❁

At home, Maji immediately retired to the puja room where she allowed grief to spill from her body unchecked. Pinky had been found and the divinities were duly thanked, but Lovely was still missing, maybe even dead. *Had she really run away and—my God—with a boy? Had she asked Pinky to cover up for her actions?*

It would be too risky to question Pinky further in the hospital, Maji decided; she'd wait she until she could bring her back to the bungalow. Alone now in her sanctuary, Maji grieved for her friend Vimla. *The past can never be undone,* she lamented. Vimla, poor dear Vimla, would now have to experience that same pain, the terrible penetrating void within oneself.

Death or disappearance? Maji considered. *Which is worse?*

If Lovely had indeed run off, nothing could repair the damage done to the family's reputation. But what if, what if, somehow Pascal was right? What if Avni was involved? What if she had somehow persuaded Lovely and then Lovely had accidentally been hurt? Tears filled Maji's eyes as she beseeched the holy trinity—Brahma, Vishnu, Shiva—to somehow, miraculously, return Lovely alive.

I was right to bargain with that Pascal, to save my family's reputation, she told herself as she wiped her eyes with the end of her sari *palloo.* Whatever happened to Lovely, nothing could be gained by linking Pinky to her. Nothing but trouble.

After clearing her face of emotions, Maji called to Jaginder who was pacing the parlor in a sullen silence. "We need to talk."

Closing the door behind him, Jaginder stood uncertainly, his wounded arm tucked behind his back. They stared at each other for a long moment, a look that said, *We're in this together.*

"I think all this stress is starting to affect Savita," Jaginder began to babble. "Her mind. Wasn't her great-grandmother, mad too? Didn't you tell me that she talked to ghosts, too? Are these thing hereditary?"

Maji cut him off. "Your wife's stronger than you think, and smarter. You could learn something from her."

"Ha!" Jaginder roared. "You want smart? I won't let you put Nimish in charge of the business. I'll bloody disinherit him first. Ha!"

"So that's what's on your mind?" Maji asked, unfazed. "I thought you cared more for the well-being of your family. Don't you remember your father's dying words to you?"

Jaginder did. *Son*, Omanandlal had said, *shipbreaking is not just a business. It is the sacred way of fulfilling your duty, your dharma in life. Your mother has a direct phone line to God—put it to full use.*

He had glanced toward Maji, as if to ask her to ring up the divine on the spot, to request a barter of a new body for his old soul, one at the very least destined to become a Congress Party cabinet minister or perhaps even a film star on a par with Jubilee Kumar or playback singer Kundan Lal Saigal. As if on cue, he began to hum the lullaby, "*So Ja Rajkumari*" from the 1940s hit *Zindagi*. *Sleep, princess, sleep. Sleep and sweet dreams will come. In the dreams, see your beloved. Fly to Roopnagar and be encircled by maidens. The king will garland you.*

The tune floated from his lips. Maji's dark eyes glistened as she watched her husband close his for the very last time. Jaginder, for his part, never had the heart to tell his father that their phone line did not reach the gods but at best, when they were working, to the Walkeshwar Temple down the street.

"He said it was my duty, my dharma," Jaginder said. Maji had pulled the well-being-of-your-family card. *Damn, damn, damn.* He quickly restrategized.

"Well there's no need to tear apart the family that I've worked all my life to keep together," Maji continued wearily. "One needs a certain cunning to survive in business now. Cunning that Nimish, unfortunately, does not possess. Tufan, perhaps, he's like you, but he's still too young."

Jaginder felt his spirits lifting. "Tufan?"

"Enough of this drinking. I will no longer turn a blind eye, do you understand?"

"Yes."

"Until the day I die, I am still the head of this family, do you understand?"

"Yes."

"Now, listen carefully. You are to meet Inspector Pascal at the Asiatica restaurant near Churchgate at five p.m. tonight."

"Inspector Pascal!"

"He has agreed to keep Pinky's name out of this mess, to straighten things out in the press, in exchange for some—" Maji rubbed her thumb and forefinger together.

"What! You want me to get involved in something like this?"

Maji raised her eyebrows. "You're no stranger to illegal activities. It's not like we're harming anyone. He'll give you a package. Bring it straight to my room, understand? Take the money from my cabinet."

Jaginder hesitated; his arm throbbed with pain as the thin material of his shirt dried into the congealing wound. "What's in the package?"

"Nothing that you need know about."

Jaginder searched his mother's face for clues but found none.

"A worthy man will do anything to protect his family," Maji added, her gaze falling upon Jaginder's hurt arm. The damn family card again. He had no choice.

* * *

Maji took her place in the parlor upon her ornamented platform and called everyone to her side. Jaginder sat and began wiping the sweat from his brow. The boys arrived still munching on stuffed potato flatbread. Savita languidly sauntered out and promptly curled up on a sofa, refusing to open her eyes. Parvati and Cook Kanj appeared with trays of cool green sherbet drinks for the adults and yogurt *lassis* for the boys.

Gulu settled onto the floor, eyes darting back and forth. Ever since Pinky's disappearance, he had felt an overwhelming need to find Avni. Now that Pinky was found, he was certain that Avni was hiding somewhere nearby. This morning he had decided, come what may, he would find her. His childhood friends—Hari Bhai in Dharavi, Bambarkar in the police force, and Yash in Kamathipura—would all be willing to do him a favor.

"A darkness has descended over our household," Maji began, shifting uncomfortably. "Beginning last night—Dheer's choking, Pinky's abduction . . ."

"Lovely's disappearance," Nimish added.

Tufan squeezed his thighs, hoping that his bed-wetting would not be included on the list. It had happened again that morning.

"I have prayed for an answer and I have found it."

Savita opened one eye.

"For four nights, every drop of water in the household must be eliminated."

Jaginder had no idea what Maji's solution might be, but her *pani-hatao* plan, her order to eradicate water was so far from anything he could have reasonably expected that he let out a snort. "It's the bloody monsoon season for God's sake."

"I'm aware of that," Maji replied with narrowed eyes. "But we must get rid of the ghost."

"Ghost?" Jaginder said, letting out a long fart as if he had been pricked by a pin.

Tufan ran for cover.

"Now you believe me?" Savita shot back.

"What killed the baby now sustains the ghost," Nimish said, remembering the tantrik's enigmatic declaration.

"But why do we have to get rid of her?" Dheer asked, mouth full of potato.

"The tantrik gave us another choice," Savita said, sitting up.

"Replace her pain with its cosmic counterpart," Nimish cited once again, "and one day she'll go on her own."

Everyone stared at him blankly.

"Love," Nimish explained, "is the cosmic complement to pain."

"Let's just love her then!" Savita cried out, squeezing Nimish's arm in gratitude.

Jaginder burst out laughing.

"This is a proper Hindu household," Maji said.

"Proper?" It was Savita's turn to laugh.

"*All* of you would need to love her," Parvati chimed in from her spot on the floor, "before she'd be willing leave."

"Well *I'm* not going to," Tufan declared.

"Please, please," Dheer begged. "Why can't we try?"

"Why? Why?" Jaginder hauled himself from the sofa and slapped Dheer across the head. "Because it almost killed you, you bloody idiot."

"Look at all the trouble your ghost has caused already," Maji said. "If we back down now, it will take over! And then what?"

"She's only a baby!" Savita said desperately. "She's never had parents to guide her! I could teach her!"

"Have you lost your senses?" Jaginder cut in, glaring at his wife. "Don't eat garlic, fine. Put bloody marks behind our sons' ears every morning, fine. Hang turmeric stones above our bed, fine, fine. But I draw the line at this!"

"It's been decided—*bas*," Maji boomed. "I will not tolerate your impertinence, Savita."

Savita bit her lip, humiliated. Her deep, dirty longing worked its way up into her chest where thick, white milk still flowed unchecked. *In four days hence*, she silently vowed, staring at her mother-in-law, *if you take my daughter from me, I will seize the bungalow from you.*

Maji held out a fistful of black strings. "The tantrik gave me these, to tie onto each and every faucet in the bungalow to dry them out."

"My bath!" Tufan said.

A chorus of 'mine too' followed.

"Take your baths!" Maji sighed irritably. "But before night falls, the faucets will be turned off for the next four days."

"No need for all of us to suffer," Jaginder said, striding to the phone. "I'll book us rooms at the Taj for the duration."

"Stop!" Maji ordered. "The tantrik said that each of us who was here when the baby drowned must bear witness to the ghost's demise."

"I have to miss my classes?" Nimish asked, thinking about getting back to Pinky at the hospital. She was the last one to see Lovely. She knew what had happened to her. He felt it in his bones. She knew.

"No one can leave for four days," Maji answered, pointing her cane at each of them. "NO ONE."

A loud collective gasp filled the room as each member of the household reflected upon the implications of this injunction.

"Parvati," Maji said, "the laundry will have to be sent out each morning. Kanj, you need to set up a makeshift kitchen in your quarters out back."

"We can't be haunted back there?"

"Where's your brain?" Parvati clucked at her husband. "The ghost can't leave the bungalow. Tantrik Baba himself made sure of that."

"Gulu, go pick up some food staples from the market. Kanj will give you a list."

Gulu nodded, silently thanking his patron god, Ganesh, the remover of all obstacles. This outing would be his chance to escape, to find Avni at last.

"Kuntal, Nimish, Dheer, Tufan," Maji continued, "every drop of water from ceiling leaks has to be immediately wiped away. No liquid of any kind will be allowed in this house. Do you understand what this means? And, lastly, we all have to share the servants' toilet out back."

At this Savita almost fainted, "I would rather die."

"You have no choice," Maji said. "You must adjust."

"What about Pinky?" Dheer asked.

"She'll stay at the hospital."

"What!" Savita began to weep. The injustice of the situation was too much to bear. "She gets waited on hand and foot while we live like street urchins?"

"She wasn't here when the baby drowned."

"Well," Jaginder said, trying to sound lighthearted. "I'm off!"

"Off?" Savita demanded. "Where are *you* going?"

"Tying up some loose ends at the office before our imprisonment," Jaginder lied, feeling the ironic sting of his words.

"I'll go with you Papa," Nimish said. He had to get out of the house.

Jaginder snorted.

Nimish turned to Gulu. "I'll come with you then."

Gulu's eyes grew wide. He'd be damned if Nimish was going to spoil his plan of escape.

Maji stepped in, guessing what Nimish had in mind. "You stay right here, young man. When everything is settled, then we'll talk to Pinky."

"But she was with Lovely last night!"

"No," Maji said, already spinning the agreed-upon lie. "Inspector Pascal found her alone and unaccosted last night and took her straight to the hospital. She had nothing to do with Lovely."

Nimish dropped his face. *I must get out tonight. I must,* he thought.

"Be back before nightfall." Maji turned to Jaginder with a wagging finger, "The gates will be chained at sunset."

"No need to worry," Jaginder promised as he strode out the door. "I'll be back."

Eyeing the rectangular bulge in Jaginder's raincoat pocket, Nimish turned away, not believing for a moment that his father would return.

CRYSTAL VIALS
OF ATTAR

G ulu and Jaginder left the bungalow simultaneously but in different vehicles, and in different states of mind. Jaginder, in the black
Mercedes crouched like a lion ready to attack. Gulu sat in the Ambassador, dipping into the dimly recalled determination of his boyhood
days at Victoria Terminus, his bandaged hand cradled to his chest.
Unbeknownst to one another, they were each headed to police headquarters, Jaginder just to pass by from the outside, to take stock of
what he was about to do, and Gulu to go inside and hope for the best.

Jaginder reached it first, slowing his car just opposite the high stone
archway and Victorian columns that supported the second story of
the building. The compound itself was run-down. The thick stone
walls held together with lime were now encrusted with mold, the red,
sloping roof was missing at least half its original tiles, and the grimy
windows hid immodestly behind cracked and warped wooden slats.
Just to the left of the structure sat rows and rows of rusting metal
drums, captured during raids on illicit distilleries and left, abandoned,
for the sole purpose of impressing visiting senior officers.

To the right was a parking lot containing a number of impounded cars. The more dilapidated ones, not worth enduring a lengthy judicial process to reclaim them, simply rotted away. Others, perhaps involved in a terrible accident in which the driver or passenger had died, lay forsaken—the owners unwilling to touch a thing that had brought *panavti*, ill luck. Those particular cars would be eventually sold to a trusted *kabadi*, who regularly bought unclaimed goods from the station, stolen or otherwise, the tidy profit going directly into the senior officers' pockets.

Jaginder hesitated for a moment, checking the sign written in white letters on a dark blue board that clattered noisily with each new gust of wind. If successful, he told himself, what he was just about to do would earn his way back into Maji's good graces. If things did not go well, however, Jaginder could only imagine how his cat-and-mouse game with the inspector would end. Shrugging off his growing fear, Jaginder snorted. *Imagine Nimish being asked to cut a deal with a police officer!* His confidence boosted, he stepped on his accelerator, and drove hurriedly towards Churchgate Station. He planned to be early for his meeting at the Asiatica.

* * *

Gulu arrived at the police station and momentarily took a seat on one of the crowded wooden benches that lined the front verandah, glancing at the others waiting for the inspector's attention. A woman in a pale green sari was wailing, fist beating her chest, about her dead child. Others stared at her with blank faces. Fear shot through Gulu's body, a feeling he remembered from his childhood at VT—the vulnerability of being on the outside, of always being suspect because he was poor. He had run into many policemen back then, but Big Uncle always took care of any problems. Driving the streets of Bombay, Gulu continued to encounter the police, but they were usually lowly constables while he was firmly behind the wheel of an imposing Ambassador.

Standing now, he avoided the wailing woman, and pushed open the door, stepping into the dull aqua building buzzing with the sounds of ringing telephones, shuffling people, click-clacking typewriters—all unfazed by the ghastly screaming from the back office where a suspect was being beaten. The smallish hall, surprisingly tidy, was jammed with clerks and officers sitting at various desks. The station inspector sat in the far back corner, behind a large table covered with cotton baize. He was roughly interrogating an impoverished man whose head hung as he stood there, though there were two empty wooden chairs in front of him. To the right was a lockup for petty thieves, all men. A teenage pickpocket sat on a bench just beyond the lockup, eyeing the station inspector's shiny watch which he would later successfully steal. A very old woman with sari hitched between her legs stooped over a short-handled *jharoo* and mercilessly swept up everything in her path. With swift circular movements, she collected trash, debris, and errant *chappals* under the officer's desks and deposited them onto the wet ground just outside the station.

The wailing woman from the verandah was brought in. Immediately, she fell to her knees, pleading with an officer, her child having been run over by an imported car the previous night by a drunken teenager. The driver was standing sullenly to the side while his rich father handed over a stack of rupees, the bail to set him free.

"Very unfortunate," the surly officer was saying to the distraught woman, as he counted the money. "But the law must be upheld."

"Please sir!" the woman cried out. "What law lets a drunkard kill a child and walk away free?"

"Very old law, written in 1858," the officer said authoritatively, as if the number of years it had been in effect somehow counterbalanced its injustice. What he neglected to say was that the legislation was originally conceived to protect horse-carriage-driving Britishers when they inadvertently ran over half-naked street children. Now that the British were no longer in power, the law served wealthy Bombayites just as well.

The woman threw herself at the officer's desk, screaming, and was quickly gripped by two *laati*-wielding constables who dragged her to the door and threw her outside. The officer finished counting the money, separating the newly minted bills with a bit of reddish saliva deposited onto his thumb.

Gulu's gaze fell on a rickety wooden staircase that led to a dank hallway with stained walls. Overlapping notices, most of them outdated and unreadable, competed for attention along the stairwell where a narrow window, the only one left unshuttered, let in a rectangle of bright light. The staircase curved just above him lined with several pipes that had been painted a sickly olive. Gulu walked past the stairs, approaching a thin, frowning man sitting behind a desk against a graying wall, hunched over a pile of papers. The man wore a beige uniform, epaulets indicating that he was an A. S. I. —an assistant police sub-inspector, his pencil resentfully jabbing upwards into the air. A layer of oil and sweat covered his bald head. Behind him was a steel cabinet; a graph with pink and gray bars indicating monthly crime statistics was posted onto the wall. A khaki canvas tote bag hanging from a wooden peg was being investigated by a rather large rat.

This was the man Gulu had been looking for.

"A. S. I. Bambarkar!" Gulu said, clicking his heels and offering a casual salute with his bandaged hand.

"Yes?" Bambarkar said with annoyance. His pencil hung in midair.

"It's me, *bhai*. Gulu."

The pencil twirled for a moment in Bambarkar's hand. Suddenly the A. S. I. looked up. "Gulu from VT?"

"What, *bhai*, you no longer recognize your friends?" Gulu said cheerily, imitating the motions of shining a shoe.

"All these years," Bambarkar said in a low voice, "I thought Red Tooth had done away with you."

"I survived."

"I see that."

"I kept track of our gang, too. You in the police. Yash on Falkland Road. And Hari Bhai in Dharavi."

"Yash a pimp?" Bambarkar sniggered. "And you?"

Gulu winked, "A first-class driver."

"Something legitimate," Bambarkar bit into the pencil. "I'm not surprised."

"Listen, *bhai*," Gulu said quietly, sitting down. "I need your help."

"I'm listening."

"The family I work for, their daughter Pinky Mittal –"

"You work for the Mittal family?" Bambarkar asked surprised. "That's my case."

"Ah! Then you can tell me what happened to the ayah."

"Avni Chachar? We don't know. Her mother insists that she's dead. Suicide. There's no evidence to support that however."

"I saw her!"

"You did?" Bambarkar asked, leaning out of his chair. "Are you absolutely one-hundred-and-one-percent certain?"

Gulu searched his memory. As time had passed, he had grown unsure if the woman he saw outside the gate had been Avni. Perhaps he had imagined her. He shook his head.

"You see," Bambarkar continued, his voice lowered, "I've been requested to revise the reports, to protect Pinky Mittal's reputation. The other girl, Lovely, probably went out with some boy. As for Avni, the inspector is sending some of his *goondas* to rough up her family tonight. Get them to talk."

"I have to see Avni's mother, *bhai*. Please tell me where she lives."

Bambarkar twirled his pencil, shaking the sheath of papers, a history rewritten. Giving out this type of information was against police rules. Yet, Gulu was an old friend and a driver for a very wealthy family. Doing a favor for him might come in handy. Bambarkar was very good at cashing in favors. It had become a hobby of sorts, keeping a chart of who owed him, taking full advantage, down to the free teas the chaiwallah gave him each morning, or the ongoing access the pretty, young tenant next door gave him to the place between her legs. Yes, favors owed equaled power—juicy, spine-tingling power. Sorting through the stack on his desk, Bambarkar surreptitiously handed Gulu a sheet of paper.

❦ ❦ ❦

The earth had but a few hours to dry before the afternoon sun was eclipsed by the gathering monsoon haze. As the sky darkened and the shadows grew long, the clouds finally burst with a terrible roar, pouring rain into the waterlogged city, sending people running for cover, forcing the sun into retreat.

Night fell swiftly. The Mittal family, freshly scrubbed from their baths and satiated by an early dinner, gathered now in the parlor, nervously watching shadows grow in the corners of the bungalow. Savita had locked herself in her bedroom, waiting until the last possible moment to empty her bladder in her western-style toilet before Parvati tied the black string around the pipe and rendered it useless.

Not wanting to face her parents during Maji's *pani-hatao*, "remove-water plan," she had called them upon their return from Goa, saying that she would visit them the following weekend. *Do you realize whom we were vacationing with?* her mother had asked angrily. *Bipin and Monu! They were just received by the Prime Minister last weekend—Mr. Nehru himself! And now you tell me that your Pinky has been found and there's no need for us to visit?*

Savita had simply replied, *She's not my Pinky.*

"Mummy come," Nimish called gently from the door.

"Coming."

Savita sat at her vanity and stared at her vast collection of Indian attars, turning a crystal vial in her palm, holding it up to the light, tilting it this way and that, fascinated by its dazzle one moment, its flatness the next. She pulled the stopper out and held the vial under her nose. The sandalwood fragrance was stale, the liquid a sickly yellowish brown. Savita remembered receiving it the morning after their wedding. Jaginder had driven them to Colaba Causeway for lunch. In the car on the way there, as Savita sat stiffly in the front seat, Jaginder had shifted the gears and rested his hand upon her leg, touching her for the first time. It was an affectionate gesture, one that had brought a giggle to her lips. And then after lunch, Jaginder had proffered the crystal vial in a silk bag. *My favorite scent,* he said, his voice a rumbling purr. *I would like to smell it on you tonight.*

Savita carefully placed the vial back in its place, the first one in a line of them that marched across her vanity table, each one a precious memory, a possibility, a building block of her Number-One-First-Class-Life. She scanned the bottles, fingering them for the briefest of moments, allowing their fragrances to envelop her in a bouquet of nostalgia. The weeks after her wedding floated by in a cloud of Rose attar, the scent of love. Aphrodisiacal Amberi attar had been her loyal companion afterward, reducing Jaginder to an animalistic state during their lovemaking. When she first became pregnant with Nimish, Maji had given Savita musky Mitti attar distilled from the sacred earth at the Ganges River for the rebirth of life. And after her daughter died, Kuntal dutifully rubbed Shamana attar onto Savita's motionless body for her spiritual protection. On and on, Savita touched each crystal: Gul Hina attar for balance, Champa for purification, Agarwood for meditation, and White Lotus for enlightenment. And her favorite: Saffron attar, embodiment of Lakshmi—goddess of wealth and prosperity—the fragrance itself emitting a striking, golden glow.

She struggled now with an urge to refill each of her vials with water, to thwart Maji's plan and keep her ghostly daughter with her.

"Where are you?" she whispered, gazing around the room. " Come," she pleaded, "come to me so I can save you."

Nothing happened.

"Mummy," Nimish knocked on the door again. "Do you need anything?"

Darling Nimi, Savita thought, *my darling son.* "Nothing, *beta,* you go now."

Savita sat motionless at her vanity, weighing the consequences of disobeying her husband and mother-in-law. Who would she be if she were not Mrs. Mittal, lovely wife of Mr. Jaginder Mittal of Mittal Shipbreaking Enterprises? How could she even consider going against Maji's decision? Despite Savita's entreaties, her daughter had not come back to her, had not even shown her face, choosing instead to make herself visible to Pinky and Parvati. *Of all people, my undeserving niece and the maid!* A surge of jealousy gripped at her.

"It's not me you want, is it? Is it?" Savita cried out. And then, before she could control herself, she flung the Indian attars one by one, shattering the crystal vials against the wall. They released a cacophony of scents so noxious that she barely reached the bathroom before vomiting.

"What's going on in there?" Maji yelled from the parlour when the first vial hit the wall.

"Mummy!" Nimish raced to the bathroom. "Are you okay?"

The twins followed with equal anxiety, pawing at the door with sticky fingers.

"Go!" Savita hissed to all of them. "Just leave me alone!"

She wiped her face, brushed her teeth, and then urinated—scanning the small, neat room with a sad whimper, as if to refuse the degradation the next four days would bring. She wondered now what her life might have been had she accepted one of the other marriage proposals that had arrived before Jaginder's. One had been seriously considered by her parents, a boy with first-class biodata whose father wielded considerable influence in the Congress Party. Savita's mother had been thrilled. But when Savita saw the boy, secretly spying on him at a social event, she flatly refused. *He's too short!*

So what? her mother had responded, regaling her with the story of Lord Vishnu's fifth avatar. *Vamna conquered the universe in only two strides and he was a dwarf!*

As Savita stood and retied the *nala* of her pants, she tried to recall what exactly about Jaginder had made her say yes. His photo, though fair and handsome, had not made her heart flutter. Nor had his bio-data. Simply put, she had acquiesced because there was no apparent reason to say no. And here she was so many years later, having successfully delivered three sons and ensured the continuation of the Mittal family for another generation. Here she was, too, forsaking her daughter because the sacrifice required to do otherwise was too great. Savita pulled the chain and watched intently as the last bit of water in the household was flushed away.

❀ ❀ ❀

The ghost woke in the bathroom pipe with a start. Usually she found a short nap to be refreshing, soaking up residual moisture while she slept. But this evening she felt strangely lethargic, and terribly thirsty. She slid through the length of the pipe, searching for relief, but unbelievably, the entire length of the cylinder was dry. The ghost squeezed herself through the faucet and landed in a blue plastic bucket. The effort exhausted her. She had lingered for thirteen years in the bungalow, she and the other inhabitants coexisting by some strange set of rituals—a bolted door, a memory repressed. Then, Pinky!

Pinky had unbolted the door, had discovered her, and had kept coming back to the bathroom, again and again, determined. And the ghost grew stronger, nourished by her presence, by her story, until she was ready to reveal the truth of her death. But when that moment arrived, Pinky had run away, not wanting to believe her. Hurt and angry, the ghost had struck back. And from that moment, the bungalow had spiraled into devastation.

The ghost wanted everything then, she wanted her family to suffer and she wanted the power only the monsoons could give her. With that power, she intended to inflict harm to the core of the Mittal family.

She vowed to kill Maji.

In the parlour, Maji called to Nimish, "The sun has fallen, chain the gates."

"But Papa?" the twins cried out in union.

"And Gulu," said Parvati. "Neither has returned."

"Chain the gates," Maji ordered. Her mouth held steady in a thin line, but the crevices that surrounded it deepened.

"He didn't come back!" Savita cried out, wanting to curse Jaginder, wanting to yell out, *That lying, cowardly, bloody bastard!*

Tufan began to cry. Nimish put on his boots and walked into the twilight. He opened the gate and peeked down the road. *Now's my chance,* he thought, *to put one foot in front of the other, to find Pinky, to know the truth.* Behind him, the bungalow clawed at him, suffocating him with the sufferings of its inhabitants. The storm lashed at his face, smearing his spectacles. Nimish stepped out onto the street. Ahead of him, the empty road beckoned. A row of gates in pinks, greens, and blues, illuminated by winking yellow lamps, stood barricaded to the night. There was so much he wanted from his life, yet he remained trapped within the tiny confines of the bungalow, within the tightly knit expectations of his family.

He stood in the middle of the road and lifted his arms up to the heavens. For a moment, he allowed the rain to drench his upturned face, washing away his responsibilities, freeing him to walk down the street and out of his family's life. *You mustn't put off what you think right,* E. M. Forster's character had said. *That is why India is in such a plight, because we put off things.* That line from *A Passage To India* had stayed in his head, finally goading him to action on this rain-swept night.

I have to find Lovely! he resolved.

He grasped at the memory of their encounter under the tamarind tree, the silkiness of her *dupatta* against his cheek. He couldn't possibly sit around the bungalow for four days while Lovely was missing and put his foolish faith in the Bombay police. Unexpectedly hearing the sound of an engine approaching from the main road, he dropped his arms. The headlights of a familiar car came careening towards him. In that moment, as Nimish realized he might be crushed under its wheels, he had one thought—

She will die without me.

The Mercedes skidded to a stop.

"Nimish! Nimish!" Jaginder urgently rolled down his window. "What the bloody hell are you doing in the middle of the road?"

"What are *you* doing here?" Nimish shouted, his whole body straining as if bracing for the impact of the car.

"I was taking care of some things." Jaginder said, shielding his face from the rain. "I thought I was too late."

"You *are* too late! I'm going!"

"Going? Going where?"

"Lovely's still missing!"

"*Arré*, hero," Jaginder said as he hopped out of the car. "How do you plan on finding her, eh?"

Nimish cast his face down to hide the torment in his heart.

"Be sensible, *beta*," Jaginder said, putting his arm around his son's shoulder. "Inspector Pascal's one of Bombay's best. You know nothing of police work."

Nimish felt his father's words mocking him, once again pointing to his inadequacies. *You mustn't put off what you think right.* He shrugged off his father's arm. "I'm going!" he yelled, dashing away.

"Nimish!" Jaginder called out, running after him. "Stop! Don't be a bloody fool!"

Nimish ran faster. In front of him lay possibilities: hidden, unknown, exhilarating.

"Nimi!" Savita came screaming into the driveway. "*Beta*, come back! Come back!"

She will die without me, Nimish thought again, realizing with a shock that the *she* was not Lovely as he had imagined, but his mother. He felt his determination falter. Involuntarily, he slowed. Jaginder came charging up behind him, pouncing upon him with his burly arms.

"Let go!" Nimish fought back, punching his father in his chest. "Let me go!"

Savita caught up and threw herself upon her son, clasping him to her. "You're the only one who cares for me," she whispered into his neck, "the only one." And then, coldly, to her husband, "You came back?"

"I promised, didn't I?"

"Come, *beta*," Savita said, pulling Nimish onto the driveway while Jaginder firmly gripped his arm from the other side.

There was nothing more Nimish could do. Fighting back tears of shame, he watched as Jaginder chained the front gate, trapping them all within the bungalow's merciless grip.

The deluge struck against the windows of the pediatric ward at Bombay Hospital, lulling some of the children into torpor, and frightening others into crying frenzies. Pinky slept through it in a feverish delirium. She woke sometime in the middle of the night, droplets of water beading her face. The barred window just next to her cot seemed to have blown open. A chilly breeze rapidly worked its way under her blankets. Pinky threw them off. *Now*, she thought, *I have to go now.*

There was still a way, still some hope, Pinky believed, recalling how she had once thought of the ghost as a sister, her cousin-sister. There had been love then, in the tiny space of the hallway bathroom, a coming together across boundaries, across fear. And then Pinky had refused to accept the image with the disembodied hand, refused to believe that the drowning could have been anything more than an accident. And that's when the ghost broke away from her. Now, faced with Lovely's terrifying disappearance, Pinky was willing to do anything to find out the truth.

Outside, a mimosa tree strained against the wind, its branches scraped against the black window-bars, depositing a flurry of leaves just inside. In the flash of lightning that followed, Pinky thought she saw something hanging from the tree but couldn't be sure as the moon was shrouded by clouds. The only light came from the little lamp that stuck out from the pillar behind her cot. She was tired, so tired as she bent down to slip on her sandals. The branches swept against the window, as if reaching in to grab her. Pinky glanced around the room, confirming that all its other occupants were fast asleep before standing in front of the open window. She looked outside at the tree, feeling something familiar—a dark, frightening presence. A voice whispered to her, *Come, come*. It was deep, gritty, unmistakable. The grill fell away, the tree beckoned. *I have to escape,* Pinky told herself, *I have to reach the ghost before it's too late. And Nimish, I have to find him too.*

She squeezed through the window opening, assessed the darkness below, and jumped.

SCRIPTURES & SEX

⁓

Gulu made his way to Falkland Road in the red-light district of Kamathipura, north of Victoria Terminus train station, to find Chinni. She would be the only one, he knew, able to comfort him in his troubled state. The gloomy road was lined with decaying wooden buildings, painted in greens and blues, covered in thick layers of grime, rust and urine; the ground-floor doors were heavily padlocked. The lower section of the structures consisted of open windows fitted with bars, cages behind which cheaper prostitutes beckoned, pulling up their garish pink saris to expose their legs. The upper stories had open windows with shutters, each sporting a red Chinese lantern upon which the brothel's license number was pasted. Girls leaned out alluringly while plaiting jasmine into each other's hair. Equally dilapidated hotels were nestled within the street, their owners selling cold drinks on the front steps and illegal country alcohol from special rooms in the back.

The road itself was packed with taxicabs, stray goats, water-carriers, *chaiwallahs*, the homeless street prostitutes forced to rent cots, and enterprising vendors, one selling a grayish solution in a vial promising an extra burst of vitality to the men entering the brothels. *Paanwal-lahs* sat by their carts offering *chara-ki-goliyaan*, balls of hashish and opium, some with a pinch of cocaine, along with less hallucinogenic offerings and the suggestive "bed-breaker" aphrodisiac, *paans*, each wrapped in a thick, moist leaf. Men squatted over card games just in front of the brothels, gambling away what little money they had earned that day. Others were lined up at the cinema, Pila House—the venue of Parsee theater a hundred years ago before its decline—lured by a poster depicting a leggy Hollywood blonde reclining on a divan, even though the exiting crowd had been visibly disappointed by the Indian Censor Board's extensive cuts. *Filmi* music undulated onto the streets along with *hijras* flaunting their bodies, teasing homosexual customers back to their own special brothel.

The doorway to 24 Falkland Road where Chinni lived reeked of waste: garbage festered in the corners with swarms of flies lifting up and settling back down in unison, vomit swam in the gutters, and cigarette butts littered the entrance. Used and discarded FLs–French letters–floated in the slime, little opaque vessels carrying human seed into oblivion. The paint had long ago peeled away from walls, bodily fluids: urine, spit, semen had rotted the wood underneath. Rats scurried along the open drain gang-style, leaving their telltale crisscross graffiti upon a man slumped in a stairwell. A street-hardened prostitute, no more than fifteen, stood at the doorstep smoking a *bidi*, her arm thrown back to accentuate her breasts in their tightly darted blouse. Gulu nodded to her familiar face, as he climbed the narrow staircase to the third floor where Chinni spent the majority of her life, on-duty from 6 p.m. until 1 a.m., the rest of the time undergoing a torturous process of tweezing, bleaching, waxing, and applying stinging creams all in an effort to rid her body of unsightly hair, especially in the nether regions. Only when she was deemed hair-free and thus, clean, could she begin servicing her clientele: exceptionally hispid men whose breath smelled of rancid mutton.

The top of the third-floor stairs led into a impossibly narrow hallway connected to a small, dimly lit room festering with the smell of unbridled sex.

"*Ay bai,*" Gulu called to the grossly overweight madam who was chewing a *paan* while reclining on a low, brightly covered sofa. "*Darwaza khol.*"

The madam briefly studied Gulu in the dim light, deciding whether or not to open the folding iron gate.

"It's me, Gulu," he said, exasperated by the unusual scrutiny. Normally, during his regular visits every other Tuesday, the gate was thrown open and Gulu welcomed in as if he were family.

"Oh ho," the madam teased, "why didn't you say? I didn't recognize your *kalia* trouble-making face. Today's not Tuesday, is it?"

The wall behind her was a shiny mustard yellow with a lamp hanging in its center. Heavy, velveteen drapes hung from the ceiling to the linoleum floor. A brass statue of Lakshmi, goddess of wealth and prosperity, adorned a cabinet on the far end of the room. A puja vessel with a lighted candle and a steel container of crimson-colored powder rested on a side table. The madam had just finished blessing her staff, as she did every evening before the start of their work. Two of her six girls, both wearing low-cut blouses, sat on the torn, green, Rexene-plastic covered sofa with her—one massaging her back, the other her feet while waiting for customers. One squatted as she cleaned the floor with a soiled rag. The other three, including Chinni, were already working in the back cubicles, each separated by six-foot tall wooden partition.

"*Chaiwallah bulao,*" the madam ordered one of her girls who leaned out of the balcony window and called for tea while expertly flirting with a potential customer.

Gulu sat on a rickety chair, waiting for the chai, listening to the low moans and high laughter, a subtle backdrop to the more blaring sounds emanating from the street. He touched the *Bhagavad Gita* tucked into his vest. Gulu was illiterate but Chinni had studied through primary school. It was she who, postcoitally, read verses out loud to him from the holy scriptures.

The chai boy came and went. Gulu sipped slowly at his tea while the other girls teased him.

"Why only Chinni all the time?" one halfheartedly said. "We are also sugary-sweet."

Gulu smiled and shook his head at the dark-complexioned girls, both *devadasis* from the villages of Karnataka. They had been dedicated by their parents to their local temples out of devotion to the Goddess Yellama or of a need for money, and subsequently sold to the Bombay brothel.

Just then, a young man appeared, sporting a crisp *dhobi*-washed white shirt, perfectly creased wool and terylene pants, Zodiac leather belt (still unbuckled), and polished black Bata shoes—the standard attire for boys from decent families or medical students from the nearby Sir J. J. Hospital.

Gulu self-consciously smoothed his shirt, dark so it could be worn for several days without needing washing.

The madam's eagle-eyes momentarily rested upon a young pros-titute, assessing her. "Go wash up," she ordered before leaning on a button which buzzed insistently by Chinni's cot. "Chinni's fat fellow's taking too long," she said sourly. The corners of her mouth perma-nently curled downwards.

Soon thereafter, her client waddled into the room, hastily tying the dhoti over his flabby gut and rushed out the door before the madam could charge him extra. Chinni followed, wiping his saliva from her face with the end of her *palloo*.

"You?" she said, surprised when she saw Gulu. He had never before visited her during one of his working days.

He nodded.

"Oh pho!" she exclaimed, noticing his tucked away hand. "What happened?"

"Nothing. Small accident."

Chinni shrugged her shoulders and walked back to her cubicle, Gulu following just behind. Usually, when he visited her, he paid thirty rupees to keep her to himself for the duration of the evening. Now, smelling another man's sweat on her, he felt repulsed, nauseated. The dirty green walls closed in around him, the dingy floral bedspread felt warm, damp.

"Go clean up." Gulu ordered her to the back where a filthy toilet pit, a tub of cold water, and a cement drain served as the commu-nal bathroom. There purple crystals of potassium permanganate were diluted in water every evening as a postcoital antiseptic or, in more concentrated doses, to induce abortions. Babies, although plentiful in the brothels, spelled nothing but trouble for prostitutes. A Falkland Road woman need not be pretty, need not even have all her limbs. But youth, extreme youth, and virginal tautness were their most coveted assets.

"What," Chinni said scornfully, "so you can pretend I'm not a whore?"

Nevertheless, she washed and changed into a fresh sari, reappearing with a strand of jasmine in her hair. Gulu relaxed, reaching into her blouse to pluck its juicy contents.

Chinni had been the wife of a lowly bank clerk, living with her husband in a one-room *chawl* in Byculla. She was sold into prostitution upon his untimely death and her infant son taken away from her. Afterward, Chinni's first thought was to kill herself. But the madam, experienced with breaking-in girls, chained her to the cot by her ankles and made sure she was watched all the time. *You're missing your son,* nah? she had asked Chinni after several weeks had gone by, knitting together her overplucked eyebrows in an effort to appear sympathetic. Sunno, *be a good girl and I'll arrange for you to see him after half your debts are paid off.*

Chinni naively relented, sending her parents a one-anna plea for money, penned by a letter-writer who sat under pigeon-shit-streaked canvas roof near the General Post Office with a blackened tin box of sealing wax, kerosene, a wick lamp, and matches. She could very well have written the letter herself but needed to borrow his anonymous return address as her own. Namaste *Amma and Baba,* she dictated to the felt-capped man who unhurriedly plucked at the skeletal Remington typewriter, adjusting his half-moon spectacles at each new mark to scrutinize the paper for accuracy. *Husband has died, please send money. Will visit soon with baby.* She signed it, *your loving daughter, Chinta,* using her given name, not the name it had been changed to in the brothel: Chinni, meaning sugar. Her parents never wrote back.

Gulu used to frequent the Nepali whores, most of whom had been kidnapped from their homes, when he was a shoe-shine boy at VT because they were the only ones he could afford. After securing his job with Maji, however, he gladly left them behind, choosing to move up a class, to the lower-middle-class prostitutes. He had imagined himself one day trying out the Eurasian whores in the most expensive brothels, gated establishments set off the main street and run by French-speaking madams, but he had never possessed the money or courage. He had started seeing Chinni the very first time he visited 24 Falkland Road, spying her in the window as another girl plaited her hair, though she was not the most attractive woman in the brothels. In fact, as he passed by, looking upward to consider the wares, she had spat a blob of reddish saliva at him.

When he entered her quarters that first time, Chinni didn't toss off her clothes like the prostitutes he was used to, immediately baring her breasts and inviting him to squeeze them as if they were guavas at the market. Gulu had simply tipped her onto her back and gone about his business. Sex with Chinni was slow, predictable, almost boring. But after his childhood in poverty, living in the streets and then in the train station, never knowing where his next meal would come from, he took pleasure in her familiarity and even in the reluctance with which she surrendered her body to him.

Now that so many years had passed, she had begun her decline, one that happened with alarming speed on Falkner Road. She was twenty-eight and frequently suffered from high fevers. Most prostitutes, he knew, did not live past thirty: victims of filth, violation, disease, and malnutrition. Gulu continued to visit Chinni, less for pleasure these days and more out of an intense need to discharge accumulated tension from his body into hers. Meanwhile, Chinni continued to be teased by the other girls for her relentless ire, *Oi, Chinni, your name is sugar but the men still can taste your bitterness.* Even so, she tempered her wrath when she was with Gulu. He had been her most loyal and longest customer, their relationship was almost like that of husband and wife. After their lovemaking, they often went to a popular local eatery and shared a bowl of trotters, pigs feet stewed in chili-pepper soup.

"You usually come on Tuesdays," Chinni now said as she pulled the dirty sheet across the doorway to enclose them in her cubicle which was only big enough for the bed upon which they sat.

Gulu clasped his hands in his lap, not looking at her, not touching her.

"Tell me what happened to your hand, *nah?*"

"I'm responsible for someone's death," Gulu finally said.

The brothel's clientele included gangsters, hit-men, and criminals, so Chinni was not alarmed. But she was surprised that Gulu was involved in such an activity. She knew that he assiduously followed rules, believing that they kept him out of trouble since breaking them had kept him on the run during his shoe-shine days. As far as Chinni was aware, *she* was his only vice.

"You're no longer a driver?"

"No," Gulu said, tightness in his chest threatening to overwhelm as he thought of his small living quarters in the back of Maji's bungalow, his extra *dhoti* hanging from the clothesline, his Cherry Blossom poster on the wall and the dried marigold tucked under his mattress. "Not after today." He told his whore about the girl he had once been in love with. "I had went to Colaba to search for Avni's mother, Janibai. I had to find out if Avni had returned to Bombay. Against Maji's orders I went."

"And?"

"And she told me about a morning thirteen years ago, the morning just after the monsoon season ended. Nariyal Poornima Day. She had gone to VT to sell her wares, arriving later than usual. She saw Avni, standing there by the tracks and went to her. And that's when she jumped."

"In front of the train?"

Gulu dropped his face. "All these years I hoped she would come back. I never knew that she had died. If I had known what she intended, I'd have never let her go." For a grotesque moment, he envisioned the spectacle on a big screen, changing the ending to assuage his guilt. In his *filmi* version, he arrived at the platform at the last moment and pulled Avni from the metallic clutches of death as the music welled to an emotional crescendo.

"You loved her?"

"Yes."

"Did she love you?"

Gulu paused. He hadn't considered this before. Since Avni lived inside the bungalow and he on the outside, they had had very little interaction. In fact, aside from the few words they exchanged as he drove her to the train station, he had never spoken with her at all.

"She didn't love you," Chinni declared, waving her hand. "Otherwise, she wouldn't have taken her life. She would have asked you to take her away, to leave your job, to run away together."

Gulu was stunned. His fantasies had never taken this into account.

"She chose death because she had no hope," Chinni said, knowing that hope was what had foolishly prevented her from killing herself, keeping her chained to the brothel all these years. She had witnessed other, younger girls buy their freedom after sleeping with fifteen men each night, even during their menses, and mixing their menstrual blood into the food they served the most lucrative clients in order to bewitch them. But Chinni serviced three or four men a night at the most; her seething hostility scared most of them away. All these years, she had never saved enough to buy her freedom. And now her son had come to this very brothel, just a few weeks ago, a shiny shirt tucked into his girlish waistline, pimples dotting his adolescent face. Hope was no longer enough to sustain her after this latest, most bruising humiliation. Chinni touched the Rampuri knife tucked into the side of her cot. She wanted revenge.

"Yes," Chinni reaffirmed almost gleefully. "She didn't love you."

"*Chup kar!*" Gulu ordered. With a violent shove, he pinned her to the bed and poured his rage, guilt, and loss between her legs.

Afterwards, as usual, he tossed her his tattered copy of the *Bhagavad Gita.*

Without looking at him, Chinni smoothed her petticoat over her legs and opened to a page.

"'Perfect bliss grows only in the bosom tranquilized, the spirit passionless, purged from offence,'" she began and then hurled the book at Gulu's head.

"*Kya?*"

"Go," Chinni said, eyes blazing.

"Listen—"

"Go! I don't want you to come back ever again."

"But how will you manage without—"

"Without you?" she snorted. "You think you've kept me in comfort all these years? Half my earnings go to Madam Ganga Bai, another percentage for rent and food, and then there is the *hafta,* to bribe the *bhenchod* police. You pay me just enough to survive, never enough to buy my freedom."

Gulu looked away.

"You promised to take me away one day," Chinni reminded him. "But all this time you've been in love with Avni. She's dead but I'm the one who's a ghost to you."

"No, no," Gulu insisted. "This time's different. I can never go back to Malabar Hill. I'll take you away from here. I promise."

Chinni did not believe him but allowed herself to be pulled into his embrace, into a temporary illusion. Gulu rested his face in her hair, smelling the jasmine wreath that had been mangled during their encounter. It would not be so easy to cut himself off from Cook Kanj, Parvati and Kuntal, even from the Mittal family. Malabar Hill was his home, more than the teeming slum of his childhood, more than at VT where he'd spent his transient years. It beckoned to him now, even as Chinni began to speak of the flat they would rent in the northeastern suburbs of Bombay.

"Brand-new Devidayal cooking utensils and a proper bathroom," she recited. "And quiet all night, not even a dog passing by before the morning."

Gulu nodded his head, "Yes, yes, everything."

But his mind settled on something he had done that fateful drowning day so many years ago, after the sun had given way to night and the sky was black but for a thin sliver of moonlight. Shame, intense and unrelenting, had forced him to repress the memory, to forget that desire could lead him to such a dark place. Since then, he had clung to his foolish hope that Avni would one day return. But, now, now that he knew that she was dead, his shame gave way to anger. And a sickening fear. The thirteen-year-old memory loomed like a poison-tipped dagger.

"*Kya?*" Chinni rankled. "You're not even listening."

Gulu involuntarily shivered.

"Tell me."

"Something I saw long time ago on the day of Avni's death," Gulu said. "A secret I've kept for all these years."

"What?" Chinni said, eyes gleaming with this tidbit, "You have some dirty-dirty secret about your boss-sahib? Or something about the other servants?"

Gulu lowered his face to hide the sudden wetness in his eyes.

"Tears?" Chinni asked, surprised. "So don't tell your precious secret, *nah*, ask them for money to keep quiet."

"Blackmail?"

"This is our chance," Chinni insisted, turning to face him. "A little extra money from your boss-sahib or the other servants is all we need to set up our new home. Better if the secret is about Mr. Boss, then you can ask for a *lakh*."

"No, no, no," Gulu cried out, tasting the salt on his lips. "You don't understand." Unwanted memories floated in his head: the eerie quiet of an abandoned cargo hold at VT, a crackling fire smelling of death, a dank breeze against his sweating skin.

"What's to understand?" Chinni demanded, swatting at his face. "You think you are big-big movie hero but you're too cowardly to even kill a fly."

Gulu pushed Chinni away with rough hands, his expression hardening.

"Didn't your madam throw you out?" She laughed cruelly. "You have no one now, except for me."

Gulu felt himself shaking.

"Go," Chinni ordered, whipping the nine-inch knife from its hiding place. "I don't care what your little secret is. Go bring the money. If not, I'll kill myself."

"What?"

"I will kill myself," Chinni said more slowly, pressing the blade's pointed tip against her heart. "And, I swear, *my* ghost will haunt you till the day you die."

Seeing a startling line of crimson appear at her breast, Gulu hastily retrieved his *Bhagavad Gita* and ran out, wondering what unfortunate alignment of stars had befallen him that day. He had not stopped Avni from killing herself, would he now also turn a blind eye to Chinni? How could he live with one more death on his soul? As he stood amidst the filth on Falkland Road watching a caged girl unclasp the first eyelet of her straining blouse, the wails of Kamathipura's inconsolable phantoms rose all around him. His shameful secret, if told, would not only land him in jail but surely would tear the Mittal family apart, felling Maji's grand bungalow to the ground.

PHANTASMAL FOG

That first night, Maji barred herself in the puja room while the boys raced around the bungalow with rags in their hands, eliminating every trace of water. Tufan had never had so much fun in his life, pouncing on drips with the verve of his favorite *khustiwallah*, Dara Singh, India's very own Wrestling World Champion.

"*Dekko!*" Tufan yelled gleefully, bounding from one sofa to another, flattening a puddle with a towel tied to his chest. "I got another one!"

"What's there to be proud of, you idiot!" Jaginder said, glancing up from his newspaper. "Unless you want to be a bloody *bhangi*, sweeping toilets all day long."

"But I'm Dara Singh," Tufan protested.

"He drinks milk with honey and crushed almonds every morning for breakfast," Dheer chipped in, having memorized the famous wrestler's diet.

All the wet rags were deposited in the back of the bungalow, just outside Parvati and Kanj's living quarters. There the boys stood shivering under umbrellas, while they drank their boiled buffalo milk and lined up to use the latrine, a smelly box that contained nothing but two ridged, shoe-shaped ceramic footrests astride a cavernous hole and a recalcitrant faucet dripping into a plastic cup.

Savita exited the latrine looking faint, a white cotton handkerchief held to her nose. As she stepped inside the bungalow, enraged by this fresh humiliation, a scheme for seizing control of it finally crystallized. She threw the handkerchief, hand-embroidered by herself in the days before her wedding with her and Jaginder's initials delicately entwined, and watched as it soaked up the brown liquid from the ground. *As pure as she appears,* Savita thought of Maji, *still she can be sullied.*

Savita noticed Cook Kanj hunched just outside his garage smoking a bidi. He had been watching her and only dropped his gaze when Savita met his eyes. But it was Savita who was more embarrassed, thinking that somehow he had read her rebellious plan on her face. They both stared at the dirtied handkerchief. Finally, Kanj stood up with a grunt and plucked it from the puddle.

"Throw it away," Savita ordered before walking back inside and locking herself in her bedroom. She retrieved a bottle of Royal Salut from inside one of the cabinets, the only one that had been over-looked during the purging of the bungalow. Savita hadn't known why she had held onto it then but now, as she undid the cap, she realized that she wanted to discover its secrets, to understand why it possessed her husband so.

She tipped the bottle to her lips, wetting them, allowing the fumes to assault her nostrils. Then, more bravely, she took a sip. The liquor burned in her mouth and throat, filling her belly with fire. *So this is its power.* She took another sip, allowing her unspoken desires to take hold of her. She was tired of being a daughter-in-law, an outsider even now. She wanted to sit upon Maji's regal dais, issuing commands and receiving visitors.

She had been the one, after all, who had warned her family about the otherworld's presence while Maji had written off ghosts as mad-ness. *Now look at her,* Savita thought savagely. *Suddenly she's following the tantrik like a fool.* It would not be much of a stretch to insinuate that her mother-in-law had finally lost her mind, nurturing a rumor among the servants and then, more cautiously, among her children and husband. And once Maji's powerful grip on the household began to slip, Savita would make her bid for absolute power.

She drank several more capfuls before hiding the Royal Salut in the cabinet again. She realized that she needed to reclaim her husband's loyalty first. In the early years of their marriage, Jaginder had always taken Savita's side during conflicts with Maji. But slowly, slowly, as their relationship disintegrated, Jaginder began to cater to his mother as if he were once again her little boy, becoming so intertwined that it blinded them to the other's faults. *I need to win Jaggi back*, Savita decided, thinking of those four days when the monsoons first burst in which they had come together, she seducing him, he forgoing Rosie's *adda*. Feeling the alcohol's unfamiliar tingling in the back of her head, the sudden rush of daring in her heart, Savita steeled herself for what she would do next. She would repress her loathing and surrender herself to her husband. She would raise him up so that he would no longer crave his mother's approval. She would make him hers.

She lay down on her bed, pulling a thin cotton sheet over her body. Her head had begun to spin pleasantly as she remembered that there was one more thing she needed to do to ensure the stability of the household. She thought about Nimish, her first and favorite son. He had always been a quiet, reflective child, delving into books, never causing any trouble. It was he, rather than Jaginder, who had taken care of her after the baby died, wiping away her tears with his little hands, reading her stories in his sweet little voice. Even though he was only four back then, he had accepted the burden of tending to Savita in her fragile state, viewing his own needs, desires, and wishes as less important.

I can't live without my Nimi.

Though she loved her younger sons as well, she found them lacking, especially when it came to potential to take over the family business. Dheer was always sniffing her perfumes like a girl and hovering around the kitchen as if it were *he* who needed to learn cooking to please his future spouse. And she had little patience for his softness, his big, droopy eyes peeking out from behind chubby cheeks-begging for her attention. Savita had no doubt that if Dheer were to lead Mittal Shipbreaking Enterprises, he would be cheated in broad daylight by Laloo and the entire *bhenchod* lot. Tufan, on the other hand, would most certainly know how to bully the sniveling sycophants that flocked around Jaginder like flies. Even as a little boy, he had been cunning, able to manipulate the servants to his advantage. But still, Savita feared that her youngest would make decisions on impulse rather than after deliberation, squandering their family fortune in the process.

Yes, yes, our future hinges on Nimish.

She recalled the wild look in Nimish eyes, panicking that she had lost him when he ran from the bungalow into the night, shouting about Lovely. *Lovely?* The realization that the seventeen-year old girl had usurped Nimish's affections dawned on Savita with crushing force. She had raced into the street to hold him back, her good will towards their lifelong neighbors vanishing in an instant. *That shameless girl, driving off in the middle of the night to meet God-knows-what kind of boys, and trying to corrupt my innocent son!*

But even more than the threat of Lovely, Savita feared that Nimish would insist on leaving the bungalow altogether. He had always wanted to complete his education in England, to study at Oxford as if Bombay's universities were all second-rate. If he were to go, Savita knew, he would never come back. *He will lie in bed with those brazen white girls, convert to Christianity, and eat fish and chips!* She forced herself to slow her breathing, realizing that above all she needed to keep her eldest securely planted in Bombay, tethered to their household for another generation. Sure, she allowed, Nimish was only seventeen, but the time had come. As soon as she could arrange it, she would get him married.

Yet, she knew he would not simply agree to her wishes in this matter, especially now that Lovely was in the picture. No, she had to trap him. And luckily for her, she knew exactly how.

Having finally spelled out her plan to herself, Savita fell into a pleasant, buzzing sleep for the remainder of the night, her door still locked. Jaginder and the boys slept together in the parlor, huddled onto thick mattresses. Parvati and Kanj, on water-elimination duty for the first half of the night, prowled around the bungalow with a stash of towels. Maji remained in her puja room, eventually slumping forward against the altar, exhausted. And the baby ghost hovered just outside, still ignorant of the plans for her imminent demise, waiting patiently for the Mittal's' powerful matriarch to emerge.

In the darkened hallways of Bombay Hospital, as the surly pediatrician took advantage of the quiet night and of a perky nurse named Nalini, Pinky felt herself falling from the window through a flickering, phantasmal fog, falling into a dark, timeless place. Winds whispered and moaned. Palm trees tossed above her.

A desolate coastline curved until it disappeared from sight. A skyful of black storm clouds held the moon hostage. The ocean surged towards her, flooding her feet in stinging salts and debris. Pinky kicked off her sandals and stepped across the sand with her bare feet. Just fifty meters further on, long wooden canoes with fierce, hand-painted red eyes on either side, rocked in the wind watching her like a row of demons trapped underneath jute netting.

Icy winds gusted through her thin, cotton pajamas where they encircled her ankles like lead weights. Up ahead, a skeletal trawler tilted precariously against a dilapidated jetty, bobbing and creaking with every wave. A terrible stench of fish carcasses and rotting jambul fruit filled the air.

I jumped, didn't I? Pinky tried to place herself. *Where am I?*

Even as her mind raced with these questions, she knew that she was wide awake in a nightmarish reality. A gritty voice whispered all around her, the very one that had come out of Lovely's throat the night she took Pinky from Malabar Hill.

There's no other way out, Pinky decided, *I must find that voice.*

※ ※ ※

The green bungalow gate stayed firmly chained shut all morning, the only item to venture past it was the morning paper. A small item in the *Indian Express* read: *The daughter of Mr. and Mrs. Jaginder Mittal of Mittal Shipbreaking Enterprises was returned unmolested to her home last night by Bombay's intrepid P. I. Pascal. She was found alone on her street and taken to the hospital where she was diagnosed with a severe case of pneumonia.* A separate article described Lovely's continued disappearance. A suspect had been arrested, a St. Xavier's College student by the name of Inesh Lele. The piece ended by summing up Inspector Pascal's impressive track record of convictions.

Jaginder stared at the photo of the young man whom he had first seen at the Asiatica restaurant on Churchgate Street and felt a sharp stab of guilt. He wished that he had not revealed the boy's name during his meeting with Pascal. Initially their exchange had not gone well; the inspector's tone had been cold and hostile, almost as if he were interrogating a suspect. *Take your niece's case to the courts where it will rot long after your children are dead,* Pascal had said when Jaginder had tried to bargain down the amount of the bribe. *There are two crores—twenty million—cases backlogged in the courts. If you want justice, you have to either come to us or the underworld. Take your choice.*

His pulse racing, Jaginder had felt the bat-wing doors of the private booth closing in on him, giving him the sensation that he was in a cell, his jailer sitting across the table from him. Briefly, he considered approaching the Anti-Corruption Bureau, thrilled at the idea of catching Pascal at his game. But if the ACB sleuths were to be involved, they would only focus more unwanted attention on Jaginder's family. Pascal swore and stood up to leave. Without further delay, Jaginder slid the bundle of rupees across the table and gave up Inesh's name.

Stupid boy, Jaginder thought, imagining Inesh and Lovely sitting across one of the Asiatica's newspaper-strewn tables, he reciting a badly written love poem while she demurely sipped her tea. Jaginder couldn't conceive that the boy, so innocent in his lovelorn state, had lured Lovely into harm's way. Yet, without another suspect, the blame would have rested on Pinky and, by extension, his own family. P. I. Pascal, Jaginder gathered, was one of those cutthroat, overly ambitious types who had his eye on the top post of Police Commissioner. He could ruin Jaginder and his family without blinking an eye. He even had a paid contact in the press, Jaginder surmised, while scrutinizing the byline of the article, someone who was retained to make him into a veritable celebrity in the eyes of Bombay's masses. *Yes,* Jaginder told himself, he had done the right thing.

He folded the paper testily, placed it under his arm, and wished for a cup of warm chai. But chai was no longer freely dispensed in the household. Jaginder had to haul himself to the back garage where Maji had organized their meals on a strict schedule. Tea at 9 a. m. , breakfast at 10. Lunch followed at 1 then tea at 4, dinner at 7, and tea again at 9. There were to be no snacks in between, no cool drinks, no Duke's sodas, not even water, nothing that was not regulated.

"Kanj! Kanj!" Jaginder roared irritatedly from the back steps, vigorously rubbing his chest hair. "I need some chai."

"It's only 8:30, Sahib," Cook Kanj called from the interior of his garage in his most deferential voice while a nude Parvati nibbled on his ear. "So sorry, Sahib, Maji's orders."

Jaginder cursed. "What more do I have to bloody tolerate?"

Even now, Jaginder had difficulty believing in Maji's story of ghosts and whatnot. *Is she turning senile?* Yet, something *had* happened the previous night. Savita's breasts. He remembered the thick milk in his throat—choking him—and vowed to behave for the four-day purgatory. It was a test just like Princess Sita's trial by fire to prove her fidelity in the epic *Ramayana*. In the end, Jaginder wanted his past misdeeds to be cleansed by his current suffering. And so he sat impatiently, on the steps, halfheartedly reading about the world outside the green gates, while casting furious looks at Kanj and Parvati's garage where, if he strained his ears, he could hear the rolling sounds of laughter.

Cook Kanj finally emerged at 8:45, languidly retying his *lungi* and offering Jaginder a satiated smile before setting the pot to boil. The rest of the household was slow in arising. Yet, when Kanj called out "Chai!" at exactly nine o'clock, eyes flew open and family members ran outside, elbowing each other as if they were trying to board a crowded bus.

"It's worse than a bloody canteen!" Jaginder spat out, swatting Tufan out of the way with a sweep of his arm.

"What a disgrace," Savita said in a martyred voice. "My sons think only about themselves."

Duly chided, Nimish grabbed the first steaming cup right out from under Jaginder's nose and handed it to his mother.

Jaginder's face grew tight. Wasn't it his right to be served before his wife? And yet, even as he thought this, he felt shamed by his selfishness. He bit his tongue, remembering his resolution. Perhaps Nimish was testing him. In fact, Jaginder thought with growing interest, if he categorized all the things that irritated him about his family as tests of his newfound resolve, they were somehow easier to bear.

"Come, darling," Savita said to her husband, handing him her cup. "You're the head of our family after all."

Delighted by this unexpected deference and grateful that his mother was not around to hear it, Jaginder accepted the steaming cup with a puff of his chest. Savita smiled.

Maji limped out to the back steps. She had not slept well the previous night, uncomfortably curled into the tight rectangle of the puja room. Yet, somehow, she felt safe in there with the gods watching. And whenever she woke to shake out a sleeping leg, she conveniently rang the tiny silver bell on the altar and said a quick prayer. Surely the gods would reward such piety.

Savita eyed her mother-in-law, noticing her fatigue. "Perhaps you should rest Maji," she said sweetly. "You look ab-so-lute-ly worn."

"I'm just fine."

"Come, Nimi," Savita said, beckoning him to her side. "Read your Mummy something from one of your books and make this day pass more quickly."

Surrounding her like bodyguards, all three boys escorted her back into the bungalow where she promptly marked their ears with black dots and kept them close until breakfast was served at ten.

* * *

Hovering just inside a window, the baby ghost watched the family's new routine with curiosity. Except for Savita and Maji, all the other members of her family now slept in the sitting area. And instead of using the dining hall, they took their breakfast outside. The bathrooms, the toilets, and the sinks remained stubbornly dry and the kitchen and storage room had been emptied of all liquid contents. Even Savita's breasts had begun to dry up. The strength that the ghost had gained since the outbreak of the monsoons had already begun to wane without continued intake of water. This new weakness made her feel frightened, territorial.

She watched intently as Cook Kanj served breakfast outside, dipping a steel cup into a large urn of water. Her eyes were fixed on the clear liquid, shimmering with a thousand colors. Slowly, she gathered herself to go outside. True, it was daytime and her powers were at their weakest. Even a sprinkling of haze overhead would have lent her strength. But there was not a single cloud in sight this morning. She knew, however, that she might not make it through the day without water. So hesitating no more, she drifted towards the open door and toward her salvation.

An unbelievably searing pain made her jerk back in panic. She tried again to cross the threshold and again she was repelled by a terrible burning. She let out a long, gasping wail while her glossy mane coiled around her body as if a sheath. Just then, she noticed a faint trail of ash at the door's threshold that snaked its way along the bottom of the bungalow wall, creeping up and down at regular intervals to the windowpanes. The baby ghost followed the ash around the entire bungalow until she ended up once again at the back door. Suddenly she understood. Black Magic. Maji had used sorcery to trap her within the waterless bungalow.

A single tear fell from her wide, dreamless eyes. And then it turned silver like a moonlit lake, like the merciless glint of a sword.

She was being sacrificed.

THE HAUNTED COASTLINE

The phone call from the hospital came just as they finished break-fast, striking Maji like Lord Indra's thunderbolt. *How could she have been taken?* she shouted into the phone to a trembling Nurse Nalini. *Weren't you on duty? Weren't the windows barred?* And because the reply to all three was affirmative, there was no doubt in Maji's mind that Avni was responsible. Avni, their former ayah, who had been blamed for one granddaughter's death, now seemed intent on destroying the other.

Marooned on the haunted coastline, malevolent whisperings all around her, Pinky took a heavy step forward. Wet algae grabbed her feet, slowing her down.

Coconuts, hundreds of them, lay in the sand decaying. Some were cracked open, the flesh eaten away by sharp-beaked birds. Others were still whole and hirsute. She bent down now to grasp one, and was surprised to find it warm, hot even, as if it contained fire. She clasped it to her chest, the heat entering her body.

The coconut contained a memory of a long ago day, the morning of Avni's birth, when her father saw her for the first time. Nothing, not the rush of the water, the thrill of pulling up a net straining with fish, nor the rise of the sun on the ocean's surface compared to seeing this creation of his.

See, the blind midwife spoke, pointing to the infant's extra toe. *An inauspicious sign.*

He placed his roughened hand on her silky scalp, determined to counteract her prophesy with his will.

Avni's mother, still shaking from the after-pains, called out to him; *Don't go today*, she implored, too ashamed to tell him that the sea inside her had spilled out, that his newborn daughter had already defiled the ocean goddess. *The goddess was not pleased; my prayers were not finished.*

But Avni's father, secure in the ancient belief that a fisherman is safe at sea as long as his wife remains chaste, smiled and said, *Today the gods have blessed us with a child. The seas, too, promise to be bountiful.*

Then he took with him a coconut as an offering to the mighty sea god Varuna.

The morning sky turned gray, the winds grew fierce.

Storm! Storm! the midwife called from the front *oti*, pointing to the skies.

Hours passed agonizingly until it was time for the canoes to return to the stone-and-wooden jetty. The women set forth in the rain to meet them, clapping their hands with relief when they spotted the boats struggling to shore amidst the formidable waves. Once they finally arrived, the women eagerly claimed the first catch of the season: pomfret, lobsters, *saranga, surumayi, kolambi,* and *bangdi* from the bigger boats; clams, prawns, *jhinga, manderi,* and *bombil* from the canoes. The women sorted the catch right there on the jetty, chatting excitedly, despite the rains whipping at their faces.

Avni's mother stood alone, eyes on the horizon searching for her husband, until night. When she returned home, the midwife was standing at the front *oti*. Her tobacco-stained mouth hung open as if it could not contain the proclamation it held. *The child's cursed*, she said, handing Avni back. *She cannot stay here past the day she begins to bleed.*

Please—

She must go when she bleeds! The midwife spat a glutinous blob of saliva upon the sand. *Otherwise, she will bring disaster upon us.*

Avni's mother stood with head lowered, accepting the indictment

against her daughter, and believing in a dark corner of her heart that
it was somehow true.

※ ▲ ※

Pinky crouched down, gently placing the decaying coconut upon the
sand where it blended in with the hundreds of others. Her eye caught
a glint of green further down the shore, the sole raw coconut upon the
desolate beach, and she was inexplicably drawn to it. As she grasped
it to her chest, a memory of a recent day unfolded inside her head,
witnessed as if from a perch in the tamarind tree.

A window opened and Lovely climbed out, her dupatta *fluttering
around her like a golden halo, her lips stained red.*

*From the adjoining wall further back in the garden, Nimish emerged
into the downpour, his white kurta soaked, ghostly in the night.*

*They came together under the tamarind tree, its branches swaying
mournfully in the deluge.*

They stood, heads pressed together.

And then, a kiss.

*Thunder shook the earth as if Lord Indra were riding his regal chariot
across the heavens, his mighty lightning bolt striking the earth a devastating blow.*

*With a snap of wind a branch reached out, its mossy oval leaves
caressing Lovely's blushing cheek, its sharpened end cutting into her
luminous skin.*

*A darkened spirit slipped from the inauspicious tree like falling rain,
moistening her face, working its way into her delicate jaw, across her
earlobes dangling with enameled gold, and then downward, downward,
trying to find a way to her heart.*

Lovely abruptly pulled the dupatta *tightly against her shoulders, racing
from the tree, from him, from the smoky blackness spreading down her
throat.*

*Inside the bungalow, hidden behind a window, a third figure awaited—
Harshal—his ugly face twisted in rage.*

*Lovely climbed into her room, to gather the courage to carry out her
plan, to run away, to leave Nimish behind.*

Unexpected fingers grasped at her neck, throwing her onto the bed.

Hands clutched at her breasts.

A tongue invaded her mouth.

She fought back.

Possessed by his lust, his fury at her affections given to another man, Harshal ripped at her salvar *pants.*

The darkened spirit readied itself, poised.

With full erection, he thrust himself into his sister.

A hymen was torn.

At the outpouring of blood, impure blood, the darkened spirit drew power enough to complete its task.

Lovely stopped thrashing.

With a muffled cry, she surrendered her voluptuous, desired, beautiful body at last.

Not to her brother but to a fisherman's daughter, an outcast.

To Avni.

※ ※ ※

Dropping the coconut and the memory it contained, Pinky fell to the sand gagging, understanding at last Lovely's words, her wild eyes, her bloodied leg, her unnatural powers. She felt sick, unfamiliar cramping in her belly, an ache in her back.

Up ahead she noticed a small flickering light on a decaying trawler and began to run towards it, losing her footing in the sand.

"'I believe,'" she heard herself strangely reciting from the Lone Ranger Creed, *"'that sooner or later . . . somewhere . . . somehow . . . we must settle with the world and make payment for what we have taken.'"*

Yes, something had most certainly been taken. The baby's life. Possibly Lovely's life.

And now as she ran towards the eerie lantern glow, the ocean spray spitting at her face, Pinky knew that the time of reckoning had finally come.

※ ※ ※

The bungalow became a crucible, a vessel heated beyond the boiling point by the fears of its inhabitants, by their strained propinquity, their battle to cull away the perceived pollutants in their holy brew.

Finally understanding the plan to desiccate her, the ghost prowled the bungalow for water, absorbing it into her body with the palms of her tiny hands or with a sweep of her effulgent mane. The monsoons broke over the bungalow once more, angry and full as if Mother Nature was attempting to rescue one of her own. Rain lashed at the bungalow's windows, dripped from the ceilings, pooled onto the floor.

The makeshift canteen out back grew perilous; each family member was forced outside, one by one, to consume watery vegetables and drink lukewarm tea. Except for Dheer, most lacked the energy to eat. The latrine began to overflow. Bodies emitted stale, sweaty odors. Greasy farts hung in the air, pungent and toxic. Tufan continued to be betrayed by his bladder, wetting his pants at the most inappropriate times. Each accident was repaid by sharp slaps from Jaginder who was sure that Tufan's incontinence was deliberate so he didn't have to use the fetid toilet.

Savita rarely left her room, not even to eat, drink, or urinate. Kuntal secretly brought water and a bit of *roti* to her, and emptied an urn of Savita's waste in the latrine out back. Savita, meanwhile, refined her strategy to erode Maji's authority, regain Jaginder's loyalty and marry off Nimish.

That afternoon she pulled out her own wedding jewelry, setting aside pieces to pass to Nimish's future wife. *What better way to spend an afternoon,* she thought, delighting in sorting through her glittering collection and estimating how much it was worth—how much *she* was worth. Briefly she thought of her lost daughter, of how they would have sat together sifting through the gems, her little Chakori pleading, *Mummy, I want this one. Save this one for my dowry please?* And Savita would have laughed. *Of course my moon-bird, you are more precious to me than any daughter-in-law could ever be.*

"Oh," Kuntal gasped, averting her eyes from the jewels as she walked into the room.

"Come and see." Savita laughed carelessly. "No need to feel ashamed."

Kuntal approached tentatively, allowing her gaze to fall upon an exquisite raw-diamond and Burmese ruby necklace.

"All this is meaningless if Maji's plan doesn't work," Savita said, gingerly choosing her words. "She's not looking well these days."

"Maji's not well?"

Savita clicked her tongue. "So much strangeness going on, *nah?* How could it not affect even the strongest person's mind? Now tell me which necklace you like. I'll give it to you when you get married."

"No, no," Kuntal backed away, shocked. Savita had made wild promises before, all of them contingent on Kuntal getting married, the likelihood of which dimmed with each passing day.

"You mustn't tell Maji that we're all concerned about her," Savita added. "Otherwise she'll be angry."

Kuntal nodded. She had so fully believed in Maji's invincibility that the possibility of her incapacitation had never crossed her mind.

"Now come here," Savita teased. "Let me try this necklace on you." She draped the jewels across Kuntal's dark neck; a ruby dangled at the curved entrance to her bosom. Kuntal shyly pulled the *palloo* of her sari across her face. For a moment, neither spoke. And then Savita clapped her hands. "*Wah!* You look like a bride."

Kuntal stole a glance at the mirror. *Would she really give this to me?* She thought of Avni. *Has she come back for me?*

"Now go," Savita said, taking back the necklace. "Go ask Jaginder Sahib to come here and then see if Maji needs anything."

Kuntal retreated reluctantly. She enjoyed taking care of Savita, draping her slender, fragrant body in silk saris, putting away the open tubes of lipstick and overturned tins of kohl on the vanity after Savita had gone out, touching each one with rapt attention. Taking care of Maji, on the other hand, was like trying to tend to a beached whale. Her massive flesh made even the simplest tasks difficult, from soaping the sagging areas of her body that Maji could no longer reach to wrapping her dull white sari around her enormous hips. And through it all, especially while Kuntal was massaging her, Maji rarely spoke unless to give a command.

Oh pho! Kuntal thought, if Maji was falling ill then she would have even less time to attend to anything else. It wasn't just Savita's chattiness that assuaged Kuntal's loneliness but something more, something intangible, unspeakable. In the past few days, when she changed the stained *dupatta* from around Savita's breasts, she had let her gaze fall on their moist fullness. She told no one of her thoughts, not even Parvati whose growing waves of nausea caused her to throw up in wide arcs across the muddy back driveway.

Jaginder knocked on his bedroom door hesitantly, not knowing what state he'd find his wife in. This past week alone she had morphed into more avatars than Lord Vishnu had in the time span of the universe. He was able to deal with her wounded-bird incarnation, tears brimming in her eyes as she quivered under his harsh words. And he heartily welcomed the Savita who seduced him in bed for several nights. But her most recent manifestations threw him for a loop: the bitter woman who told him to go to hell the other night and the doting wife who served him his chai this very morning.

Jaginder was in no mood for his wife's games; dealing with his addiction now was challenging enough. A terrible thirst had gripped his body causing his head to ache and his fingers to tremble. A thick fog had settled in his head, making it difficult for him to think clearly. Pinching the throbbing tension lodged in the base of his neck, Jaginder pushed the door open a crack. "Savita?"

"Come, darling."

He saw his wife lying on the bed, jewels piled around her. The effect of all that glistening color in the austere room was stunning.

"What's the meaning of this?"

Savita motioned him over, "No hello-how-are-you first?"

Jaginder cracked his neck, his back, and all his knuckles before sitting on the edge of the bed, touching the silvery sheeting of the bed frame. At one point in his life, this furniture had thrilled him. The colorlessness of it immediately drew his eyes to Savita. Recently though, he realized that it had the opposite effect on him. He, in his monochromatic kurtas and pant suits, all but disappeared.

Savita leaned her shoulder and head against his broad back. "I'm worried about our Nimi."

She began dusting off his shirt with her hand.

"What's to bloody worry about?" Jaginder said gruffly. "He's a normal boy with normal urges."

"But what's this nonsense with Lovely?"

"He wants to be a hero, that's all."

"Nothing more?"

Jaginder clicked his tongue, "I'd be worried if he didn't go *pagal* after such a beautiful girl."

Savita stiffened. "Yes. So we must get him married to a nice Punjabi girl *fut-a-fut.*"

"Married? But you're the one always saying that he must study."

"Study, yes," Savita said, starting to massage Jaginder's shoulders. "He can still study, but a wife will keep him grounded, *nah?*"

"But—but."

"But nothing," Savita interrupted. "With Maji barely able to manage the household and all the terrible events of these past days, don't you think a daughter-in-law would bring us happiness?"

Jaginder remembered the first moment after his own nuptials when Savita had been brought from the marigold-garlanded car into their home. The entire driveway and interior of the bungalow had been strewn with rose petals. She had been so beautiful, so coy, so perfect, auspiciously scattering a handful of rice placed at the threshold with a kick of her bejeweled foot, foretelling the prosperity her presence would bring. The desire he felt for her at that moment was indescribable; she had been the answer to all his adolescent dreams. *Let Nimish bloody rot a bit,* Jaginder thought, jealous that his son would experience that rapture soon. "He's too young," he protested, aware of Savita's warm fingers pressing into his shoulders. "Best that he's several years older than his wife so he can mold her to his liking."

"But I already have the perfect girl in mind and we don't want her to be snapped up by someone else," Savita said. "Juhi Khandelwal."

"Falgun's daughter?"

"Yes," Savita said excitedly. "She's also seventeen and very fair. And very shy. She wasn't even interested in attending college. And from what I hear, she's a very moldable type."

Jaginder remembered going to Falgun's home for dinner once, when Savita had taken the boys with her parents on vacation to Goa. Juhi was a young girl then, no more than twelve, but even so her face was striking. In a city of overwhelmingly brown-eyed people, Juhi's emerald green eyes burned into his memory. *And now,* he thought, *now she could be my daughter-in-law.*

"Let's talk more once things settle down."

"Settle down?" Savita asked. "What if Maji's plan fails?"

"It won't fail," Jaginder said, growing tense. "The tantrik said four days."

"He also said that we all must be here now, all of us who were here when our baby died."

"So?"

"So, Gulu's not here. And that wicked ayah's not here either."

Jaginder cracked his knuckles again.

"What if our baby lives," Savita suggested, wishing it to be. "Then what? Maybe she'll kill all of you who wanted to get rid of her."

"Use your head! Do you think we'd be able to control the bloody ghost if it were to stay. No! It would only grow bolder until it certainly killed us all, you included."

"Oh, Jaggi," Savita switched tactics, "aren't you tired of this water shortage? Of being humiliated in front of the servants?"

"We must see this through," Jaginder said with less certainty, his headache growing stronger. "No matter how long it takes. Otherwise, it will be a sign of weakness."

"Please, Jaggi," Savita pleaded, pressing her fingers into his neck. "Please let me make some inquiries about Juhi."

"Fine, fine," Jaginder conceded, waving his hand dismissively.

Savita gave Jaginder a squeeze of gratitude. "She'll be perfect for Nimish. I just know it!"

"Now don't be crazy. We have to ask Maji first."

"She has so much on her mind these days," Savita said. "Haven't you noticed how drained she looks?"

Jaginder remained motionless, not willing to concede this to his wife nor to betray his mother. His fingers began to shake again. His body felt fatigued. He clutched his hands together, willing his muscles to obey him. *A cool sip of whiskey!* He conjured the image in his head unaware that a solitary bottle of Royal Salut lay stashed just behind the thin metal of Savita's cabinet. *Just one little sip.*

"You must get her to do less, to rest more," Savita continued. "We can manage things."

"But still we must ask her," Jaginder insisted wearily.

"*Hai! Hai!*" Savita lamented. "You're always taking the fun out of things. Now tell me, which diamond set shall we give our daughter-in-law for the engagement?"

Jaginder looked blindly at those on the bed. He pointed to the one closest to him.

"Oh my God!" Savita shrieked. "How can you even think to give her such a simple set, they will think we're paupers!"

Jaginder managed a smile as Savita gave him another squeeze. "Oh, Jaggi," she cooed. "Nimi will be so happy."

Jaginder puffed out his chest, absently scratching at it as he thought about Nimish's recent rage at him. Savita was right, he grudgingly admitted to himself, all the boy needed was a wife. Jaginder had been embarrassingly tense at that age, spending much of his allotted private time addressing this imbalance. *Yes, Nimish needs a wife to relieve his tensions.* And once Juhi came to their home, it would only be a matter of time before Nimish would agree to forgo his wild plans to study abroad and his romantic delusions about Lovely and instead settled down to family life as expected. *Maybe I'll even be a* dadaji *in a year's time,* the thought momentarily chasing away the thirst in his throat. *Imagine that! A grandfather!*

And then, unwillingly, his mind settled on Savita's warning: *What if Maji's plan fails?* He had been willing to endure the four days of suffering, believing that salvation lay just on the other side. Now, for the first time, he considered they might be trapped by the spiteful ghost in this indefinite state of hell. *If Ma fails us,* he swore, *I'll sell this bloody bungalow.*

Savita fell into a contented sleep, surrounded by her jewels. In her dream, her daughter came to her again, sucking at her breast as if she were starving. *Drink, drink,* Savita whispered softly to her daughter, the skin around her delicate features turning a translucent pink, miniscule beads of sweat peppering the arc just under her eyes, hidden shyly under a veil of thick eyelashes. But then, without warning, the dream turned into a nightmare. The baby looked up gasping, eyes hollow. With horror, Savita realized that her traitorous breasts were barren once more.

Her baby was going to die.

☼ ♀ ☮

Nimish spent the afternoon alternately pacing about his room, phoning the police precinct, and pushing the side door open whenever the rains broke to take a peek at the Lawate's tamarind tree that could be seen shimmering over the wall. "Lovely, Lovely, Lovely," he intoned like a prayer, "come back to me." And then, equally fervently, he called out to Pinky, ever more fearful for her safety. *Had she really been abducted again?* And then, more terrible thoughts invaded his mind. *What if Lovely had intended to run away? What if she really was meeting another boy? What if her promise by the tamarind tree had been nothing more than a lie?*

With a violent swing, Nimish shoved the door shut. As it screeched in protest, a locked-away memory suddenly broke into his consciousness, filling him with a surge of intense pain. He had been only four then, asleep in his bed until the creak-crack of the very same door had pulled him from his slumber. He remembered hearing footsteps in the hallway and assumed that they belonged to Maji whose morning rounds usually lulled him back to his dreams. But that morning Nimish had remained awake, unexpectedly alert. There had been wisps of a melody in the air and then his father's booming voice. And then more footsteps, fast ones, along with other, more indistinct sounds.

Frightened, but unsure as to the reason, Nimish had thrown his legs over the side of his bed and considered calling for Avni or Kuntal. After what felt like an eternity, he slid from the mattress and, peeking from behind his door, saw his grandmother lead the ayah from the bathroom and out towards the front of the bungalow. *What had happened?* Nimish padded quietly to the bathroom. As he approached the brass bucket, he saw his sister blue-faced, towel wrapped around her body, lying still as a stone upon the wooden stool.

Wake up! He had cajoled her, every hair on his body tingling with dread. *Wake up! Please wake up!* But his sister remained motionless. Nimish heard the front door close and raced back to his bed, flinging his covers over his head as his heart thudded violently, fearing that he would be caught. He stayed there, fighting back tears, even as his one-year-old brothers awoke and began to cry, hoping that what he had seen could be erased if only he remained immobile.

Nimish felt a sob emerge from deep in his throat. *So much had been lost.* He had been awake when his sister died, just a few meters away in the adjoining room. *If only,* he told himself, *if only I had gotten out of bed earlier, I could have saved her from drowning and none of this would be happening.*

He slumped against the wall, recognizing at last the cumbrous guilt he had carried all these years. *That's why I've always taken care of Mummy. Because I failed her then.* Nimish's anger at his father had taken root that day, too. It was his father who had called for the milk-production cereal and set the juggernaut in motion. And it was Jag-inder who took up drinking afterwards, wallowing in self-pity rather than attending to the emotional state of his family as he should have. Everything had fallen apart after the baby's death. But even that was not enough. Now she had returned as a ghost to wreak further ven-geance. And what better way to make Nimish pay than to take Lovely away from him forever?

Nimish slid down the wall until he crumpled onto the floor. "Please," he called out to his ghostly sister, reaching out to the intangible oth-erworld, an action he would have considered unimaginable only a few days earlier, "I was only four then. Please don't take Lovely."

Just on the other side, ensconced in the bathroom, the ghost opened her eyes.

Water, she whispered to her eldest brother, her diaphanous hair bil-lowing like a pure, barren cloud.

Water.

A TRAWLER & TRUTH

P arvati touched her belly, awed that new life was forming inside her awaiting ensoulment in the next days and then, according to the ancient *Vedas*, its consciousness at seven months gestation.

"My little *pakora*," Cook Kanj said, affectionately calling his future child a fried ball of chickpea flour.

"Can you believe that after all these years without a child," Parvati said, her hard edges already starting to soften, "she'll be here before the next monsoons?"

"She?" Cook Kanj was offended. He spat, pulling the twig of *neem* with which he had been cleaning his teeth from his mouth. "It will be a boy."

"And how can you be so sure?"

"The baby inside you is like dough, *nah*? Add sugar and you have sweet *puras*, good for only breakfast and snack. But add a bit of salt and you have *roti*, the staple of life. My seeds are salty-salty boys, I have no doubt."

Parvati laughed. She and Kanj had been the only ones to retain their sense of humor these past days, buoyed by their pregnancy and by the unbelievable change the household had experienced, rendering the Mittal family virtually homeless. Just yesterday morning, in fact, Jaginder had practically begged them for a cup of tea.

"I'll be sad when the ghost goes," Kanj said wistfully. "I've never had so much fun in my life."

"Oh ho!" Parvati said. "Why take such pleasure in others' sufferings? Your own cooking has become so watery that it should be served in a glass."

"What do you expect when I have to cook in the rain?"

"Oh ho! no need to get upset. The ghost will be gone by end of tomorrow and everything will be back to normal."

"Fine, fine," Kanj said. "The ghost will be gone, but what about the ayah?"

Parvati shifted uncomfortably.

"She's come back for some reason, too."

"If she comes near my family, I'll kill her."

"What is it? Has she reason to harm us?"

"No," Parvati said, turning away. "Go, it's almost time for morning chai, you better go."

Kanj's joints creaked as he swung them over the bed and stood up. *She's not telling me something,* Kanj thought as he adjusted the *dhoti* over his bone-thin legs, realizing once again that there was a part of his wife that he would never be able to access. She had other secrets too, he knew, dark secrets from her childhood in Bengal. He had accepted those mysteries when he married her. Yet, this more recent concealment was more difficult to overlook, souring his affections.

During the three years that Avni had been part of their household, Parvati had complained endlessly about her, growing combative, hostile, almost paranoid to the point that Kanj spent his free time in the storage room sorting canisters of lentils just to escape his wife's tirades. Parvati's bond with Kuntal also suffered, their sisterly affection strained almost beyond repair. When the baby drowned and Avni was thrown out, Kanj had not felt grief or sadness but relief.

He absentmindedly threw tea leaves into the pot of milk, crushing five cardamom pods to toss in afterwards while standing under an improvised canopy that did little in the way of shielding him or his cooking from the rain. A disturbing thought came to his head:

Does Avni know about Parvati's pregnancy? With the comings and goings of all the vendors, relatives, and friends, it was not difficult to conceive that a vengeful Avni had been watching them all these years, paying someone for news about the household. *Everyone has a price*, Kanj thought, casting his net of suspicion onto each and every person who had been by the bungalow since Parvati's morning sickness began.

Vimla Auntie's son Harshal, Kanj knew, was just the type of bastard who took pleasure in bringing misery to others. *And Gulu, the jackass,* he silently cursed, *would have driven the Ambassador over his foot for Avni.* And what about that pimply-faced U. P. dairyman who drove over in a corporation van every third day with sealed bottles from the Aarey Milk Colony? Before the establishment of the government-run Colony several years back, the very same man would teeter over on his bike with two aluminum vats of diluted milk swaying from his rusted handlebars. *Sister fucker,* Kanj remembered resentfully. *And he'd still charge full price! I'll fry him up like onion* bajji *the next time he shows his face!*

As the chai began to heat, forming a thick skin of fat across the top, Kanj felt certain that Avni knew about their pregnancy. *Why else would she have returned at this time?* He had no idea what had transpired between Parvati and Avni just before she was fired, but he was sure something had happened, something so terrible that even after all these years, Avni burned to retaliate. *And,* Kanj decided with a grunt, *his wife knew all this.* That was the only explanation for her behavior this morning.

"*Bas!*" Kanj said out loud as the boiling milk frothed over the top of the pot in a violent surge. He was tired of Parvati's secrets. He might only be an illiterate cook but he was no fool. Before the end of the day he wanted to know everything about his wife's past. A line had already formed for morning tea. Kanj deferentially handed Jaginder the first tall tumbler but his eyes were on the person standing unassumingly in the back of the line. With just the right combination of sweet and salty, Cook Kanj decided, he would coax Kuntal into telling him the truth.

The only member of the household who seemed untouched by the increasing chaos was fourteen-year-old Dheer. Left on his own, he wandered around the bungalow like an inflatable life raft, rescuing chocolate bars from long forgotten locations. "Here," he said, venturing into the abandoned hallway bathroom and placing a slim package of Danish chocolates in the bucket, "for you."

The ghost shifted from her position atop the pipes and eyed the chocolates with suspicion. Despite the monsoon's increasing wrath the last several days, she had grown weaker. Maji's power was too pervasive, too deadly. The baby ghost cast a forlorn look at Dheer, who sat against the wall pushing a half-melted chocolate into his mouth, swallowing the barely chewed pieces in large gulps. She was too weak to make herself visible to him now; her body was already losing its form as if reversing the process by which she had originally appeared. Strands of silvery hair molted from her head and floated in the air, sticking to the bungalow walls like curling filaments of moonlight. One fell onto Dheer's lap. Wiping his chocolatey hands on his trousers, he ventured to touch it and was immediately struck by a deep sadness.

"When Pinky first told me about you"—he began to weep at the mention of her name—"I didn't believe her." He squinted up at the ceiling, seeing nothing but a bit of peeling plaster. "I don't remember you," he continued. "I was only one when you died. And now you're back, but I can't see you." He sighed. He too had felt invisible these past few days as the household was too caught up in its own misery to notice him anymore.

Yesterday Dheer found Nimish slumped in tears against the side door and just earlier today he heard Cook Kanj talking with Kuntal in loud, angry whispers in the closed-off living room. No one cared to make sure Dheer ate or was dressed; it was as if he was were on his own. The only bit of attention he received was when his mother momentarily emerged from her room to order them all to take baths. *Maji may have forced us to live like street urchins,* Savita had yelled at them when she knew that her mother-in-law was safely ensconced in the *puja* room, *but I won't tolerate you smelling like one!*

In the next moment, they were duly stripped down to their underwear and shoved behind a strung-up tarp attached to the side of Gulu's garage, giving it the appearance of one of the ubiquitous shanties that lined the streets of Bombay. They were each given one bucket of cold water and told to wash from head to toe. The only concession Savita had made was to personally attend to Jaginder's bath, waiting under an umbrella with his fresh kurta pajama, and ensuring that his water was heated.

Dheer shuddered at the memory of the cold water on his back. After their baths, they were forced to stand outside until their toweled-off hair completely dried. Even Dheer's extra layers of fat hadn't protected him from the chill he felt then. Yet no one took pity on him as each of them were lost in their own miseries.

Tufan had stood by the latrine, shivering under an umbrella.

Nimish, too, had been in his own world, his eyes glazed over behind his spectacles, reading *A Sketch of A Bombay High Caste Hindu Young Wife*, not even shrugging Dheer away when he read over his shoulder, trying to catch his mother's attention. *Whose happy rule in my dear native land*, Dheer had quoted in his loudest voice from the dedication to Queen Victoria, *is brightening and enlightening the lives and homes of many Hindu women.*

Savita snorted. *What nonsense are you reading today Nimi? As if that meat-eating* ferengi *knew anything about us Hindu women.* Nimish closed the book with a snap and stared out at the Lawate's tree with unfocusing eyes.

What about me? Dheer had silently pleaded to his mother, but she had not even seen him.

Fat tears began to roll down his cheeks at the memory. Even a slap across his head would have been better than this total inattention. Sitting against the bathroom wall, he tried to wrap the strand of ghostly hair around his finger but it dissolved into nothingness. Things were supposed to be better by now, the third night. *Yes*, he thought, *some things were better.* His mother no longer tied a *dupatta* tightly across her chest, his father was not as prone to unsolicited slapping, and Cook Kanj's cooking had even thickened. But Pinky had not been found. And as each day went by, the chances of her being so grew slimmer.

"Please," he began to beg the ghost, "you're the only one who can save Pinky. You have powers." Dheer had never disobeyed an elder in his entire life; it simply was not in his nature to do so. But his cousin's life was at stake.

"Promise me that you'll save Pinky," he said. "Promise me this. Kemosabe, and I won't let you die." And then as if to make good on his word, he reached into the bucket and opened the Danish chocolate box that he had stolen from his parents' locked cabinet. A row of chocolates, each filled with watery liquor, glinted back at them.

Maji emerged from her puja room visibly strained, and immediately phoned the priest. She let out a great sigh and stumbled into another prayer, knowing that the wheels of karma had not yet finished churning. Despite her life-long piety, the Gods jealously continued to guard the bungalow's destiny within the multitude of their arms, balancing a brilliant pearl conch shell in one hand, a diskette of golden fire in another, the fate of the ghost in a third, and that of Pinky in a fourth.

Pinky staggered down the abandoned coastline and onto the jetty. The dilapidated trawler was tossing in the howling gale. The glowing light she had seen earlier vanished as she stepped onto the boat, her toes curling as they touched the molded, rotted floorboard. Darkness surrounded her. The boat lurched and Pinky threw her hands out to steady herself. She took another step. A gust of wind whipped through the trawler. The decayed frame moaned as the boat tossed back and forth, back and forth, in a mournful rhythm. Somewhere beyond, Pinky heard a distinctive splash-splash over the ocean's crash. She took another step.

Then the smell hit her, the ghastly stench of rotting fish.

Pinky doubled over, gagging.

A voice said to her from the darkness, *My father survived it by drinking fermented jambul fruit. So strong it was, it could flatten an elephant.*

The clouds parted. In a sliver of moonlight, Pinky spotted a sari-clad figure hovering at the stern of the boat dropping coconuts one by one into the water as if to dispose of them. One of the coconuts rolled to Pinky. She bent to pick it up and found herself enveloped once again by a strange heat.

Another memory.

A train approached, its front headlight illuminating the tracks. Passengers surged forward, holding themselves inches away from the platform's edge.

A unfamiliar voice rang out: There is one way, but it involves an exceptional sacrifice. You must be strong, unwavering.

And then a jump. The tracks seemed to lift up to meet Avni's falling body.

Hard, metallic, fast, the train approached like a bullet, a harbinger of death.

Instantly there was a rush of blood, the beginnings of a scream, then nothing, nothing at all—the remnants of a body reduced to its elemental parts.

Hair, flesh, blood, bone.

☙ ❦ ❧

Pinky dropped the coconut. It fell to the ground with a sickening crack.

That was my sacrifice. The voice was close, far too close.

Pinky opened her eyes.

Avni stood right in front of her, sari consuming her like a fire, eerily obscuring her face. Her feet were bare, powdered with dust and dirt, a single silver toe-ring her only adornment. Her arms were muscular, with a tattoo etched into her skin—a holy mark that ensured entrance into God's abode. *Godhun aali ki choruni?* she will be asked at heaven's gate. *Do you bear the mark of God or are you sneaking in?* A sharpened sickle-shaped *koyta* swung at her waist.

I had to give my life to obtain certain powers. And then I waited thirteen years, chained to the platform where I died, her gritty voice hissed, *but I wasn't alone. There were other transitory souls, a parallel otherworld.*

The boat rocked violently. Pinky backed away.

I became part of them, the boundaries of flesh no longer a barrier to our unions, Avni continued, *but I had only one true desire.*

Her gaze fell upon the cracked coconut upon the floor. *I'm drowning them,* she confessed, pointing to the other coconuts rolling about the stern like marbles. *Drowning them so I won't remember anymore.*

And then, hurling the cracked one off the boat, she turned back to Pinky.

There was one boy, a tea-boy known as Crazy-One. I ventured into him the very day I died. And then it became easier: the drug-addicted, the mentally ill, the poor, anyone with weakened defenses.

"But why?"

Avni cackled, a sound like merciless winds upon a desolate ocean.

To practice so I could find a way back into the bungalow when the time came. I needed a body to inhabit, a body already inside the bungalow so my spirit would be allowed passage.

Pinky took a step back, her heart pounding in her chest. "So it was you in the boat! It was you inside Lovely!"

I draw power from impure blood, vaginal blood. I waited, waited in the tamarind tree. Your Maji is old and no longer bleeds. And Parvati is pregnant. And you are still a girl. And Kuntal . . . I could never violate her. That left only Savita. So I waited, waited for her cycles, waited for her to come out of the bungalow. Then Lovely came to the tree. And she was so beautiful, so pure, her heart so very open. I wanted her, even if just for a moment. It was not the time of her cycles so I had to find another way.

Pinky cried out, hand over her mouth. "You took her but it's me you wanted!"

You were the one who came outside, who came to me in the street. But you are strong. I could not get into you, even in the canoe when I tried to weaken you. I had to wait, to bring you here.

Pinky felt the unfamiliar cramping again, the ache in her back. A soreness in her breasts. And then, the faintest trickle of something between her legs.

She had to get away, get away before it was too late, before Avni sensed it.

She took another step back, then another.

"Where's Lovely?" she cried out. "Tell me! Is she here? Is she alive?" Her eyes frantically searched the trawler, the jetty, the coastline curling into eternity.

Avni smiled. *She found her freedom. I could not take that from her.*

She then plucked a coconut from her sari, not a dried one like the others but raw, smooth, green. *You've not come for her but for this.*

"A coconut?"

The truth.

"No!" Pinky cried out. Another step back. And another.

You must drink it in you.

"No! Just leave me alone, leave my family alone!"

I'll not go away. I'll never go away. If not you, then Savita, then Parvati after she gives birth.

Pinky hesitated. She had turned away from the truth once before, in the bathroom with the ghost. Her decision resulted in devastation. *If only I had stayed, listened, believed, the ghost would be okay. Lovely would be okay.*

Despite every desire to do so, she could not turn away again.

Since ancient times, she knew, coconuts were offered to the gods, the hard-shelled nut representing the human skull, the home of the ego. To crack it open at the feet of a deity, to consume its milk or meat, meant to surrender this ego-self, to become a willing vessel for the divine, the all-encompassing Truth.

She seized the coconut from Avni's hands, closed her eyes as Avni brought the *koyta* down upon it with a thwack, and lifted it to her lips.

The milky liquid slid into her throat.

Pinky fell to her knees, her mouth foaming, a scream bubbling upon her lips.

Avni had done it.

She had finally claimed Pinky.

SILVER *PUJA* VESSEL

A thin, flushed figure approached Maji's green gates, hidden behind vines of bougainvillea. The figure held out a hand to the gate, then hesitated, looking upwards to the sky. Rain fell lightly this morning.

Sitting inside the bungalow, the lethargic inhabitants heard the dull slap-slap of a flattened palm against the gate. They waited for the sound to stop, to disappear into the background of other noises that filled their morning. But the slapping grew more insistent. A voice called out. Parvati went to investigate.

"*Kaun hai?*" Maji asked wearily, waking from a doze upon her dais.

"Gulu."

"Tell him to go."

"He insists on talking with you."

"I have nothing to say."

"He has something to say about the day the baby drowned."

Maji froze, the flesh around her jaw the only part of her body that continued to sway. Then she slowly pulled herself erect and, taking her cane, walked to the gate, firmly closing the door behind her.

"I did not come a few nights back," Gulu started, eyes peeking from between the iron arrowhead caps jutting from the top of the gate, "because I had to find Avni. I had to know if she had really come back after all these years."

Maji's jaw tightened, "She's of no concern to you!"

"I went to her mother's home," Gulu continued, shoulders heaving with emotion. "She told me everything."

"She's of no concern!"

"She died!" Gulu's mouth opened wide with the terrible words. "Thirteen years ago, she threw herself in front of the train the very same day you sent her away."

Maji heard Parvati gasp behind her.

"If she died, I had nothing to do with it!"

"You sent her away!"

Maji furiously undid the lock and, throwing the chain onto the driveway, yelled at him to step inside the gate. She stood just an inch away from him, the fury contained in her enormous body causing his own scrawny one to shake. Instinctively, he tucked his wounded hand under his armpit.

"What should I have done?" Maji spat, aware that her entire family stood on the verandah intently listening in to their conversation. "Kept her here after what happened? I could have sent her to jail or had her beaten but instead I had you take her to VT, even gave her money to start a new life. My only instruction was that she leave Bombay and never come back."

"She was not to blame for what happened!" Unabashedly weeping, Gulu opened his mouth as if to allow the words, trapped deep within his body, to come pouring forth, fueled by Chinni's threat. What would happen if he were to tell his terrible secret, about what he had done after the baby and Avni had both died?

"Remember this Gulu," Maji said furiously, pointing a finger so close to his eye that the tip of it touched his eyelashes. "You were nothing more than a street urchin when I took you in. I gave you food, shelter, a job, a second life. I gave Avni another chance, too. It was *she* who decided not to take it. Remember this. Now *jao!* Go away from my home!"

Gulu took a step back as if he had been slapped. What had he been thinking, to confront Maji like this? If Chinni were watching, she would have had a cruel laugh at his expense. Bhenchod *fool!* she would have spat in his face. *Can't stand up to a woman!* It was true, Maji had given him a second chance, a life better than the slums into which he had been born. What would he gain by telling her now, after all these years? The threats that had been lodged in his throat died away. "Please forgive me," he whispered.

Maji snorted.

"There's nothing left for me out there," Gulu said, his shoulders hunched, his chest caved forward in defeat. *Will Chinni really kill herself?* he thought.

Maji looked up into the misty sky. The rest of the household stood on the verandah watching, waiting for her verdict. It was Savita who unexpectedly stepped forward to plead his case. "A good driver's difficult to find these days."

"Yes, yes," said Jaginder feeling as if his position as man of the house was at stake. "He's been with us since he was a bloody boy, after all."

Despite his support, Gulu couldn't help but to feel a sting of hatred towards Jaginder.

"Pleasepleaseplease," the twins chorused from the verandah.

Parvati, Kuntal, and Cook Kanj remained silent, reminded once again of how uncertain their own livelihood was, how their presence in the bungalow on Malabar Hill was only on sufferance, as workers but never as its rightful inhabitants.

"Go from here," Maji commanded. "Never return."

Gulu stopped himself from crumpling to the ground.

"If I see you here again, I'll call the police," Maji threatened before turning back to the verandah where the rest of the family stood in shocked silence, not one daring to question her decision.

"Wait!" Nimish called as Gulu walked away. "Was there any news of Lov— of Vimla Auntie's daughter?"

Gulu shook his head.

The gate was bolted once more.

* * *

As the sun began to set on the fourth day, the Mittal household heard yet another hollow knock on the gate. "That's it," Maji said, reaching for her cane, "I'll thrash him myself. Come Nimish, come with me."

As she unchained the gate, however, she saw it was not Gulu who stood before her, but Pinky. Pinky in wet and dirty pajamas, crusted coconut milk upon her face. She fell, shuddering, to the ground. For a blessed moment, Maji found herself unable to speak and crumpled to the ground beside her. Without a thought for his grandmother, Nimish hastily carried Pinky to her room, where he laid her down on the bed and closed the door.

"Tell me quickly before they all come," he whispered to her. "Tell me where Lovely is!"

Pinky looked at him with lifeless eyes.

"Please," he begged, caressing her hair. "Please."

At his touch, she began to laugh, a horrific, gleeful cackle. She yanked him towards her, her breasts rising to meet his falling hands, her lips crushing his.

Nimish fought back but could not break from her unearthly grip. Her wide open legs clamped around his hips.

Kuntal stepped into the room and gasped, her hand flying to her mouth.

Pinky turned her wild eyes upon her and pushed Nimish away.

She reached out to Kuntal, her fingers splayed back.

"Oh my God," Nimish cried out, moving backwards to the corner of the room, panting breathlessly, "oh my God!"

Kuntal took a step forward.

Pinky lifted herself off the bed and began to sway.

Tears began to fall from Kuntal's eyes. She stretched her arm toward Pinky.

Parvati rush in and stopped. "Move away!" she yelled. "Kuntal!"

Kuntal dropped her arm.

Maji finally arrived at the room and tried to push Parvati out of the way. "Pinky!"

"She's possessed!" Parvati yelled, grabbing Maji. "Kuntal, get out now!"

Pinky's sunken gaze fell upon them, a low growl rumbled in her throat.

"No!" Kuntal said, "I'll stay with her."

"No!" Parvati yelled, instinctively protecting her belly. A familiar hate rose up in her chest. "Look at her eyes, I've seen eyes like that before!"

"It can't be!" Maji cried out.

"Leave me!" Kuntal pushed her sister away.

"The doctor can't save her!" Parvati yelled. "Your prayers can't save her! There's only one who can!"

Maji gaze fell upon her granddaughter, her malevolent eyes, her chilling stare. "Go," she whispered, backing away, *"tantrik ko bulao."*

Kuntal closed the door in her sister's face and locked it.

"No!" Parvati cried out, pounding on the door. "NO! NO! NO!"

Kuntal stood inside the room, pressing her back against the door, the thump-thump of Parvati's banging resonating up her spine. "What have you done?" she whispered to the figure upon the bed, to the reckless spirit inside Pinky. A desperate look appeared in the girl's shining eyes.

"This is not the way," Kuntal cried out, biting her lip. "This is not the way to come back to me."

The girl reached out, a rumble in her throat.

Kuntal sat on the bed next to her, her face filled with grief. She unwrapped the sari *palloo* that she had tied to her waist and moistened the end of it with her tongue. Tenderly, she pressed it to the girl's face, annointing her forehead, her lips.

"What do you say when you want a lifetime," Kuntal said, looking into those eyes through which she could glimpse her beloved, "but must say good-bye?"

The pounding continued unabated, the rattling of the doorknob.

Kuntal took a breath and continued. "I'm so sorry—"

The eyes flickered, Avni's eyes.

"You must leave this child," Kuntal managed, beginning to weep. "You mustn't harm her. Please."

And then, she lay her head upon the girl's heart and closed her eyes. If only she had the power to stop time, to make these precious seconds spin out, out, out, to infinity.

"I'm here with you now," she whispered.

There was nothing more to say.

The tantrik arrived, his rosary swinging angrily upon his ash-covered chest, bells clanging around his ankles. He sat cross-legged on a sheet laid out, not on the front verandah this time, but right inside the bungalow's central location, the parlor.

Without uttering a word, he fell into a deep meditation, his back remaining upright, spine etched deeply into the tight muscles of his back. The coil of hair upon his head was the only part of him out of alignment. His son lit a small *diya* and incense sticks and placed them next to statues of Hanuman, Lord Rama, Goddess Sita, and Lord Shiva and brought from the *puja* room in order to create a temporary shrine in the parlour. Then he pulled out a steel container of vermilion and turmeric, hues that were typically shunned by evil spirits, and laid a similarly colored thread near the shrine. Glass containers of *ghee* and asafetida were unpacked, the latter sprinkled around the perimeter of the sheet. The tantrik began to sing a *bhajan*, a devotional song to the gods, as he rang a brass bell.

"Is that all he's going to do?" Tufan asked, clearly disappointed.

"Shut up," Savita hissed, cuffing him across the head.

Just then there was a honking outside the gate.

"Panditji!" Maji exclaimed, remembering that she had called him the day before.

Nimish raced outside to open the gates for the priest's saffron Impala.

For a whirling moment, Maji almost yelled at Nimish to send him away, to make any excuse so that he would not witness the tantrik in her home but then she realized she could no longer hide from shame. Panditji swept in under the cover of a huge umbrella, not even the small tuft of hair on the back of his head moistened by the pouring rain.

"Please," Jaginder said greeting him at the door. "Have a seat."

"What's the meaning of this?" Panditji demanded when he saw the tantrik sitting in the dead center of the room, surrounded by the gods.

"Panditji," Maji wearily brought her hands together in namaste, "Pinky's very sick."

"So you insult our gods with black magic?" Panditji's bare chest quivered with indignation. Oh ho! What a secret this was! *Jadoo tona,* how he would make them grovel to keep his mouth shut!

"We need you both."

"Both!" the priest huffed. "I communicate with the divine. What does *he* do? Conjure evil spirits?"

"I bring the divine into the human body," the tantrik shot back, lifting his scarlet-rimmed eyes to the priest. "Divine communication and divine possession are complimentary, Panditji. Surely you must have learnt this as a boy while memorizing your Sanskrit *slokas.*"

The priest raised one of his contoured eyebrows, quickly inventorying the dullness of his mind for a suitable reaction. He could storm away in anger, forcing Maji to appease him with expensive gifts, maybe even one of those newfangled refrigerators to keep his lime sherbets cool in the temple's back room in between prayer sessions. Or he could stay, not allowing this filthy, serpent-tongued sadhu to show him up. Making up his mind, he adjusted his silk *dhoti* and plopped himself onto his prayer mat.

"Bring the girl," the tantrik ordered impatiently, gesturing to the space in front of him.

"Yes," Panditji said loudly in his high-pitched voice. "Bring the girl."

Nimish stood up, his face pale, and hesitated.

"Oh, for bloody sake," Jaginder grunted, heaving himself up.

The priest quickly busied himself with opening jars of *ghee*, sweat dripping from his protruding belly onto the floor.

Jaginder carried Pinky into the room, Kuntal holding onto her hand, and Parvati clutching at Kuntal. He placed her upon the sheet.

The tantrik's heavy lids flickered open. "Move away," he growled at the family. "You." He pointed to Maji. "You come."

"What's the nature of her illness?" the priest inquired, feeling faintly hungry despite the three samosas he had consumed on route.

"She won't talk," Maji said. "See how she's sweating."

"She's in God's hands now," Panditji said, evading any commitment as to her fate. With that, he emptied the contents of one entire jar of *ghee* into the iron *kund* and lit the match against the floor.

The tantrik passed a hand over Pinky's body. A low chanting emanated from his mouth, a guttural sound—*ma*—that grew in intensity, sounding more like a wail, and finally culminating in a terrifying scream.

Panditji nervously attended to his flickering fire, speedily muttering

prayers as his fingers fumbled with a bag of *puja samagri*. His eyes
kept going askance to the tantrik as if with a will of their own. The
rest of the family drew back, chilled, their hearts beating faster and
faster. Maji looked from the priest to the tantrik as if she did not know
which one to put her faith in. Tufan stopped fidgeting and hid his face
behind Savita's sari *palloo*.

Rain poured down outside, thunder growling.

The chanting continued again, faster this time, clashing with the
priest's equally urgent prayers. Maji found herself rocking back and
forth as if trying to keep up with their frantic pace.

The sacred fire suddenly leapt from the iron *kund*, singeing the
thick patch of hair at Panditji's navel. He yelped and dabbed at his
belly with an oily cloth.

The tantrik took some black ash from a pouch and drew a line
around Pinky's neck to trap the spirit within her body while he questioned it. He uttered a mantra, blowing a spell from his mouth onto
Pinky's face.

She opened her eyes as her body began to shake.

"*Bolo!*" the tantrik commanded, eyes blazing, thick matted beard
twisting ferociously. "*Suchh bolo!* Speak the truth!"

As if being physically assaulted, Pinky began to writhe on the floor,
screaming.

Panditji began to hyperventilate, his chest moving in and out with
the intensity of a hummingbird's.

"Kuntal," Savita managed to whisper, her face devoid of color.
"Take the boys out of the room."

Kuntal nodded but Nimish, Dheer, and Tufan refused to move,
entranced by the scene unfolding in front of them.

"*Kali Mata ki jay, Shankar Bhagvan ki jay.* Victory to Goddess Kali!
To Lord Shiva!" the tantrik chanted in a low, hollow voice that echoed
endlessly against the parlor's tapestried walls.

"*Ki jay,*" Panditji echoed, grasping the tantrik's familiar words.

Maji felt something grip in her throat, an incalculable fear that
grew more and more insistent. It moaned in her ears, an unearthly
sound like spirits swirling around and around her head, wailing their
ancient laments.

"*Bolo!*" the tantrik commanded again. "What do you want?"

Pinky's lips parted, a deep, gritty voice unlike her own moaned, "To belong!"

"Why did you enter this girl's body? She did not call you!"

"She! She!" the voice howled in accusation.

"Who are you?"

"Avni!"

Savita screamed and threw herself around her boys, "You can't have them, you witch! You took my daughter, filled my life with misery. Isn't that enough? Isn't that enough?"

Jaginder pressed a trembling hand against Savita's back, his other hand curled into a fist ready to strike at that voice, so strangely familiar, to save his family whatever it took. She had come back, the ayah. She had defied them and come back. He had a sudden understanding of the wheel of karma, of its mercilessness

Kuntal continued to weep, her hands covering her face. Cook Kanj pushed his wife behind him, brandishing a rolling pin in an upraised hand. Parvati held her belly fighting the urge to vomit.

"Make her go!" Maji demanded. "She's no right to be in this household! Make her go!" She touched her rosary as if it were a weapon, her lips moving silently as she prayed to the gods and goddesses for their merciful protection. Outside, the sky turned dark, casting the inside of the bungalow in a long shadow. Rain pelted the roof, the window, the doors, as if insisting on being let in.

The tantrik gazed at Maji for a long moment, then closed his eyes. The room filled with an unearthly vibration as if a wrong chord had been plucked on a sitar and then amplified. Tufan covered his ears with his hands. Nimish adjusted his spectacles, watching Pinky with horror. Jaginder furiously scratched at his chest hair, then pulled Savita tight. Panditji abandoned his sacred fire and prostrated himself in front of the idols, the rump of his enormous bottom heaving up in the air.

The tantrik continued to gaze at Maji, his heavy lids closing so only white showed where his iris should have been.

"Make her go!" Maji repeated.

The tantrik wiped the ash from Pinky's neck and tied the twisting red and yellow *mauli*, the sacred thread, upon Pinky's fragile wrist. "Go!" he commanded. "*Kali Mata ki jay! Shankar Bhagvan ki jay! Vishnu Bhagvan ki jay!*"

"Hail to God!" Panditji wept.

Pinky's body writhed, her arms flinging back and forth, out of control. Her eyes rolled back, her mouth opened and words in an indecipherable tongue, poured forth unchecked. Then she abruptly sat up, her body still violently shaking, and cast her eyes around the room, looking at the people who were her family. Dark shadows encircled her eyes, making them appear demonic. Gazing at Parvati, she lunged at the person closest to her, hands gripping Maji's throat.

Nimish leaped to grab Pinky from behind, to pull her away.

"Go!" the tantrik yelled, jumping to his feet, bringing down the bullwhip with a sharp crack. "What you seek is impossible because your violent acts have tainted you, but what can be given, will be. Now GO, leave this innocent child!"

Pinky became still, falling backward into Nimish's arms, eyes rolling back into her head. She uttered a low moan and then was silent. Maji grasped at her throat, breathing heavily, as Jaginder helped her onto the couch. Panditji tentatively pushed himself back to a seated position and wiped his face with his oily cloth.

The tantrik stood, legs splayed, sweat pouring off his body. His hair had come uncoiled and now swept across his body in thick ropes. His whip was held in the air, ready to strike again if necessary. He gazed down at Pinky, his fierce scarlet eyes scanning her body. Then, slowly, he glanced up at the ceiling and lowered his whip.

"She is very weak," he finally said. "She will die tonight."

"No!" Maji sobbed. "No! No! No!"

Dheer and Tufan began to cry.

"The ghost," the tantrik pointed, seeing her curled up in a tiny ball, hanging in the corner of the hallway like a desiccated spider. "By midnight, *she* will die."

Panditji cast his pale face upwards and passed out cold.

Afterward, Pinky was laid gently on Maji's bed for the night. Only a few hours were left until midnight, until the fourth day was done and the little ghost was forever banished, her soul cast back to the other side to make its way alone in the undulating layers of gray, to be reborn.

The ghost had curled up dizzily in the plastic bucket next to the broken chocolate pieces. She had sucked the alcoholic contents dry but had not quenched her thirst as she had hoped. She waited to die. *Hear me*, she whispered, the first and only words to escape her lips. The utterance, a spinning, silvery filament, traveled upon the tissue-thin wings of a moth, fluttering through the dining hall where they momentarily circled a dimming bulb before pressing on, beyond the dark hallway, to Pinky's ear. And there the moth flapped its tiny wings, disturbing the air so slightly that only the lightest strands of hair on Pinky's head, the fine ones nearest her cheeks, rose in response. But that, that rising was enough to make Pinky move her hand to brush it away, to stir and wake. To hear the plea, or warning, humming in the night air.

She glanced at the mound that was her grandmother, her stony face made gentle by sleep, her jaw drooping onto the pillow. She reached her hand to Maji's face until she could feel warmth emanating from it. Then, without a sound, she slid off the bed and crawled down the hallway like someone dying in a desert. When the effort grew too much, she laid her head on the cool floor and caught her breath, then continued in this way until she reached the bathroom.

Once there, she pulled herself up and peeked into the bucket. The baby ghost opened her eyes and looked up as if she were drowning in air. She was almost bald, her lustrous mane having fallen out and scattered across the bathroom except for a few, sterling strands that glimmered weakly like perishing fireflies.

"Don't die," Pinky whispered.

But the baby ghost only stared at Pinky with empty, water-seeking eyes.

Pinky staggered to her feet.

She turned on the tap but nothing came out, not even a drip. Then she pulled herself to the sink in the hallway, then to the kitchen. She felt dazed, confused, and so very tired. She dropped to her knees. A thought came to her. Again she stood and made her way to the east hallway. Quietly, fearfully, she opened a door.

It was almost midnight when Pinky returned to the bathroom. "Baby ghost?"

This time, the ghost did not stir, its body having dissolved into a formless mass except for two tiny fists and two eyes, shut tightly against the world.

Pinky held a silver urn in her hands, an urn that contained three sacred *tulsi* leaves and the holy water that Lord Krishna and Radha had frolicked in that very morning. Lord Krishna, incarnation of Vishnu the Preserver, preserver of life, preserver of the universe.

"Don't die," Pinky called again. And then she poured the entire contents of the urn, water blessed by the mighty gods, into the bucket. Exhausted now, she dropped the vessel. Reaching into the liquid, she touched the ghost's fingers with her own.

Then curling herself around the bucket, she fell asleep.

STORMY RETRIBUTION

Pinky woke the next morning in the parlor. Sunlight cast its flutter-ing radiance upon her face as the willowy curtains embraced and parted with the morning breeze. Slowly, bits and pieces of the previ-ous night came to her, like petals dropping from the jasmine vine. Avni was gone. Her cough had vanished. She was home. Other petals of memory, the most painful ones, had blown away as if by an unex-pected gust of wind. She could see them, faintly pink in the distance, swirling out of her grasp. And then they faded away. Pinky could no longer remember anything of her abduction beyond climbing onto Lovely's Triumph. The truths that had once traveled through her body had evanesced.

She sat up, surprised at her strength, as if she had once again crossed the chiasmus between the living and the dead and had returned to the side of the living. Pinky suddenly panicked. She ran to the hallway bathroom where she discovered the bucket, overturned against the wooden bathing stool. The silver urn from the *puja* room remained in a corner near the far wall, where it had rolled the previous night.

"Baby?" Pinky called. "Where are you?"

She turned on the faucet and yellowish water spurted and spluttered out onto the floor. Pinky stood there, watching as the initial outpouring grew into a pool that covered her toes. The lightness in her chest began to grow dark. Something was not right.

"*Hai, hai,*" Kuntal said kindly. "Silly girl, you'll flood the bungalow!"

Pinky looked up and watched Kuntal lift the hem of her sari as she tiptoed through the water to turn off the faucet.

"No bath for you until your fever's gone," Kuntal chattered on, though her normally cheery voice carried an edge of strain.

"What happened?" Pinky asked. *Did she die?*

"You must get to bed," Kuntal said, ushering Pinky from the bathroom. "You'll need your strength."

Just before Kuntal closed the bathroom door, her eye came to rest on the *puja* vessel. A slight frown creased her forehead.

"Where's the ghost?" Pinky demanded. "She was here last night."

Kuntal reentered the bathroom and picked up the vessel. One solitary *tulsi* leaf was dried onto the lip, leaving no doubt as to the vessel's origins or its prior contents. "So it was you," she said softly.

"There was no water. The ghost was dying."

Kuntal nodded.

Footsteps sounded in the hallway. Kuntal hastily hid the vessel under her sari *palloo* and pushed Pinky out of the bathroom, before disappearing in the direction of the *puja* room to surreptitiously return the stolen contents.

"You're awake?" Dheer asked, kurta sagging over his belly, hair an oily mess atop his head.

"Yes."

"Cook Kanj made first-class *puras* for breakfast," Dheer said, though his announcement lacked its usual enthusiasm.

"The ghost? Where is she?"

Dheer shook his head, scratching his scalp with both sets of fingers, "I found you last night and carried you to the sofa."

"Last night?" Pinky asked. "Why were you awake?"

"Papa came into the room yelling. He woke us all up. He wanted Nimish to go with him," Dheer said, his bulky chest heaving with emotion.

"What happened? Tell me!"

"Maji—"

"Maji?" Pinky ran back to the parlor. The dais was empty. Savita sat on one of the sofas drinking chai, looking surprisingly resilient.

"Maji!" Pinky shouted. "Where's Maji?"

"*Beti*," Savita said beckoning her forward. "We think it may have been a stroke."

"That's not what you said before." Tufan bounded into the room, wiping a smear of *ghee* from his cheek.

Savita stiffened, "Go finish your breakfast, Tufan. Pinky, *beti*, she called out sometime in the night in pain. Your uncle and I ran to her."

"What happened?"

"Uncle and Nimish took her to the hospital, but . . ." Savita turned away. "Maji's not so strong anymore."

"She's stronger than any of you!" Pinky shouted.

"But she's very old," Tufan said.

Pinky pushed Tufan so hard that he fell backward and hit his head upon a chair.

"Shameless!" Savita jumped off the couch but Pinky was already running down the hallway.

"Do you want to know what Mummy said last night?" Tufan yelled after her as he had regained his balance. "She said that the ghost killed her!"

Pinky ran into Maji's room and shut the door. Tears rolled down her cheeks.

Dheer knocked gently on the door and entered.

"Go away!"

"Tufan's right," Dheer said grudgingly. "Papa came running into our room last night. He needed Nimish's help. We all ran to Maji's room. She was shaking and moving her arms from her chest into the air like there was something heavy on her."

"The ghost?"

"I think so."

"How would you know? You never saw her before."

"Maji was talking to *someone*," Dheer insisted. "I heard her begging for forgiveness."

"Why would she do that?"

"She wanted to get rid of the ghost. That's why we had to turn off the water for four days."

Silenced ensued while Pinky registered this information. Dheer plopped down on the bed and began to babble. "We all thought the ghost was dying. I put chocolates in the bathroom. It was my fault."

"Ghosts don't eat chocolates."

"I know," Dheer said, digging a chubby finger into his belly button. "But these had Papa's tonic in them."

"She needed water."

"I was only trying to help."

There was a long stillness.

"Me too," Pinky said in a small voice, realizing the enormity of what she had done.

"You too? But you were in the hospital."

"I gave her water last night," Pinky confessed, "from the *puja* room."

Pinky thought about what had taken place after she had emptied the urn into the bucket, a coming together of the otherworld and the divine, a union so powerful that it lasted but for a fleeting moment. But long enough to restore Pinky's health and perhaps to have killed Maji.

"I thought she was my friend," Pinky said.

"She was," Dheer realized. The ghost had kept her end of the promise, she had given Pinky her life back. He slid next to Pinky and, with an awkward clutch of his chubby arm, held her to him, not caring that the door was closed nor that it was the first time they had ever embraced.

❋ ❂ ❋

Savita called Panditji who at that moment was having his fleshy feet expertly kneaded by his assistant. He had slept badly the previous night, the events at the bungalow spooking him in the darkness of his chambers. In an attempt to quell his fears, he had wandered to the temple sanctuary but the steely idols scared him, their oversized arms and legs jeered at him, causing him to race back to his bed as fast as his pudgy legs could carry him. *This is my reward for a life of servitude? To be defiled by tantriks and their black magic tricks?* he had thought angrily.

"When can you come?" Savita asked him, explaining the situation.

The priest fingered his Favre-Leuba wristwatch as he lay back in his bed, feeling emboldened by the claims engraved on the back of the watchface: *Antimagnetic. Waterproof. Shockprotected.* He felt betrayed, made a fool of by Maji. Her current dire condition was evidence that she had fallen prey to the dark forces of the universe. He wanted nothing more to do with her or her family nor with a flat full of demons and whatnots, the promise of a new Electrolux refrigerator be damned. "I'm busy-busy all day."

"But my mother-in-law needs you," Savita explained. "I'll make a most generous offering."

Panditji rolled his eyes. Nothing, not even the promise of good money was enough to make him return to that godforsaken, haunted bungalow. "I will break a coconut for her here at the temple," he offered, plucking a *laddoo* from a silver tray as he hung up the phone.

"Idiot," Savita huffed as the dial tone droned in her ear, rankled that she did not have the same sway over the priest as Maji. Carefully, she replaced the receiver and then called her mother in Goa. Soon enough, the extensive network of friends and family would find out about Maji's condition and flood their home once again. This time, Savita, seated prominently in the parlor to receive visitors' condolences would be the one to carefully orchestrate the event. There was so much to plan, from the food to the most appropriate sari for her to wear, something subtle, perhaps in a soft pink to suggest hope. In Maji's absence, everyone would be looking to her to set the tone. Savita felt a delightful shiver in her spine. Finally, finally, the bungalow was becoming hers.

* * *

Gulu stood outside the green gates smoking furiously as he paced in the thickening rain, berating himself for being so weak. Yes, he thought, the gods were making him suffer for his weakness. Isn't that why Avni was dead? And why he stood outside Maji's bungalow like a stray mongrel? He kicked at the ground, cursing under his breath. He, who had stood up to Red Tooth back in his shoe-shining days, had been felled by three women—one old and fat, another a prostitute, and the third, dead. The shame caused him to spit a glutinous blob of saliva at the gate.

"So *you've* come back?" Parvati clucked disapprovingly as she opened the gate, proffering a tiffin of roti and green beans.

Gulu stared at her for a moment, anger and lack of sleep plastered his features into hard, ugly crevices. He had spent the night pacing the wet streets of Bombay, gazing despondently at every passing Ambassador. Gratefully, he accepted the tiffin. "My Cherry Blossom poster."

"Is that why you returned, for that?"

Gulu thought of that marigold flower, pressed in newspaper, hidden under his cot.

"I can't believe she threw me out," he said, hoping that perhaps Parvati could find a way to get him back into her good graces. Of all the servants, she was the one who had Maji's ear.

"You're the one who left," Parvati said, hand on her hip. "I wouldn't let you back either."

"Whose side are you on?"

"I'm speaking with my brains, not my loins, you fool. You men are all the same, two-two *lingams* each, one in your head, the other in your pants. Both *ee-qually* dull. You let Avni go, you idiot, and now thirteen years later you want to chase after her ghost? You've thrown away your future. And for what? A dead Koli girl."

"I didn't know she was dead," Gulu said. "All these years I thought she'd come back."

"For what?"

"For me."

At this, Parvati let out a laugh. "Believe me *yaar*, you weren't her type."

Gulu felt the heat rise in his face.

"You'd better go," she said, turning to look over her shoulder, "before someone finds out you're back."

Gulu took the tiffin and squatted against the gate, ravenously dipping his fingers into the curried green beans. He ate in large gulps, barely tasting the food that he had become accustomed to for so many years. The *roti* filled his belly, warming his body and assuaging his desperation. Sighing, he let out a roaring burp and lit a *bidi*, intently drawing in the smoke and remembering the quiet hand of fate that had led him to the Maji's bungalow in the first place.

Since first stepping behind the wheel at age fifteen, Gulu maneuvered the city streets as if he were Lord Krishna entering the battlefield upon his glowing chariot. Battling the demons who obstructed his way, he mercilessly honked at slow-moving bullock carts, cut off motor scooters whizzing by with entire families precariously balanced atop, out-revved BEST buses, and sent bicyclists scattering as if they were panic-stricken birds. He thought of himself as a warrior, scoffing at those who relied on their turn signals or brakes, the Ambassador's metal providing a solid layer between him and the unfortunates who littered the road.

Now, after all these years, he had ended up on the street again. *How did this happen?* he asked himself.

The answer hung in the air for some time, curling in the smoke, before he dared to acknowledge it.

Avni.

It always came back to her. Like the cycle of karma, Avni was without beginning or end. She was everywhere.

He had forsaken her. He could have stopped her from dying. But that was in the past now. He pondered on his favorite verse from the *Bhagavad Gita*: *Let right deeds be thy motive, not the fruit which comes from them.* Back then, that fateful drowning day, he had failed to follow this sacred command.

Gulu spat again. He was not going to let himself be thrown out, after all he had done for this family. Damning his shame and his vows of loyalty to the Mittal family, he finally made up his mind. He would reveal what he had seen thirteen years back. He would do as Chinni asked. *Blackmail.*

He weighed the options in his mind, deciding that approaching Jaginder was his best choice. He was just the type with whom to play such games, if only Gulu could face him with the conviction needed. *Red Tooth*, he repeated over again like a mantra; Jaginder was nothing compared to his old shoe-shining adversary. And, if everything went according to plan, Gulu consoled himself, he could start over on his own terms. Maybe buy a flat in the suburbs and even purchase a taxi of his own. Nothing would please him more.

Gritting his teeth, he stood and prowled by the gate, resisting the urge to storm inside and confront his boss face to face. He slapped on the gate with his flattened palm until Parvati appeared.

"Where's Jaginder Sahib?"

"He left early this morning."

"*Achha?*" Gulu tried hard to contain his disappointment. It was so unlike Jaginder to leave the bungalow before ten.

"What do you want with him?"

"Urgent business."

"Well, it'll have to wait."

"*Very* urgent."

Parvati shrugged.

"I'll go inside if I have to."

"*Arré*, hero," Parvati said, "and do what?"

Gulu cast his face down. "The four days are over now, *nah?*"

"Yes."

"The ghost gone?"

"Yes."

"Has something more happened?" Gulu asked, noticing Parvati's swollen eyes and the flush in her cheeks. "Is Pinky-baby okay?"

Parvati nodded. "Tantrik Baba came yesterday. It was Avni. Avni was inside her."

Gulu searched Parvati's eyes for signs of disbelief. "Where's Avni now?"

"Gone," Parvati said. "For now."

"You think she'll come back?"

"I think she attacked Maji last night."

"Maji?"

"She's in the hospital," Parvati said, sighing. "We're waiting for Jaginder's phone call."

"You should leave the bungalow."

"Where would I go that she couldn't find me?"

"Or me."

"She already got you, didn't she?" Parvati said. "She maimed your driving hand, didn't she?"

"You're more vulnerable."

"I'm not afraid of her," Parvati's eyes flashed with anger. "I won't let her hurt my child."

Inside the bungalow, the phone finally rang. Savita ran to answer it as the rest of the household crowded around. "Yes, yes," she said breathlessly.

Maji had survived.

"Cerebral thrombosis," Savita announced gravely after she hung up the phone.

"Will she be okay?" Pinky asked.

"It's too early to tell," Savita said as if she had a physician's insight. "She can't speak."

"Can't speak?"

Savita arched one of her manicured eyebrows as she patted Pinky on the head. "Don't worry. We'll make sure she has the best care, your uncle has already hired a full-time *malishwallah* to come home with her."

"She won't like that," Pinky shouted, angry that Maji was at the mercy of Savita's care. "She only likes Kuntal to do her massage!"

Savita's face stiffened. "Pack up Pinky darling," she hissed, her mouth curling into a smile. "Guess what? I'm sending you to boarding school."

RETURN OF THE AYAH

Jaginder lay in bed and threw his limbs in four opposing directions until he felt his spine deliciously crack. "We must arrange for more help," he said to Savita who sat next to him, her baby pink sari *palloo* falling against his cheek.

"Yes," Savita said. "The *malishwallah* will come starting tomorrow. But Maji needs round-the-clock care now."

"What about Kuntal?"

"I need Kuntal for myself," Savita said, caressing Jaginder's cheek. "She knows exactly where everything goes, what I need. I can't start with someone new, not with all this responsibility on my shoulders now."

"Of course," Jaginder said, feeling intoxicated by Savita's touch. Despite the recent stresses of alcohol withdrawal, confinement within the bungalow, and his mother's stroke, he had fared quite well. In fact, he had not felt so good for a long time. His family was coming back to him, looking to him for leadership and reassurance and, what was more, Maji could never threaten his place at the helm of Mittal Shipbreaking Enterprises again. Silently, he promised himself that he would not let Savita down this time, he would run the business as his father had and make his family proud. The recent shine in his wife's eyes had even tempered his craving for alcohol though, in the late hours of the night, haunting visions of Rosie's *adda* still beckoned to him.

"Jaggi?" Savita abruptly asked, tucking a bit of her sari into the corner of her mouth. "Do you think that our little Chakori is free now?"

"She's free now to be reborn, isn't that what the tantrik said?"

"She was with us all these years," Savita said with a shudder.

"You weren't able to let her go," Jaginder said, pulling Savita against him. "Just as I can't let you go."

Smiling, Savita allowed herself to be enclosed in Jaginder's furry arms wanting, praying, that their latest tenderness would prove itself lasting. *I've won*, Savita told herself, pushing away the dreadful thought that her formidable mother-in-law might unexpectedly recover. *I've won!*

Her first decision, the day of Maji's stroke, was to rehire Gulu. She had spotted him lurking behind the green gates waiting for Parvati to slip him a tiffin of food. Maji had been foolish to let him go, Savita thought, to breed resentment amongst the other servants. *And finding a good driver is so difficult these days!* But most importantly, in bringing Gulu back into the fold, Savita knew that she had earned the other servant's silent appreciation, not for Gulu's sake but for their own. *What better way*, she had thought, *to begin the bungalow's new regime?*

A terrible thought unexpectedly sliced through her sunny mood. She sat up, pushing Jaginder away.

"What is it?"

"Do you think the ayah's really gone?"

"The tantrik sent her away, didn't he?"

"But what if she comes back?"

"She won't," Jaginder said, pulling Savita back to him. "There's no reason to anymore, is there?"

"No, no, no reason." Savita tried to allow her husband's words to sooth the panicky flutter in her heart. "Maybe we should have the boys sleep in our room for a while, just so, you know."

"Absolutely not," Jaginder said firmly. "I want to be with you. Just you."

※ ※ ※

Maji arrived by ambulance the following week. Jaginder spent the better part of an hour fighting with the medical workers as to the best way to transport his mother inside the bungalow. Finally, after the promise of an extra five-rupee tip for each of them, the workers ingeniously strapped her to a chair and carried her to her bedroom, their muscles straining with the massive undertaking.

Maji was laid upon her bed, her thick body propped up on its side by bolsters. Her right arm was drawn close to her side, elbow flexed, and the right half of her face drooped where a small pool of saliva collected at her lips. After everyone had left, Pinky closed the door and curled up beside her, their faces just inches apart.

Maji clumsily brought her hand to rest upon her granddaughter's face. Pinky looked away, not able to confess what was really on her mind, that Savita was sending her away to boarding school. With remarkable efficiency, Savita had made the necessary phone calls, proffered generous bribes, and secured a space even though the school year had already begun.

Pinky could not even appeal to Nimish to intercede. He was never around anymore, skipping classes to search for Lovely during the day, walking the broken lanes of Colaba showing passersby the black-and-white photo of her he had once discreetly hidden underneath his "An Ideal Boy" chart. By the time he reached home late in the evening, heartbroken and worn, it was not Ackerley or Arnold he reached for in his vast collection of books but the neglected copies of Rabindranath Tagore and Mulk Raj Anand.

He didn't know what to do, where to go, he read from Anand's *Untouchable* late into the night. *He seemed to have been smothered by their misery, the anguish of the morning's memories. He stood for a while where he had landed from the tree, his head bent, as if he were tired and broken. Then the last words of the Mahatma's speech seemed to resound in his ears:* May God give you the strength to work out your soul's salvation to the end.

And then gently closing the book and drifting off to sleep, Nimish could no longer deny that a single shelf of a good Indian library was worth more to him than the whole native literature of England.

Alone together, Pinky breathed in the scent of her grandmother, so familiar, so comforting. All these years, she had needed Maji's love, to tuck herself into her strong, magical presence, to be tended to with unconditional love.

Pinky had striven to make herself indispensable, to carve out a rightful place, to belong. But Maji's stroke laid bare the truth of her situation, that Pinky was expendable, inessential, removable; that the bungalow was only a temporary home and not a place that she could claim as her own. Among all the fearful scenarios that she had conjured of being married off or sent away, she had never once imagined her grandmother falling ill or dying. Maji was the bungalow's anchor, like a banyan tree that grew and grew, dropping roots into the ground from its branches, its expansive foliage providing shade for their entire family. But Jaginder and Savita had been waiting in the banyan's broad shadows all this time, Pinky realized, biding their time.

Maji's eyes fluttered open and closed, her hand weighed heavily against Pinky's cheek.

Pinky struggled to hold back the flood of sadness for everything that had been lost. *Somehow, somehow,* Pinky thought, though her memory of the abduction had been mercifully wiped away, *I'm responsible for it all.* She had befriended the ghost. She had ridden with Lovely on the motorbike before her friend disappeared. And she had been the one to give the ghost water the night that Maji was rushed to the hospital. "It's all because of me," she whispered to her grandmother.

But Maji did not speak, did not move or even crack open an eyelid. Exhausted by the effort of being transferred from the hospital, she had already fallen asleep.

Pinky stood and, from the enameled teak chest, pulled out the photo of her mother, which was in reality the publicity shot of the actress Madhubala. She folded it to her heart. There was only now a rectangular-shaped darkness in the teak chest. An emptiness.

※ ※ ※

The next morning was a blur of activity. By the time Maji woke and, furious, had the bony *malishwallah* thrown from her room, it was almost time for Pinky to leave. Painfully pulling herself to a standing position with Nimish's help, she limped to the parlor, her semi-paralyzed right leg remained extended, foot flexed towards the ground so that she had to rotate her leg outwards in an uneven gait in order to move forward. After finally being seated, not upon her dais as usual, but on one of the low sofas, she gripped her cane in her left hand and watched dully as Pinky's suitcases were brought from the room and placed by the front door.

"It's just until you're better," Savita said to Maji in an overly loud voice as if she were deaf.

"But *you* said she was going there forever," Tufan chimed in.

Savita shot him a withering look.

"So, *beti*," Jaginder said, searching for something appropriate to say when Pinky finally walked into the room, her hair pleated into one long braid that was elegantly coiled at the nape of her neck. "So . . ." he trailed off, feeling somewhere deep inside as if he were betraying his dead sister. He gratefully plopped down with a glass of *jal jeera*, a refreshing concoction of lime, mint, and rock salt.

Gulu entered to retrieve the suitcases and froze when he saw Maji on the sofa, her unfaltering gaze upon him.

"Don't bloody dilly-dally," Jaginder ordered, slurping loudly. "We might as well get this over with."

Gulu dropped his head and lifted the bags with his good hand, expertly shuffling back and forth out the open door.

Kuntal appeared with a hot tumbler of chai which she lifted to Maji's lips. Maji shook her head, pushing the tumbler away with a shove so violent that the glass slipped from Kuntal's grasp and broke upon the floor.

"Oh pho!" Savita reprimanded Kuntal. "You must be more careful with her now. She's not able to control her muscles."

Kuntal nodded as she kneeled and swept up the shards. The scent of cardamom rose into the air.

"Well," Jaginder grunted at his boys, "say your good-byes now."

Pinky looked around the room as her cousins approached awkwardly. Tufan reluctantly handed her one of his *Lone Ranger* comics, a double of one he already had in his collection. Dheer began to blubber, pressing his favorite Cadbury chocolate into her hand.

Nimish peered at Pinky with a thousand unspoken questions about the night Lovely had vanished, knowing somehow that she was the only one who could shed light on what had really happened, if only he had some way of jogging her memory. He had questioned Pinky earlier in the week but she had simply shaken her head. *I don't remember anything Nimish* bhaiya, *only that she had taken me on a motorbike. After that, everything's blank.* "If you remember anything," he said quietly, his arms strangely bereft of a book.

Pinky nodded. "I'll write and let you know." She fleetingly gazed upon his soft lips, feeling strangely that she knew how they might taste.

Savita pushed forward. "You can always visit during holidays," she offered magnanimously.

Pinky fell at Maji's feet, her face pressed against her sari, now smelling of the spilt tea. "Maji," she whispered, her voice choking with emotion as an overlooked piece of broken glass cut into her knee. "I want to stay. Just tell them. They have to listen to you."

Maji looked at Pinky, her eyes dull and flat, her hands motionless. With supreme effort, she turned her body from Pinky, refusing to give her blessings.

"*Jao,*" she slurred almost inaudibly, almost indecipherably. "Go."

❦ ❦ ❦

Gulu peered in the rearview mirror, watching with a pained expression as Pinky turned away, her face stony. Unwittingly, he remembered when she had first arrived at Maji's home, a sickly infant.

As she grew up, he had fallen into a routine, taking her to school in the mornings and returning in the afternoon with a steaming tiffin of lunch. His favorite time of day had been picking her up from school when she jumped on the springy seat pleading, *Gulu tell me about the time you stole an entire flock of birds from Crawford Market to feed your family.* And, thus invited, he had spun tales of heroics that held Pinky entranced and made him feel a little like a movie star. On these drives home, he was no longer Gulu-the-Compliant-Driver but Gulu-the-Fearless-Hero who braved physical injury and death to provide for his destitute family.

In the past months, when Pinky no longer had time for his tales and was content to give him her school satchel instead of her ear, the stories that had come so vividly to Gulu's lips wasted away in his head. And with them, the daily escapes into a world of possibility. "Pinky *didi,*" Gulu said tentatively, "did I ever tell you the story of when I scavenged through a garbage heap to find bits of metal to sell as scraps in Dharavi? It was the time of the monsoon flooding when cholera spread through the slums like a bullet. *Hai Ram,* my youngest sister was so sick, almost dead. My mother went to the temple with my sister a limp bundle in her arms, and gave our last five rupees to the *pujari.* But his prayers were in vain. Goddess Lakshmi did not take pity on us and my sister grew worse, loose motions and vomiting all the time. I was desperate for money to pay for rehydration salts. Did I tell you—" He halted, embarrassed at his attempt to somehow right the present, to push away the pain with a rusty story.

Pinky did not respond.

Gulu's heart sank. "Is Maji okay? They said she can no longer speak."

She can speak, Pinky thought, remembering Maji's cruel word to her—*Jao,* go—as she rubbed the cut on her knee where a circle of blood now stained the *salvar.*

Gulu was trying his best to appear concerned. Maji's tragedy had been his salvation, his opportunity to remain with the Mittal family, to keep his job, to go on as before without having to resort to Chinni's threats or to reveal his shameful secret. Who knows what Jaginder would have done if he had told him? He could have sent Gulu to jail or had him beaten, disfigured even, left on the streets to die.

Gulu recalled seeing his friend Hari's father who had once been detained for several months in Arthur Road Prison. Upon his release, the father had stopped by VT to see Hari, ribs jutting from an emaciated frame blanketed in sickening bruises and pussing wounds. *Don't let the* bhenchod *police ever get you,* he had warned Hari, his eyes lifeless, spirit broken. *Kill yourself first.*

How stupid I almost was, Gulu silently chided himself. *I would rather die before telling my secret.*

His deformed hand began to throb, blood pushing against the delicate stitches. He winced as he pressed it into his armpit. But the pressure continued to build, the pain traveling up the length of his arm, into his chest. He proceeded to weave in and out of the traffic when suddenly, in a flash so fleeting that he might have missed it, he saw a young woman lit by a blinding aura, her fiery red sari flaming as she ran in front of his car. The Ambassador veered into the next lane of traffic, almost crashing into an oncoming bus.

"Oh no!" Pinky gasped.

"A woman just ran in front of the car!" Gulu cried out, his heart thudding in his chest as he realized that he had just seen Avni. The phantom pain in his missing finger was so intense now that he felt as if he might pass out.

Pinky pressed her face up against the glass, watching the sari-clad figure flash in the sun as she came toward them again, like a storm. The apparition lifted her face, allowing the *palloo* to slip from her head. Pinky's nose skidded across the window. *She will never leave us.* And suddenly, seeing her face, she remembered how she had drank the coconut elixir and how Avni had seethed within her.

"Oh God! Oh God!" Gulu shouted, grinding the gears as he tried to get the car moving again while frantically steering it with his good hand. *She's trying to kill us!* Sweat poured from his face, dripping into his eyes, obscuring his vision. "Oh God! Oh God!"

"You can't outrun her!" Pinky yelled, climbing into the front seat. "She'll never leave us, never. Unless . . ."

Gulu gunned the engine, driving as if on a race to hell.

"Say it, Gulu, you must say it to save yourself!" Pinky knew what he struggled to contain, she had drank it inside her that fearful night.

It was still there, she realized, if she just listened hard enough.

THE VAMPIRE CURSE

They had been together, Avni and Gulu, one final time after he had left her at the train station that fateful day of the baby's death. He had gone back, searching the platforms, calling her name. And then, rushing towards him was the tea-boy, the Crazy-One, his legs infected with scabies, the sores pussing despite white benzyl benzoate that powdered his skin. "You, you there," he called to Gulu, "she sent me to fetch you."

"I'm not meeting anyone."

"Oh yes," the tea-boy insisted. "She knew you'd be coming back. She's waiting for you."

Apprehensively, Gulu followed the boy, past the station and into the deserted backyard where cargo cars rusted upon abandoned rails. Climbing into one of the empty compartments, he hesitated, fearfully scanning the desolate landscape. When he was a shoe-shine boy, his friend Bambarkar had been brutally sodomized in one of the empty cargo trains. "Where is she?"

"She's in here," the tea-boy said, one hand on his hip, the other neatly placing the tea carrier upon the ground before he climbed aboard. The dark, empty hold echoed with shrouded susurrations.

"Where?" Gulu called out. "Where? I can't see her!"

Over here, came her sweet-gritty phantom voice in the hollow darkness.

Gulu stretched his hand out, walking towards the voice in anticipation. She met him, slender arms enclosing him, soft cardamom-scented lips pressing against his. *Leave them,* she whispered, her hand running down his chest, hovering at his waist. His trousers fell away. *Leave them for me.* A mouth tightened around his tumescence.

He writhed and moaned, body tensing with acute urgency. "Please," he begged, "I can't just leave. Where would we go, how'd we survive? Please—"

All at once she was gone, leaving him clawing at the dark, his fingers scraping at the fetid air. *Go to the cemetery by the sea,* she commanded, her voice now cold and far away. *See the baby. Only then will you understand.*

Gulu fell to the ground, panting.

She did not die because of me.

He grasped at the voice, falling against the metal siding.

It was not an accident. Find the amulet tied around the baby's neck at her birth. It was meant to protect her from evil spirits. But it failed to protect her from something more powerful. It fell off before she was buried. Find it. Find her. Her whispered commands issued forth until they overlapped like waves, echoing against the sides of the hold, distorted. Gulu senselessly flung himself at the voice.

All at once, the tea-boy screamed, his unearthly howls exploding within the cargo hold.

"Avni!" Gulu cried out.

A deathly silence followed.

Suddenly, a sweaty hand grabbed his. "Come," the tea-boy urged.

"Where were you all this time?" Gulu asked, shaking him. "Where did she go?"

"You must do as she asks," the tea-boy said, jumping onto the tracks, lifting a cup of cardamom tea from his carrier and taking a sip.

* * *

"Say it!" Pinky said shaking Gulu's shoulder while he madly drove as if to elude Avni's spirit, to escape the searing pain in his hand, his arm, his chest. "You went to the cemetery, didn't you!"

"You know?" he gasped as the Ambassador shot ahead.

"You dug up the baby!"

"No, no, no!"

"You did! I know you did!"

"I can't!" Gulu shouted, his face contorted, corroding into defeat.

The Ambassador swerved from lane to lane, horns blaring and brakes screeching in its wake.

"Don't you see?" Pinky beseeched. "You'll never be free until you do! Say it or she'll kill you! She'll kill me, all of us!"

The secret that had been lodged inside Gulu for thirteen years all at once came to his lips.

"Your final story!" Pinky shouted as Avni's blinding aura descended upon them like cyclone, like a spinning, spiraling harbinger of death. "Say it! Say it now!"

And then Pinky closed her eyes and let the devastation crash upon her.

☙ ❧ ☙

It began with a song, not an ancient one but one that told an ancient story. One that ended in Lahore, a full circle back to Punjab, Pinky's birthplace, at a tomb bearing the inscription: Could I behold the face of my beloved once more, I would thank God until the day of resurrection. The tomb had been built by a lovesick prince, destined to become Jahangir, Conqueror of the World. His beloved was a dancing girl, her beauty such that she was named after the exquisite pomegranate flower, Anarkali. Their love was doomed: she was buried alive. But their story endured on the big screen as *Mughal-e-Azam*. Gulu sang one verse from the hit single *"Pyar Kiya To Darna Kya"*—Now That I Love, Why Should I Fear? and then plunged the Ambassador and its passengers headlong into the truth.

☙ ❧ ☙

Two black crows sat in the crook of an ancient peepul tree, cawing to each other as if feuding, the sheen of their wings visible in a faint shaft of moonlight. The tree, devoid of its red flowers and fleshy fruit, stood behind a tall wall, its thin branches hanging over the top, beckoning. Gulu stood before the entrance to the Hindu burial ground and recalled the grim story of King Vikramaditya who was said to have carried a vampire corpse for four miles to the *shamshan*, burning grounds by the riverbank, in order to rid himself of an ancient family curse. Upon entering the *shamshan* on that moonless, stormy night, the king was greeted by the ghastly sight of wolves, fur alight in a bluish blaze, and monstrous bears, pawing at the newly-buried. Malignant spirits crawled upon the ground in reddish mists, massive black snakes hissed as they swung from naked branches, and goblins danced upon the burning pyres. Shanta-Shil, the fearsome yogi, sat in the middle of the debauchery, blood-stained and ash-smeared, invoking Kali, the Goddess of Death.

The chilling story of King Vikramaditya froze Gulu at the cemetery's gated entrance. He took another sip of the country *daru* he had procured. He had rarely imbibed alcohol since starting his work with Maji and the concoction went to his head, strengthening his resolve. A chilling fear ran along his spine as he slipped through the opened gate, recalling Avni's words: *See the baby. Only then will you understand.*

Possessed by love or madness and wanting nothing more than to bring Avni back to him, Gulu took another step, staring fearfully at the impure ground in front of him. The two-acre, walled compound was paved in black macadam, broken stones jutting from the numerous cracks. The fluorescent tube lights that normally lighted the area had shorted out in the rain, drenching it in darkness. In the center of the lot two *doms,* untouchables, walked around the crematorium sheds, where dead bodies were placed, each surrounded by four-hundred kilograms of firewood. The smell of the bodies brought in by grieving sons and brothers, and cremated that day, now thickened the air with a forbidding gloom.

Just beyond the small crematoriums on the far end of the grounds, Gulu spotted the small patch of soft earth where babies and young children were buried, wrapped in woven bamboo matting. The area was surrounded, almost enclosed in a thicket of trees whose verdant branches obscured the moonlight peeking through the clouds. Trying to talk himself out of what he was about to do, he murmured a verse from the *Bhagavad Gita*: "'As often as the heart breaks wild and wavering from control, so oft let him recurb it, let him rein it back to the soul's governance.'"

But even as he spoke the words, he knew that he had not the strength. He was entranced by a more potent verse, one as old as time: *Now that I love, why should I fear?* He crept around the periphery, his back against the wall, eyes on the two muscular *doms* who squatted by the crematoriums, stirring the red-hot embers to ensure that the remains burned to completion. The blazing pyres of the afternoon had since crumbled into flaring ashes and bits of bones, which cast flickering patterns of light upon the men's blackened faces. Gulu could hear the low tones of their conversation, every once in a while punctuated by a fit of coughing.

He glided past the concrete benches where mourners sat before sunset to watch the pyres burn, and past the row of taps where they washed their hands and faces afterwards. Gulu waited, hidden by the trees until the untouchables turned their backs to him and then quickly made his way to the far end of the compound, heart pounding in his chest. There were no gravestones, no markers of any kind to indicate where dead babies lay. The earth itself was saturated, making it nearly impossible to discern a freshly dug grave. He fell to his knees, clawing the mud. And then, as he almost gave up hope, his hands sticky with foul-smelling earth, his fingers grasped a tiny, gold-and-black-beaded amulet.

As his hoe hit the ground, the peepul tree directly above him shivered. Gulu froze, thinking that a ghost was hanging in the branches observing him. The mighty peepul also known as the bodhi, under which Prince Siddharatha found enlightenment as Buddha, was also considered home to ghosts, ghouls, and evil spirits, its quivering leaves a telltale sign of their presence. Gulu remembered Big Uncle's warning about the dwarflike *virikas*, with their blazing red skin and pointed teeth, who hovered above those who were just about to die, all the while jabbering feverishly. *I hear them all night long,* Big Uncle had told his frightened gaggle of shoe-shine boys just before his own death. *They ferry wicked souls across the Vaitarani River and into utter darkness.* Were the *virikas* now waiting in the tree above for Gulu? The skin on the back of his neck prickled in fright, a salty breeze from the Arabian Sea reached into the walled compound to lick the sweat from his back as if it were the blood-stained tongue of Goddess Kali herself.

Gulu once again fell to his knees as a cacophony of wails and howls sounded. Thunder rumbled above and stray dogs began snarling and snapping on the other side of the wall. He was certain that Kali, who dwelt in cremation grounds surrounded by a horde of mythical female jackals, was eyeing him, waiting to kill him and gorge herself on his blood. The untouchables broke from their conversation to glance in his direction. Gulu halted, terror-stricken. And then the thought of Avni filled his chest with a pulsing heat, and his hoe struck the ground once more.

He thought of his father, a cart puller who was attacked one winter night by a *mumiai* ghost, an invisible being who grabbed at him from behind with long, skeletal fingers and curling nails that dug into his ribcage. He was found dead the next morning at the crossing of Churchgate Street and Esplanade Road, his head submerged in Flora Fountain, torso torn apart as if by an unearthly predator.

Gulu's hand grasped at something rough. Though it was dark, he could make out the woven texture of the bamboo mat that enclosed the baby's body. The smell knocked him back as he pulled the mat away and held the tiny bundle in his arms. And then, tears streaming down his face, his trembling fingers undid the cotton *khadi* cloth, letting it fall to the ground.

The baby was still beautiful, a thick mound of hair covering her head, long, black eyelashes sweeping across her cheeks. Her fists were curled tightly, the decaying stump of the umbilical cord jutting from her belly. *What have I done! Oh Lord, what have I done!* And then, remembering Avni's command, he clenched his jaws and pulled the stiffened legs apart.

Oh God no!

Gulu dropped the baby, falling backward in shock.

All at once, he understood why Avni had to go.

And why he must stay.

For, despite the elusive promise of her love, Gulu would not be able to clear Avni's name. Even at his death, he knew that he could never reveal that the beloved baby, the family's little moon-bird, was a *hijra*. Not completely female, nor completely male, but somewhere in between, she had no rightful place, no rightful future in the Mittal bungalow.

He wept then, hidden in the shivering thicket of peepul trees as tears rained down his cheeks, splashing upon the baby's exposed body, violated in life, violated in death. He would carry this burden always, this shrouded story, this one film-worthy drama he starred in—not in glory as he had dreamed, but in disgrace.

Avni had told the truth. The baby's death was not an accident.

* * *

Sitting in the careening Ambassador, eyes still closed, Pinky witnessed the final piece of the truth unfold. Possessing a resolve befitting mighty Lord Shiva and a love like that of his divine consort, Maji had pressed her hand to the baby's face and drowned her. And then, the cosmos shamefully reordered, she continued on with her rounds, heading for the parlor, the bungalow's shattered heart.

A SCALDING SACRIFICE

Opening her eyes, Pinky realized that she was sitting in a train, her satchel clutched in her arms. She had known all along. *I tasted this truth, took it inside me. And fought to keep it there.*

Somewhere within the impenetrable haze of shock at her grandmother for what she had done, she felt compassion. She stood up. "I won't. I won't leave."

"But . . . but . . . but they don't want you," Gulu said nervously through the window.

The wheels on the train began to creak forward.

"I belong here!" Pinky cried out. She had always relied on Maji to grant her a place in the bungalow. She knew she must claim it herself now.

The train began to move. Pinky ducked out of the window and ran to the open doorway, throwing her suitcases down to the platform.

"They'll be angry with me!" Gulu cried out, dodging the flying luggage. "You have to go!"

"I have to stay!"

And then, as rusted wheels ground against the iron tracks, she jumped.

The train dissolved into a feverish blur of careening metal.

As silence ensued, Pinky became aware of her pounding heart. *Oh Lord, what have I done? How can I walk back up those verandah steps? What will Nimish and Dheer say when they see me? And Maji? Maji!*

Gulu retrieved the scattered suitcases, staring at Pinky with wide, startled eyes.

Pinky tried to take a step but remained rooted, her ears awash with the ghost's final whisper—*Hear me.*

Her eyes welled and she wept for the baby, born a *hijra*. She had seen *hijras* all her life, the same shadowy figures that had descended upon the Empress café, offences to the natural order. Born high-caste or casteless, they shared a destiny as outcasts, denied their humanity.

A deep, shuddering sigh filled her chest as she bore her part in the drowning's ill-fated chronicle.

For she, she too, had turned away from truth, from possibility. She had succumbed to the seductive lure of belonging.

Gently, Pinky grasped the magazine photo of her mother tied to the end of her *dupatta*.

And then, wiping the tears from her face, she lifted up her chin.

"Home, Gulu, take me home."

EPILOGUE

Each morning Pinky woke early and helped her grandmother walk around the bungalow, managing five, maybe ten, rounds before Maji insisted on retiring to the *puja* room for her prayers. Over time, Maji grew stronger and was even able to speak again, but she never tried to regain her place as the head of the family. Instead, she chose to spend the majority of her days in her darkened bedroom or the *puja* room, away from the bungalow's throbbing center. Savita had Maji's ornamented dais disassembled and carted away from the parlor, choosing instead to receive the bungalow's visitors from a thickly-upholstered, golden divan imported from Europe.

Occasionally, Vimla Lawate from next door came visiting, using the front gate like a proper guest instead of their private backyard passageway which, due to neglect, had rapidly been choked by thick brush and curling vines, rendering it impassable. The two women, each broken by tragedy, did not talk as they once had done. The effort proved too much for Maji. And Vimla simply had nothing more to say. Instead, they offered the other the silent comfort of their presence before draining their tea, leaving only a bit of sugary sludge in the bottoms of their porcelain cups.

❦ ❦ ❦

Pinky continued to tend to her grandmother in much the same way as she had done for most of her life: writing letters, looking after the *puja* room, relaying messages to the servants. In other unspoken ways, though, she became so much more. When she had returned to the bungalow that fateful day, determined to carve out her own destiny, she had claimed her rightful place in the Mittal household at last. Through the many days and nights that followed, she never ceased to wonder how Maji's life-giving hands, hands that had brought her so much comfort and love, could have also inflicted so much suffering.

❦ ❦ ❦

Inspector Pascal never solved the case of Lovely Lawate's disappearance and was forever haunted by this, his single glaring failure. He once thought he spotted her walking along Colaba Causeway in the middle of the night, pausing in front of the Sweetie Fashions as if remembering something. "Miss Lawate!" he had called out, racing towards her, "Miss Lovely Lawate!" Before he could cross the street to reach her, however, she vanished. In the weeks that followed, he received several reports from colleagues in Madras and Pondicherry that they had seen her along that coast, too.

❦ ❦ ❦

And perhaps they had. For Lovely had been given an unexpected gift by Avni that terrifying night on the Arabian Sea, the instant she had plunged into the chilly, depthless water. The power to grasp her destiny—her truth. To be free.

❦ ❦ ❦

Because Lovely was never found, the newspapers had written only that she had mysteriously disappeared, her story inked into the pages of the city's history. The insinuation was that she had run away with Inesh, the owner of a ruby red Triumph 500cc, reported missing the very same night of Lovely's flight. Inesh was bullied, reprimanded, and eventually discharged in return for an exorbitant bribe paid by his frantic parents, never to be reunited with his beloved motorbike again.

Harshal Lawate believed that his sister had run away to spite him, to crush his obsession. He unsuccessfully squandered a vast amount of the family's fortune on a private detective who spent his retainer on the pricey European whores in Kamathipura where, just down the lane a bit, an aging prostitute took her own life after murdering her adolescent son and his uncle with a nine-inch Rampuri knife.

Finally, after months of research and an abrupt cut-off of his generous allowance, the detective submitted a portfolio of his findings to Harshal. In the detailed report, he quoted the *Manu Sutras*, the first Laws of Man, blaming the fifth mode of marriage, called the *isachavivaha*, for Lovely's disappearance. "In this mode," he wrote, "the lover lures a girl with the use of talismans and black magic and marries her without her parent's consent. It is of my opinion that whoever lured her away that terrible night was none other than the devil himself."

The report was burnt, more out of fear than rage. Harshal, after all, still suffered from an invisible bruise deep inside his bowels, inflicted by Lovely herself the night he raped her. Just once he had penetrated her, just once. And then she had inexplicably risen up before him, thrown him onto his belly, and pierced him from behind. With what, he never knew, but he felt it, the inward thrust, the tearing of skin, the unimaginable violation. He began to bleed from his rectum, never again having a bowel movement without intense suffering. *Yes*, he thought fearfully, *something had possessed her. Something utterly evil.*

Vimla spent long afternoons meticulously reorganizing the cherry-colored satchel of Lovely's marriage proposals, keeping track of which suitors had become hitched and which were still available. Month by month, the number of eligible bachelors dwindled and with them the hope that her daughter would ever return. Somewhere in her heart, she believed Lovely was alive; she believed because she was the one to discover that the golden dowry pieces she had been saving for Lovely's marriage were missing. Only Lovely had known where they had been hidden. And this knowledge, that somehow her disappearance had been purposeful, was the most painful part of it all.

The tamarind tree was uprooted, chopped into pieces and hauled away, paid for with two of Vimla's resplendent saris. A mango tree was planted in its place but it never grew, nor did the neem or guava trees. Finally, the patch of land was abandoned, a startling circle of decay embedded within the succulent green paradise of Malabar Hill.

※ ※ ※

Lovely's golden *dupatta*, which Jaginder had retrieved from Inspector Pascal, was locked away and forgotten in one of Maji's steel cabinets where it remained until Nimish was moved into Maji's room after his wedding to Juhi Khandelwal. One cool waning winter morning, while Juhi opened Maji's chinoiserie cabinets, replacing the motheaten widow-white saris with her own vibrant, new-bride ones, she found the *dupatta*—delicately embroidered with emerald petals, strangely smelling of the sea. The *dupatta* felt old, weighty, as if it had held something vital within the weft of its fabric.

"This is strange, *nah?*" Juhi held the cloth out towards Nimish, who was reading a text of Jawaharlal Nehru's *Tryst with Destiny*.

"'A moment comes, which comes but rarely in history,'" Nimish read from the historic speech, "'when the soul of a nation, long suppressed, finds utterance.'"

Juhi searched her husband's face in the mirror of her dowry vanity, a heavy imported teakwood set with matching dressers and bed frame. "It was folded between Maji's old saris," she tried again, determinedly shaking the *dupatta* at him. "Was it hers?"

Nimish caught the metallic flash in the small oval mirror in front of him, the million gemlike petals floating in a sea of gold, a tiny bird drowning within its depths. A terrible ache clutched his chest, pressing into his heart like a blade as a memory descended upon him: Lovely standing underneath the rain-swept tamarind tree, the very same *dupatta* cascading over her bronzed skin, her plump breasts, her satiny forehead which she had touched to his own.

"I don't know," he said. The book slipped from his hands onto the floor. "Must have been Maji's."

But even as he said this, Juhi noticed the boyish blush on his cheeks, the same awkward redness that had overpowered him during their very first nights together as husband and wife. Flashing her emerald green eyes at him, she hurriedly pushed the *dupatta* onto a heap of Maji's old saris, feeling a pang of uncertainty grip her. "I've asked Kuntal to take these away since Maji has outgrown them," she said, tying up the bundle and crisply leaving the room.

Nimish sat on the bed and stared at the sack of clothes, fighting the urge to pull out the remains of a lost past and, just for a moment, hold it to his cheek. After so many desperate months had passed without any sign of Lovely, his mother had secretly set up a meeting with Juhi and her family. As he sat across from her at the restaurant, his cheeks aflame with anger, he knew that he had been trapped, for once a boy meets a girl face to face, they are as good as engaged. As the potential groom, he had the right to say no, but to reject the girl would ruin her reputation, and Nimish simply could not bring himself to cause such humiliation. Savita had known that her eldest would put the girl's honor above his own desires, and had used it against him. And so the marriage took place. Deep inside, Nimish struggled to let go of the past for the sake of the future, for the sake of his new wife whom he genuinely adored. Still, in the thick of the night as they made love, it was Lovely's face he saw. Always hers.

He fought the overwhelming urge to undo the bundle's knot to let go of the moment under the tamarind tree, a remembrance so precious, so breathlessly divine, that he sometimes wondered if it had happened at all. "Juhi," he finally called to his wife in a strained voice, standing up as he hastily wiped tears from his eyes. "Juhi, I must be off to the university."

And then tenderly touching the bundle of saris as if it were Lovely's silken cheek, he turned and left the room.

"Nimi," Savita called after him, sitting regally at the dining table, a plate of golden pastries at her side. "Come have your breakfast."

"I've made your tea the way you like best," Juhi added faintly, holding out a cup.

Nimish shook his head at them and walked out of the bungalow, asking Gulu to drive him to the tram stop at Dhobi Talao, where if he rode all the way to King's Circle and back, he had more than two full hours of uninterrupted reading time.

Savita glared at Juhi to hide the sinking feeling in her own chest. In the months since his marriage, Nimish had closed himself off from his mother, his affections towards her visibly diminished though his dutifulness never once wavered. His turning away was a daily reminder that, although she had won the bungalow, she had lost something even more precious.

❀ ❀ ❀

Jaginder finally accepted his part in the baby's death. Maji had come to him the day his daughter had been born, showing him the truth of her being. But he had refused to look, refused to believe that such a deformity could be born of him.

What can be done? he asked, his dreams for his daughter dying. There would be no marriage, no dowry, no grandchildren, no legitimate life.

The hijras *will take her,* Maji said, *we can only hide it for so long. And the law does not prevent them.*

No! he gagged. *It's better that she doesn't live.*

Their eyes met then, filling the space between them with infinite sadness, helplessness. Maji pressed the baby to her bosom, inhaling the sweet, milky scent of her skin. She could not see a way into light, into possibility.

She thought of her childhood friend who had been widowed.

This child should not know that suffering, the world's unforgiving cruelty, she said, waiting for his consent.

Anguish bore down upon him.

He had to save his child from a fate worse than death.

He nodded.

❀ ❀ ❀

The golden *dupatta* traveled along with Maji's old petticoats, out of the bungalow, out of their lives. The silken utterance of Lovely's story, the sweeping rectangle of cloth that held the tainted memories of a beloved girl, was too much of a threat to Juhi's fragile heart and too painful for Nimish's broken one.

So it vanished.

Along with a million other stories that haunt Bombay in its darkest, deepest, most naked core.

❀ ❀ ❀

In March, the month in which Bombay's balmy winter fully surrendered to summer's pushy heat, Parvati gave birth. From her body, marked by the ravages of history—colonialism, famine, orphanhood, rape, servitude—a baby emerged, an infant girl with thick hair and coffee-dark skin just like her own. Parvati named her Asha, meaning "hope."

In her first days of life, the baby cried relentlessly while she slept, her tiny face contracting with pain, eyes still not ready to produce tears.

Savita sent Gulu to procure some imported Woodward's Celebrated Gripe Water.

"She's reliving her past," Parvati comforted an ashen-faced Kanj who stood guard with a pot of freshly boiled fennel water for signs of a gassy tummy. "Let her say her good-byes, let her come to us unburdened."

And with that, she tucked an iron key under the mattress where the baby lay to help her make the final steps into her current life, locking away—finally—the sufferings of her past life.

After four days, the baby miraculously settled, happily suckling at Parvati's breasts and sleeping a deep, untroubled sleep. Sometimes, Kuntal brought her inside the parlor on a blanket while she cleaned. Asha gazed at the room as if it was strangely familiar.

The baby refused to go to Maji, however, screaming if she was even taken near her.

"Frightened by the smell of old person," Kuntal reasoned.

"Of sickness," Cook Kanj corrected.

"Of death," Parvati concluded.

The baby ghost never returned to the bungalow. Once in a while, Pinky called to her in the hallway bathroom, praying that her troubled soul had finally found peace.

That first monsoon, however, as the ambrosial summer purred into slumber, Parvati saw it.

And Pinky did too.

For a fleeting, almost imperceptible moment, when the weighty clouds relinquished their heavenly abode to the moon's graceful light,

And the sky spread with the bluish hue of new beginnings,

Little Asha's hair shone silver.

ACKNOWLEDGMENTS

I would like to thank all those who came into my life during this journey to lend their expertise, provide me with a precise detail, or assist me along the way. I would especially like to thank the following:

Satti Khanna and Miriam Cooke at Duke University, for unveiling the beauty of literature.

The presenters and judges of the 2003 First Words Literary Prize for South Asian Writers, for recognizing the potential of my manuscript in its early stages.

Sai-ling Michael, Heather Onori, Rajshree Patel, Kim Pentecost, and Lawrence Taw, for sharing their wisdom and helping me navigate the formidable voyage to health.

Ghalib Dhalla—my writing comrade of many years, Aimee Liu—mentor and friend, and Tonia Wallander.

My girlfriends, for supporting me in innumerous ways and celebrating the milestones with me.

My family in India for sharing their stories, especially of Partition, and their generous affection.

Kim Witherspoon and all those at Inkwell for helping bring my book to fruition, most especially Alexis Hurley for her dedication and determination.

Laura Hruska for her warmth and guidance, and my community at Soho Press, including Sarah Reidy, for their enthusiasm in launching my book.

My siblings Ajay and Sonal, and their families, for their wholehearted support.

Vinod Agarwal, my fellow writer and uncle, for his insightful letters that came to me as if on angel's wings, bringing an insider's eye to Bombay in the 60's.

Mom and Dad, for guiding me always with love, entrusting me with their memories, and giving me their blessings to follow my heart.

James and our daughters, for illumintating my life with their love, and for believing in me through these long, long years of writing.

Over the course of writing this book, I have consulted many theoretical, historical, and reference texts along with interviews, old colonial guidebooks, and letters. In lieu of listing an extensive bibliography, I would like to acknowledge the following people and their works which have been especially invaluable resources: Benedict Anderson's *Imagined Communities*, K. Asif's film *Mughal-E-Azam*, Julian Crandall Hollick's *Apna Street*, Sir Richard Francis Burton's *Vikram and the Vampire*, Partha Chatterjee's *The Nation and its Fragments*, Graham Dwyer's *The Divine and The Demonic*, Eicher's *City Map of Mumbai*, Zia Jaffrey's *The Invisibles*, Sashi Prabu Joshi's knowledge of the *Vedas*, Mary Ellen Mark's *Falkland Road*, Ashis Nandy's *The Intimate Enemy*, Julio Ribeiro's *Bullet For Bullet*, Kalpana Sharma's *Rediscovering Dharavi*, Gillian Tindall's *City Of Gold*, and *The Traveller's Literary Companion to the Indian Sub-continent*.